AL

The Loveless Brothers

Enemies With Benefits

Best Fake Fiancé

Break the Rules

The Hookup Equation

One Last Time

Wildwood Society

The One Month Boyfriend

The Two Week Roommate

Dirtshine Series

Never Enough

Always You

Ever After

Standalone Romances

Ride

Reign

Torch

Safekeeping

The Savage Wild

Convict

USA TODAY BESTSELLING AUTHOR

ROXIE NOIR

Cover designer: Najla Qamber Designs
Editor: Edits in Blue
Proofreader: Gem's Precise Proofs

CHAPTER ONE
VIOLET

This is going off the rails.

I don't want it to. I wish it wasn't, because I started this date the way I start every date: with unbridled optimism. Before I actually go on a date, I'm always overflowing with excitement and the soul-deep knowledge that somewhere out there in the mountainous wilds of southwestern Virginia lives my Prince Charming, ready to show up and whisk me away.

Okay, that's overstating things a little. I have zero interest in an actual prince, and being whisked sounds like it's some kind of baking-gone-wrong incident, but I'd like to have a life partner. When done properly, it seems like having one is nice.

I'd like someone to make me look forward to going home at the end of the day. Someone to make me laugh on long car rides. Someone to snuggle during the long mountain nights, preferably someone warmer than me.

I just don't want the *wrong* life partner.

"You've never been here before, huh?" Todd asks, looking at his menu and not at me.

"No, but I've heard good things," I say, keeping it upbeat.

"Yeah, I figured you hadn't," he says, finally glancing at me over the menu. He's smirky and smug. Smugky? "You should've seen the look on your face when I said where I was taking you, like I'd just told you it was Christmas morning."

I want to give him the benefit of the doubt. I keep reminding myself over and over not to judge a book by its cover. People are invariably deeper and more complex than they seem at first.

After all, he took me to *Le Faisan Rouge*, the fanciest and only French restaurant in Burnley County. He opened his truck door for me when he picked me up. He pulled my chair out for me when I sat down in the restaurant. He settled my napkin on my lap with a flourish, like a perfect gentleman.

But the smug smirking. The fact that he corrected my pronunciation of *Le Faisan Rouge* with a pronunciation that was completely incorrect. I've never been to France, but I did take a semester of French in college, and I know how to say *rouge*, thanks.

"Don't get to go to many five-star restaurants, I assume?" he asks, smugly sipping his water.

Optimism: slipping.

"I've heard the steak is good," I say, deciding I'm going to keep having the conversation I'd rather not be having. "Maybe I'll get that."

Todd just snorts, then leans across the table like he's got a secret he wants to tell me.

"The steak's the best thing on the menu but that doesn't mean it's very good," he says, looking around. "I heard a rumor that the chef made *friends* with the restaurant reviewer when they were in town, if you know what I mean. One of the perks of being a female chef, I guess. Garçon!"

There's so much going on with that statement that I just stare at him for a moment.

Did he really just shout at the waiter?

And insinuate that the chef slept with a reviewer?

"I hadn't heard that," I say, my voice getting brittle. I keep scanning the menu, reminding myself: book. Cover.

But of course, none of the menu items have prices. My heart curls into a little ball, because I have very firm beliefs regarding first dates: I pay my own way.

I don't like being paid for. I don't like feeling as if I owe someone something. I don't like feeling like I shouldn't order gold-plated lobster with a side of caviar if I feel like it.

Not that I ever do. I've got a budget.

"Well, you wouldn't unless you're really tuned into the local restaurant scene," Todd says. "I'm personal friends with a few other chefs around town, and that's the rumor going around. *Garçon!*"

Optimism: running on fumes.

"Any chance they're all men whose restaurants got lower ratings?" I ask. At this point I'll do almost anything make him stop shouting *garçon* like that. With his accent it sounds like *gar-sawwn*, and it grates on my ears every time he does it.

Todd ignores my question completely.

"GAR-SAWN!" he says, even more loudly than before. From the corner of my eye I can see the people at the next table over look at us. I don't look back. I'm too afraid I'd recognize them, even though we're in Grotonsville – one town over from Sprucevale, where I actually live – and then I'd have to acknowledge that I'm here with Todd.

That's when it happens.

Todd snaps his fingers at our server.

I swear the sound echoes in my soul.

And now I'm forced to acknowledge that this date is in salvage mode. Todd is no longer *a guy with some issues but maybe we'll get to know each other over dinner*; he is now *someone I actively hope to never see again after tonight.*

I know that everyone has flaws — I'm flaw central over here — but after a year of waitressing during college, with God as my witness, I'll never fall for someone who snaps at the waitstaff like they're dogs. Not that I was in danger of falling for him anyway.

Showing a strength and integrity of character I can only dream of having, the waitress comes over with a smile on her face.

"Hi there, I'm Stephanie, can I get y'all started with something tonight?" she asks, never once betraying that I'm sitting across from a monster.

I give her the most intense *I'm sorry he snapped at you* look I can.

Todd doesn't even look up.

"We'd like a bottle of the two thousand twelve *Deux Canard* Bordeaux, along with the three-cheese *gougères* and the duck *rilletes*. That'll be all for now," he says.

"Thank you!" I call as she walks away. Todd looks at me like I told a mildly amusing joke.

"I can't believe I still have to ask," he says, settling back into his chair. "I'm a regular, they know what I'm going to want. Always the 2012 Canard Bordeaux. It's the best wine in the house, not that their wine selection is anything to write home about."

I take a long sip of water. I consider just standing up and leaving, but I don't want to be rude. I don't want everyone in *Le Faisan Rouge* to stare at me as I walk out.

I also am not having a good date.

So I smile, shrug, and say, "They only got five stars because the chef slept with a reviewer, but you come here all the time?"

Todd smiles. His teeth are an untrustworthy white.

"Where else am I supposed to go around here?" he asks. "You think I'm gonna go to Louisa Mae's for meatloaf?"

"I don't see why not. At least it's good," I point out.

"The only wine they have on the menu is merlot and chardonnay," he says, like that's some unspeakable crime. "At least here I can eat my decent steak with a *very* good wine."

My heart skips a beat at that *very*. Did Todd just order us a hundred-dollar bottle of wine?

Maybe just this once, get down off your feminist soapbox and let him pay for the date?

This was his idea, after all.

My palms are still sweating when the waitress comes back with the already-opened wine, because I'm still trying to figure out how much I'm going to be paying for it. Fifty dollars? Seventy-five dollars?

It's your own fault now for not saying something, I remind myself.

Or you could just let him pay for the stupid wine that he wanted in the first place.

They go through the whole sniff-swirl-taste-drink-nod thing that wine people love to do, and the waitress pours both of us a glass. I sample mine.

It tastes like wine.

"Are you ready to order?" she asks, still smiling.

"We'll both take the filet mignon, medium rare," Todd says, and reaches for my menu.

I pull it back and look up at the waitress myself.

"Actually, I'd like the coq au vin, please," I tell her. This guy has already gotten me wine that's definitely too expensive. The hell I'm paying for dumb steak I don't want, too.

"The filet is better," Todd says, looking at me like I've just said that I'll be dining out of the dumpster.

"I'm not in a steak mood," I say,

"You should be."

I hand my menu back to the waitress and smile at her. Todd just shrugs.

"Your loss," he says, which I very much doubt, and drinks some more of his fancy wine.

He then launches into a one-sided conversation about golf. I have no opinions whatsoever on golf, so I drink my overpriced wine, nod sometimes, and think about what I'm going to tell Adeline about this date, since she set me up in the first place. Todd is her cousin's cousin's friend or something.

Our food comes. Todd slices his filet mignon like it's done him wrong, and I eat my chicken as politely as I can. When we're finished, the waitress clears our plates. I thank her and he doesn't. After she leaves, he refills my wine glass, even though I haven't even finished my first one.

Then he leans in, smirking smugly, holding the stem of his glass between his fingers.

"So," he says. "Your place or mine?"

I nearly choke.

"What?"

He smirks, though this one comes out more like a snarl. It's not a good look.

"Come on. Your place or mine?"

I set my wine glass gently on the table.

I'm not having sex with him. I'd rather get into a

bathtub full of wolverines, and for a long moment, I just stare at him in disbelief that any human being can think that this date was heading that way.

It's on the tip of my tongue: *I do not want to have sex with you; rather, I would prefer to get the check, split it, and amicably go our separate ways.*

But at the last second that seems rude, so what I actually say is: "No, thank you."

"You sure?" he asks. "I thought that was a pretty nice dinner."

He spins his wine glass between his fingers, the red liquid sloshing around inside. I want to tell him about preferring the wolverines, but I control myself.

"I'd prefer to go home alone, thanks," I say. "I need to get up early in the morning."

It's still too polite, too *nice*, because it's been bred into me since I was old enough to say *goodness gracious*.

"It doesn't have to take a long time," he says, like this somehow makes his offer better.

I wonder how I ever felt optimistic about him. I wonder if my optimism meter is broken, or at least seriously damaged.

Todd's face changes in a way that reminds me of a five-year-old about to have a tantrum in the toy aisle at Walmart. He snaps his fingers in the air again, and this time, I swear I flinch.

"Check," he says as the waitress comes over, and she nods, then leaves.

He looks at me. It's calculating look, like he's tallying up how much money he just spent not to get laid.

The almost-tantrum look on his face intensifies.

"I'll be right back," he says, and heads toward the men's room.

The moment he's gone, I breathe a sigh of relief.

I should have ended the date the first time he snapped at the waitress. I should have told him I wasn't interested instead of that I have to get up early tomorrow. I should have been polite but firm and just walked out of there, figure out my own way home.

I shouldn't have let him pick me up for this date in the first place.

Todd takes his sweet time in the bathroom. I pull out my phone and text Adeline.

Me: Don't trust your cousin's cousin again, for the good of womankind.

She doesn't text back, so she must be at work already. I flip through Pinterest on my phone. There are some cute pictures of hay bales decorated for a wedding. I pin one to my work account.

I wait for Todd to come back. I wait for the check. I wait and I wish that Todd had taken me for meatloaf at Louisa's instead. I also wish that Todd was someone else entirely, someone I'd actually want a second date with.

Maybe I should stop dating for a while, I think. *I keep getting disappointed. Maybe I need a hiatus.*

The waitress flits over, dropping a smile and placing the check on the table, enclosed in a leather-bound folder that matches the menus. My heart ties itself into a knot but I look up at her, smile, and say thanks. She smiles back.

Thank God.

I mentally brace myself before I open it.

$254.09.

I close it again, like there's a poisonous snake inside it, my heart beating way too fast. I thought it'd be expensive but not that expensive. Good *God*, was his steak plated with gold? Was my chicken encrusted with pearls and I didn't notice? What exactly about that wine was worth $125 anyway, and can I re-cork it and take the rest home with me for that price?

I drink the rest of my glass of wine, pour myself a few more ounces, and drink that too.

Just let him pay, I tell myself. *This was all his idea.*

I wish I could. I wish to high heaven I could be one of those girls who just hands over the check and acts like it's the natural order of things, but I can't. I hate feeling like I haven't paved my own way, like I don't deserve whatever I get.

I grab my purse and start fishing through it for my wallet. My palms are getting sweaty, and I feel like I just had four espressos instead of wine.

Two hundred and fifty dollars. Two. Fifty.

Still no Todd. There's a second panic, low and steady, eating at the bottom of my stomach but I ignore it because I really need to take one disaster at a time.

The waitress walks by. I'm now elbow-deep in my purse because my wallet has apparently migrated to the very bottom. I pull the thing onto my lap.

I shove some stuff around in there. Still no wallet, but I tell myself that of course I can't see it — it's dark in here, and besides, the interior of my purse may as well be an abandoned coal mine.

I still don't find it.

I start pulling stuff out.

An eyeshadow palette I've used exactly twice. A tube of mascara. A tube of mascara that has *old - do not use!* written on the side. Three tubes of chapstick, a tube of tinted chapstick that's supposed to give you a healthy, vibrant glow but in fact does absolutely nothing, a bottle of Advil, and a water bottle cap.

No wallet.

One earring. Foundation. A plastic bangle bracelet. Eyeliner. A pack of unopened index cards, two dry-erase markers, and a tiny notebook that's rubber-banded shut. A used paperback copy of *East of Eden* and also a used paperback copy of *Shopaholic Takes Manhattan*, because I'm a woman of complicated tastes.

Still no wallet. Still no Todd.

I'm panicking. My insides are tied in knots, and my hands are trembling with the adrenaline that's shooting through my veins as I think *this can't be happening* again and again.

No wallet means asking Todd to cover the whole bill. No wallet means I'm not the self-sufficient go-getter I like to think I am. No wallet means relying on someone else's kindness, and I already know that the price tag for Todd's kindness isn't one I'm willing to pay.

I paw through everything on the table. I pat down the lining of my purse and run my hands over the straps, *just in case* my wallet has wormed itself into a strip of leather one inch wide.

It's not there. My whole body is hot with embarrassment. I ignore the sidelong glances from the couple at the next table over as I shove everything back into my purse and wait, trying to slow my heart.

I look at my phone to text Adeline again about my *hilarious* date mishap and realize it's been ten minutes since Todd went to the bathroom.

Well, he's either dead or gone.

Or playing Candy Crush on the toilet because he's a rude jerk.

I flag the waitress down. Politely.

"I'm so sorry," I start, meaning I'm sorry for what I'm about to ask, and also, I'm sorry in general about Todd. "My date went to the bathroom about ten minutes ago and hasn't come back, and I'm starting to worry he's had some sort of emergency. Could you ask someone to go check?"

I'm talking way, way too fast, my words coming out in a frantic rush. Her eyebrows knit together in a look of waiterly concern, and she glances back at the bathrooms, like maybe we'll both get lucky and he'll waltz out at this exact moment, looking only slightly worse for wear.

Todd does not waltz.

"I'll find someone," she says. "Be right back, okay?"

"Thank you!" I call after her, my heart thumping too loud in my chest.

Please be playing Candy Crush like a jerk.

Please.

A minute later the kitchen door swings open, almost smacking into a busboy.

A tall, dark-haired, annoyed-looking man comes out and strides toward the bathrooms.

I stare.

I forget about Todd.

I forget that I'm on a date.

In fact, I forget everything I've ever learned about how to act in public because I unabashedly ogle this man as he crosses the room.

Did I mention tall? Dark hair and light eyes? Handsome as the devil himself, with sharp cheekbones and a hard jawline, wearing a white chef's jacket over broad shoulders?

It takes him about three seconds to disappear into the men's room, but it's a *very* good three seconds. My heart *flutters*. It flutters enough to make me feel guilty for looking at this man while on a date with Todd. It even flutters hard enough to distract me from my current situation.

Then he's gone. I turn around and try to act like I wasn't ogling.

Except there's something else. Something scratching at the back of my mind, a sneaking suspicion that I *know* the handsome man currently finding out whether my date is pooping and playing games on his phone.

I don't know how. I'm not even sure whether I really know him, or whether my processing centers have been scrambled by this disaster.

You know how it's hard to recognize someone out of context? Like when you were a kid and you saw a teacher in the grocery store or something, and it would take you a minute to figure out who they were because they weren't at school?

It's like that. He looks vaguely familiar, but in this tiny town, *everyone* looks vaguely familiar.

Thirty seconds later he comes back out of the bathroom, shaking his head at my waitress as he crosses the room.

I get another great three seconds, and then Hotface McChefsalot is gone. My waitress is frowning.

Shit. *Shit.*

"Nobody's in there," she says, and my stomach clenches anew.

"He's not in a stall playing Candy Crush?" I ask, just to be sure. My voice is high-pitched, strangled.

"Um…" she says, glancing toward the kitchen door, where the man I just ogled disappeared. "I don't really…"

"I'll check!" I say brightly, and jump out of my seat in a burst of oh-God-I-have-to-do-something energy, and charge for the bathrooms.

Several people watch me as I hustle across the dining room and into the hallway with the bathrooms, where I knock on the door to the men's.

No answer. I shove it open, bracing myself for someone to shout at me, but no one does.

That's because there's no one in there. The bathroom only has one urinal and two stalls, and the moment I open the door it's clear that they're all unoccupied.

I back out. My mind is racing. There's a trickle of panic-sweat running down the back of my neck.

Can I barter a dog collar and some paperbacks for dinner and some overpriced wine? Maybe my phone? It's a year or two old, but I've treated it well.

Just for good measure, I check the women's bathroom. There's a middle-aged woman applying lipstick in the mirror. No Todd.

I keep going down the short hallway, round a corner, and there it is: a giant green EXIT sign. Just like that, I *know*.

I push the door open. The cool night air feels good against my overheated, sweaty skin. The stars above twinkle merrily as I scan for Todd's truck: unnecessarily huge, the kind of truck that belies its owner's insecurities about his dick.

It's not there. I double-check. Still nothing.

I start laughing, the sound of sheer nerves making their way out of my body via my mouth. I shove my hand against my mouth, trying to muffle the sound, but I can't stop giggling.

Oh, my God, I'm losing my mind, I think.

Another giggle escapes.

I'm the one who was having a bad time. I was a perfectly good date. I should have been the one to walk out. Todd was a dick, why does he get to do this, too?

I snort. It's not a good sound.

The door opens behind me, and the sudden sound is finally sobering. I take my hand off my mouth and stand up straight, the giggles finally gone.

The waitress clears her throat quietly.

"So the check…" she says, her voice trailing off.

I gather all the nerve I can muster, even though I feel like there's a hand around my windpipe, and smile at her.

"Could I talk to the manager and maybe work something out?" I ask.

CHAPTER TWO

ELI

"You got that thing ready?"

"Yup. Smoke detector's off?"

"Yeah."

I pause for moment, crouching in front of the glass-doored commercial oven, wearing an oven mitt and holding tongs.

"You are sure that thing's a jury-rigged kitchen blowtorch and not a pipe bomb, right?" Travis asks. He's standing slightly to one side, holding a fire extinguisher at the ready.

"I'm about ninety-five percent on that," I tell him. "It looks a lot more like a kitchen torch than a pipe bomb, that's for sure."

"You've seen a lot of pipe bombs?"

"No, but I've seen a lot of kitchen blowtorches," I say, adjusting the oven mitt over my hand.

I discovered this gem a few minutes ago, since I'm the last person in the kitchen tonight. I'm usually the last person in the kitchen, the one who makes sure that all the food is put away according to protocol, the one who makes sure every surface is wiped down, ready for the next day, even though none of that has been my job for years now.

Tonight, that seems to include getting a jury-rigged kitchen torch out of the oven. Travis is Le Faisan Rouge's bartender, and he was unlucky enough to still be here when I discovered this gem.

"You're here as a last resort," I remind Travis, who looks like he wishes he'd left ten minutes ago. "Oven's been off for an hour. I'm pretty sure nothing's going to happen."

"All right," he says. "Let's do this."

"On three," I say, putting my free hand around the oven door handle. "One. Two. *Three.*"

I jerk the door open. Travis holds out the fire extinguisher like he's using it to ward off a vampire.

Nothing happens.

"Definitely a kitchen torch," I say, reaching in with the tongs and grabbing it. "Or at least a former kitchen torch."

He just whistles, lowering the extinguisher.

"The hell?" he asks.

I stand and walk it to the sink, placing it carefully inside.

"I believe," I say slowly as I examine the thing, "someone's duct-taped a propane canister for a camp stove to the blowtorch we used for crème brûlée."

We both stare down at the thing in the sink, arms crossed. It's not pretty: the propane canister is about twice the size of the kitchen torch, the nozzle stuck into the bottom. The entire package is mummified with duct tape.

"And why was it in the oven?" he asks.

"If I had to guess, I'd say whoever came up with this idea also figured that ovens get very hot, and therefore, if something went wrong with the torch, the oven would be the best place for it," I say. "But that's just a guess."

There's a brief silence as we both try to wrap our heads around this particular conundrum.

"Blow torches don't even use propane, do they?"

"Nope."

"So…" Travis says, then trails off. "Why…?"

"Why did someone in a busy kitchen take the time to cobble together a solution that clearly didn't work from camping supplies and duct tape instead of asking someone where the butane refills were?" I supply for Travis. "Beats me. I didn't even know we had duct tape."

Now Travis laughs.

"Course we have duct tape," he says. "You need anything else?"

"Nah, I'm good," I tell him. "I'm gonna dismantle this thing and then head home."

"Have a good one," he says, already walking for the swinging kitchen doors. "I'll see you around, right?"

"Right," I call after him, and then he's gone and I'm alone in the kitchen again.

I look around for another moment, soaking in the quiet, empty kitchen. The gleaming surfaces, the clean floor, the labeled canisters and jars on the shelves. The sense of stillness only possible in a place that's normally busier than the Tokyo subway at rush hour.

Aside from this kitchen torch incident, my last night at Le Faisan Rouge went beautifully. All my staff turned up when they were supposed to. Only two wine glasses got broken, which is pretty good. Not a single diner sent their food back, which might be a record.

I did have to check the men's room for a dead body, but even that was a false alarm.

I sigh and lean over the sink, the stainless steel edge cool against my palms, and contemplate the masterwork of redneck engineering inside.

I liked this job, I think, surprising myself.

When I took it, I wasn't sure I would. It was a three-month temporary gig while the head chef was on maternity leave — decent pay, a decent restaurant, but the real reason I applied was for the chance to go home for a while. That's what I wasn't sure I'd like, but I guess I did, because I'm starting a permanent gig next week at a wedding venue in town.

I grab the contraption out of the sink and start unwinding layer after layer of duct tape from it, the whole time wondering who on earth did this and then left it in an oven. That's the really baffling part — I've been around plenty of rednecks in my life, so I'm familiar with the mindset that leads someone to duct-tape together a misguided solution rather than ask for help, but the oven is the real kicker.

I'm just lucky that nothing melted. Then I'd be on the phone with the owner, trying to explain what happened while trying to guess who should be fired. Truth is, there are a couple of candidates, and I'm not at all sorry that it'll be someone else's problem.

But despite all that, I did like it here. I like being home more than I thought I would.

Finally, I remove the last of the duct tape and the propane canister falls away from the kitchen torch, both things scratched up pretty good. I don't really trust the kitchen torch anymore, so I grab it and the mass of duct tape and push open the door to the dishwashing room, where the back exit is.

I stop in my tracks.

There's a stranger washing dishes.

That isn't what's peculiar. A dishwashing position in a restaurant tends to have a near-weekly turnover rate, so more often than not the people in it are strangers to me.

Infrequently, they're female.

But never before has a dishwasher been wearing a turquoise sundress and heels. At least, not that I've ever seen.

I've also definitely never seen a woman who looks like *this* washing dishes. The dress hugs her perfectly — small waist, full hips, *great* ass — but doesn't go into detail, so I've got an idea of what's going on but not the full picture.

It's a great dress. It's an even better rear end, and as she turns to the left, hoisting another huge stock pot into the industrial sink, I've practically got my head tilted like a curious cocker spaniel, watching her.

She shoves her hair back off her face with her wrist, tilting her head side to side, like she's trying to work some tension out of her neck. She balances on one foot and then the other while she leans slightly forward, waiting while water runs into the pot.

I stare. I memorize. I practically take notes. I don't know what it is, but there's something in the way she's standing, the way she moves, that sings to me. There's poetry in the flick of water off of her yellow dishwashing gloves as she shuts off the water, starts scrubbing out the pot.

I lean against the doorframe, busted torch and duct tape still in my hands. I drink in the way the hem of her dress skims her knees, the tilt of her body over the sink, the muscles in her shoulders working, until I can't stand it anymore.

"Leave it for the morning crew," I finally say.

She jumps. The pot clatters back into the sink, splashing water on her already-wet dress as she whirls around, startled.

The front of her matches the back, only better: big blue-gray eyes and high, wide cheekbones, her honey-brown hair pulled it into a messy knot on top of her head, strands flying wild around her face.

She's beautiful. She's otherworldly, even standing there in the bright fluorescent light of the restaurant's back room, so much that it shocks me into silence for a moment, doing nothing but appreciating her face.

Then I realize she's something else, too.

She's familiar.

She narrows her eyes with equal parts wariness and suspicion, and it only makes her look more familiar. My stomach tightens for reasons I can't quite name, a bad feeling quickly rising inside me.

How the hell could I forget someone who looks like that?

Her lips part slightly. She takes a step back, toward the sink, her hands coming together in front of her, still yellow-rubber-clad, and we just look at each other for a long, long moment.

Finally, she speaks first.

"Eli?" she says.

Just like that, I know who she is. The cold, hard ball that's been gathering in the pit of my stomach falls straight through to my guts and rolls around in there.

"Violet," I say, and stop. For once, words fail me.

Violet could always smell weakness like a shark smells blood in the water. Give her an opening and she'll bite your leg off. I'm already tense, alert, the duct tape squeezed tight in my fist.

"What the hell are you doing washing dishes in my kitchen?" I finally ask.

I try to sound casual. I'm not sure it works.

Violet gives me a full-body, floor-to-head once over and she takes her sweet time about it. Her eyes are the color of sharks. I feel like they're circling me.

"It's a long story," she finally says. "What the hell are you doing back home?"

I give her a once-over, too, just to see how she likes it, and because I like it pretty well.

"Did you try to dine and dash?" I finally ask.

She snorts.

"Of course no—"

"You tried to dine and dash and got busted, didn't you?" I ask. "Crime never pays, Violet."

She rolls her eyes and turns back to the sink.

Then, suddenly, I put two and two together.

"Sure," she says. "That's me, some kind of—"

"Your date ditched you," I say.

Violet says nothing.

"He ditched you, you can't pay, and *that's* why you're here," I say.

She sloshes water out of the huge pot she's washing and glances over her shoulder, eyes blazing at me.

"And I assume you're here because you're all done with med school and you're just killing time between shifts as the top-rated neurosurgeon in southwestern Virginia," she says.

Scrub. Slosh.

"Or did that not work out as planned?" she finishes.

Her voice is sharp. Cutting. I don't want it to hurt but it does, like a scalpel on scar tissue.

I remind myself that she's clearly having a shitty day.

I remind myself that I'm nearly thirty years old and I shouldn't react to her like we're both in middle school, because I've matured past that. I remind myself what my mother always said about flies, honey, and vinegar, but all the reminders in the world can't override my gut reaction to Violet.

"It's working out about as well as law school and moving to New York seems like it has for you," I say.

She heaves the pot onto the drainboard, obviously pissed, and reaches for the last one. The ball of duct tape is clenched in my fist, bits sticking between my fingers, but I can't unclench.

"I'm not the one who swore on his father's grave that he'd leave Sprucevale forever if it took every cent he made," she says, her back still to me, her voice placid with forced calm.

Something tightens in my chest. I clench the duct tape harder, knuckles starting to ache. I still feel bad about that particular oath, even though it was fifteen years ago.

I feel worse that Violet remembers it.

"What *do* you say to a man to make him leave in the middle of a date?" I ask, leaning against the door frame, pretending to be casual despite my death grip on the duct tape.

She doesn't answer me. I snap my fingers like I've just remembered something.

"Did he order the wrong wine, so you called him a backwoods pigfucker who could barely add two and two?" I ask.

Violet ignores that, but I can see the muscles in her back tighten. I'm clenching the duct tape so hard my hand is shaking.

"Or maybe you told everyone on the debate team that you'd seen him drinking beers in the 7-11 parking lot with his brother so they would vote for you to be captain instead," I go on.

"No, and I also never told him that the reason he got into college was a cute face and a trailer trash sob story," she snaps back.

I ignore her.

"*Or*, you told him that he'd always be a moron who

couldn't tell Togo from Trinidad when you won the geography bee the day after his father died?"

There's a savage delight in this. I know there shouldn't be, but there is.

I'm enjoying seeing Violet Tulane, legendary know-it-all and the bane of my existence from ages five to eighteen, knocked down a peg or two.

Violet dumps the pot out violently, splashing water far enough that some gets on me, five feet behind her.

"I didn't know he'd died when I said that," she gets out between her teeth.

"And it's such a lovely thing to say otherwise."

"Fuck off, Eli."

"No, thanks."

"Great," she says, sarcasm dripping from her voice. "Glad I can entertain the guy who spread the rumor that he saw me making out with a golden retriever. Was being eighth grade class president worth it?"

"Hell yes," I say, because honestly? It was.

She slams the huge pot upside-down on the sideboard, precariously stacked next to all the other pots, and whips the yellow rubber gloves off.

"*Wonderful* to see you again, Eli," she says, already walking for the back door. "I had a super nice time chatting. Bye!"

Violet disappears. Seconds pass. The door slams. I'm vibrating with unreleased tension and the force of acting casual about this.

Slowly, I unclench my fist full of duct tape. There are red lines crisscrossing my palm.

It takes about twenty seconds before I feel bad about riling her up. I'm nearly thirty. I'm grown. I know better.

But I never could help riling up Violet Tulane. I never

could help holding it over her head when I was in a better position than her.

We tortured each other growing up. Sprucevale's a tiny town with one elementary school, one middle school, and one high school, so for thirteen years she was omnipresent.

She always had to be the very best at anything, and woe to anyone who stood in her way — usually, me. She was mean. She was petty. She was a bossy know-it-all who treated everyone like they were morons, and she always seemed to get what she wanted.

I had no idea she was still in Sprucevale. I have no idea *why* she's still here.

I had no idea that she turned into a gorgeous, sexy-as-fuck bombshell.

I'd assumed she was gone, probably doing some big important pain-in-the-ass job in a city somewhere — D.C., New York, Philadelphia. I didn't care where she was, so long as I wasn't there.

After a minute, I follow her out the door and toss the duct tape and defunct torch into the dumpster. I don't see her. Good.

I head back into the kitchen, grab the propane canister, and leave it on the counter along with a note. There, now it's someone else's problem.

Then I exit through the side door, slipping out into the night and the quiet parking lot.

It's Violet-free.

Perfect.

CHAPTER THREE

VIOLET

I don't make it five feet outside before I tear my shoes off.

After standing in heels for five hours, lifting heavy pot after heavy pot, the cool asphalt feels like pure heaven on my toes. This parking lot could be a chewing gum, broken glass, and cigarette swamp and it *still* would be heaven.

I walk around the side of the building, pull out my phone, and hit the button.

Nothing.

I hit the button again.

You have to be kidding me.

Of course my phone is dead. *Of course.* That's the day I'm having, obviously: bad date, Eli, repentant dishwashing, Eli, no ride, *stupid Eli*, dead phone.

Fine. That's fine. I'm prepared, and I reach into my purse and fish for my backup battery, which I keep for exactly this scenario.

As I fish, Eli's face appears like it's etched on the insides of my eyelids. A tiny dark tornado erupts in the pit of my stomach.

Don't let him get to you.

Don't do it.

God, I didn't even know he was back. The Sprucevale gossip machine hasn't said a peep about Eli Loveless's return, and the gossip machine normally has a *lot* to say about the Loveless boys.

I haven't seen him since we graduated high school. I knew he went to college. There was a rumor he dropped out, but I never knew whether that was true, and by then, my mom was sick and I was too busy to find out.

Besides, I was happy enough to lose track of him because Eli Loveless was an infuriating, cocky, competitive asshole who would stop at literally nothing to one-up me my whole life and *oh my God, where the hell is my phone battery?*

My empty hand hits the bottom of my purse for the second time that night.

This can't be happening.

In desperation, I rifle through everything in my purse one last time. My formerly-cute sundress is sticking to my back. There's sweat trickling down my butt crack, and it's grossing me out. I'm tired and angry with Todd and angry with myself and somehow, angriest of all at Eli Loveless for existing at the worst possible time.

"Fucking Eli," I mutter to myself.

It does make me feel a little better.

I take a deep breath and close my eyes. I drop my stupid purse to the stupid ground, and lean my head back against the brick wall. It's after midnight and I've got no money, no phone, and no ride.

I'll just walk, I think.

It's warm enough. The town's safe enough and small enough. Home is close enough — Four, maybe four and a half miles.

Besides, I'd rather walk than hitchhike. Even if my

phone was working, Adeline's at work with her phone off. The cab company here has one driver and he's probably drunk right now. This place is way too podunk for a ridesharing app.

I toss my shoes into my purse. I spent every childhood summer running barefoot on gravel. I'll be fine. It'll be an adventure.

I take off along Main Street, heading south.

Downtown Grotonsville is quiet, illuminated only by the orange glow of the streetlights and the lights of McMahon's about a block away, but even that is pretty quiet right now.

I walk one block, then two. Grotonsville is even smaller than Sprucevale, the town where I actually live, so I'm already close to the edge of it.

I start to relax a little. It's a nice night. The stars are out. The two traffic lights on main street change from green to yellow to red and back in a soothing, predictable rhythm.

And I do not think about Eli. Not even a little.

I don't think about the fact that his stupid smirk is actually hot as hell, about the fact that I want to shut him up by putting his mouth to better use, or the fact that his thick, ropy arms make me want to climb him like a tree.

Of all the people to turn out hot, I think, stomping along the midnight sidewalk. *I'd rather it was literally anyone else.*

I'm so focused on being irritated at Eli that I don't hear the engine until it's right behind me, and then all the hairs on the back of my neck stand up, my sense instantly whipping into sharp relief.

It's loud and guttural and someone's revving it.

Has anything good ever come of loud, revving engines at midnight?

I steel myself, fighting the adrenaline rush and glance over my shoulder. There's a huge pickup truck about a block away, and it's got at least four people jammed into the cab and a couple more riding in the bed.

Don't look scared, I tell myself as a vortex forms in my stomach. *They're probably just gonna shout at you and looking scared will only make it worse.*

They're drunk, hooting and hollering to raise the dead. They're likely coming back from McMahon's, the only place besides Le Faisan Rouge that's open this time of night.

I steer my steps closer to the buildings. I stand up straighter and I act like I'm not scared.

I am.

The truck comes closer. I glance over my shoulder at it, hoping for *nonchalant* instead of *lonely victim.*

I'm practically hugging the closed cafe to my left when the truck comes up alongside me and slows.

"Whachu doin' out here alone like this?" a voice says. "Come on, get in."

"I'm fine," I say, still walking. I'm scanning for exits, somewhere that I could go that the truck couldn't follow, my heart pounding.

"Shit, she ain't even got shoes on," one of them says to another. I still don't look over. "She got kicked out with no shoes!"

I can smell the alcohol from here, and I scan the buildings faster, looking for any route of brief escape. I see it: up ahead, there's a narrow passage between two buildings, too narrow for the truck.

"We can give you a ride if you want," says the first voice.

Drunk men laugh.

"A real good ride," he goes on. More laughter. I don't look over.

Then: "Come on, sweetheart."

"Where you walkin' barefoot, anyway?"

"Awful late to be out here alone."

I walk. I don't look over. I pretend I'm alone, even though I'm trembling, knowing how badly this could end.

I can't believe I thought this was an okay idea.

"Come on. Come on. Come on, I know you like this."

I glance over. I don't even mean to, I just do.

One of them has his dick out. The other three are laughing hysterically, slouched around the bed of the truck as the first guy waves his dick back and forth.

My heartbeat skyrockets, but I force my eyes forward again. I want to run but I don't. I can't show any sign of fear.

"Fuck off," I call.

More laughter. They holler something I can't even make out, and then the engine throttles. It might be the sweetest sound I've ever heard, because a moment later the truck is pulling away, down Main Street, blatantly running a red light.

"Bitch!" I hear one last, high-pitched yelp.

Then, sweet silence.

I stop. I take a deep breath, eyes closed, and get a hold of myself. I lean against a brick wall until I stop shaking and I can trust myself not to cry.

The hell was I thinking, a woman walking alone at night?

New plan: go back. McMahon's, the sports bar, is at the other end of town but it's still open, and I'm going to walk there, ask to use their phone, and call everyone I know until someone comes and gives me a ride home. Screw politeness. I don't give a damn who I wake up.

Before I can turn my steps, I hear the engine behind me again.

Every muscle in my body tenses. The gap between the

buildings is still up there, too small for a vehicle, and it probably connects to the alley behind the buildings where I can lose them.

The engine growls behind me, closer, the rednecks silent this time.

I run.

"Violet!" Eli's voice shouts.

I stop, whirl around, and there he is. He's driving an ancient Ford Bronco, the windows rolled down.

It might be the first time in my life I've been glad to see Eli Loveless. He rolls up until he's beside me, leaning over the passenger side

"Get in," he says.

"With you?" I ask.

My heart's still pounding. My hands are still shaking, even though I've got one clenched around the strap of my purse, and even though I'm fully prepared to walk to a bar and call everyone I know for the next hour, I don't want to show Eli any signs of weakness.

We lock eyes. He just gives me a *look.*

"You're walking barefoot along main street at midnight with no shoes on like some redneck hooker because your night's going well?"

I ignore *redneck hooker* and take a step toward the Bronco. My face barely comes up to the bottom of the window.

"Just get in," he says.

"I know better than to get into cars with strange men at all hours of the night."

"Good thing it's just me, then."

"You're plenty strange."

"And you're plenty stubborn. Get the hell in the car, Violet, you really think I'm gonna let you walk home alone at this hour? You're not even wearing shoes."

I clench my jaw and look away, down Main Street. He's right and I know it, but Lord I hate admitting it.

"You know if you don't get in, I'm still gonna follow you going two miles per hour because I can't have your murder on my conscience, right?" he says.

I glare at Eli. He glares back. *Handsomely,* the most irritating way for him to glare.

Then I jerk the passenger door open and climb into the cab.

"*Thank* you," he says, just a hint of humor in his voice as I buckle my seat belt.

His truck smells like grease, leather, and old car. He wrestles the gear shift back into drive and glances over at me, the flicker of a smile on his face.

I feel that flutter in the pit of my stomach, ignore it, and double-check my seatbelt.

"This thing street legal?" I ask, looking around the inside of the car, because I really need to look at something besides him.

"Near enough," he says, shifting back into drive with a *clunk* and a faint grinding noise. "Why, you worried about a few bumps?"

"If I lift up this floor mat, am I gonna be able to see straight through to the street?"

The Bronco shudders forward. From the corner of my eye, I see Eli smile. It twists my stomach again. I keep ignoring it.

"Sorry, the clutch sticks sometimes," he says. "Actually, the clutch sticks all the time. Don't touch that mat."

I don't touch the floor mat. For a few minutes we drive in silence, and I stare ahead through the windshield. There's a long crack running half the length of it, about an inch above the dashboard, and I entertain myself by wondering what caused it.

You're both adults, I tell myself. *It's been ages since you've seen each other. There's no earthly reason that Eli should still get on your nerves like he used to. I'm sure he's changed. You've both changed.*

The window's down and I lean into the wind, because my face is too hot. My whole body is too hot, the air in this ancient Bronco humming, vibrating. He shifts gears again and I try not to notice that he's got rugged hands, scars across the back, the muscles in his forearm flexing in a way that makes me cross my ankles.

"Where am I taking you?" he asks, his deep voice harmonizing with the throaty growl of the engine.

Oh, God.

I clear my throat.

"Same place, actually," I say, forcing my nerves back down. I don't look at his reaction.

There's a beat of silence.

"Oh," he finally says.

"It's a right turn onto White Oak in about a mile and then a left at the sign," I say.

I tense, despite myself.

Say it. Say it, I dare you.

He doesn't say a thing. We drive out of town, his headlights swiping across tree trunks like a barcode in the forest.

"How's your mom?" he finally asks.

I glance over, but he looks sincere. Serious. I swallow.

"Gone," I say.

He looks over at me for a second, taking his eyes off the road.

"Shit, I'm sorry," he says. "I didn't know."

There's a raw note in his voice I don't recognize, and my heart twists in my chest.

"Thanks," I finally say. "It's been a couple years."

"What happened?"

"Lung cancer."

I leave it at that. There's more to it than *she's gone, lung cancer*, but I still don't know how to tell it. I don't know if I ever will, but right now I sure haven't figured out how to say *now I just want another day with the mother I spent so much time resenting* or *sometimes I wished it would kill her faster and I still can't forgive myself* or *I don't know if I'll ever stop blaming her.*

"That's a hard way to go," he says.

"It was," I say.

We're quiet for a long time. What do you say after that?

"How are your brothers?" I finally ask, just to change the subject.

"Mostly staying out of trouble," he says, making the right turn onto White Oak, trees flashing in his headlights. He sounds relieved.

"Mostly?"

"Mostly is about all you can ask for," he says, a smile in his voice. "Besides, I imagine you know better than I do."

He's probably right. The five Loveless boys are beloved by the Sprucevale rumor mill, who have deemed them simultaneously handsome, eligible, and unsuitable.

Levi, the eldest, is brown-haired and brown-eyed, has an impressive beard, and lives in a cabin he built himself up on a mountain. He's the chief arborist for our part of the Cumberland National Forest, a vegetarian, a slow talker but a quick thinker, and knows more about lichen than I do about anything.

Eli's younger by two years. He's an argumentative asshole who's vexed me since we were in the same kindergarten class. Enough about him.

Daniel's only a year younger than Eli. He's got light brown hair, crystal-blue eyes, and a six-year-old daughter named Rusty with a woman who, when she bothers to show up in her daughter's life, is at best a shrieking hell-banshee and at worst, a drain on society. He's the master brewer at Loveless Brewing, which he owns with Seth.

Seth, the fourth, has dark hair and gray-green eyes, and he's unsuitable because he's never going to settle down. At least, he's too charming and too flirtatious for the Sprucevale gossip machine to approve of him. He's likely to show you a fantastic time and then never call again, which got him labeled ungentlemanly — and worse — but he doesn't seem to mind. He runs the business side of the brewery he owns with Daniel.

The youngest, Caleb, has dark hair and blue eyes, and last I heard he was in grad school up in Charlottesville getting his doctorate in some kind of theoretical mathematics. If I remember correctly, he's spending his summer break hiking some long-haul trail out west.

"Levi's wrestling bears or climbing trees or whatever he does up there. Daniel's making beer and ferrying Rusty to ballet class. Seth's doing the paperwork and trying to stay out of trouble. Caleb's in California, hiking part of the Pacific Crest Trail before he starts working on his dissertation this fall."

"And your mom's still teaching at the college?"

"Still teaching," he confirms. "Still trying to figure out if the universe is getting bigger or smaller."

There's another long pause. I take a deep breath. I relax a little, even though the air in here is still humming.

Maybe the past can be behind us. Maybe Eli and I can peacefully co-exist as adults.

But then he glances over at me again, smiling that half-smile he's always had, only now it's handsome and it hits me in that soft spot right below my sternum.

Something's coming and I'm not gonna like it.

"So, what *did* you say to that guy?" he asks.

I slouch against the passenger seat, face in the wind

again, ankles still crossed. The nice thing about the giant Bronco is that Eli's about ten feet away from me, so it's not too hard to avoid looking at him.

I sigh.

"He was a dick," I say, resigned.

Eli laughs.

"If that's what you said, I'm not surprised he bailed."

"He bailed because I wouldn't sleep with him."

"My cooking didn't get you in the mood?" Eli asks.

A quick tightness knots in my stomach. I look over and he's half-smiling, watching the road.

"It wasn't *that* good," I say.

"I was voted the panty-droppingest chef west of the Mississippi two years running," he says.

There's that knot again, along with the fervent wish that I had a harder time believing it.

"Too bad we're east of the Mississippi."

"I must have had less competition in Sonoma," he says with a smirk that says *I know full well I didn't.*

"I imagine it's against the editorial standards of the Journal-Bulletin to print the word *panty*, so I doubt you'll get that particular honor while you're here."

"Too bad, because meanwhile I'm ruining dates left and right."

"You're giving yourself entirely too much credit."

"You don't believe in the power of a good meal?"

I turn my head and look at Eli, his face glowing in the reflection of the dashboard lights, blue and green shining off his dark wild hair. My stomach flutters. I cross my ankles a little tighter.

I wonder why he's so interested in how my date went wrong. I wonder how we haven't managed to strangle each other yet, though we came close in the kitchen.

"He snapped at the waitress," I finally say. "There's no meal powerful enough to make up for that."

Eli just whistles low.

"Bad, right?"

"I'd hate to be the man trying to impress you," he says, shaking his head.

"You approve of snapping at the waitstaff?"

Eli brakes, turns, his headlights washing across the sign that reads *Pine Estates Mobile Home Park*. I swallow the rising tension in my throat.

"Hell no," he says. "But all the same, the man was in a bad position."

"He snapped at the waitress like he was trying to train a dog, then ditched his date, and *he* was the one in a bad position?"

Eli slows, turns right down a row of mobile homes, chuckles again. Heat's creeping up my neck, my body rigid.

Don't let him get to you. Don't.

"I'm not excusing him," he says. "Just saying I don't envy him."

I crack a knuckle. *Don't let him get to you.*

"The position of taking me out on a date?"

"The position of thinking there's anything he could do that would impress you enough to have sex with him."

He points at a trailer on the outside of the loop, with a car in the parking spot, two potted flowers on the tiny front porch, Christmas lights neatly strung around the top, and no rust spots.

"Even I know that's a hopeless cause," he goes on. "That's you?"

"That's me, and you don't know a *thing* about me," I said as he slows to a stop.

"I know you still live in the nicest trailer in Pine Estates," he says.

Every muscle in my body tenses, the defensive anger whooshing through me like a flame as I open my mouth, ready to light him on fire.

"And I know anyone trying to buy their way into your good graces is likely to be disappointed," he goes on before I can say anything.

"Oh," I say, caught off guard, my anger deflated.

He didn't say it.

Eli props one elbow against the window, leans his chin on it, and grins.

I don't hate the grin, though I do hate the way my stomach feels like it's sliding around inside my body when he aims it at me.

"Have a good night, Violet," he says. "I'm sure I'll see you around."

I pull at the door release. Nothing.

"You gotta —"

I tug on it and the door jerks open.

"Right," he says.

"Thanks for the ride," I tell him.

"Told you it wouldn't be so bad."

I hop out and heave the door shut without responding, because anything I say will lead to us arguing in a truck, in a trailer park at almost one in the morning, and that's how an episode of *Cops* starts.

My heart is still beating a little too fast as I mount the aluminum steps of my mobile home and unlock the door. I can still feel Eli's eyes on me, even though I don't look back.

It's not until I close the door behind myself and lock it that I hear the guttural sound of his engine revving, the slow crunch of his tires on the gravel as he leaves.

He didn't say it.

Of course he didn't. You're adults.

You know he still thinks it, though. Deep down, you know that.

I put my shoes on the rack next to the front door, slide my slippers onto my feet, and head into the kitchen where I pour myself a glass of water.

I drink and the years slide away until I can practically hear him.

I know where you live.

Trailer trash.

He didn't say it, but he didn't have to say it. I heard it so much in middle school — sometimes the full moniker, sometimes *T. T.* for short, if the teachers were around — that it's practically engraved into my soul.

In the years since then, I've been valedictorian of Sprucevale High. I got a full ride to college. I took care of my mom and still graduated Summa Cum Laude before finding a good job in a town that doesn't have too many of those.

All that, and I still live in Pine Estates.

All that, and I'm certain Eli Loveless still thinks I'm trailer trash. I've got a knot in my chest. I've had the stupidest day and I just want to cry, the pressure behind my eyes demanding release, but I don't.

I wash out the glass, put it in the drying rack, wipe down the counter, and go to bed.

CHAPTER FOUR

ELI

Just as I make the turn, the Bronco slips into neutral.

"What'll you give me?" the small voice asks from the backseat.

I grit my teeth together, silencing a string of muttered curse words, grab the gear shift, and hit the brakes. The Bronco jolts to a stop, half on the road and half on the gravel driveway of Loveless Brewing. It's got a tiny hill that's five degrees at most, but I'll be damned if my car doesn't do this every single time.

I really, really need to get second gear checked out. I've been putting it off for two months now, but sooner or later I'm going to have to take the Bronco in.

"What do you want?" I ask as I muscle the gear shift into first, then hold it there as I ease off the clutch and onto the gas. Lucky for me, my brothers' brewery is just past the edge of town right off Highway 39, so there are no other cars in sight.

"Wedding cake," she says, like she's been thinking about it.

The Bronco growls, the engine making a guttural

clanking sound that doesn't thrill me. I give it a little more gas.

"I don't have any wedding cake," I say.

I give it a little *more* gas and the Bronco practically leaps forward, shooting up the tiny hill and into the parking lot, gravel crunching beneath the tires.

"I mean after a wedding," Rusty says, sounding exasperated in that way that only kids can.

I don't answer her right away, just park next to Daniel's old blue Subaru wagon. Since it's three on a Monday afternoon, there aren't too many other cars here — Daniel's, Seth's Mustang, Levi's Forest Service truck, a beat-up Ford F250 that looks familiar, and a gleaming, brand-new white extended cab Ram that doesn't.

I turn the car off, remove my seatbelt, and turn around to look Rusty in the face. The kid is sitting in her booster seat like it's a judge's bench, both her hands on the padded bar in front of her.

"Just to be clear," I say. "You want a piece of wedding cake after the first wedding at my new job."

For the first time since these negotiations began, Rusty looks uncertain, like she thinks I might be trying to get one over on her. I'm not. I just want to make sure that our terms are absolutely clear, because the kid drives a hard bargain.

"Dad said you were going to a lot of weddings at your new job," she says, her fingers intertwining in front of her. "You can get wedding cake, right?"

"Of course I can get wedding cake," I tell her, even though I'm not exactly certain, given my new job doesn't start until tomorrow.

"Okay. That's what I want."

I nod once, all business.

"Deal. I'll come around to unbuckle you and we'll shake on it."

I hop out of the driver's side and head around to the back door, only to find Rusty looking at me quizzically, the expression making her look almost exactly like her dad.

I fight back a grin, because I don't want to put our bargain in jeopardy by making her think I'm laughing at her. Six-year-old egos can be delicate.

"All right," I say, holding out my right hand. The Bronco is so big that, in her booster seat, Rusty's nearly eye-level with me. "I'll get you a piece of wedding cake on Saturday, and you don't tell your dad about the words you heard me say."

She looks from my hand to my face, her big eyes wide, her golden-brown curls wild around her face. The curls are from her mom, but the rest of her is pure Loveless.

Including the negotiations. She may look just like her dad, but she somehow got my personality.

"An edge piece," she says, still not taking my hand. "With a lot of frosting."

I narrow my eyes at her like I'm thinking.

"And a frosting rose. I want a frosting rose and I won't tell my dad."

I withdraw my hand, cross my arms over my chest. Rusty looks nervous, one dangling foot kicking in the air.

"Not all wedding cakes have frosting flowers," I tell her. "You're gonna have to take your chances on that one, kiddo."

A tiny frown crosses her face, but then she nods.

"Okay," she says.

We shake on it, and the deal's official: I steal her a sugar bomb from work, and she doesn't tell my brother Daniel what I said when my damn car stalled out five times in a row going up the hill by the old Whitman place.

As soon as I lift her down, she's off like a shot, running for the front door of Loveless Brewing, her wild hair bouncing and waving. I watch until she disappears through the front door, then heave the car door shut.

"Eli," another voice calls. "Come give me a hand."

I turn to find my brother Levi standing behind his truck, watching me.

"She's fine, Seth and Daniel are in there," he says. "Take one of these in, will you?"

I walk over to Levi's dark green Forest Service truck. He's bent over the back, pulling a box out, the tailgate down. He looks like he's just come from work, still wearing the gray-green Forest Service overalls that say *Levi Loveless* over one breast pocket, and his work boots. He drags a cardboard box from the bed and hands it to me.

It's surprisingly heavy. I tilt it one way and then the other, getting a better grip on it, while Levi watches me skeptically.

"You got that?"

"What's in here?" I ask, securing it with an arm underneath. It feels like the bottom of the thing is about to fall out, and it smells like gin. I know he's got a still somewhere out near his cabin, hidden in the forest, and I half-wonder if he's bringing bootleg hooch to the brewery.

"Juniper berries," he says, grabbing an identical box from his truck. He balances it on the side while he pushes the tailgate up, then lifts it onto his shoulder.

"From where?" I ask.

"From *Juniperus virginiana,*" he says with the same flourish he always uses when he gives the Latin name for something.

He gives the Latin name surprisingly often.

I don't respond, I just wait. Levi is accustomed to telling you what he wants you to know in his own sweet time.

"Commonly known as Eastern Red Cedar," he goes on. "Daniel and Seth asked if I could find some juniper berries. They're making an IPA."

With his other arm, he gestures toward the door that Rusty disappeared through, the movement surprisingly graceful and courteous, especially for someone who looks like birds could nest in his beard if he isn't careful.

Levi and I probably look alike. We're brothers, after all. He's the oldest and I'm two years younger, but unless he shaves his beard and cuts his hair or I cease my personal upkeep for a few months and start wearing a top knot, we aren't going to find out how much alike.

Half the time he's wearing the exact same thing he has on right now: dark green Forest Service coveralls, the sleeves rolled up to the elbow, and thick work boots. He lives way up in the Cumberland National Forest, in a cabin he built himself, and works as the forest's Chief Arborist.

I hoist the box of juniper berries onto my shoulder, and we head through the front door of the brewery. Inside it smells sweet and bready, the scent of half-finished beer flooding my senses. Levi leads us wordlessly to the walk-in cold storage, takes my box, and carefully stacks it atop his.

"Hope that's enough," he says, eyeing them. "If they need more, they can pick the things themselves."

"Anything else in the truck?" I ask, brushing my hands off, though I'm sure they'll smell like cedar for the next few days regardless.

"That's all for—"

"—strongly advise that you take this offer now because there won't be another," a voice says suddenly, echoing from somewhere outside the cold storage room where we're standing.

The voice is too loud to be polite, and sounds as if it belongs to a man unaccustomed to being told *no*.

It's also very, very familiar.

Levi gives me a glance and walks past, heading for the door and seeing what all the commotion is about. I follow on his heels.

"We'll take our chances," comes Daniel's voice, calm and laconic as ever. "Thanks for stopping by."

"You're going to regret this," the other voice goes on. "Do you know—"

"Get out."

That's Seth, his voice flat and hard, an edge to it that instantly makes me nervous. Levi and I exchange glances as we walk quickly out of the cold storage, between two huge steel tanks, and skirt a puddle of something on the concrete floor.

"—I could crush you like—"

"Out!" Seth shouts.

Levi and I break into a jog, tanks and nozzles and hoses all hissing away above us in the vast brewery. He rounds a corner and I'm one second behind.

Then I nearly run into his back, skidding to a stop.

Seth is nose-to-nose with Walter Eighton, the biggest landowner in Burnley County. Rather, he's nose-to-forehead, given that Seth towers over almost anyone who isn't related to him.

"I suggest you do as he says," Levi tells him, walking forward slowly, his arms crossed over his chest.

Walter just snorts, still looking up at Seth. He's wearing a suit that looks expensive but poorly tailored, nice fabric that doesn't fit him quite right, like he doesn't even have the patience to get something fitted.

"You don't scare me," he says. "None of you inbred rednecks are gonna—"

"You pompous shit sack—"

Daniel steps neatly between them before Seth can get

any further with his insult, holding his hands out. Behind him Seth's jaw flexes, his eyes flashing. Levi unfurls his arms and eases to his younger brother's side, ready to catch him before he can do any real damage.

"You can go on your own or you can be escorted," Daniel says flatly. "Your pick, Walter, though I think you might not enjoy your escort."

Walter finally takes a step back. He adjusts his suit jacket, an ugly tie underneath it, and he looks at all four of us with flat eyes.

"I'll get what I want," he says, voice brimming with as much menace as he can muster. "Even if it means going through the lot of you."

He stalks off toward the exit. Levi and I exchange a glance, and Levi follows him, a few paces back, just to make sure the man doesn't get lost on his way out. Seth, Daniel, and I watch them disappear.

"Fucker," Seth mutters.

"What was that?" I ask.

"That was a rich, entitled asshole who thinks that the world should fall at his feet just because his daddy owns a chain of grocery stores," Seth says.

Daniel doesn't say anything. He just frowns after Walter and Levi, like he's thinking.

It's par for the course. Daniel's normally placid as a lake on a windless day and calm as a toad in the sun, while Seth is fiery and mercurial. He's always the first to jump into a fight, but also the first to laugh long and hard at a good joke. It's a wonder they can work together, but Loveless Brewing had a banner year last year, so I guess something is going right.

"It's not even our land," Daniel says, half to himself. "It's Mom's."

Levi comes back around the corner and walks up to us.

"He out?" Seth asks.

"Yeah, but not before giving me the hard sell on selling him a hundred and fifty acres of Mom's land," he says, frowning.

"I'm starting to feel left out," I say.

"Yeah, you should be real bummed about that jerk not getting in your face," Seth says.

"Rusty made it in here, right?"

"She's on the office couch reading *Little House on the Prairie,*" Daniel says.

Then he shrugs, runs a hand through his hair, and looks from Levi to me and back again.

"You bring the juniper berries?" he asks.

· · · · · ★ ★ ★ ★ ★ · · · · ·

"THAT SLIMY BASTARD," my mom fumes, slamming open a cupboard. "That backstabbing, underhanded, weasel-faced no good son-of-a—"

"Mom!" Daniel shouts.

"I'm not listening," Rusty says.

She's sitting at the kitchen table, carefully coloring a pony with an electric blue mane and bright green hooves, looking innocent. It doesn't work on me. Rusty is *always* listening. That's why I owe her cake.

"Sorry, baby," my mom says, pulling out a big pot and filling it with water. "But I can't believe that—"

She takes a deep breath, then sighs, clearly thinking of all the words she'd rather be using.

"— That *jerk* thought that just because I said no, he could go behind my back and work up some kind of deal with you all," she says, slamming the faucet off and yanking the pot out of the sink so fast it sloshes onto the floor.

I grab a hand towel and dry it, a few steps behind my mom.

"That sneaky, good-for-nothing, two-faced little man has always been an absolute prick —"

"Mom."

"— Prick's not a bad word, Daniel, he's always been a prick who thinks that he farts rainbows. You remember the time he failed algebra and his daddy got him that remote control airplane to make him feel better?"

"No," says Seth, with the air of someone who's had this conversation before.

He's just here for the food and has his own place in town. Daniel and Rusty live here, since my mom's helping raise Rusty. I've got the attic room on a temporary basis, until I find my own place to live.

"You were a baby," my mom says authoritatively, turning on the stove under the pot of water. She stands there glaring at it, like that will make it boil faster. From the table, I hear the distinct sound of Rusty trying not to giggle.

"And then he crashed it into the river?" Seth asks, knowing what comes next. Mom gets on a tear about the Eightons sometimes, so this is all familiar.

"So his daddy bought him a remote control helicopter," Mom goes on, slamming open cupboards again. "He should have given him a whipping instead. Or an algebra tutor, for heaven's sake, the man is nearly forty and I doubt he could graph an equation if his life depended on it."

"I don't think I could graph an equation," I offer, still standing in the kitchen. Any time my mom starts cooking, I get nervous.

She turns and looks at me, disbelief written all over her face.

"I'm sure you just need a refresher," she says, grabbing

down a jar full of sugar. "Whereas Walter Eighton needs someone to remove his head from his colon."

"Mom, that's —"

She dumps the sugar into the water, then screws the top back on, jamming it back into the cabinet.

I sigh.

"He thinks just because he's got money, he can get whatever he wants, whenever he wants. Just walk all over other people like they don't matter," she fumes, slamming open another cabinet and grabbing a package of spaghetti.

"Mom, that was sugar," I say, coming toward the stove.

"It's spaghetti, Eli," she says, holding up the pasta.

I walk over and gently take it from her hand.

"You just dumped sugar in the water," I tell her. "Come on. I'll make dinner."

She huffs, glaring at me with her steely green eyes. I stare back, raising one eyebrow.

"Fine," she says at last, ending the stare down. "There's garlic bread, too."

"No problem," I tell her, steering her toward the kitchen table. As soon as she turns away from me, I make the universal *get her a drink* motion at Seth, who rises and grabs the bottle of good whiskey.

"That's a beautiful horse, honey," she says to Rusty. "Have you named it?"

"This is Gertrude," Rusty answered.

I dump out the water, wash out the pot, refill it and put it on to boil while Mom continues half-ranting about Walter Eighton and half-talking to Rusty about her coloring book. While that's going on, I grab some eggs, onions, bacon, and parmesan, and get to chopping.

Walter Eighton offered to buy our family land. That, in and of itself, isn't a problem. It's not the first offer we've gotten for the hundred and fifty acres that border on the national forest, and I doubt it will be the last.

It's the fact that when Daniel and Seth said no, things got ugly. Walter got pissed and threatened them, said he'd take the land one way or another if he had to. He swore that he *knew a guy* from up in Richmond and he also swore that he'd sue us into oblivion, so it doesn't sound like he's made up his mind on how to do us in just yet.

Unbeknownst to any of us, it wasn't the first offer he'd made on the land. A few weeks before he'd offered a lower price to my mom, and when she declined, he called her a senile old fool who'd regret turning him down.

Clarabelle Loveless is many things — bad cook, accomplished astronomer, doting grandmother — but she's not senile and she's *certainly* not a fool. She's angry about the name-calling, but she's *furious* that he went behind her back and tried to make a deal with Seth and Daniel.

Walter wants to build some sort of shopping center on the land, calling it 'phase one' of a project that will 'bring economic opportunity to Southwestern Virginia,' which sounds like bullshit to me. He wants to raze acres of perfectly beautiful forest for some outlet malls, followed by a ski resort and a waterpark.

We all know full well exactly who'd profit in that scheme. By and large, it's not the people of Sprucevale.

Except the Eightons, of course. They'd profit while the rest of us would be lucky if the capitalist megaplex didn't bleed us dry, put all our stores out of business, and ruin our beautiful countryside while they were at it.

"His mother's a piece of work, too," Mom says, the ice clinking in her glass. "Remember for Walter's wedding about ten years back, she insisted on importing the lawn from somewhere in Kentucky?"

Seth snorts.

"How'd she import a lawn?"

"In sod chunks," Mom says. "On a flatbed truck. Bluegrass. All the way here from Kentucky. No wonder he thinks the world is his for the taking."

"Did it look good?" Daniel asks. He sounds baffled.

"It looked like grass," Mom says, shrugging. "At least when I saw it a week later."

"Plus, she parks like an asshole," I add. I remember Rusty's presence one second too late.

"Oh, come on," Daniel says.

"Sorry. She parks like a butthole."

Daniel just sighs.

"Every time I see her Mercedes at the grocery store, she's parked diagonally across two spots," I say, tearing open the package of spaghetti, the water close to boiling. I'd already put the garlic bread in the oven, and a pile of bacon and onions on low heat on the next burner.

I'd also quietly thrown away the jar of pasta sauce that my mom had gotten out, since I'd given it a taste test and I was pretty sure she'd made it with mint. Spaghetti carbonara was a much better option.

"I know it," my mom says. "Last week when I was there, I parked right up next to her, not a foot away from her driver's side door. Bet she had to get in the other side and crawl over."

Seth snickers. They keep on talking, moving from Walter to his parents and then finally off the topic completely. I boil pasta, crack eggs, and try to keep my mind from wandering to Violet and how much her continued presence in Sprucevale vexes me.

I have no idea why she's still here. By rights, she shouldn't be — when we were growing up, she never liked this place to begin with, and even if I don't like her, I can recognize that she's meant for bigger and better things.

I know she'd gone to college nearby, but even though I lost track of her after my own disastrous college experience, I just assumed she moved on. People like her don't stick around a tiny town in the middle of nowhere; people like her move to big cities, Richmond or D.C. or maybe even New York, and they get high-powered jobs and wear suits and make conference calls.

It bothers me that she hasn't. I know she wanted to. If anyone deserved to move on from Appalachian Nowheresville, it's her.

I finish the pasta, make a quick salad, and pull the garlic bread out of the oven while the rest of my family chats around the kitchen table. I make myself stop wondering what Violet's deal is, since she's not my problem and, with any luck, I won't be seeing much of her.

"Eli," Seth says when we all sit down a few minutes later, mouth full of garlic bread. "Tell us about your new job."

CHAPTER FIVE
VIOLET

I flip through the pictures one more time. There's the airy, bright loft space. There's the small-but-modern kitchen, complete with a farmhouse sink. There's the open plan living and dining room; also small, but bright, sunny, welcoming, and all the things that my trailer isn't.

Last but not least: there's the view of Deepwood Lake, shot from the cabin's deck, the day outside perfectly cloudless and beautiful.

I bet it's always sunny at this cabin, I think wistfully, sitting in my tiny office. I lean my chin on my hand, staring at my computer, phone held to one ear.

I bet the neighbors there never shoot beer cans off the top of a fence post with a BB gun at three in the morning when they've been drinking for twelve hours straight.

Also, nothing there leaks when it rains. Ever.

I glance at the price one more time. $97,000.

I'm so, so close. And yet…

"Thank you for holding, Miss Tulane," a voice on the other end of the phone line says, jerking me out of my cabin-by-the-lake reverie. "And thank you for confirming that you did *not* purchase the Wet And Wild Pool Party Floating Mechanical Bull With Real Bull Sound Effects And Bonus Accessory Drink Floats."

"Not a problem," I lie. It's actually been at least three days' worth of problems, but given that it seems like my stolen credit card woes are coming to an end, I let it go. I've already requested replacements of everything else in my wallet and this is, at last, the final piece.

I'm pretty sure I left it on the counter at the Mountain Grind on Friday morning when I got coffee. Someone must have taken it. I'd love to know who so I could give them a piece of my mind, but I'll settle for having fraudulent charges removed from my credit card.

"Now, just to check, these other purchases on your card are correct, yes?" she asks.

I frown. I froze all my credit cards first thing when I woke up Sunday morning, and at the time, the only suspicious purchase was a floating mechanical bull.

I don't even understand how a floating mechanical bull works. Doesn't it capsize and dump its rider directly into the water the moment it starts moving? Doesn't the bull have to be braced against something more substantial than water?

Though maybe that's the point. Maybe it's some sort of special fraternity edition, used for wet t-shirt contests on spring break or whatever it is fraternities do. I don't know. I went to a frat party once for about five minutes before some guy asked me if I had any Alpha Pi in me, then asked if I wanted some. It didn't even make any sense.

"Miss Tulane?" the woman on the other end of the phone says, pulling me from my mechanical bull contemplations.

"What other purchases?" I ask, wondering what one buys to go with a floating mechanical bull.

"There are just a few," she says, and I hear clicking in the background. "A fuel purchase in Iron River, Wisconsin for forty-two fifty-four, a charge for one hundred nineteen dollars and three cents at Mickey's Candy Castle in New Haven, Connecticut, and another charge for three seventy-five and seventy-four cents from We Love Wrapping Paper Dot Com."

For a moment, I'm speechless. Whoever stole my card has been getting around, and they've been buying some weird stuff.

"Was it all wrapping paper?" I ask.

"I'm sorry?"

I glance at the clock. I'm supposed to be at the all-staff meeting in seven minutes, but I also really want to know how much wrapping paper three-seventy-five-seventy-four buys. A lot, right?

"Did someone use my card to buy almost four hundred dollars' worth of *wrapping paper*? From We Love Wrapping Paper Dot Com?"

There's a pause.

"I'm afraid I can't tell from this transaction report," she finally says.

I look around my office, crammed full of wedding ephemera for the upcoming weekend, and wonder exactly how much wrapping paper that is. Maybe whoever stole my credit card really, really likes giving gifts. Maybe they're going to wrap several cars in wrapping paper as a prank. Maybe they have a fetish and need to be wrapped before they can achieve orgasm.

If it's that last one, I actually kind of feel bad for them.

"Can I assume that you didn't make any of these charges?" she prompts.

"Yes," I say, my mind still half on the possibility of wrapping paper fetishes. "I mean, no, I didn't make any of them. I thought I froze my cards on Sunday morning, so I'm not sure how those charges got there in the first place."

"Thank you. Do you mind holding for one more minute?" she asks.

The hold music starts before I can say *please don't make me hold any more*. I sigh and go back to flipping through the pictures of my dream cabin: a bathroom with a real bathtub. Hardwood floors. A big oak tree out front. Sure, it's only about a thousand square feet, but I can deal with that for that kitchen and that *view*.

Besides, I really, really don't want to live in the trailer for much longer, but it's cheap while I'm saving up. In a few more months, I'll have the down payment and then it's sayonara, Pine Estates.

Someone knocks on my door, and a moment later, my intern Kevin pokes his head in.

"Paper lanterns are here?" he asks.

I point to a corner of my office, the one I use as a staging area for the upcoming wedding of the week. It's piled high with brightly-colored seat cushions — the bride didn't like the standard colors that we offered — sparkly gold tablecloths, five-foot-high glass tubes to hold flower arrangements, the lanterns Kevin is looking for, and bags upon bags upon bags of M&Ms with the bride and groom's initials on them.

To my credit, I've eaten absolutely none of them even though there are way more than they're going to need and I've been on hold for what feels like a year.

Kevin grabs the lanterns and takes off, leaving me still on hold. I glance up at the clock again: five minutes until the meeting. I squeeze my eyes shut to quell my rising anxiety, because if I weren't stuck on the phone, I'd be there already.

I like being early, by at least five minutes if not a little more. I don't like feeling as if people are waiting on me, and I especially don't like that feeling if some of those people are my bosses.

The seconds tick down on the clock. I have visions of all my coworkers arriving in the meeting room, milling around, getting coffee. Calmly putting their folders and notebooks down on the table. Everyone perfectly relaxed, knowing that they still have several minutes before the meeting begins. Everyone but me, because at this rate I'll probably run in there two minutes late, with a post-it probably stuck to me somewhere.

I check myself for stray post-its while I wait. None.

Finally, after another excruciating minute, the other end of the line clicks.

"Hi, and thanks for holding," says a brand-new voice. "All right, Miss Tulane, I'm happy to tell you that we've updated your address on file and sent it to Pool Accessories On Fleek LLC, and it looks like the Wet And Wild Pool Party Floating Mechanical Bull With Real Bull Sound Effects And Bonus Accessory Drink Floats will be on its way to you very shortly."

"What? No," I say, sitting up straighter in my chair. "There's been a mistake. I didn't order that, my card was stolen and I asked for it to be canceled."

He just makes a noise. It sounds dubious, and not terribly unlike a bull. I think.

"Please don't send me a mechanical bull," I say, starting to panic. "Or a thousand pounds of wrapping paper. Or a ton of candy. I've got absolutely nowhere to put it and I really, really don't want it."

"Hmmm," the new person on the phone says. "Can you hold for a moment?"

"Yes," I say, but the hold music is already on again.

I look at the clock again. Three minutes until the meeting. I could hang up right now, but then I'd be throwing thirty minutes of wait time down the toilet, and I don't like that possibility either.

You can be a minute late, I tell myself. *You've never been late before, and besides, it's an all-staff meeting. Montgomery won't even start the thing until five after and no one will notice when you walk in.*

I get out of my chair and start pacing my office as far as the phone cord lets me, which isn't very far.

Two minutes. I remind myself that thousands of people all over the world are late to meetings all the time and usually nothing bad happens.

At last, the line clicks on again.

"All right, ma'am, I've spoken with a representative at Pool Accessories On Fleek and apprised them that you do *not* want the mechanical bull," he finally says.

I sigh in relief, leaning against my desk and slump over.

"Thank you," I say, looking at the clock. If I power-walk, I'll still be exactly on time.

"However, they asked me to tell you that if you *do* receive a mechanical bull, you can just ship it back at no cost. Just give them a call and they'll pick up the tab."

"No!" I say, too loudly.

"I'm sorry?" he asks.

They're going to send me the damn bull. I know it. I know, deep down in my bones, that there has been some sort of deep rift in communication in the depths of this particular financial institution, and I'm going to get a floating mechanical bull in the mail. With bonus accessory drink floats.

Also, I have one minute to get clear across the building to the wedding season kick off all-staff meeting, and I'm going to have to run.

"Listen," I said, standing up straight. "I would very much appreciate it if you could make it clear to the bull company that I do *not* want a mechanical bull. I don't have a pool. I don't like bull riding. I have absolutely no use for a mechanical bull and if you send me one, I'm not going to send it back. I'm going to keep it, put lipstick on it, name it Martha, and *never ever pay for it, is that clear?*"

I may have gone slightly off the rails there at the end.

There's a long, long pause, and I start to wonder if he's hung up on me for being a lunatic.

"Yes, ma'am," he finally says.

Another pause.

"Is there anything else I can help you with today?"

I thank him, get off the phone as quickly as I can, grab my notepad and pen, and book it out of my office.

The biggest conference room, where the all-staff meeting is taking place, is clear on the other side of two former dairy barns. Sometime in the 1970s, when Bramblebush went from being a working farm to the venue and inn that it is now, the space between the two was enclosed and the whole thing turned into one big building that houses staff offices, storerooms, and the kitchen.

I break into a half-walk, half-jog, my heels clicking on the tile floor. Every office I pass is empty. It doesn't help the anxiety slowly blossoming in my chest, so I pick up a little speed, rounding a corner.

Right into a brick wall.

I bounce, then flail backward, stumbling several steps before finally landing on my ass, my notebook and pen flying in opposite directions.

"Are you okay?" the brick wall asks.

It's not a literal brick wall.

"I'm fine, I'm fine," I say, already collecting myself, grabbing my notebook and pen from where they flew, my face red hot with embarrassment already. "Sorry, I was in—"

Hold on.

I look up. I've heard that voice recently, like *last weekend* recently.

"No," I say, my gaze crashing into his.

Eli's mouth hitches up on one side, both eyebrows rising.

I wish for the thousandth time that he hadn't turned out so damn *handsome*, because I definitely feel that smirk somewhere deep inside me that Eli isn't supposed to have access to. Somewhere personal.

"Yes," he says after a moment.

"What are you doing here?"

"Well, I *was* having a leisurely walk down a hallway, when —"

"I mean *here* here. At Bramblebush."

"I work here. What are *you* doing here?"

I'm still on the floor, butt still throbbing. I've managed to sit up cross-legged while I stare up at Eli Loveless, who's claiming that he works here after showing up in my life for the second time in four days.

Also, he still has that expression on his face. The obnoxious one that gives me some funny tingles that I do *not* approve of.

"No, you don't," I say, ignoring his question.

"Yes, I do."

"No, you *don't.*"

Eli leans down, offering me one hand. I look at it. He rolls his eyes.

"It's my hand, not a cobra," he says.

I put both my hands to the floor and push myself up, ignoring Eli's outstretched hand out of sheer pettiness, brushing the floor dust off my black pants.

I silently offer a quick prayer of thanks to whichever deity oversaw my wardrobe decisions that morning. I wore pants and not a skirt. If Eli ever saw my panties I'd probably have to murder him, and then I'd have to spend the rest of my life in jail because I'm not the kind of person who could get away with a murder. The police would look at me sideways and I'd break down in tears and confess, I'm sure.

"What do you mean, *you work here*?" I say, ignoring my now-sore butt in favor of the uneasiness crawling into my chest.

"I'd have thought it was self-evident," he says, crossing his arms. "But if you'd like, I can really break it down for you. See, I've got what's colloquially known as a *job*, where I come into a place of business and exchange my services for money —"

"You don't have to be a dick about it."

"*I'm* being a dick about it? You just crashed into me and then told me I was wrong about working here before you'd even gotten off the floor," he says.

"Why were you standing in such a weird place?" I snap back. I'm losing the argument and I know it, and that annoys me more than almost anything else.

I hate losing. I hate being wrong, I hate being late, and I definitely hate literally running into my former nemesis when I thought I was safe.

Also, if we're listing things that I hate: his smirk, the way his forest-green eyes feel like they're looking straight through me, the way his button-down shirt is an iota too tight, the fact that Eli clearly works out and isn't at all bad to look at.

Too bad about the personality, though.

"You mean, why was I walking through the halls of my workplace in a perfectly normal manner?" he says, still sounding calm. "I'm going to a meeting. Though now I'm going to be late."

Tell him it's in another building, I thought, suddenly feeling devious. *Then he won't show up at all and maybe his boss will realize he's not there and then he'll get fired and you'll never have to see him again.*

I take a deep breath, exhale, and remind myself that I'm twenty-nine, not fourteen.

"The all-staff meeting is the other way," I say. "You're staff?"

"That's what I meant when I said *I work here*, yes," he says. "I'm the new Executive Chef. And I thought the meeting was in the Cumberland conference room, over that way."

I decide to be an adult and bite back a retort to the first part, even though every fiber of my being is itching to further the fight.

"It's in the other building, but they have the exact same layout. It's confusing," I offer. "Come on, I'm going there too."

I walk ahead of him, quickly, because I don't want to look at Eli any more than I have to. He follows me down the hall, through the glassed-in atrium, and to the other barn-turned-offices.

Mercifully, he doesn't say a word, and neither do I.

You're adults now, I remind myself over and over. *He's not going to call you names or tell anyone about your farts.*

No one is asking you to be friends. Just do your job, Eli will do his, and it'll all be fine.

Right?

I'm a grown-ass woman. How hard can it be?

CHAPTER SIX

ELI

"—Third floor is currently being renovated, adding a state-of-the-art spa and two new hot tubs, so if any guests wander into the gated off area, please redirect them," a voice inside the room says. "Bramblebush currently has a zero-fatality record, and we'd like to keep it that way."

Polite laughter ripples through the room just as Violet pauses in the doorway. I pause behind her. I'd walked behind her for the length of two barns now, and I'd been staring at her ass for an unspecified percentage of that time.

It was above fifty percent.

Okay, it was above eighty percent. Maybe around ninety. It's a good ass, and it looks good in those pants, even if the fact that it belongs to Violet Tulane is kind of a boner-killer.

Somehow, she grew up to be attractive, which still blows my mind even though I've had two days to get used to the idea. It just doesn't jive at all with my memories of her, all elbows and glasses and crooked teeth that her mom couldn't afford to have fixed, usually telling me why I was wrong about something.

At least that last part hasn't changed. If it had, I'd wonder if she'd had a lobotomy.

I glance down at her ass again just for good measure. She shoots me an annoyed look over her shoulder, obviously annoyed that we're late.

Those shark-gray eyes send a quick shock through me.

Fine, make that *very attractive*. Physically, at least.

Personality wise, she's still Violet Tulane, as evidenced by our interaction when she headbutted me in the hallway and then interrogated me about my presence at my own job.

She steps into the room and I step in after her, standing against the back wall, behind a few other rows of people, also standing. Violet shoots me another annoyed look, craning her neck to see Montgomery Tanner, our boss, as he goes on about the renovations currently being done at the Bramblebush Inn. Even in heels she's too short to see over the people in front of us.

Don't, I tell myself. *You're at work. Be a goddamn professional, Eli.*

Violet cranes her neck harder, still trying to see over the people in front of her.

I lean down, knowing full well that I should keep my mouth shut.

"Want a boost?" I ask, keeping my voice low, my lips closer to her ear than they should be. Her hair just barely whispers along my cheek, a tingle echoing down my back. It smells nice.

Violet jumps, then shoots me yet another look from her arsenal of glares.

"I can put you on my shoulders," I whisper, leaning in even closer, her hair tickling my cheek even more. "You seem to be having some trouble."

I wouldn't mind that at all, wrapping her legs around my head. Just as long as she didn't talk.

"Shut *up*," she hisses as another woman glances over. I give her a quick, professional nod, and she looks away.

"I'll take a look and tell you what you're missing," I tell Violet. She pretends to ignore me, but a muscle twitches in her jaw.

I grin. I can't help it. If she's going to be obnoxious to me, I'm going to be obnoxious right back.

"And finally, John wants me to remind you all that the golf carts are *not* for guest use," Montgomery says, standing up front. "Make sure to take the keys with you when you get out, we all know what happened last year."

More polite laughter.

"Don't let guests use the golf carts," I quickly whisper to Violet.

She glares daggers. Poisoned daggers, with barbs in the tips. It sends a vicious thrill through me.

"Just trying to help," I say.

"*Shut. Up*," she whispers through her teeth.

She's still standing on her tiptoes, inside her heels, craning her neck like there she's missing out on a glance at the Hope Diamond.

She's not. It's just Montgomery, my boss and, I assume, also hers; a sixty-something Southern man with an accent and personal style that's much more *Gone with the Wind* than *Duck Dynasty*.

It's fitting, given that he runs Bramblebush Farm and has apparently done so for about twenty years. The whole place is also much more *Gone with the Wind* than *Duck*

Dynasty, even though it's at odds with everything else in Sprucevale.

When it was founded, Sprucevale was a coal mining town. Or, at least, it was until the coal ran out. Ever since then it's been trying to recover.

Bramblebush is beautiful. It's opulent. It's luxurious. It's exclusive, an escape for the upper class, where they can come and have their every whim catered to without ever having to see any of those *poor people* they've heard so much about.

Sprucevale, on the other hand, isn't opulent or luxurious or exclusive. It's a working-class town filled with working class people who figured out how to survive once the mines shut down. It's small. It's tight-knit. Everyone feels like family, for better or for worse.

Admittedly, Bramblebush Farm's existence probably helps. A beautiful, secluded retreat for the one percent, it mostly functions as a wedding venue. Despite having a price tag of $150,000 — just to use the space, nothing else — I learned that morning that it was currently booked almost every weekend at least two years in advance.

Four years for summer wedding dates. I can't imagine either of those things: paying that much for a wedding or wanting to wait four years to get hitched once I decide to do it.

Not that I'm in any danger of deciding to get married. Not that I particularly suspect I ever will be, given that I'm nearly thirty and I've never gotten remotely close.

Marriage seems nice, but it also seems like it's for other people.

"All right. John, you got anything else?" Montgomery asks, looking off to one side.

I resist the urge to tell Violet what he just said, because

I think she might actually strangle me if I do. Besides, sooner or later I should remember that I'm at work.

"Nothing here, Montgomery," says a voice I assume is John in an old-school, charming, laid-back southern accent.

"I guess we're on to the main event," Montgomery says.

The assembled staff members — fifty or so — all go perfectly silent and still. Even Violet stands up straighter.

I slip my hands into my pockets, wondering what *the main event* is.

"This year we've got quite a slate of weddings on our hands," Montgomery says, his aristocratic voice flowing out over the audience. "In fact, I daresay this is going to be our biggest wedding season ever."

He pauses. You could hear a pin drop in the silence.

It's obvious that something big is happening, and I've got no idea what.

"Among other guests, we'll be hosting the wedding of the tech billionaire Sergei Volkov's son, and the heir to the Pillsbury flour fortune."

The room shifts impatiently. I wonder what kind of appetizers the Pillsbury heiress will order. If you're heir to a flour fortune, do you love baked goods, or are you tired of them?

"And of course, as many of you already know," he goes on, "this August, Bramblebush will be hosting its first-ever royal wedding."

Gasps arise from the crowd. Violet doesn't seem to react at all. I wonder what kind of royalty is getting married in an out-of-the-way spot in southwestern Virginia. Probably one of those tiny countries in Europe — San Marino or Luxembourg or somewhere inconsequential that still has a royal family by accident.

"Now, I can't tell you all *who* the royal wedding is for until we get a little closer, but I *can* tell you that this year the bonus for the MVP staff member is a little bit higher than it's been in the past," he says, still in absolutely no rush to get to the point. "This summer is going to be a whole lot of hard work, but maybe this'll spice things up a little."

The room practically hums with anticipation.

"This year's," he says, giving his words the weight of an announcement. "Most Valuable Player Bramblebush Staff Star Award. Will be. In the amount of..."

Everyone holds their breath. I hold my breath.

"Twenty thousand dollars!"

Everyone gasps. The room is instantly in an uproar. The guy next to me whistles. Violet claps both her hands to her mouth. The woman next to her turns and asks Violet if Montgomery really said twenty *thousand*, and Violet just nods.

"Okay, everyone!" Montgomery calls from the front of the room, waving his hands like that could calm us down from the revelation that twenty big ones were up for grabs. "You've all got a royal wedding to thank, they're *very* interested in maintaining their privacy. All right, folks, there's pie and coffee along the back wall. Here's to wedding season!"

I don't move. I'm too stunned. Twenty grand is a whole lot of money: enough to move out of my mom's place. Enough to buy a new car.

Enough to fund at least six months of travel to somewhere that *isn't* Sprucevale. Enough to start my own business if I feel like it.

Shit. Twenty thousand dollars.

This is a hell of a first day on the job.

The people around me start talking to each other excitedly, drifting toward the pie and coffee, but before I could go anywhere Violet turns. She catches my eye.

And gives me a *look*. A look I'd know anywhere, any

time, in any country and on any continent. I'd know it because I used to stay up late studying or practicing or honing my debate skills, fantasizing about finally wiping that look off of Violet's face.

I'd like to say that, as a grown man, I rise above that.

I don't.

"They didn't mention a twenty thousand dollar prize in my interview," I say, as casually as I can manage.

"Last year it was two thousand," she says. "And I thought *that* was cutthroat."

"Who won it?"

She cocks one eyebrow, and that's how long it takes me to know the answer.

"Guess."

I glance around, unwilling to fall into her trap right away.

"Naomi," I say, watching the sous chef chatting with someone from Maintenance, cheerfully grabbing a piece of cherry pie.

Violet doesn't bother answering, just looks skeptical. The sharks in her eyes circle.

"Janice," I said, naming our wedding cake person.

"She's not even staff, she's an outside vendor," Violet says, like she's explaining something to a four-year-old.

"She's right over there," I say, nodding in her direction.

"She probably likes pie," Violet points out. "I like pie. Presumably you like pie, unless you really *are* that difficult."

"Difficult?" I ask, putting one hand to my chest. "Violet, I'm anything but."

"Could've fooled me."

"I'm a team player. I'd even say I'm a *valuable* team player," I go on.

Her eyebrows rise, and I swear the side of her mouth

twitches like she's about to smile. In the corner of my vision, I see Montgomery — my new boss and presumably also hers — coming toward us, probably so he can introduce us.

You know, *professional* stuff that sounds a lot less enjoyable than giving Violet Tulane hell.

"Maybe even the *most* valuable player," I say.

"Not a chance," Violet says, deadpan.

"Best be on your toes, Tulane."

She takes one step closer, eyes flashing, and suddenly this feels *very* unprofessional. It feels profoundly personal. It feels like a long-held grudge coming back to life and blossoming in the pressure cooker of the first day at my new job.

Also, god*damn* she's pretty.

"You'll win this over my dead body," she says quietly.

Montgomery closes in. I force myself to keep my cool, even though inside I'm close to my boiling point.

I want to tell her that shit has changed in ten years. That I'm back and I'm going to knock her down a peg.

I want to tell her that I'm going to win that twenty grand, buy myself a big-ass pickup truck, and drive it by her trailer with the radio blasting fifty times a night just to rub it in her face.

But I don't say that. I clench my fists in my pockets and make myself smile.

"Hope you don't mean that literally," is all I say.

Then Montgomery is there, his good-old-boy smile blazing away. Violet steps back, her face softening, and she makes herself smile.

"I see y'all have already met," he says, clapping both of us on the shoulders at the same time. "But just in case, Eli, this is Violet, our Lead Event Coordinator. Violet, this is

Eli, our new Executive Chef. Eli, did you meet Martin yet?"

"I don't think so."

"Martin!" Montgomery calls, his hands still on our shoulders.

Violet makes a face. It's subtle, and she controls herself almost instantly, but it's a face.

Another man saunters over. He looks to be about our age, with dark blond hair, blue eyes, and a sharp nose. His button-down shirt has a Polo logo on one pocket.

Between the look he gave me and the face Violet made, I already don't like him.

"Martin Beauregard," he says, taking my hand and pumping it vigorously. He's got a smile that doesn't reach his eyes, and I give him back the same.

"Martin here is in charge of the guest experience," Montgomery says. "You have any questions about that, just let him know."

I'd like to know what, exactly, being *in charge of the guest experience* even means, but I decide to figure it out on my own.

"Fantastic meeting you," he says, giving me that insincere smile again. "I'm looking forward to our working partnership. Nice seeing you, Violet."

"Nice seeing you too," she says, her voice pure ice.

"Fantastic," Montgomery says to Violet and I as Martin steps away. "Eli, let me steal you away so I can introduce you around. Have you had any pie yet? They're from Ruth-Ann's and her strawberry rhubarb is simply out of this world…"

Violet turns. Montgomery leads me away, still going on about the pie, but my mind isn't on pastry at all.

It's on Violet, and the twenty grand, and Violet. It's on

how if Violet wins it, I may as well move out of Sprucevale again because I'll never hear the end of it.

Right now, I know two things.

One, that money is mine.

And two, Violet is going *down*.

CHAPTER SEVEN

ELI

I open the hood of the smoker and a plume of smoke erupts out and floats upward, smelling of pure heaven and burning my eyes. I wave it away and stick a thermometer into one thigh.

One-sixty. About another hour at least before I can pull the duck out and let it cool.

I glance over my shoulder and back into the big, bustling industrial kitchen from where I'm standing on the grilling patio, a concrete slab that holds five different grills, a tandoori oven, and a giant smoker that's nearly the size of my first car. I'm sure if a guest ever requests such a thing, we'd dig a pit and roast a whole pig for a luau.

Actually, that sounds kind of fun. I've never roasted a pig in a pit before.

Automatically, I start going through my mental checklist. The duck will be done in about an hour. I've got one sous chef baking the hand-turned sesame crackers and the other making almost a thousand wild mushroom ravioli by hand. There are six different sauces reducing on the stove, and in another room, the pastry chef, Janice is baking hundreds of macarons.

It's Thursday afternoon, and things are looking good. Not only is everything going perfectly for my first Bramble-bush wedding as Executive Chef, I've barely seen Violet since the meeting on Tuesday.

Which is ideal. If we have to work at the same place, at least it's big enough that we don't really have to see each other. At this rate, we'll both survive the summer.

I turn to head back inside, but before I make it, the door opens and Violet comes marching out.

"Welcome to the patio," I say, one hundred percent cheerful and professional. "How are you doing?"

"I'm fine," she says carefully, looking at the collection of grills and smokers and outdoor ovens. "But Kevin said there was a problem with the menu that I needed to come talk to you about?"

I take the hand towel that I always have hanging over my shoulder and wipe my hands with it out of habit.

"Right. The mac and cheese balls," I say.

"What's the problem?" she asks. "Did your order not have the ingredients in there? I know Louis, the old chef, was having some issues when deliveries didn't have the right—"

"I'm not making them," I cut her off.

She pauses. Something glints in her gray-blue eyes.

"No?" she finally says.

She doesn't change position, but her entire body tenses and I *feel* the fight coming on the way you can feel a thunderstorm.

"No," I say, crossing my arms in front of myself. "They're a travesty of an appetizer and this kitchen won't be making them anymore."

Violet gives me a long, up-and-down look like she's assessing me for something and finding me unfit.

"They're on the menu," she finally says, her voice full of forced patience. "The bride and groom ordered them months ago. They specifically asked to have the mac and cheese ball appetizers, because I guess the groom's brother went to a wedding here a few years ago and they were so amazing—"

"Well, the groom's brother is wrong because they weren't amazing, mac and cheese balls are *never* amazing, and I'm not in the business of making non-amazing food."

She snorts.

"You're a wedding caterer," she says. "Where do you think you are, some Michelin-starred restaurant in Paris? Make the mac and cheese balls."

Anger bubbles up inside me, fast and hot because Violet is exactly the same as always: infuriating.

"Bangkok," I say.

"What?"

"The Michelin-starred restaurant was in Bangkok."

Violet raises one eyebrow, but I can tell she's surprised.

"Kham Na. I was a sous chef. We were one of three restaurants in the city to get a star," I tell her.

Violet looks at me, her face unreadable.

I want her to be impressed. Despite everything, I do. As much as I want not to care what Violet thinks about *anything*, as much as I want to never give the girl's opinion another thought, I also want her to be impressed.

"And how, exactly, does that prevent you from making the appetizer that's on the menu which was finalized several months ago and which someone has paid *four hundred thousand dollars* for?" she asks.

"If someone paid that much for mac and cheese balls they really overpaid."

"You know what I mean."

"You sure this place isn't laundering money? If I saw appetizers with that price tag, that's the first thing I'd think."

Violet doesn't say anything.

"It's impossible to make good mac and cheese balls," I finally say. "If you can get the cheese thick enough that it'll stick the macaroni together properly, it dries out in the deep fryer. In order to make the macaroni pliable enough to form a ball in the first place, you have to overcook it, and then when you fry them they get even *more* overcooked and the result is a sticky, gloppy, textureless mess that tastes okay but that everyone only wants for the novelty of having macaroni and cheese in ball form, because for some reason Americans have a raging hard-on for all their childhood favorites. Next you'll be asking me to make chicken nuggets and tater tots fancy."

"No one ever complained about Louis's mac and cheese balls," she says. "They were fine. More importantly, he made them and didn't try to mess with a menu two days before a wedding!"

"Just because no one complained doesn't mean they were good," I point out. "No one ever complains about vanilla ice cream but that doesn't mean it's *good*."

"I like vanilla ice cream."

"I'm sure you do."

"What's that—" Violet stops suddenly, narrowing her eyes. "No. We're not doing this."

I fight back the urge to smile.

"Doing what?"

"We're not getting into a fight over this. We are *at work* and we are *not fighting* and you're going to make the balls because that's what they've ordered and that's what's on the menu and *that is all, Eli.*"

She doesn't wait for a response, just jerks the door open and walks back into the kitchen. I'm right behind her, but I stop just inside as she makes her way between people, dodging a rack of pans and neatly stepping around a sous chef as he pulls a sheet of pasta from the pasta maker.

"I'm not making the balls!" I shout after her, over the din.

Violet turns around at the far door and smiles at me. It's a dangerous smile.

"Yes, you are!" she shouts, and then she's gone, the door swinging shut behind her.

In unison, everyone in the kitchen looks at the door.

Then they turn to look at me.

"What? It's fine," I tell them. "Keep cooking."

They all go back to their jobs. I stand there for a few more moments, telling myself not to let Violet get the best of me.

Then I go back to work.

CHAPTER EIGHT
VIOLET

I stare down at the seating chart instructions, wondering why the bride and groom don't just do this part themselves. Most do, but for some reason, Emma and Ashton decided that leaving me three full pages of instructions about who should be seated next to whom and who *absolutely should not be seated next to whom* would be easier for everyone involved.

Maybe they really enjoyed typing out all their family drama, past and present, for a complete stranger. I don't know. I just know that Emma's college roommate, Julie, should *not* be seated with the bride's sorority friends, that the groom's brother can't be in the same half of the room as the bride's coworker Della, that Emma's cousins on her mom's side all need to be seated at separate tables because of something that had happened in the nineties, and apparently the groom's boss and the bride's uncle, Jim, will get along famously and should be seated together, but *absolutely not* near the bar.

I'm starting to get a headache when there's a quick knock on my half-open door.

It swings open before I can say anything, and there stands Eli.

He's tall, dark, annoyingly handsome, totally interrupting my train of thought, unlikely to make my afternoon less of an exercise in frustration, and holding a plate of something.

"Come on in, I'm not busy," I say, eyeing the plate. It looks he's brought me mac and cheese balls, but I know Eli better than that.

After our earlier disagreement, he'd probably rather drink rattlesnake poison than make mac and cheese balls. Unless, of course, he's bringing me mac and cheese balls laced with rattlesnake poison.

"Good," he says, crossing my office in a few steps and putting the plate on my desk, right on top of the seating charts that I'm trying to work on. "Here."

There are four breaded, fried balls, each about an inch and a half in diameter. They're obviously fresh and, to be honest, they smell *really* good.

Briefly, I wonder if Eli knows how to get rattlesnake poison at an hour's notice.

His older brother, maybe?

Would anyone in town be surprised if Levi knew how to get snake poison in sixty minutes?

Unlikely, though. I'm pretty sure Eli wouldn't try to murder me. Even for twenty grand.

I pick one up between my finger and thumb. Poison or not, they smell amazing, and I'm pretty much incapable of resisting a tasty fried treat.

"Careful, they're hot," he says, folding his arms in front of himself. He's still wearing his chef's jacket, still has a kitchen towel slung over one shoulder. "Fresh outta the deep fryer."

Another, non-snake-poison possibility presents itself to me.

"Did you make terrible mac and cheese balls just to prove your point?" I ask.

"Do those *look* terrible?"

"I can't tell, they're fried balls."

"Just eat one before they get cold," he says.

I keep considering the fried ball without putting it my mouth. I know they're not actually poison, but I hate giving Eli the satisfaction of telling me what to do.

"What are they?" I ask, just to delay another moment.

"Delicious. Which you would know if you ate it," he says, the faintest hint of amusement around his mouth.

He's watching me. Not glaring, not rolling his eyes, just watching my face with his intense, deep green gaze.

I gaze back, the ball still held between my fingers.

For a split second, time freezes. I feel stuck, unable to move, pinned under the weight of his intensity and his attention. He watches me like a boxer watches his opponent: wary but ready, practically begging me to take my next swing.

I blink. Then my heart kickstarts. The moment is over.

I bite into the fried ball, my teeth crunching through the outer layer and sinking into the middle, savory flavors flooding my mouth as my eyes go wide.

It's good. *Really* good. So good that for a second I forget where I am and who I'm with.

"Mm*gaw*," I say. "Thishi *mazin*."

Something like relief flickers across his face and then it's gone, replaced by his usual half-hitched smile.

"Told you so," he says.

I don't bother arguing. The ball is crunchy on the outside and chewy in the middle, light and fluffy and bursting with flavor all at once with notes of lemon, garlic, thyme, and a dozen other things I can't even name. Plus, the center is filled with perfectly melty mozzarella, pulling from my mouth to the other half of the ball, still in my hand.

I shove the rest into my mouth before I finished chewing the first half. I can't stop myself. I want a dozen more.

"What *are* these?" I ask, swallowing and taking another one off the plate.

"Better than mac and cheese balls," he says.

I just chew, swallow, take the third one off the plate, and wait for him to answer my question.

"They're called *arancini*," he says, pronouncing it errran-cheenee. "They're Italian. Sicilian, I think. It's mozzarella in the middle of a ball of risotto, covered in breadcrumbs and deep fried."

"So, basically a mac and cheese ball," I say, biting and chewing. I manage not to moan.

Eli snorts.

"They're nothing like mac and cheese balls," he says. "There's no mac. Completely different."

"Please, they've got all the same stuff," I go on, contemplating the half still in my hand. "Cheese, carbs, they're fried…"

"Except mac and cheese balls are bad, and these are good," he points out. "Porsches and Chevys have all the same parts, too, and you'd never call those the same."

"They're both cars. They'd both get me to work and back."

"*You* might not notice a difference, but I wouldn't show up in Monaco with a Tahoe."

I chew. I was on my third, contemplating the fourth, but I need to save it.

"You still have to make mac and cheese balls for the wedding," I tell him.

He shifts his stance, his body tensing into a fight mode. Despite the years since high school, I'd know Eli Loveless's fighting stance anywhere.

"That thing is ten times better than some gummy, overworked and undercooked monstrosity of Americana and you know it," he says, eyes flashing.

"It's good," I say, shrugging. "But it's not on the menu."

"So change the menu."

"Menu's not up to me," I say. "It's up to the bride and groom who, I'm sure I told you this before, *decided on it months ago* and aren't even here to approve changes."

"When do they get in?"

"The menu's done."

"When?"

Eli is quiet, intense, and he's still standing tall and rock-solid in the middle of my office, not giving an inch. Not that I'd expect him to. As far as I know, the man's never backed down from an argument in his life.

"They're not interested in last-minute menu changes," I finally say.

"Are you this sure about what everyone wants?"

Hell no.

"You're acting like I haven't been doing this for years already," I say, finally in danger of losing my cool. "People don't want to worry about picking appetizers the day before their wedding. Just make the mac and cheese balls. You're not going to ruin your reputation or whatever it is you keep going on about. Sometimes people like bad things, just let them be happy."

"That doesn't mean I have to make bad things for them," he says, uncrossing his arms.

"For fuck's sake, it's one appetizer."

"Just tell me when they get in."

I take a deep breath, my spine ramrod-straight, and remind myself that it's a reasonable question from a coworker.

"Friday morning. They're driving down from D.C.," I say.

"Was that so hard?"

I resist the urge to throw a pen at his head, even though he's being a dick.

"Don't fuck this up," I tell him instead.

One eyebrow twitches.

"By trading out appetizers?" he says.

"By doing something flashy and dumb to prove to everyone that you're some *amazing* chef even though you're running the catering kitchen at a wedding venue," I tell him. "If you fuck something up and it comes back on me, Eli, I swear I'll—"

Eli snags the plate off my desk, one fried ball still on it.

"—hey!"

Still smirking, he pops it into his mouth whole.

"No promises," he says, turns, and leaves my office. I jump to my feet, leaning forward on my desk.

"—Shove those things so far up your butt that you'll—"

Another head pops into my doorway. I stop short.

"Everything okay?" Kevin asks, looking half-puzzled and half-frightened.

I swallow hard. I smile. I compose myself.

"Everything's fine!" I say.

CHAPTER NINE

ELI

The three of us all look down at the tiny glasses in front of us, concentrating for a moment. There are fifteen in total, five in front of each, and I'm not sure any of us were listening too well.

"Run through that one more time?" Silas says, eyebrows furrowed in concentration.

Standing across the table Daniel exhales, his hands on his hips in his classic slightly-annoyed-but-trying-to-look-perfectly-calm pose.

"It's in the same order as any tasting menu," he says, like that makes it obvious. "From left to right, you start with the Chardonnay, then you move to the—"

"Do you have anything we can write with?" asks Levi.

"It's not that hard," Daniel says.

"Chardonnay's the bubbly wine you drink at celebrations, right?" Levi asks.

Silas, Levi's best friend, is trying not to laugh. Daniel rolls his eyes, but he ducks into a back room and comes back with a few stubby pencils and some scrap paper. We each take one.

It's Saturday night, and we're at Loveless Brewing, standing around a high table off to the side of the main room because Daniel asked us last-minute if we could come sample some beers he's been working on.

The real reason, of course, is that Rusty's at her first-ever sleepover tonight and Daniel needs something to distract him.

"Okay, in order, from left to right," Daniel starts again, slowly this time. "Chardonnay. Pinot Grigio. Merlot. Oak. Bourbon. Eli, you're not gonna write this down?"

"I know how tasting menus go," I say.

"How do you spell oak, again?" Silas asks.

Now Levi's the one trying not to laugh.

"Never mind, figured it out," Silas says, flashing Daniel a shit-eating grin.

"Let me know if you'd ever actually like to sample the beer," Daniel says, forced calm radiating from every pore of his body. "Maybe sooner or later we can actually get around to—"

"Dan, she's fine," I finally interject. "Right now they're probably eating ice cream, jumping on a couch and watching *Frozen.*"

"I'm not worried," he protests, crossing his arms over his chest.

"Is that why you're being an uptight prick about an informal beer tasting?" I ask, leaning both my elbows on the bar.

Daniel sighs. He shoves one hand through his floppy light-brown hair.

"Okay, I'm sorry," he says. "I just thought that tonight would be a good time to get some opinions on this project."

"Any time you want us to come drink your fancy beer for free, just let us know," Silas says. "I'm happy to be a guinea pig."

"Thank you for your service," Daniel says dryly.

I hold up the first glass, the dark liquid inside it glowing faintly red in the light. It's a stout beer that's been aged for a couple of months in Chardonnay barrels, part of a new experiment that Daniel's trying at the brewery.

"Here's to Rusty's first sleepover," I say.

Everyone holds up their own tiny tasting glass. We clink them together. We each take careful, thoughtful sips.

I hold the beer in my mouth for a moment, thinking, before I swallow it.

"Not that one," I tell Daniel.

"No," agrees Silas. "That one's weird."

"I like it," Levi says, contemplatively taking another sip. "It's unexpected."

"The fruity, sharp overtones from the chardonnay barrel clash with the roasted baseline of the stout, and instead of each enhancing the other, they just get in each other's way," I tell him. "The two flavors don't really pair well."

I take another sip, though. It's free beer.

"Yeah, it's weird," Silas says. "What Eli said."

"I think it's a good weird," Levi says.

"You can't listen to him, though," Silas tells Daniel as he drains the tiny sample-size glass. "He likes orange-vanilla Coke, too."

"It's refreshing," Levi protests.

"It tastes like a melted popsicle that someone found beneath a Slurpee machine," I say.

"And why do you know what that tastes like?" Daniel asks.

"It's an educated guess," I say.

"How educated?" Levi asks.

I drain my own beer glass and ignore him, but I'm glad I came tonight and not just for the free beer.

I'd forgotten how much I missed my brothers by being away. Sure, I'd visited while I was gone, and we kept up well enough, but it wasn't the same. A phone call has nothing on Sunday dinner, or drinking lemonade on the back porch, or just shooting the shit while you're ignoring the nightly news on television.

When I got back, I slotted right back into their lives like I'd never been gone.

"Okay, next up is the Pinot Grigio," Daniel says, cutting off Levi and keeping us on track.

"Which one is that?" Levi asks.

Daniel just points and sighs.

· · · · ★ ★ ★ ★ ★ · · · ·

WHEN WE'RE DONE TASTING, Daniel rewards each of us with a free beer that's not experimental and we stay at the table while Daniel keeps an eye on things.

"So far, so good," I say, in response to Silas's question about my new job. "Well, except Violet Tulane works there."

"Who?" Levi asks.

"Oh, Jesus," Daniel mutters.

"You know Violet," Silas says to Levi. "She organized that charity auction for the firehouse a few years ago, the one where Kim Fortner and Mavis Bresley got into a bidding war over your mom's blackberry pie?"

"Oh, *Violet*," Levi says. "What's wrong with Violet?"

"Nothing," says Daniel.

I take a good sip of my beer.

"We don't get along," I say, as diplomatically as possible.

"You don't remember?" Daniel asks him. "Every time

Eli had a test in school, we'd have to hear for a week about how he wanted to get a better grade than her, and then God forbid she got a ninety-seven and he got a ninety-six, we'd hear for another week about how awful she was for that one point."

"That's because she was always awful about it," I say, starting to feel defensive. "You'd think that the difference between an A and an A-plus was equivalent to rescuing a bus full of orphans—"

"Oh no," Daniel says, holding up one hand. "Not today you don't."

"She's always seemed perfectly nice to me," Levi muses. "Smart, too. We had a very stimulating conversation about moss one time."

I frown into my beer and take another sip. Something about Levi calling Violet *stimulating* really rubs me the wrong way.

"Well, yeah, she's *smart*," I say, because I think that much is obvious. "I'm not denying that. She's just also the worst."

"Because you were perfectly nice to her at all times," Daniel says sarcastically. "You, Eli, were certainly never a dick."

"I was a dick in self-defense," I say.

Daniel just snorts. He's only a year younger than me, so he got the full brunt of my high school angst. Levi, on the other hand, is two years older and apparently wasn't paying us much attention.

"Is she the girl who got into the National Junior Honor Society when you didn't?" Levi asks.

I swear I have a full-blown flashback to eighth grade when every day for at least two weeks, Violet waved around her National Junior Honor Society invitation letter and asked if mine had come yet. It hadn't, because it never did, because I didn't score quite highly enough on a test.

"Yes," I say tersely. I drink some more beer.

"I do remember that," Levi says, still sounding contemplative. "How odd. She's always been very nice to me."

"And me," Silas volunteers.

"That's because Violet's nice," Daniel says.

"You're all wrong," I mutter into my beer.

We're all quiet for a minute, the low buzz of the brewery filling the silence. It's not crowded, but the main room is about three-quarters full of people sitting at long communal tables, drinking beer, some playing board games. Along one wall, there's shuffleboard and pool tables. Outside there's cornhole and croquet.

Basically, it's a chill place to spend a Saturday and have a beer, and plenty of people from Sprucevale and the surrounding areas take advantage.

"Question," Silas says, after a bit. "Is that Violet playing darts over there? My contacts are kinda dry."

My heart stomps at my chest. I hold my beer glass a little tighter, scanning the opposite wall as I half hope that it's her and half hope that it's not her.

It's her. She's laughing, her hair in a high, messy bun. She's with a redhead who I'm fairly certain is Adeline Mathers, another girl from our high school class.

Violet's got a beer in one hand as she grabs darts out of the dart board with the other, saying something over her shoulder to Adeline.

Then she bends down to grab a dart off the floor. It takes a split second but I swear my mouth goes dry, and then she's upright again, strolling back to where Adeline's standing.

Everything about her is entirely familiar and entirely

alien, all at once. She's still Violet. She still looks like Violet and sounds like Violet and God knows she still *acts* like Violet, but in some indefinable way, she's different.

I never wanted her before, even a little, but now the same movements as ever have me wondering what it would be like to take her by the hip and push her against the wall. She looks at me the same way as always but now there's a challenge in it, like she's daring me not to wonder what her skin tastes like.

"…entered some sort of angst-fueled fugue state — oh, he's back," Daniel is saying.

I shoot him a glare. He gives me a perfectly neutral look. I don't like it.

"Yeah, that's her," I say, and shrug. My knuckles are still pale around my glass.

"That's already been established," Levi says. "The conversation has moved on, Eli."

"To what?"

"I was asking after Silas's sister, June," he says. "Apparently she's doing well for herself, down in Raleigh."

"I can't stand her boyfriend, though," Silas says.

Levi makes a sympathetic noise. Across the room, Violet takes a sip of her beer, leaning against the bar-height table, one leg cocked under her. Adeline says something and Violet laughs, spreads her fingers, then says something back.

She cocks the other leg, shifting her hips. It's perfectly casual, just a girl standing around, talking to her friend, but I have to tear my gaze away before I get any further down this rabbit hole.

"—Can't just tell her that, though, you know how June is. Besides, she'll just think I hate him because I'm her big brother—"

"I gotta take a leak," I say, standing and putting my nearly-finished beer on the table.

"Do you?" Daniel asks.

As I walk away, I turn and give the table a winning grin.

"Of course," I say, and leave.

CHAPTER TEN

VIOLET

The dart bounces off the board and falls to the ground.

"—Last time I ever take Cash's suggestions, I swear," Adeline says.

I'm silent for a moment, focusing as I throw the last dart.

It sticks in the sixteen wedge of the dartboard. Good enough.

"I should have known when I saw the truck nuts," I say. "I'm pretty sure their existence makes it my own fault. Like, if I somehow took this to court, the judge would throw it out on the basis that I should have known he was terrible because his vehicle *had testicles*."

I walk to the dartboard, yank my darts out and pick the final one up from the ground.

"No," Adeline says. "How are you supposed to find someone to date who doesn't have truck nuts around here? You make a 'no truck nuts' rule and there goes at least fifty percent of the eligible population. Maybe sixty."

I sigh and lean on the table.

"Adeline," I say. "I think I'm ready."

She's got a dart between her fingers, about to throw, when she looks over at me.

"For truck nuts?"

"For spinsterdom."

"Oh, good Lord," she says, and throws a dart. It lands on the twenty.

"It doesn't seem so bad anymore," I say. "Yes, sure, a life companion sounds nice, but at what expense, Adeline? *At what expense?*"

She throws another dart. Seventeen. She's absolutely smoking me at this game.

"Statistically speaking, there have to be at least a few guys with truck nuts who are also perfectly decent people," she says, readying the third dart. "Maybe some of them just think truck nuts are funny."

She pauses, considers the dart board, then looks over at me.

"I mean, they're kind of funny," she says, and throws her final dart.

It's a bullseye. I have no chance of winning.

"No, they're not," I call after her as she retrieves the darts.

"Yes, they are," she shouts, grabbing the darts, then returning and putting them in my outstretched hand. "Violet, that's, like, rule number one. Testicles are *always* funny. Unless they're abscessed or something, that's not really funny."

I give her a horrified stare, and she wrinkles her nose.

"Everything okay at work?" I ask. Adeline works the night shift at the county hospital, so abscessed testes are, unfortunately, a possibility at her workplace.

"Oh, that was a couple of years ago," she says, waving one hand. "It just stuck with me. Anyway…"

I walk to the line for the dartboard, weighing the darts in one hand as I try to visualize the perfect throw and also *not* think about abscessed testicles.

"Anyway," I echo, "Todd was a jerk who both had truck nuts and had opinions on wine vintages, which should be illegal, and then he left without paying and screwed me over. And I had to get a ride home from *Eli Loveless*, and now I'm just going to embrace hairy legs and microwave dinners for one," I say, and unleash a dart.

It sticks in the cork right outside the dartboard.

"At least Eli was there," she says, as if that helps.

"I didn't even know he was back," I say, throwing another dart.

"I'd have told you but I didn't know you cared," Adeline says.

"I don't *care*," I say, and throw the last dart, which hits the number seventeen. *Finally*. "I just like to know when evil is lurking."

Adeline and I went to high school together, but we were barely acquaintances at the time: I was in the National Honor Society and co-captained the debate team; she was on the cheerleading squad and got invited to parties. A couple years ago we reunited at the DMV — the number-giving system was down, and we took it upon ourselves to prevent total chaos in the line — and have been friends ever since.

"He used to help me with my trigonometry homework," she says. "I'm pretty sure I only passed because of him."

"Did you have to pay him in blood?"

"No, but I invited him to one of Tony's field parties once," she says. "I don't remember whether he came."

Field parties are, as the name suggests, parties that take

place way out in a field. There's usually a bonfire, lots of pickup trucks, and beer.

"Eli got invited to a party?" I ask. "I never got invited to a field party."

"I went," a voice says behind me. "I even drank half a beer that Josh Stipe gave me."

I whirl around and he's standing right there, one hand in a pocket, hair a little unruly and green eyes blazing, his *Big Al's Western Emporium* t-shirt tight across his shoulders and biceps. Suddenly, it's too hot in here.

"You were supposed to tell me when evil was lurking," I say to Adeline.

"Sorry," she says.

"I wasn't lurking," Eli says. "I just came over to say hi and see if you needed any help."

I grab my beer and take a long, suspicious sip. I'm not surprised that he's at his brother's brewery on a Saturday, but I don't like it either.

"Hi, and no, I don't," I say. I don't even know what he's offering help with.

"Hi, Eli," Adeline says. "How are you?"

"Good, thanks," he says. "Yourself?"

"I'm well," she says. "I'm gonna go grab another drink, you two want anything?"

We both decline, and Adeline walks toward the bar, leaving me alone with him.

"I think you need some help," Eli tells me the moment she's out of earshot.

"Did you know she thinks you're *nice*?" I ask, ignoring him. "I can't imagine."

"I used to help her with her homework," he says, shrugging. "She was cute. And all the cheerleaders wore those skirts—"

"Okay, okay," I say. There's an unpleasant, boiling sensation rising through my stomach. "God, I get it."

"This one time, she put her hand on my arm—"

"I don't want to hear your high school *Letters to Penthouse*," I snap.

Eli just laughs.

"I won't even tell you what went on at that field party," he says. "Did you know that some of our classmates were having *sexual relations*?"

My face heats up slightly at the phrase, and I cross my arms in front of myself like I can ward it off.

"We graduated ten years ago and you're still bragging about how you got invited to a single party?" I shoot back.

"It's one more than you got invited to," he points out.

I go get my darts out of the dart board. For a moment, I consider throwing one at Eli, but with my luck I'd either murder him by accident or maim someone standing behind him.

I don't want to murder him, just show him I mean business.

"You don't know how many parties I got invited to," I say.

"Zero," he says, holding out his hand.

"You don't *know* that. What do you want?"

"Give me a dart, and yes I do," he says.

"Why?"

"So I can throw it and show you how it's done."

He's right about the number of parties. I always heard about them Monday morning: who hooked up, who got drunk, who invited their hot twenty-two-year-old cousin, who got into a fight.

I still can't believe he got to go to one, and I'm way, way more annoyed about it now — over a decade later — than I should be.

"I know how it's done," I tell him. "You stick the pointy end in the board. It's not rocket science."

"Okay, impress me," he says, hands on hips.

"No."

"Because you can't."

I've got the three darts clenched in my hand, the plastic digging into my palm. He's standing closer to me than he should be, and it's setting off proximity alarms in every single part of my body — only instead of sending an alert, every single one is reminding me how long it's been since an attractive man touched me.

The answer is *a while*. Like, maybe a year. There's been a dry spell, filled only with dates that go nowhere. Hell, right now might be the closest I've gotten to a man in a few months.

"Because I have no interest in whether you think I'm good at darts or not," I say. "And I don't want your dart lessons."

"My dart lessons are only for people who I think can be taught," Eli says.

Now I'm clenching my other fist, too.

"Then are you just here to tell me I'm shitty at darts?" I ask. "Yes. I know. I'm shitty at darts. Happy?"

He doesn't answer, just steps around me and grabs Adeline's darts off the table. I don't know why he didn't just borrow those in the first place.

Well, yes, I do. Because Eli delights in being difficult. That's why.

"Follow through," he says, standing on the line, dart in hand, making a throwing motion slowly. "Just look where you want the dart to go and don't forget to follow through."

He throws the dart. It lands in the ring right outside the bullseye.

"You missed," I say.

He throws another one, and it lands in nearly the same place. I'm impressed for a moment, and then I remind myself not to be.

"I wouldn't *take* lessons from you," I say.

He releases the third dart. This one hits the bullseye, and Eli looks over at me, grinning.

"Feel free to show me up any time," he says. "I've got all night. I can wait."

"Congratulations," I say sarcastically. "You're good at darts."

"I know."

"Do you want a prize?"

"I think I'm getting it right now."

A pain shoots through my hand, and I look down, unclenching my fist from the darts. Oops.

"You okay?" Eli asks, and takes my hand.

It feels like every cell in my body is a compass, and he's magnetic north. There's a pull so strong that I almost step forward to be closer to him.

I jerk my hand away. I swallow hard. I stare at him, wide-eyed, my breath caught somewhere between my mouth and lungs.

For one split second, his green eyes flick to my lips. The compasses jerk, tug, and this time I take half a step forward.

Then I catch myself. I breathe. I clench my fist.

"I'm fine," I say.

I walk away. I don't know where I'm going, I just know I need to get away from Eli Loveless before I punch him or kiss him or, possibly, do both at the same time which seems like it would be impossible, but I wouldn't put it past myself right now.

There's a hallway. I hurry in there, still trying to regulate my breathing, and duck around a corner. The women's room is here, but so is a door with a green glowing EXIT sign over it so I pick that, and suddenly I'm outside and in the near-dark.

I step to one side. The door closes. It's warmer and stickier out here than it is inside, and I breathe the humid air in deep. I'm standing on grass, facing the forest that's the constant backdrop of southwestern Virginia. I can barely see the edge of the floodlights over the parking lot, around the side, but they don't reach back here.

Don't let him get to you, I tell myself, but it's a feeble attempt because he's already gotten to me. Eli's been getting to me since we were five years old, and platitudes aren't going to help the situation now.

Just don't do anything stupid, I tell myself, and that one seems much more reasonable. That one seems like something I can handle.

The door opens. I brace myself. If I had a shield right now I'd put it up.

"Violet?" Eli asks.

God*damn* it.

"Yes."

"You okay?" he asks, for the second time in two minutes.

"I'm *fine,*" I say, all the pent-up anger and irritation leaning on that second word.

"I'm just checking," he says, letting the door shut behind him. "You practically ran out of the brewery like you were going to vomit or have a heart attack or—"

"—or before I finally lose my shit with you in public for acting like I need dart-throwing lessons?"

"Well, you do," he says.

"I don't!" I say. "I don't care about darts! I don't care that I'm bad at it!"

Eli just laughs. Somehow, we've moved closer to each

other, close enough that I can feel his laughter rippling through the night air.

"Liar," he says. "You're pissed that I'm better than you at something and you're terrible at hiding it."

"No," I say, swallowing hard. "I'm pissed that you followed me out here to keep gloating."

"I followed you out here to see if I should call an ambulance," he says.

"Liar," I say.

I could swear that neither of us is moving, but we keep getting closer by centimeters, degrees. My heart feels like it's punching my ribcage, my pulse racing. I'm praying that he can't hear it and that he can't tell that I feel electrified, like if he touches me I'll spark.

I'm furious, and I want him, and I'm furious that I want him.

"You think I wasn't worried when you sprinted out of there?" he says, his low voice getting louder, irritation edging in.

"I didn't sprint."

"Do you really think I'm incapable of concern?" Eli asks, his jaw tensing, his eyes glinting, the dark making them gleam gray.

"Not incapable," I say.

I look him dead in the eye. My heart seizes.

"So I'm not a *total* monster," he says, eyes blazing, voice dangerous and low.

His anger's so real that it's almost palpable. I feel like I could reach out and grab it, wrestle it with my own.

"I didn't say that."

"But it's what you think."

His eyes flick to my lips again, like they did inside, only now they stay linger there like he can't tear his gaze away.

Please, whispers my body.

Hell no, whispers my brain.

"Since when do you care what I think of you?"

"I don't," he says, and his mouth finds mine.

It's hard and fast and above all it's hungry, his lips bruising and demanding even as I push back against him, feeling my teeth scrape his bottom lip. I want to hurt him and I want to make him regret doing this but above all, dear God I don't want him to stop.

His arm's already around my waist. My hands are already in his hair and then his tongue is in my mouth, our bodies a tangle, our skin sticking together in the humidity.

I bite his lip. He grunts, roughly pulls me closer into his warm heat. Our bodies smack together hard enough to force the air from my lungs, but I want more. I want to knock him over and tear his shirt off and leave claw marks, and more than anything I want him to wake up tomorrow and reconsider what I'm capable of.

"Tell me to stop," he says, his words blurred because his mouth is on mine.

"No," I whisper.

"Tell me," he growls, but he's already kissing me again. He's already grabbing me, walking me backwards without breaking the kiss and then I'm against the brewery wall, the wood scratchy through my shirt.

Eli keeps pushing me, my hips pinned against the wall. He swipes one thumb along my bare skin, just above the waistband of my jeans, and I gasp into his mouth, every inch of me ablaze.

Suddenly white light slices in. My eyes fly open and I freeze, both hands in Eli's hair as he's over me and we both stare toward the open door.

"Sorry," Daniel's voice says, trailing off.

Eli steps back, out of my grasp, and all of a sudden,

everything is normal again and I wonder what the hell I just did.

You made out with Eli and you liked it.

You made out with Eli and you liked it and he's absolutely going to use this against you in the future. Every single day he's going to smirk at you and remind you of the time you kissed with tongue and —

I bolt. Daniel steps out of the way just barely in time as I shove through the door, and flee back down the hallway. I grab my purse from the table where I shouldn't have left it, pulse racing. I feel like I'm swirling down a drain as I glance around for Adeline.

I find her. She's talking to a few other people, laughing, having a good time like I didn't just fuck up so bad they must know about it in China by now.

"Something came up, I gotta go," I tell her, breathless, without even saying hi to her conversation partners.

She frowns.

"Are you o—"

"Fine! Talk to you later!" I say, and practically run out the door and to my car, where I crank the radio, drive too fast, and try to tell myself that none of that just happened.

CHAPTER ELEVEN

ELI

"Question," Daniel says, finally breaking the silence. We're in his car, nearly home, and I'm in the passenger seat staring out the window as the trees fly past.

"Yeah?"

"Are we going to pretend I didn't catch you making out with Violet back there?"

"Yes," I say.

After he opened the door, Violet *ran*. She didn't walk. She didn't hurry. She straight up *ran* to get away from me. By the time I'd made it back inside, she was gone and Adeline was giving me weird looks.

And then I had to replay it over and over until Daniel finally decided it was time to leave. The softness of her lips paired with the brutal way she kissed me back. Her hands in my hair, hard enough to bring tears to my eyes, the way she grabbed like she couldn't decide if she wanted to rip me apart or hold me.

I really fucking wish I hadn't done that, because I don't think I'll ever get it out of my head.

"Good," Daniel says. "I think denial's really healthy."

"Could you not right now?"

"I'm just saying that you're going about this the right way," he says.

"People drunkenly make out by accident all the time and it's no big deal," I say. "You run a bar, how do you not know this?"

"You drunk?"

"Yeah. Blitzed outta my mind."

"Wow, your tolerance has really gone down," he says.

"Shut up," I mutter, and turn back to the window.

· · · · · ★ ★ ★ ★ ★ · · · · ·

"What are these called again?" the maid of honor asks.

"Arancini," I tell her. "They're a Sicilian delicacy."

She plucks a third from the platter and popped it into her mouth, her eyes rolling slightly as she chewed.

"They're *amazing*," she says, adjusting her huge sunglasses, propped on her head. "Emma. These are *amazing*," she says again, holding one out to her sister, the bride.

"I've already got one," the bride says, holding up half a fried ball in her hand. "They're really good."

"*So* good," gushes the maid of honor, her cheeks flushing slightly pink.

It's Friday afternoon, and I'm standing behind the bar in the Fox Hunt Lounge. It's a swanky spot in Bramblebush Lodge filled with overstuffed rich leather armchairs, an antique wooden bar running along one wall, dozens of bottles of expensive whiskey behind it, a humidor full of cigars in one corner.

Violet's avoided me all week, and I've avoided her right back. If she's got a question for me, she sends Kevin, her intern. If I've got a question for her, I send Zane, one of *my* underlings, and that way the two of us never even need to be in the same room.

And I haven't thought about the kiss at all. Not once. Certainly not a hundred times a day when I should be doing something else.

Right now, I'm watching the bridal party make arancini disappear. At this rate they won't last another two minutes, which is fine with me.

I won't be making mac and cheese balls, and Violet can't do a thing about it.

Point: Eli.

"Glad you like them," I say, smiling at the bride as she delicately eats the other half of hers. "And again, I'm sorry about the situation with the mac and cheese balls," I lie.

The situation being that I refuse to make the damn things. I don't mention that part.

"Honestly, these are better than what we sampled when we came down a couple of months ago anyway," the bride says, carefully wiping crumbs from her fingers. "Thanks for taking the time to make some for us."

"Yeah, that was *so* nice of you," the maid of honor adds. "I think I could eat about twenty!"

I eye the empty glass next to her at the bar. I'd watched her drink at least two gin and tonics from it in the space of ten minutes, and based on how unsteady she seems on her barstool, I suspect she's had more than that.

Based on the look her sister keeps giving her, I suspect the afternoon might get interesting.

"So, Elliott, are you coming to the wedding? Will I see you tomorrow?" the maid of honor asks, her long fake eyelashes dipping and bobbing.

"It's Eli, and I'm afraid not," I say, still leaning against the bar. "They pretty much keep me locked in the kitchen."

The maid of honor sighs dramatically, her long, shiny black hair spilling over one exposed shoulder.

"That's too bad," she says. "I bet you're great on a dance floor."

The eyelashes bob again. Emma, the bride, is sitting ramrod-straight on her barstool, the other bridesmaids off to the sides, going over something on a sheet of paper.

Emma takes a deep breath, closes her eyes for a moment.

"Susan," she starts. "Why don't you—"

The door to the lounge swings open behind them, and they turn as Violet and her intern step through.

I swear that there's a hitch in her step when she sees me. I swear her eyes blaze with fire for just a second before she puts up her professional veneer, smiling at the room.

I smile back, and now we're putting on an excellent show for the bridal party who paid an obscene sum of money to be here.

I'm fully aware that, in the scheme of things, switching the appetizers from one kind of fried carbs with cheese to another doesn't matter. Chances are that no one but me, Violet, and *maybe* the bride and groom will even know. Tomorrow, during the cocktail hour, exactly zero guests are going to think to themselves, *I was expecting mac and cheese balls.*

Birds will still sing. Rivers will still flow. The world will keep on turning.

But I've won a battle, and I *never* win battles against Violet. I think I could count the times I've bested her on one hand, and God knows that for most of my life I tried at least once a week.

"—Help the girls with their hair and makeup schedule," Emma finishes, still talking to her maid of honor.

"Hi there!" Violet says, walking toward us. "Welcome to Bramblebush. Congratulations!"

She's all smiles and professionalism, warm and no-nonsense.

Until she glances over. *Then* she feels like a firestorm as she takes in the scene and last of all, me. There's a look. I forget to breathe for a second as I run through it all again: *lips, tongue, teeth, hands, wall. Tell me to stop. No.*

I don't laugh at my victory. I don't even grin. I just smile at her, polite and professional as you please, and I resist loudly telling her about the recent appetizer change on the menu. It's immature and petty, but damn, it feels good.

Besides, dear *God* Violet is pretty when she's mad. She's pretty all the time, but anger sparks something in her eyes that makes her light up like a human flame, burning and flickering from the inside, dangerous and alluring all at once.

This feels dangerous in a way it never has before. Her anger's always been dangerous, of course, but now there's something about it that shakes me to the core.

Violet makes me unsteady. She makes it feel like the ground under my feet is treacherous, like I'm exploring new and uncharted territory.

I don't hate the feeling.

But I can't stop. If she's the flame, I'm the moth, and despite myself, I want to see her light up again and again.

"Thanks, Eli, I've got it from here," she says, giving me one last burning glance before turning to the assembled bridal party. "It's so nice to finally meet you in person. Shall we finalize everything for tomorrow?"

· · · · ★ ★ ★ ★ ★ · · · ·

ONCE THE BRIDE and groom retire with Violet and Kevin to the other side of the lounge to talk logistics, I'm left with the bridesmaids.

Things go dramatically downhill.

Six of the seven bridesmaids are sipping on drinks, standing around, casually chatting. They seem like they're having a lovely time getting ready for their friend's wedding.

The maid of honor — Susan — has had another gin and tonic, and she's sitting on a stool, half an arancini between her fingers, leaning on the bar, telling me about her life.

I have work to do. I'd love to get out of here, but I'm new at this whole *create a good guest experience* thing. Does ditching a drunk girl create a poor guest experience? Will it cost me twenty grand?

Hell if I know.

"So anyway," she says, the eyelashes dipping and bobbing dramatically. "I'm a free woman now, just in time for my little sister's wedding. Cheers!"

She holds up her glass, then takes a long pull from it.

"I think I should go to Paris," she says. "That's *exciting*, right? Paris?"

She takes another sip.

"Or Bangkok. Or Abu Dhabi. Or Moscow. Those all sound like places someone *exciting* and *adventurous* would go, right?"

"I hear Moscow is nice in the summer," I say, staying as neutral as possible. "I wouldn't go in the winter."

Susan laughs. She laughs way too hard.

"You're *funny*," she says, putting a hand on mine.

Shit.

"Or maybe I should go to Sicily and get some more of these tasty balls," she says, finally picking up the last one and holding it in front of her face like she's divining her future in it. "I'll just get as many tasty balls as I can handle, I bet that's *fun* and *exciting*."

Then she pushes the whole thing into her mouth, chews, swallows. When she finishes she licks the crumbs from her top lip, making eye contact with me the whole time.

I have a vague sense of foreboding.

Maybe she'll just leave, I think.

"Got anything else for me?" she asks, reaching for her glass and missing. Her hand bangs against the bar, and she sighs and frowns at it like it's a misbehaving pet.

"That's all I made tonight," I say, clearing away the platter.

This is your chance. Deposit her with the other girls and get out of here.

"Boo," she says. "Does that mean — um, so, you know, are you off now? Like, are you doing anything?"

She tries to lean her chin on her hand, but misses and goes off-balance, nearly careening off her bar stool.

Shit. This girl is about five minutes from full-blown drunk disaster, something that would almost certainly create a *poor guest experience* for everyone else in this room.

Trust me, I bartended near the oil fields in North Dakota for a while. I know from drunk disasters, though those disasters were usually much burlier than Susan. Compared to them, she'll be a walk in the park.

"Sorry," she breathes, her hand in mine as she finds the floor with one foot, then the other. "Sometimes your hand's not where it's supposed to be, you know?"

She tries to shake her hair over her shoulder again, but it sends her off-balance, stumbling into me. I steady her with a hand on her back, her hand still gripping mine for stability.

"Thanks," she says, closing her eyes for a moment, fully leaning on me. "You know, you didn't answer me."

"Let me help you to your room," I say, still holding her up.

This girl needs to be in bed before she can cause any damage, preferably with a trash can next to her and a glass of water on her nightstand. If I had Gatorade and Advil, I'd leave that too. How's that for *guest experience*?

"You're coming to my room?" she says, her words getting blurry, still leaning against me.

I don't answer her, just walk her through the lounge and to the elevators opposite the door. I feel bad for her. She seems like a nice girl who's having a rough time right now, and to top it all off, she has to stand up at her little sister's wedding, probably while half her family wonders why it's not *her* up there.

"You're nice," Susan says, leaning her head against my shoulder, sliding an arm around my waist. "*So* nice."

She sways again, and I prop her up with an arm around her shoulder. She's too warm, and I'm trying to hold her up while I touch her as little as possible. I've always felt bad for girls when they drink, just because it seems like they go from "slightly tipsy" to "puking in the gutter" so fast.

The elevator dings. The doors slide open. I carefully guide Susan across the threshold, because in her current state, even that seems like it could present a problem.

Just as I face forward and hit the button for the third floor, the door to the lounge opens, right across from us.

Violet steps out, alone. She stops. She looks at me. Susan hugs me tighter, her arms around my waist. She buries her face in my shoulder, my arm around her so she doesn't fall over.

Violet's eyes lock onto mine as the elevator doors slide

shut. It feels like it takes a year for them to close and the whole time, she doesn't look away. Her expression's unreadable, but I still feel it deep inside myself, twisting me in a place I didn't know I had.

Then the doors close and I stare at myself in the dull reflection, Susan snuggled against me, head now against my chest, my arm still around her shoulders so she doesn't fall over.

"This is nice," she murmurs.

I don't answer her.

CHAPTER TWELVE

VIOLET

I stand stock-still in the doorway as the elevator closes, my brain unwilling to process what I just saw.

Eli. And the maid of honor who's been sloppily hitting on him for the past fifteen minutes, in the elevator, their arms around each other, her head against his chest.

Going upstairs. Where there are beds. Six days after he kissed the hell out of me, he's going upstairs with this girl who's clearly handsy as fuck and who's also pretty cute.

If I were a dude, I wouldn't turn her down. My heart feels like a fist.

"You forget something?" Kevin asks, shaking me out of my reverie.

"Nope!" I say, sounding way too perky. "Just standing here. You ready?"

Kevin gives me a weird look, but doesn't say anything as we head back to the office barn, talking over the final few preparations for tomorrow.

When the linens get here, we need to make sure they match.

Eli is banging the maid of honor.

The bride brought last-minute chair-hanging nameplates for the entire wedding party, so someone should make sure that those go in the right place.

Does he do this all the time? Does Eli have a new girl every week and I didn't know? Am I already old news and he's on to the next thing?

We'll need to do a dry run of the butterfly release before the ceremony, and *Eli is banging the maid of honor. Oh my God, why is he doing this and why do I care? Stop caring. Now.*

We reach my office. Kevin hands over the iPad and says goodnight. I act normal and also say goodnight, then gather my things, and prepare to head out.

And I keep thinking about Eli. In the elevator. About the look he gave me, the smug way his eyes lit up when the maid of honor snuggled harder against him, his arm around her shoulders. I'm pretty sure she was grabbing his butt.

You are being ridiculous, I tell myself.

You saw two people in an elevator, one drunk and one not. You have no idea what happened afterward.

Except they looked so *cozy* together, and she was definitely into him, and they were touching and he gave me that *look* as the doors closed, the one that was smoldering and high and mighty and smug and hot.

The same look he gave me Saturday night right before —

"Stop it," I say out loud, in my empty office, like a lunatic.

Then I clear my throat, hope no one heard me, grab my stuff, and leave my office.

As I'm walking down the hall, something else occurs to me.

Sleeping with a guest is unprofessional as hell.

I don't know if it's specifically in the employee handbook. I read it cover-to-cover when I started this job, of course, but I didn't memorize it and it's been a few years. But there's no way that's proper, condoned behavior.

It's possible that I could get Eli fired. It's probable that I could get him in hot water with Montgomery.

It's almost certain that I could knock him out of the running for that twenty thousand dollars.

I stop again, right in front of the door to the employee parking lot, and I back up a few steps until I can look down the hall, toward Montgomery's big corner office.

The door's open. The lights are on. If I listen really closely, I think I can *just* make out the sounds of typing.

And I can't get the elevator scene out of my head: the way they were intertwined, all over each other, her hands everywhere. Most of all I can't get the look on his face out of my head, like he's mocking me, challenging me.

I'm not jealous. I'm not. Kissing him last weekend was a dumb mistake and I don't want to do it again, no matter how good it felt, because Eli and I don't get along and there's no point in making out with someone you don't even get along with.

Therefore, I can't be jealous. Logic dictates it.

I'm still standing here. I'm still staring at Montgomery's open door, thinking about how much harder I could probably make Eli's life if I just walked down there and told him.

But you didn't actually see anything, a voice whispers in the back of my mind.

You saw Eli and a drunk girl. That's all. Everything else is pure conjecture.

God, sometimes I hate it when I'm right.

I stop looking at Montgomery's office and go home.

· · · · ★ ★ ★ ★ ★ · · · ·

I STARE UPON THE MONSTROSITY, uncomprehending.

It's so tall I can't even see the top, tiers and tiers of cake reaching heavenward, festooned with endless swirls and whirls. Flowers drip from every layer, each one more dramatic than the last.

"How much of it is cake?" I finally ask, gobsmacked.

Janice, Bramblebush's pastry chef, leans in, squinting. We're standing right outside the wedding barn, where the dinner has finished and now everyone is dancing. This small, green courtyard is lit only by dozens of string of fairy lights looped overhead and around a row of potted trees in a complicated, swirling pattern. It's romantic, but also hard to see.

Janice points at a layer, still squinting.

"I'm pretty sure that from here down," she says, "is the stand, and everything on top of that is cake. I *think*."

I continue to stare. My job is mostly logistics, but every so often, I'm presented with some very interesting problems that require creative solutions.

Right now seems to be one of those times. Frankly, I wasn't expecting it — after the butterfly release and the choreographed bridesmaids' dance went off without a hitch, I thought I was in the clear.

I was not. I was unaware that there existed a wedding cake too tall to fit through a barn door, but you learn something new every day, I guess.

"If we split it in two and only leave on the top layer of the base, can we put it back together inside?" I ask, looking from the cake to the door and back. "People might see us, but…"

I shrug, the universal shrug of *I think this is our only option.*

"As long as we're careful, I think so," Janice says, still moving around the cake. Here and there she takes the stand in her hands and wobbles it very, very carefully, checking its structural integrity. "The only other option is to serve the cake out here, and…"

She gestures around the small outdoor barn entrance area, clearly indicating *four hundred people won't fit out here.*

"We'll use the cake dolly," she goes on. "Brandon and Zane can handle it, don't worry."

I just nod, still looking up at the biggest, most elaborate wedding cake I've ever seen. Apparently it's the groom's grandmother's gift to the couple, and she really went all-out.

Naturally, I got the cake dimensions from the bakery last week. I *always* get the dimensions from the bakery, but she ordered from a bakery I've never worked with before, one all the way up in Richmond.

When they sent the dimensions, they sent it for the cake only. They failed to mention that it was attached to an elaborate custom cake stand as well.

By itself, the cake would fit through a ten-foot-high barn door.

With the stand included, it does *not.*

It's really a hell of a cake.

"It'll be no problem," Janice reassures me, since I must look worried. "You won't even be able to tell that—"

"HEY! STOP IT!" a kid shouts, right behind the row of potted trees. Janice and I both turn, but we can't see anything through the perfectly cylindrical evergreens.

"NO, YOU STOP!"

"FARTKNOCKER!"

There's a quick scuffling noise, and we both frown.

"I'M TELLING MOM!"

"Liam, you're such a baby—"

"Take it BACK!"

There's a shout, then a grunt.

"Ow!" the other kid yells. "You little—"

A tree shakes slightly.

"TAKE IT BACK!"

There's another loud *oof.* A grunt.

Then the tree falls.

It seems like it falls in slow motion, the top wiggling before picking up speed and rushing earthward, revealing the surprised faces of two boys who can't be more than nine.

I lunge for it. Janice lunges for it, but there's no way to match the speed of the disaster.

The tree falls on the cake, the branches and needles sinking into lush white buttercream, slicing through the beautifully-wrought flowers, gouging through frosting, pushing the tiers askew, cleaving them in twain.

Then it comes to rest. On the cake. The nine-year-olds are long gone.

I can't do anything but stand there, mouth wide open, staring in horror. This feels like some sort of anxiety dream, and I swear to God I'm expecting my teeth to start spontaneously falling out any moment now.

They don't. If they did, I'd be relieved.

"Oh God," Janice finally says, her voice strangled. "Oh God. Oh my God."

Then the cake starts slipping, the tiers sliding sideways under the weight of the tree. I finally jolt out of my horrified reverie and lurch forward, panic singing through my veins.

"Get the tree!" I shout to Janice, running to the side of the cake just as a layer starts sliding off the one beneath it.

I put my hands out. I don't have a plan. I'm not at all sure that this will work, I just know it's my only option right now and this cake *cannot* hit the ground.

Instead, it falls straight into me.

Softly. Slowly. Gently, almost.

My outstretched hands are no match for the thick, soft buttercream. My fingers squish as they finally reach the cake, and the whole thing slumps against me like a sleepy toddler after a long day at Disney World.

"Help," I squeak out.

Janice grunts, launching the tree back upright, the needles and branches along one side are covered in off-white frosting. Then she turns and looks at me.

"Oh, fuck," she says, her eyes wide as saucers. Both her hands go to her temples, in the universal gesture for *oh fuck*.

"Oh fuck. Oh *fuck*. Don't move, Violet, I don't — fuck!"

Janice is freaking out as she looks at me, at the cake, at the tree, then frantically around as if someone's going to run in and save her.

I gather my wits to the best of my ability, which is not great right now.

"Janice," I say. "There's a radio on my belt," I say, sounding far calmer than I feel. "Call Lydia and ask her to get Eli out here."

I don't know why I told her to get Eli. He's probably busy right now, and he's not even a pastry chef, but that's what came out when I needed someone to come save the day.

Janice grabs the radio. The cake slumps a little further, and I try not to wonder what it's like to drown in cake.

"Hello?" she says, mashing the buttons. "We have a cake emergency at the barn. I repeat, WE HAVE A CAKE EMERGENCY."

I stand there, perfectly still. As the only thing standing in the way of a complete and total cake disaster, I can't move, so I close my eyes and try to go to my happy place.

Eli behind the brewery —

Nope. Wrong happy place.

Janice keeps talking into the radio, saying, "Yes, literally an emergency!" and "A TREE!" The cake is soft and pliable, surprisingly warm with my body heat.

Cake makes a good blanket, I think. *Who knew?*

If I ever get stuck at work overnight and the power goes out, I can just sleep in a wedding cake.

I wonder if strippers who jump out of cakes like it because of this.

"Okay," Janice says. She still sounds panicked, but at least she's making progress. "Yes. NOW. Like, *now* now! Thanks."

She clears her throat.

"Okay, he's coming," she says.

"Cool," I answer, because there's not a whole lot more that I can say, and we wait. I still have my eyes closed, the cake very slowly slumping against me more and more as I pretend that I'm actually doing something really fun that involves being covered in a warm, sticky, thick substance.

I admit that I'm having trouble coming up with something that fits the bill. A mud bath at a spa, maybe, but a pretty gross mud bath.

"Jesus tapdancing Christ," Eli's voice says, and my eyes jolt open. I didn't even hear him coming. "What the fuck happened? Did that tree fall on the cake? Give me that and take the other one to the other side," he says, not waiting for any answers.

He stands there with a huge round pizza spatula, his eyes drifting over the cake, a look of total concentration on his hot face.

Thank God, I think.

It might be the first time I've ever been relieved to see him, but I am. Eli is a lot of things, and God knows we've got issues, but I know one thing for sure.

He's gonna do his damndest to save our butts, and his damndest is a *lot.*

"Zane, get on the stepladder and lift the top two layers. Brandon, you get the next two and I'll move this bottom one so it's centered again. On three."

I can't even turn my head without coating my face completely in frosting, but I hear the sound of a stepladder being unfolded and deployed, feet climbing up, Eli giving further instructions.

"You got it?"

"Think so."

"Okay. One. Two. Three!"

The weight of the cake lifts off me. It feels like a miracle, because it turns out cake is pretty heavy. I step back, freed, and watch as Eli carefully moves a cake layer back to where it belongs, depositing it and sliding the pizza peel from underneath it as gently as possible.

"Okay, next," he says, his voice tense. "Careful."

He guides the rest of the layers into place. I watch, still holding my breath, cake-covered. At any second the whole creation could go off-balance, topple over, and then we'd be well and truly fucked.

"Careful," Janice whispers, mostly to herself. She stands off to one side, wringing her hands, still clearly wigging out.

Zane and Brandon balance the cake. They pull pizza peels back, slowly, carefully.

The cake stands on its own. It looks like an absolute wreck — frosting smeared to hell and back, gouges of exposed sponge where the frosting stuck to me instead — but it's standing on its own, and that's step one.

I glob frosting off of my face and look around. Then I just wipe it on my pants, because they're covered in frosting anyway.

"Any chance someone from the bakery is still here?" Eli asks.

"They were gone before noon," I say.

He nods, very serious. There's already frosting in his hair and a light smattering on his arms and down the front of his jacket, but he doesn't pay it any mind as he considers the cake, eyes crawling over every square inch.

"What happens if we don't have a cake?" he asks.

My stomach flips. I think my vision narrows.

"Not an option," I say.

"I'm just asking—"

"There needs to be a cake," I say, the urgency rising in my voice. "This thing cost twenty thousand dollars, and I'm sure we could get sued for *much* more than that for ruining a five-hundred-thousand-dollar wedding."

"*Twenty thousand?*"

"At least."

"Do they know there are children starving in—"

"Eli, for fuck's sake!" I say, panic spiking through my veins again.

"Okay," he says, holding up his hands, his voice surprisingly soft.

He looks at the cake. I look at the cake. Brandon, Zane, and Janice all look at the cake, all totally silent, contemplating the confectionary disaster in front of us.

I sidle around to the other side of the cake. There are pine needles embedded in the frosting.

I hate trees.

"Janice," he finally says, still studying the thing. "Go get me all the frosting you can find or make. Buttercream, ganache, fondant, I don't care. Anything decorative that can go on a cake, bring that too. If it's pretty and edible, I want it. And every single spatula we have."

"We need to move it to the side of the barn so the guests can't see it," I say, pointing at Brandon and Zane, both college students working in the kitchen for the summer. "Do you have the dolly?"

All three of them nod and hurry off, looking rattled and shell shocked. Now it's just me and Eli and the cake.

"How are you at decorating a cake?" Eli asks me.

"Bad," I say.

"How are you at picking pine needles out of frosting?"

"As good as the next guy, I guess."

"And when are they supposed to cut the cake?"

I look at my watch.

"Now," I say.

Brandon and Zane come back, pushing a dolly in front of them.

"Push it back half an hour," Eli says.

For once, I didn't question him or argue.

I just pick up my frosting-covered radio, call Lydia, and get it done.

· · · · ★ ★ ★ ★ ★ · · · ·

I PIPE the last of the frosting into the massive cake rift. My arms are sore and shaking, because I've been doing this for twenty minutes now and it takes way more strength than I'd thought.

Bakers must be ripped, I think.

I'm sweating. I'm even more covered in frosting than before. I look like a terrifying lovechild of an ent and a yeti, because after picking tree debris out of wedding cake, I'm covered in both.

I'm halfway up a ten-foot ladder, staring at my wedding cake repair job.

It's bad.

I wasn't lying when I said I was bad at cake decorating. Things get ugly when I try to decorate cupcakes, let alone a beautiful, twenty-thousand-dollar wedding cake.

It had been my job to smash whatever chunks of cake I

could back into the rift, then patch it together with buttercream, filling in any gaps with gobs and gobs of the sticky, heavy stuff. While standing on a ladder. And panicking.

Now the cake looks like it has some sort of tumor situation, but it's probably better than what it looked like before.

I take a deep breath and lean against the ladder, dropping the icing bag to my side. Frosting blobs out of it onto the ground, but right now I couldn't care less.

Eli's head pops around the cake.

"That done?"

"It looks awful."

A smile flickers around his eyes. It doesn't last, and I barely catch it, but it's there.

"Don't worry, that's the back," he says. "Here."

He takes the icing bag and replaces it wordlessly with an offset spatula, then goes back to work on the front of the cake. I get back to smoothing out the blobs.

We work. We don't talk much. Every so often he hands me a tool, I give him a report, or say something into my radio, but for the most part, we labor in a frenzied, stress-filled silence.

I smooth. He decorates, coaching my unsteady hands even while he works, his voice surprisingly soothing, calm, and above all, *nice*.

I don't have time to think about the fact that Eli is being nice. I don't have time to think about the kiss or the maid of honor, and in that way, this disaster is pure bliss.

I only have time to fix frosting.

Finally, Eli steps back a few feet. He considers the cake, crumbs and frosting everywhere: on his clothes, streaked on his face, spiking his hair. My radio crackles again, Lydia's voice punctuating the ambient quiet.

"What's the cake status?" she asks, her voice even higher pitched than usual.

I look at Eli, covered to the elbow in white, blue, and purple frosting.

"I'll let you judge," he says.

I get off the ladder and come around the front of the cake, silently praying to the cake gods that it's not a complete and utter disaster.

Please look okay. Please look okay.

I hold my breath and turn, looking up at twelve feet of wedding cake.

It's okay.

It's not *good*. Before the tree incident, the cake was a master craft of baking design. Now it's a perfectly adequate wedding cake. Not fancy. Not art. Definitely not worth twenty thousand dollars.

But it's *fine*, not *a total disaster*, and that's more than good enough.

The air leaves my lungs in a rush, and I try to run a hand through my hair. It sticks halfway through, because both my hair and my hand are coated with frosting.

"Thank fuck," I say.

"I've seen worse," Eli says behind me as I grab the radio from my belt, smearing it with frosting.

Before I can speak into it, it squawks.

"Violet?" Lydia's voice says. "How's the cake? It's nearly nine-fifteen and I can't hold the groom's grandmother back for much longer."

Her voice lowers, like she's telling me something in confidence.

"She is *feisty*, Violet," she says, her voice tinged with panic. She's completely serious.

For a long second, I stare at the radio. Any rational response flies out of my brain, and I'm totally speechless.

My arms are so tired they're floppy. I'm covered in

frosting and totally wrung out from the adrenaline of our emergency wedding cake surgery.

I start giggling. I don't mean to. I know giggling isn't helping anything right now, but it's coming from somewhere deep inside me that's not obeying my brain, and I can't stop.

"Violet?" Lydia hisses.

"I'm sorry," I gasp, trying to control myself. I bite my lip, trying to stop the laughter.

Then I make the mistake of glancing over at Eli. A grin spreads across his frosting-streaked face.

I snort, dissolving into giggles again so hard that I have to sit down, on the grass.

"*Violet*," Lydia says, the radio crackling. "Are you okay? Are you hysterical?"

I inhale with another snort, eyes closed so I can't see Eli also laughing, and I finally get a hold of myself.

"The cake is go," I tell her, taking a deep breath. "I repeat, *the cake is go!*"

"Thanks," she says, then pulls the radio away from her mouth. I can still hear her as she speaks to someone else. "Okay, she's lost her mind but…"

A tear runs down my cheek, flowing over more frosting as I look at Eli again. He's laughing too, his arms clasped over his chest, and that only makes me laugh more.

Which makes him laugh harder, which makes *me* laugh harder until my ribs hurt and I'm lightheaded. We laugh until we're both borderline hysterical, standing in front of this perfectly *fine* enormous wedding cake.

"You're a damn mess," he finally says, still laughing.

"So are you," I point out.

He holds out his hand. I take it, and he locks his strong, firm grip around my wrist, both of us slippery with frosting, then pulls me up.

"I'm always a mess," he says, slowly letting my hand go. "You, on the other hand…"

He half-smiles, and even though we're right outside a four-hundred person wedding and there are plenty of people around, I feel like we're alone.

Then he reaches out with his thumb, swipes a glob of frosting from my cheek, and licks his thumb.

I hold my breath for a beat too long. I watch his thumb disappear into his mouth, his lips closing around it, his mouth working as he sucks the sugar off. I look back into his eyes, mossy in the low light and teasing as always.

"Delicious," he says, just as Lydia comes out of the barn.

"Oh, thank God," she says.

CHAPTER THIRTEEN
VIOLET

I lean forward into the sink, bending in half at the waist until my head is fully under the faucet as I rake my fingers through my hair.

Slowly, the globs of frosting start to come loose. They've hardened on the outside, so I massage them until the sugar melts and the fat softens between my fingers, then work them through the strands and down the drain.

It's not my favorite thing to have in my hair, but at least I'm washing it.

"I think that's a health code violation," Eli's voice says behind me, the door to the kitchen closing.

"You gonna narc on me?" I ask, working another frosting chunk out.

He comes in, tossing something onto the counter behind us. There are still people in the kitchen, washing dishes and stacking plates, wrapping leftovers in plastic wrap, but they're across the kitchen from where I'm standing over an industrial sink, rinsing sugar out of my hair.

I can see him out of the corner of my eye, standing off to the side, hip leaning against the counter, upside down and perfectly casual. He's still wearing his black pants but he's taken off his chef's jacket, wearing nothing but a black t-shirt that has a few frosting streaks on it.

It's not a bad look. Eli seems incapable of bad looks. I may be rinsing my hair under the running water for longer than strictly necessary, just getting an eyeful of him where he won't catch me.

After a minute of that, he saunters over, standing next to me.

My heartbeat picks up, despite my brain asking it not to do that.

"You need soap?" he offers, holding up a bottle of Dawn.

It's tempting. My hair still feels gross, but I can't imagine that dish soap is great for my hair either.

"I'll use shampoo when I get home," I say, still rinsing and scrubbing. "I'm just getting the chunks out so I don't get frosting all over my car."

"It's all the same stuff," he says.

I just laugh.

"Not at all," I tell him, still upside-down, combing my fingers through my hair, making sure I've gotten as much sugar out as I can. "I doubt dish soap will give me the bounce and volume I require."

"You know that's all marketing," he goes on. "Make it smell nice and promise *manageability* and they can charge you twice as much for soap."

I reach up and turn the water off, wringing my hair out into the sink. When I stand right-side-up again, Eli hands me a kitchen towel.

"Thanks," I say, scrunching my hair in it.

For a moment, I study him. He studies me, something oddly unguarded between us.

"But you can't convince me that you don't shampoo *and* condition," I say.

Eli has nice hair. It isn't showy or dramatic, but it's a brown so intense and deep it's nearly black, framing his face and flopping over his forehead in exactly the right way. There's no way he doesn't spend *some* time on it.

"And why would you say that?"

Because you look too good.

"Come on. You're *coiffed.* There's probably even hair gel or something in it," I say, rubbing the towel vigorously against my head. "Mousse, maybe?"

"Why would I put an ungulate in my hair?"

"Moose aren't ungulates," I say.

I have no idea whether moose are ungulates, but disagreeing with Eli is a knee-jerk response.

"I think they are."

"Because you're a moose expert."

"At least I've seen one," he counters.

"Did it tell you it was an ungulate?"

"It didn't have to," he says. "It was just so obvious."

I drape the towel around my neck, dragging my fingers through my hair again. It's wet and probably looks like a rat's nest, but at least it isn't sticky anymore.

Don't ask, I think. *Don't give him the satisfaction.*

"It was in North Dakota," he says, then nods at me. "You need another towel?"

"I'm all right," I say, squeezing it around the ends of my hair. "What were you doing in North Dakota?"

"Bartending," he says, then holds out a hand. "I'll take that back."

I toss Eli the towel. He catches it and walks off, heading

through a doorway to some other part of the kitchen as I look down at myself.

Even if my hair is… not clean, but *better*, the rest of me is still a disaster. Sighing, I head back to the sink, scrubbing frosting from my elbows and upper arms. More than anything, I need a shower, but I don't want to get frosting all over the inside of my car on the way home.

"Here," Eli's voice says from behind me, and I turn.

Fabric hits me right in the face. I grab at it with wet hands.

"You did that on purpose."

He grins, his face easy and relaxed as he tosses something onto the counter next to himself. It's not how I'm used to seeing him.

It's weird. It's unfamiliar.

Strangest of all, it's *nice.*

"Prove it," he says, and pulls his shirt off over his head.

I wasn't prepared.

Eli's gorgeous. He's tall and broad-shouldered, his muscles thick and ropy. Even in the ugly fluorescent light of the industrial kitchen, watching them move under his skin as he takes one shirt off and puts another on is mesmerizing.

My face is hot. I want to touch him so bad my hand twitches and I think about it all again, that thirty seconds outside the brewery, about what could have happened if Daniel hadn't found us.

I want. *I want.*

So did the maid of honor.

God, I hate my stupid brain sometimes. Can't I just ogle a man in peace?

Eli turns away from me slightly, grabbing his shirt from the counter, his back toward me.

I notice something else: Eli has a tattoo now.

There's only one that I can see, but it's big. It stretches the width of his upper back, lines and circles connected across muscle and bone and sinew. It's a good, well-done tattoo. A tattoo that clearly took time and effort and thought, a tattoo that was carefully and lovingly planned.

All at once, the enormity of the thing hits me.

Eli's changed. He's different. He left this place and then came back, and in the interim he was a chef in Bangkok and a bartender in North Dakota and God only knows what else, and he's not the same anymore.

The evidence is right there, in front of my eyes. Eli's inked his change on his skin, stark permanent lines reminding me with every inch that this Eli is a different Eli than the teenager I used to know.

A new Eli, the same in some ways but reinvented in others.

Someone I don't know. No matter how much I think I do, I don't.

His new shirt slides over his torso, and I tear my gaze away, pretending to shake out the shirt he tossed me.

Did I change?

The thought makes my breath stick in my throat, and I stare at the shirt, unseeing.

I didn't go anywhere. I haven't done anything great or interesting. I haven't gotten any tattoos.

I don't even have my ears pierced.

I feel small, immaterial. I feel rooted like a tree, stuck in the ground, doomed to stay in the same spot from sunrise to sunset every day until I wither and die. Here's Eli, tattooed and worldly, hot and knowledgeable about moose, and I still live in the same trailer where I lived in high school. It's been ten years and I've barely left the state in all that time.

I think about the elevator again, even though I'd really rather not. Eli: tall, handsome, smirking. The maid of honor: arms wrapped around him, possessive. Like they were already lovers.

She probably went to college somewhere far away. I bet she studied abroad. She probably goes on international vacations, can speak a little French, has opinions about which part of the Mediterranean is the best for yachting.

Stop it, I tell myself for the one-millionth time.

"You gonna put that on?" Eli asks, glancing over his shoulder.

My face flushes. I focus on the t-shirt in my hands, giving it another good shake.

"I keep a few extras in my locker in case I make a mess," he says, pulling his new shirt down to his hips.

I HIKED THE CANYON, the shirt in my hand brags. GRAND CANYON NATIONAL PARK.

"Did you?" I ask, even though I think I already know the answer.

"I did," he says, brushing a hand through his hair, then making a face. "Ugh," he says, looking at his hand.

I hold up the shirt.

"Thanks," I say, and head around a corner, into a pantry where I shut the door. There's absolutely no way I'm taking my shirt off around Eli, not when he's hot and tattooed and has been to Thailand and hiked the Grand Canyon.

Not when I'm just me.

His shirt smells nice. Of course it does. I ball mine up and stand there for a moment, squeezing it with my tired hands, before finally opening the door to the pantry and heading back into the kitchen.

Eli pulls a plate out of a fridge, a slab of wedding cake

on it. It's an edge piece, thickly covered in frosting. I raise an eyebrow, hoping that no one noticed him taking it.

"Come on, I earned it," he says, looking at my face. "Besides, it's not for me."

"Who's it for?"

"Daniel's daughter."

I eye the cake as we walk through the kitchen. The wedding is officially over and the party has moved back to the lodge, but the cleanup crew is still working, moving tables and chairs, packing the dishwasher, loading dirty linens into massive bags.

"She's gonna be bouncing off the walls six ways from Sunday," I say.

Eli grins and opens the kitchen door, letting me go through first.

"It's a bribe," he admits. "If I give her cake, she doesn't tell Daniel that I called another driver a fucking shithead."

I laugh.

"That sounds like Rusty," I admit.

"She's gonna get me in big trouble one of these days," Eli muses. "You going home?"

"Yeah, I think I've earned it," I say as we walk down a hallway, past closed offices. "You?"

"Yup. Need a ride?"

"No, I actually drive myself to work most days," I tease.

"Just making sure," Eli teases back. "Let me walk you to your car."

It's not a question, it's a statement. He opens the door to the outside and holds this one for me as well, the cool, wet southern night air flowing over my skin. It's late, the sky inky black, the stars bright and the moon brighter.

"I'll be fine," I say. "I walk myself to my car all the time."

"You're covered in frosting and there are bears," he says

as we cross onto the asphalt of the parking lot, the air warmer as the pavement releases the last of its heat.

"The frosting is mostly gone, and they're just black bears. If I were a dumpster, I'd be worried," I counter.

"Raccoons, then."

"I can handle a raccoon," I point out, even though we're already halfway to my car. A few spots away, Eli's giant Bronco hulks.

"Can you?" he asks, casually carrying the cake, the shirts he's taken off slung over his shoulder.

"Sure. They're small. Terrier-sized or so."

"They all have rabies. Every single one. Rabid as hell," he says. "Besides, raccoons don't give a shit that you're bigger than them. They go for the eyes first."

He holds out one hand like claws and pretends to snarl, the moonlight shadowing his handsome face, his hair falling perfectly over his forehead despite the frosting in it.

I laugh.

It's the weirdest feeling.

I'm enjoying Eli's company, maybe for the first time ever. Even though I like it, I'm suspicious. I know that next week, this spell will be broken, and we'll be back at each other's throats.

"Where are you getting your information?" I ask, digging my keys from my purse.

"Levi works for the Forest Service."

"Levi's a tree expert, not a raccoon expert."

"You think he don't know his varmints?" he says, exaggerating his accent.

I laugh as we reach my car, and I unlock the door, looking over at Eli as I open it.

"I think if Levi told you that raccoons go for the eyes, he probably had his own reasons for wanting you to think that," I say. "You want a ride to your car so they don't get yours, either?"

A smile flickers across his face, and he glances up at his Bronco, fifty feet away.

"I'll take my chances," he says, then taps the roof of my car. "See you Tuesday, Violet."

He walks in front of my car, headlights briefly illuminating his form, and then he fades into the night. I wait until I see the lights of his Bronco flick on, feeling some responsibility to make that sure he doesn't get attacked by raccoons, either.

Twenty minutes later, I pull up next to my trailer, the lamp in the living room blazing through my curtained windows. I keep it on a timer so strangers think someone is home, something I started after Mom died and I lived alone. I guess it works, because no one's broken in yet.

A burst of laughter erupts from the trailer next door. I wonder how many cases of Bud Light the rednecks have gone through tonight. Apparently this weekend kicks off the summer party season for them as well.

Before I go in, I take one last look at the stars. They're bright out here, and even though they're so far away, somehow they feel warm, friendly.

Then, it hits me. Eli's tattoo. It's a constellation.

I stare upward, wondering which one. I didn't recognize it then and I don't now, trying to recreate its shape in the heavens. I wonder if it means something, whether recognizing it would give me some insight into Eli.

I wondered if the maid of honor saw it. I wonder whether she recognized it.

I wonder what pieces of Eli she has that I don't.

I quit staring into space, open my door, and head inside to my lighted lamp and empty trailer. I strip as I head toward the bathroom and get into the shower before the water's even fully hot, desperate to feel less sticky, to wash the day off of myself.

I could have kissed him again, I think. *When he took his shirt off. No one else was there. I could have just walked over and kissed him and he'd have pushed me against the counter…*

I sigh, roll over, and get my vibrator out of my nightstand for at least the tenth time that week.

CHAPTER FOURTEEN

ELI

At seven the next morning, there's a knock on my door.

I ignore it and shove a pillow over my head. I don't do seven a.m., especially when my job means I usually don't get to bed until one or two in the morning.

The knock sounds again, louder this time. I sigh, taking the pillow off my face and flopping one forearm across my eyes.

"No," I shout.

There's a pause, and then the door creaks open.

"Come *on*," I say, fervently grateful that I'm wearing pajamas. It was the only rule my mother absolutely *insisted* on when I moved back in, and I've come to understand why.

I don't open my eyes as small footsteps pad to the side of my bed.

Much too small to be Daniel or my mom. Rusty's not the best with personal space. Like I said, thank God for pajamas.

"Did you get it?" Rusty asks, whispering so loudly they can probably hear her in the next county.

"This couldn't wait an hour?" I say, my arm still over my face.

She's quiet for a moment. I peek at her from under my arm, her serious blue eyes crawl over my face, studying me in that honest, open way that only kids can.

"Are you hungover?" Rusty finally asks.

That jolts me awake.

"No, no," I say, sitting up right, swinging my legs off the bed. "I worked late, that's all."

She doesn't say anything, just looks at me with those wide, clear blue eyes.

"I promise," I say, one hand on my chest. "Cross my heart."

Rusty just nods, and something like anger closes a small fist, deep inside my chest.

I *hate* that that's her first question. I hate that, at six years old, she even knows what a hangover is or what one looks like.

Daniel has sole legal and physical custody of Rusty. Legally, he never has to let his ex see Rusty again, but Daniel's not a monster. He still wants Rusty to have her mom in her life, even if it's not really clear that her mom wants the same thing.

She'll go weeks, sometimes even months without contacting her own daughter. Daniel's reported her missing at least twice. And then, after Rusty visits her, she comes home knowing what hangovers look like.

Sure, Daniel owns a brewery, but I've never seen him have more than one drink in a night.

"I had to hide it," I explain, still trying to clear the final cobwebs of sleep from my brain. "It's in the bottom of the fridge, behind that big Tupperware of macaroni salad that your grandma made."

Rusty grins.

"Does it have a flower?"

"There weren't any flowers," I say.

Technically, it's true: the flowers were gone by the time we actually served cake. I think most of them were in Violet's hair.

God, it was disappointing when she went into the pantry to change shirts. Not unexpected, but disappointing. Turns out she's pretty when she's laughing, too.

"I got you a corner piece, though," I say, as seriously as I can manage. "Is our deal still good?"

She nods.

I hold up one finger.

"One more thing," I say.

Rusty frowns.

"You can't eat it in front of your dad, because he'll kill me," I say. "We'll sneak it out when the time is right, okay?"

Rusty nods, grinning and rocking from foot to foot.

"Okay," she says, practically bouncing with excitement, then leaves my room.

I flop back onto my bed.

· · · · · ★ ★ ★ ★ ★ · · · · ·

"Listen, it was nothing," I say, watching the saucepan like a hawk, keeping my voice low. "You've never made out with someone at a bar?"

"Oh, I have," Daniel says, leaning over and looking into a pot. "That's how I got Rusty, remember? Well, that was step one."

Today's Sunday, and that means that today is Sunday Dinner.

If we're in town, we're expected to be there. No excuse is good enough. Anyone we want to bring is welcome. Silas is there a lot. Charlotte, Daniel's best friend, is usually around.

Since I've been back, I've taken over the cooking. Tonight I'm trying out a slightly sweet lemongrass catfish dish, and the sugar needs to be caramelized before I add it to the sauce.

"Then you know that sometimes it happens, and it's no big deal, and there's no need to talk about it because it was nothing," I say, not moving my eyes for an instant.

The sugar is starting to turn very, very slightly yellow.

"Yeah, it sure seems like suddenly getting physical with your childhood nemesis is nothing," Daniel deadpans.

"We all make mistakes," I say, trying to sound as nonchalant as I can.

Was it a mistake? Maybe. Would I do it again? In a second.

Did I come close last night?

Hell yes.

The sugar's slightly darker.

"So this was a one-time thing and I don't need to brace myself to hear even more about Violet?" he asks. "I just like to be prepared."

I quickly glance up at my younger brother, who's leaning against the kitchen counter and clearly doesn't believe a word I've been saying.

"Nope," I say.

"Well, if you're wrong, I'm here for you," he says, patting me on the shoulder. "And I promise to only say *I told you so* a few dozen—"

"Here they are!" my mom says, bursting into the kitchen, holding her phone out in front of her like it's divining rod. "Daniel, Eli, your brother's on the phone!"

"Hi," comes Caleb's slightly staticky voice, over speakerphone.

"Hey," Daniel and I say in unison as my mom hands her phone to Daniel.

"Where are you?" I ask.

"Uh, I think this town is called Idyllwild," he says. "I'm at a hostel for the night so I can take a shower and resupply, so I figured I'd call and let you know I'm still alive."

"How far have you gotten?"

"About a hundred and seventy-five miles," he says.

Daniel whistles.

"You gonna finish this year?" he asks, and Caleb just laughs.

"Probably not," he says. "The Pacific Crest Trail is longer and harder than the Appalachian Trail."

"That's what she said," I mutter.

They both snort, and my mom rolls her eyes.

"Tell him about your job," she says.

I'm still watching the sugar. It's getting close.

"I got a new job," I say.

"Doing what?"

"Cooking," I tell him.

"He's the executive chef at Bramblebush," my mom says, smacking me lightly on the arm.

"He works with Violet Tulane," Daniel says.

I shoot him a glare. He raises one eyebrow slightly, like he's challenging me.

"You didn't tell me that," my mom says.

"Is that the girl you couldn't stand in high school?" Caleb asks.

"Yes," Daniel and my mom chorus together.

"She's very nice," my mom says. "But she used to really get Eli's goat."

Daniel makes another face at me. I ignore it.

"Tell us about all your adventures on the trail," my mom says.

· · · · · ★ ★ ★ ★ ★ · · · · ·

THAT EVENING, after dinner, Daniel and I sit on a couch in the living room, watching Rusty.

She's taken all the available cushions, piled them up on the floor, and is leaping onto them from the arm of the couch. I just watched Daniel try to corral her for about twenty minutes, but it was hopeless.

He gave up, exhausted.

Rusty stands on the arm of the couch, balancing carefully, her arms held out to the side. She's tied a towel around her neck like a cape.

"Three, two, one…"

She bends her knees, crouching.

"GERONIMO!"

Rusty leaps onto the pile, already giggling.

Then she springs back up and climbs back onto the couch, ready to do it again.

"I think she's possessed," Daniel says to me. He's sprawled across the other couch, the cushion behind him missing, probably in Rusty's pile. "Is there a full moon or something?"

"That's probably it," I agree, keeping my voice totally neutral. "Kids just get crazy sometimes, I guess. So much energy."

Rusty jumps onto the pile again.

Daniel sighs.

I say nothing.

CHAPTER FIFTEEN

ELI

It's already four o'clock in the afternoon. At five o'clock sharp some pharmaceutical company's retreat is having a happy hour and raw bar on the Presidential Patio.

The oysters were absolutely nowhere to be found.

I rub my temples, looking at the guy standing in front of me.

"What do you mean, you don't *think* they're down there?" I ask Zane, one of the college kids who currently has a summer job in my kitchen.

He frowns at me like it's a trick question, real confusion crossing his face. I sigh inwardly, wondering why on earth Montgomery hired someone with the last name Payne to work a fast-paced job where he'd have to think on his feet sometimes.

Hell, a job where he'd have to think *ever*. I don't know Zane — Lord, his name is *Zane Payne*, seriously? — or his parents, but they're cousins of some of my high school classmates.

The Paynes are not known for their intellect, cleverness,

or wit, is what I'm saying, and Zane Payne seems to be performing to expectations.

"I mean…" he says, and pauses. "I don't think I saw them?"

I shiver, despite myself. We're standing in the walk-in cooler, our breath puffing up in front of us, and neither of us know where the oysters were. I don't even know if we *have* oysters, despite ordering them last week for this event.

If we don't have oysters, I don't know what the fuck I'm going to do.

"Okay," I say, and push past him, swinging open the heavy door of the cooler. The kitchen's bustling: the ovens on, pots steaming on the stovetop, my sous chef, Naomi is rolling out pasta on the stainless steel countertop for wild mushroom ravioli.

"We'll go check the loading dock," I say, striding through the kitchen. "Naomi, can you keep an eye on the au jus that's on the stove?"

"Got it," Naomi says, and I swing through the kitchen doors and into the wide, concrete-floored hallway, Zane on my heels. The kitchen is in the barn that was once a dairy barn — the other, which houses offices, was a former horse barn, I think Montgomery told me — and it still has a lot of those semi-industrial trappings.

I push open the door to the loading dock and looked around. A few pallets of stuff, all wound up tight in plastic, stand around.

There's a pile of flowerpots in a huge wooden crate. A precarious-looking plastic-wrapped stack of chairs. There's a pallet stacked high with what, on closer inspection, turns out to be plastic-wrapped sod.

We wander through the loading dock, looking for either someone who works down here or the oysters themselves.

At this point, I'll take almost anything as long as it provides a clue.

We walk between more stacked-high stuff: old-fashioned lanterns; golf cart tires; throw pillows; cleaning supplies.

No oysters.

"Right, I don't see them," Zane Payne says.

We walk around a few more piles of things — bricks, fake flowers — moving deeper into the sides of the loading dock. I pray that somehow, some way, the oysters managed to find somewhere cold and dark.

My hopes are not high. I'm already trying to think of what to serve besides oysters. We'll have to scrap the whole raw bar, obviously, but we can probably throw together some sliders, slap a few different sauces on there, and call it fancy.

That's the last resort, though, and I clench one fist as I walk around another pallet stacked high with something or other. I really, really don't want to fuck up this job on my second week here, especially not after the wedding cake fiasco of last weekend.

"This seems like it's all not oysters," Zane offers, still trailing behind me.

I move further into the loading dock, finally finding the cement wall.

"Is Zane your first name?" I ask, distracted.

"Yeah?"

Still no oysters, and I've hit the end of the pallets. I scan the docks, but it seems futile.

"You ever think about going by your middle name?"

"Not really," Zane Payne says, shrugging. "I like Zane a lot better than Gomer."

Gomer. Oof.

Before I can offer my condolences on a middle name

that makes mine sound high-class and fancy, I hear voices on the other side of a towering stack of paper towels, talking in hushed tones. They sound like they don't want to be overheard.

"Poor Violet," one woman is saying. "She must feel awful about it. Good thing Martin was there."

A prickle runs down my spine at Violet's name, and I stop.

"Did you know he could decorate cakes? I didn't know he could decorate cakes," a second woman says.

Still standing behind a stack of paper towels, I frown. If Martin can decorate cakes, I'm a warthog.

"Montgomery won't take it from her paycheck, will he?" the first voice asks, growing fainter.

Shit, they're walking away. I backpedaled, trying to stay even with them. Zane's disappeared around a corner, hopefully not lost forever in this maze.

"Oh, no," the second voice says. "It's just an accident, he would never. Still, I'm glad I'm not Violet right now."

Zane's head pops around a corner as the voices fade away, my heart beating faster, something tightening in my chest.

Why would Montgomery take something out of Violet's paycheck? She's the one who saved that stupid cake, not Martin.

"Still no oysters!" Zane reports, too cheery for my tastes.

"Keep looking," I growl, more angrily than he deserves, and his head disappears.

I keep looking too, but despite the ticking clock and the *very* imminent disaster, I'm no longer thinking about oysters.

I'm thinking that if Martin's trying to take credit for Violet's cake heroism, I'll rub poison ivy on the inside of his jacket when he's not looking. Sure, Violet's annoying, but at least she did the work instead of just trying to take credit afterward.

"No oysters here either!" Zane Payne says from behind me.

"Right. Thanks," I say, my mind returning to my current disaster.

Just as I'm giving up hope, a door in the wall opens. A man emerges: bearded, burly, wearing flannel, and about fifty. He looks like he knows what's what down here, I jog over.

"Howdy," he says, pushing a baseball cap back on his unruly hair. "Welcome to the loading docks. You here on business or pleasure?"

He grins, laughing at his own joke. I smile despite myself.

"You haven't seen a few bushel bags of oysters, have you?" I ask. "They were supposed to come in this morning, and no one's seen them."

Bearded/burly runs a thoughtful hand through his beard.

"Oysters," he says, reflectively. "Oysters. Hold on a tic, will you?"

I'm flooded with hope. This man just might be my redneck savior.

"Hey C.J.!" he shouts into the doorway from which he emerged. "Were you the one telling me you found some oysters this morning on top of those tables?"

"Yup!" a voice shouts back.

I crack the knuckles on one hand, silently praying: *please tell me you found somewhere cold to put them.*

"Where they at now?" Bearded/burly hollers.

"You know that old chest freezer down along the far wall where they took out those vending machines last year?" C.J. shouts back. "Tossed 'em in there, didn't know where they were supposed to go but figured they ought to stay cold."

Thank you, oyster Jesus.

Thank you.

"Thanks, man!" Bearded/burly calls back, then looks at me, jerking a thumb over his shoulder. "There's a chest freezer over yonder against the wall that doesn't freeze anything anymore, but it ought to have kept oysters cold enough."

I thank him profusely, then jog off to find the freezer. Zane is right behind me as I open it.

Inside are four red mesh bags, all filled with oysters. I stick my hand in to see how cold it was, but Bearded/burly is right: it's kept the oysters cold enough.

"That them?" his voice says behind me.

"Yup," I say, already heaving one out. "I think you just saved my ass."

"Don't mention it," he says, pushing at his baseball cap again. "You know, it was the weirdest thing. Found those this morning by accident. They were on top of a shipment of tables that we were about to return to a rental agency, up where no one could see 'em, only one bag happened to slide off. Figured someone must've made a mistake so I tossed 'em into the old freezer. Hell of an odd place to put oysters, though."

I glance over at Zane, the wheels in my head already turning.

"Well, you're supposed to keep them somewhere cold and dark," Zane says earnestly. "Maybe someone just got confused."

"Must have been pretty confused," B/b says.

I pull two bags out and hand them to Zane before he can offer any more thoughts, then hoist the other two on my shoulders.

"Come back now, y'all hear?" B/b calls out as we leave.

"Thanks!" I call as the loading dock door swings shut behind us.

"All right," I say to Zane, already power walking toward the kitchen, albeit carrying an extra seventy pounds. "How fast can you shuck oysters?"

· · · · · ★ ★ ★ ★ ★ · · · · ·

We finish at 5:05. I've never shucked oysters faster in my entire life, and somehow, I manage to do it without stabbing myself even once.

I guess miracles really do happen, even minor ones.

We get the oysters out the door, along with the rest of the happy hour appetizers. It's all a few minutes late, but the bar was open on time so hopefully no one noticed.

As soon as the food is out, I tell Naomi I'll be right back and book it out of the kitchen. Forty-five minutes of angrily shucking oysters hasn't done much to make me less pissed about what I overheard.

Sure, Violet's annoying, and she's a know-it-all, and she'd probably eat her grandmother's ashes if it gave her a competitive advantage in something. I don't want her to win the twenty grand at the end of the summer, because I want to win it.

But Violet at least worked her ass off. If she did win, which she won't, at least I'd know she didn't cheat.

I walk into her office just as she stands from her desk, slinging her purse over her shoulder.

"Hey," she says, then sniffs. "Seafood?"

Right, I probably reek.

"Oysters," I say. "We need to talk."

Both her eyebrows go up, and I take a step forward, lowering my voice.

"What do you know about Martin?" I ask.

Her eyes dart to the open door behind me, and she shifts her purse on her shoulder.

"He's fine," she says, her voice perfectly neutral, and nods at the door. "Why?"

I step back and close it. My heart thuds in my chest.

"He's a brown-nosing shitweasel," she hisses, dropping her purse on her desk. "Last year, the weekend before Labor Day, we were short almost fifty chairs for a wedding, and an hour before the ceremony started we *finally* found them in this old shed in the woods. Fifty chairs! In a shed, half a mile from the ceremony site."

"He stole the chairs?"

"I couldn't prove it, but I think he was trying to make me look bad, like I'd screwed up this wedding by not having enough of these fancy, special-order chairs that the bride wanted," she says, her cheeks flushing slightly pink.

I watch her, something slowly unfurling inside me. Violet is always beautiful when she's angry, but now she's angry at someone else even though I'm in the room. It might be a first.

The door's closed. I could kiss her again right now, right here. Forget Martin. Forget everything.

"How do you know it was him?" I ask, folding my arms over myself. In the past week, I've only had brief interactions with the man, but I don't particularly like him.

She shakes her head.

"It was just little stuff," she says, eyes still blazing. "When the chairs first showed up, he had all these questions about them, wanted to know where we were keeping them. For a few days before the wedding, he'd get here really early in the morning, and sometimes I'd see him using the golf cart to drive across the lawn when I was getting in, and he'd always say that he was checking in on something in the Lodge, but it never quite added up. And when we couldn't find the chairs, he seemed like he was trying to pretend he wasn't happy about it."

She slides back into her chair, crossing her arms over her chest, eyes still sparking. I force myself to look her in the eye instead of checking out the way her blouse fits her *really* well.

"And he's pulled other shit too," she says, shark-colored eyes still boring into mine. "I know he's switched orders before, hidden stuff, taken credit for other people's hard work. But no one's ever proven it, and Montgomery likes him for some reason, so he stays."

She narrows her eyes, the diatribe over.

"Why do you ask?"

"I think he's been telling people he saved the cake on Saturday," I say.

Violet goes red, her mouth a thin line. Her eyes glint dangerously.

"That lying bastard," she whispers.

I sit in the chair opposite her and tell her the whole story about the oysters: the trip to the loading docks, what I overheard, how the burly, bearded guy narrowly averted a seafood disaster.

"It's the money," she says when I'm finished.

"Really?" I ask dryly.

She shoots me a look.

"Twenty thousand dollars is crazy," she says. During my story, she'd grabbed a pen and now she's furiously tapping it on the top of her desk, scowling at the wall. "Martin was a pain in the butt last year over two grand. What is Montgomery *thinking* offering that kind of money? Someone's gonna get stabbed."

"As long as it's Martin, fine with me," I drawl.

"Don't joke like that," she says, but a smile ghosts across her face.

"I bet I could make it look like an accident."

Violet just rolls her eyes.

"We can't let him win this," she says, still keeping her voice low. "He can't take credit for our work and sabotage people and get rewarded."

"No," I agree, leaning forward in my chair. "I have a proposal."

She raises one eyebrow, turns slightly pink.

"I'm still not comfortable with stabbing," she says.

"I say we make a pact," I go on. "We work together."

She taps the pen a few more times, saying nothing.

"I only want to win this thing slightly more than I want you *not* to win," I admit, totally candid. "And I'm fairly sure you feel the exact same way, but you know what I want most of all?"

"For Martin to lose."

"Bingo."

She blows air out the side of her mouth, pen still tapping her desk, her eyes on me.

"Listen," I say. "I admit that I'll be pissed as hell if you beat me, but at least I'll know you earned it. That's more than I can say about that slimy fucker."

Violet says nothing.

"Just imagine," I say, leaning back in my chair, locking my hands together over my head. "It's the end of the summer. Montgomery calls a meeting or whatever it is he does, and with every single employee there, he announces that Martin beat you. He wins the twenty grand, and he did it because he's a backhanded shitweasel."

The pen taps faster, her face stormy. I know for Violet the worst thought isn't failing to win the money. It's the thought of someone else winning dishonestly.

"This isn't some ploy is it?" she asks, still suspicious. "Where I help you and then at the end you screw me over somehow and take it for yourself?"

"Hand to God, it's not," I say, raising my right hand over my head. "I just don't want Martin to win."

She nods, watching the pen tap against the desk.

Then she stands from her chair. She leans over and holds her hand out.

I don't look down her shirt. The effort that takes is Herculean.

"Deal," she says.

I stand. I take her hand in mine, and we shake. Her hand is smaller and more delicate than I imagined, and for a moment I wonder if I'm being too rough.

Then she gives my hand a squeeze so hard it crunches my knuckles together, and I stop wondering.

All right, if that's how we're going to do this.

I squeeze her hand back. Her jaw flexes, but she doesn't say anything. Of course she doesn't. It's Violet.

"Deal," I agree.

The shitweasel is going down.

CHAPTER SIXTEEN
VIOLET

Kevin grunts, sliding his foot into the shoe, then stands. He does a couple of deep knee bends, then takes a few exaggerated steps around the carpeted lobby before bouncing on his toes, looking contemplative.

"Yeah, I think I need a bigger size," he says, sitting back down on the bench, next to me.

I wiggle my toes in my own shoes. Bowling shoes always pinch a little bit — that's the nature of bowling shoes — but do these pinch too much? Not enough? Do I look like I'm wearing clown shoes?

Across the way, Lydia is already in one of the several lanes reserved for Bramblebush employees. We're having one of our happy hour team building outings, where Montgomery tells everyone to leave work at four o'clock and we all go do an activity together.

It's been a week since Eli and I made our pact, and it's been blissfully uneventful. No one's sabotaged anything. No cakes fell over. Last weekend's wedding was a small, intimate, relaxed affair, and I was home and in bed by ten p.m. That's practically unheard of.

Most astonishing of all, Eli and I have barely fought. Admittedly, I've been avoiding him a little, because when I see him I can't help but think of him in the elevator and then also him shirtless, and neither of those images are particularly conducive to a pleasant day for me.

I'd love to stop wondering whether he had sex with the maid of honor. I'd love to convince myself that it doesn't matter, because it doesn't, and yet I seem unable to quit thinking about it, and yet I'm *also* unable to quit thinking about how much I enjoyed seeing him half-naked.

Ugh.

I watch Lydia enter our names into the computer, a pitcher of beer on the table behind her. Her bowling shoes seem to fit fine, but she's also one of those people who could wear a paper bag as a dress and a cactus for a hat and look effortlessly stylish, so that hardly counts.

"What size were these again?" Kevin mutters to himself, flopping the shoes off his feet and picking them up.

I catch a glimpse of his feet, and then can't help but stare in horror.

"Kevin," I say.

He stops and looks at me, alarmed.

"Are you okay?" he asks.

"You're not wearing socks," I whisper, horrified.

He looks down at his toes. His naked toes. They're touching the floor without a barrier. They were *just* inside bowling shoes, also without a barrier.

My stomach recoils. I'm not really germophobic — I don't even own hand sanitizer and firmly believe that that's how bacterial superbugs are created — but I cannot handle bare feet in bowling shoes.

"Uh…" he says, glancing from his feet to my face and back.

"You can't do that," I tell him as he wiggles his toes

against the gray-blue industrial carpet. "That's horrible. *Kevin*."

He gives me a look so clueless, so deer-in-the-headlights, that it could only come from a nineteen-year-old guy.

"You need socks," I tell him. Suddenly I feel like his mother.

"I don't have socks with me," he says, like he's still trying to figure out what the big deal is.

"You can't put those on without socks," I say. I grab my purse and start rummaging through it. After a moment I find what I'm looking for and hand the small bundle to Kevin.

He takes it and holds it in the palm of his hand for a long moment.

"Are those pugs saying 'I love you'?" he finally asks.

I take a closer look at the socks I just handed him.

"Yes," I confirm.

"And you just had these in your purse," he goes on, still not putting the socks on his feet.

I bend down and tie the laces on my own bowling shoes. They pinch, but I've decided it's the right amount. Mostly because I don't feel like trying on another pair only to inevitably switch back to these.

"I don't have to explain myself to you," I say.

I wore heels to work today, and I knew I'd need socks for the bowling outing after work, so when I grabbed myself a pair of socks, I also grabbed an extra just in case someone else forgot socks.

Obviously it came in handy, because I saved Kevin from needing his feet amputating.

"They use that disinfectant stuff," he says, sounding a touch defensive, unfolding the socks from each other.

I just shake my head, tying my other shoe. Kevin slides

the socks over his feet, then looks down, wiggling his toes again.

Then he shrugs.

"Thanks," he says.

Across the lobby from us, Eli walks by. He's already got bowling shoes on, along with jeans and a green t-shirt that says *Don Antonio's* in faded script across the front.

I'm still tying my bowling shoes and through my hair, I watch him walk past the lanes while pretending that I'm not watching him. His sleeves are tight across his arms, the shoulders of his shirt slightly snug. I stop tying my shoes and just watch him as he approaches the rack of bowling balls, glancing along it before picking one up.

He tests it, facing away from us. He lifts it a few times, turns it back and forth, puts it back down. Even from thirty feet away I can see the muscles in his forearm flex as he locks his fingers into the holes, testing a few different ones.

It feels deeply, deeply unfair that he looks hot while trying out bowling balls and wearing bowling shoes. That just shouldn't be a thing.

Finally, he picks one and turns away from the rack of bowling balls, glancing at Kevin and I, seated on the bench. Eli nods hello.

I realize that neither Kevin nor I have moved since Eli started lifting bowling balls. We've just been sitting here, Kevin with his shoes in his hand, me bent over, not even tying my shoes.

Very cool of us.

I nod back quickly and sit upright, trying to hide the slight blush creeping up my cheeks. Eli heads into the lane with Lydia. Kevin still hasn't moved.

"He's straight," I say.

That shakes him out of his reverie, and he snorts.

"I know," he says.

"You do?"

For a flash, I think *yet again* about Eli in the elevator. The maid of honor. His arm around her, her head against his chest. The glowering, smoldering, victorious look he gave me as the elevator doors closed.

Something I can't name stretched and tightened in my chest, a nervous, strained tension.

Did Kevin see them in the elevator? Did he see something else?

How many people has Eli slept with at work in his first week?!

"Of course I know," Kevin says, standing. "Trust me, the first thing a gay kid learns is how to tell who's straight and who's not. I've got it down to an art. I could tell you everyone here who's ever *thought* about putting a dick in his mouth."

He stops short, looking suddenly alarmed.

"...Ma'am," he says, like he just remembered that he's talking to his boss.

"Right," I say. "Sorry."

He shrugs, then walks to the shoe counter in sock covered feet.

· · · · · ★ ★ ★ · · · · ·

"COME ON," I mutter, still standing at the very end of the lane. "Come on, come on."

My ball creeps toward the gutter.

"Don't do that," I coax. "Be a curveball."

The ball wobbles at the lip of the gutter. I cross my fingers on both hands.

It falls in with a definitive *whump*.

Dammit.

Sighing, I head back to the seats at the end of the lane, glancing at the scoreboard.

I've got sixty points. Eli's still ahead of me, with sixty-six points. Lydia's got fifty-five, and Naomi's at forty-two.

Kevin, who is wearing borrowed socks with pugs on them because he thought it was okay to wear bowling shoes with no socks, has almost a hundred and fifty points. It turns out that he was on his high school bowling team. I didn't know high schools *had* bowling teams.

I'm not annoyed that my summer intern has nearly triple my score.

But I'm *really* annoyed that Eli's beating me by six points.

"We could ask for bumpers," Eli says, sitting in the plastic seat behind the scorekeeping computer, his ankle crossed over his knee.

"Would that help you?" I say, grabbing my beer and taking a long swallow.

"Bumpers don't help if you're not throwing gutter balls," he says.

Lydia stands and grabs a bowling ball, frowning at the lane in front of her.

"Follow the arrows on the lane with your fingers," Kevin coaches, both of them ignoring us. "And make sure you follow through."

"You're six points ahead, Loveless," I say, sitting down on another plastic seat, facing him. "Don't get cocky."

"Cocky? That was an offer made from the goodness and generosity of my heart, *Tulane*," he says. "I'm not even winning. Kevin's kicking all our asses. I just hate to see you upset like this."

He leans back on the plastic seat, hooking an elbow over it. He's got that half-smile on his face, the one that reaches his eyes more than his lips. The one that makes them sparkle from within.

They sparkle with the joy of being the most difficult man this side of the Mississippi, but they *do* sparkle.

"Bless your heart, you sweet thing," I say, taking another sip of my beer. "Always thinking of others."

Eli knows exactly what I mean by *bless your heart.* His smile widens to a grin.

"All we've got to do is ask," he says, jerking a thumb over his shoulder. "I'm sure they can set 'em up in no time flat."

"I'm starting to think you want them," I say, mimicking his position, one elbow over the chair next to me. "What is it, Loveless? You think you can work the angles or something? Bounce balls off the sides better than you can throw straight?"

I drink some more beer, trying to stay cool and cover the tangle of weird emotions crawling around inside me. That results in an empty beer cup, and I spin it between my fingers, still keyed up and nervy.

"I just want to even the playing field a little," Eli says. "Obviously it won't help Kevin, but it might make things a little better for you."

I get up and walk to the pitcher of beer on the table behind us.

"As if you're not *six points* ahead of me," I call back, refilling my flimsy plastic cup. "As if my next turn couldn't completely wipe that smile right off your face."

"Not unless we get bumpers," he says, twisting around in his chair, one eyebrow raised. "Then, maybe —"

"They only give bumpers to kids," Kevin says, walking back from the lane as the machinery clears the pins. Lydia follows him, pointing at Eli.

"You," she says.

He gets out of the chair, and I sit down in it, watching

him as he selects a bright orange bowling ball from the return mechanism.

He strides forward. I drink some more beer, acting casual. He winds up, crouches, and releases the ball down the lane.

I watch his butt and keep drinking so I can pretend like I'm not watching his butt.

When his turn is over, he's gotten another seven pins. Now he's thirteen points ahead of me, but if my bowling math is right, if I get a strike or a spare for the next two rounds in a row, I could catch up by the end of the game.

He comes back and pretends not to notice that I took his chair. He's perfectly casual, sitting in the row of plastic chairs, watching me with a smirk on his face because he's throwing a ball at the floor a *tiny* bit better than me.

His eyes don't leave my face. I pretend like I don't notice, but I feel like there are heat rays on my skin. I'm practically melting under the intensity of his gaze, and I don't even know if it's bad melting, like action figures under a magnifying glass in the sun or good melting, like chocolate in your mouth.

"What?" I finally ask.

"Want to make it interesting?"

Isn't it already?

"How?"

"Ten bucks to the winner," he says, lifting his eyebrows ever so slightly.

Naomi walks between us toward the bowling lane.

"Boring," I say. I take another sip, trying to drown this mix of nervousness and anticipation and competitiveness and *meltiness* in beer.

"Twenty?"

I roll my eyes. I'm starting to feel the beer, but it's in my hand, and drinking it is a nervous tic I can't stop.

"Let's hear your idea, then," he says.

I turn my legs toward him, leaning sideways against the back of the chair. Lydia and Kevin are chatting about something while Naomi bowls, studiously ignoring us. It's probably for the best.

I think about it. Money is fine, but if this is going to be *interesting*, it needs to be something else. I take a few more sips of beer and ponder.

"Coffee," I finally say.

"How is that different from money?"

"Because the loser brings the winner coffee every morning for a month," I say.

I like the thought of having a coffee manservant. Even though I'm not particularly bad at mornings, making coffee always feels a little bit too hard if you haven't already had coffee first. It's a caffeine catch-22.

"*Every* morning, or every workday morning?" he asks, considering.

With horror, I imagine opening the front door to my trailer in my pajamas and finding Eli standing on my tiny front porch, coffee in hand, at seven on a Sunday morning.

Or, knowing Eli, he'd purposefully come even earlier. He'd probably bring me coffee at five a.m. on my days off, just to annoy me.

And Eli — a man who looks hot while testing out bowling balls — absolutely does not need to see me in my pajamas at five in the morning.

"Just workdays," I say. "I'm a benevolent bowling dictator."

"All right, Tulane," he says, leaning forward, holding out his hand. "You got yourself a deal. Daily coffee. One month."

I reach out and take his hand: warm, dry, strong. I

squeeze a little too hard and he squeezes right back, just like the last time we shook hands.

"Cream, no sugar," I say.

That sparkle lights up his eyes again, my hand still in his, and it sends a quick rush of I-don't-know-what through me.

"I'll take mine black," he says, the hint of a smile flashing in his eyes.

CHAPTER SEVENTEEN

ELI

If I didn't know Violet, I'd think she's hustling me.

The turn after our agreement, she gets a strike, then a spare. I still win by five points, but it's closer than I thought it would be.

After that, she offers double or nothing. Two months of coffee to the winner, from the loser.

I accept, exactly like she knows I will.

She wins the next round. By seven points. Somehow, the promise of having something to win makes her twice as good at bowling as she was before.

That's when Kevin, Lydia, and Naomi leave, but Violet and I barely notice, being way too involved in our bowling bet.

I offer Violet triple or nothing.

Free coffee all summer long for the winner. Hand-delivered fresh every morning, three months of coffee servitude dependent on the outcome of this final bowling match.

She accepts.

I've never bowled harder. I've never bowled with particular intensity before, to be honest — I like winning, but the last time I was here was years ago with my brothers Seth and Caleb. I don't even remember who won.

But now, bowling against Violet, I'm out for blood. Every pin she knocks down stings. Every one of her gutter balls is a victory.

Whenever I get a strike I howl with glee and pump both fists in the air, like I've just won the Olympics.

We're starting to get weird looks from the other lanes.

I don't even let myself get distracted by watching her ass as she bowls, even though it's right there. Even though I have nothing else to do on her turns, I make myself focus somewhere else.

No distractions.

No surprises.

Just victory.

Well, mostly no distractions. I do look a few times, because Violet's ass is unfairly spectacular, even when bowling, and especially in jeans.

When we get to the final round of the game, Ken's Bowl-o-rama is closing. The lights are already off over the other lanes, they're vacuuming the lobby, and the guy behind the concession stand is scraping gunk out of the popcorn machine.

We're tied.

It might be the highest-stakes, most stressful moment of my life.

By this point in the game, we're barely talking, only competing. I'm completely focused on the matter at hand, and Violet is as well, only moving to occasionally sip from her plastic cup of beer.

I declined to drink anything. I don't need alcohol stealing this victory from me.

It's my turn, the last frame of the game. I stand from

the uncomfortable plastic seat. I grab the bright orange bowling ball I've declared lucky.

I linger at the mouth of the lane, collecting every ounce of bowling savvy I've got.

Fly straight. Fly true.

I bring the ball up in front of myself.

Bring it home, lucky ball.

I rear back, crouch, and unleash it.

Eight pins fall. There's a pin still standing on either side of the lane. Laughing at me. Mocking me. I take a deep breath, shake out my hands, and ignore Violet's gaze that feels like needles pressing into my skin.

My ball comes back. I take it back, ready myself, and bowl again.

It sails straight down the center of the lane, a perfect strike ball if only the pins had cooperated.

I glare at them as the apparatus comes down, knocking them into the gaping mouth at the end of the lane.

Eight. As long as Violet scores less than eight, I'm golden.

I turn. I lock eyes with Violet. Her beer cup is empty, and she nods once, rising.

We say nothing. I sit where she was sitting, her warmth still in the plastic. Another light flicks off in the alley, but neither of us turn our heads.

She grabs the ball, steps forward. The vacuum stops. The scraping in the popcorn machine continues.

Seven pins. Two on one side of the lane, one on the other.

My heart clenches. I hold my breath. She doesn't look back at me as she waits for her ball to return, and I wonder what happens if we tie this game.

Her ball comes out of the return. She grabs it, hefts it

carefully, goes back to the lane, all without casting so much as a glance in my direction.

I'm literally on the edge of this seat as she crouches, swings her arm back, and releases the ball. It veers sideways, closer and closer to the gutter. Neither of us is breathing. I'm on my feet now, staring at the ball like I can will it into the gutter.

Halfway down, it veers back. My heart sinks. In front of me, Violet is clutching her hair with both hands, standing on tiptoes as the bowling ball traverses the lane, cutting clear across the wood.

It hits the two pins on the right perfectly, knocking them both down with a hollow *smack*.

Violet screams.

"YES!" she shouts, pumping both fists into the air. "YES! YES!"

I slide back into the plastic seat, my defeat settling over me like a heavy blanket. One pin. One *stupid* bowling pin.

It's not even about the coffee. Coffee itself isn't such a huge deal. It's the fact that I have to deliver it every morning, like I'm her personal butler or something. It's the fact that every single morning for the entire summer, I have to give her coffee and see her *I'm better at bowling than you* face.

It'll be absolutely, completely, one hundred percent terrible to see her every morning. I'm not secretly looking forward to it even the slightest amount.

I wish I could go back in time and smack myself before I offered to *make it interesting*.

She walks back, grinning. Her face is pink with glee, her hair a little wild, and she's laughing. Still cursing myself, I hold out one hand, and she shakes it.

"Good game," I say, trying to mean it.

"Cream, no sugar," she says, looking me right in the eye.

"You already said."

"Just making sure you know," she says, a glint in her eye. "And I like it hot."

"How hot?"

"As hot as you can make it."

I raise one eyebrow.

"You think you can handle it that hot?" I ask. It just slips out.

Violet laughs, though I swear she blushes, too.

"Don't worry about me, Loveless," she says, shark eyes still dancing. "I can take it."

Are we still talking about coffee?

I withdraw my hand from hers, look at her again, still flushed with victory, still breathless and wild with it.

She's beautiful like this. So beautiful that whatever I was about to say flickers and dies before I can say it, so beautiful that she lights up this dingy bowling alley.

I'm blindsided by a sudden, irresistible thought: I want to leave here and take her with me. I want us to leave Sprucevale behind. I want to bring her somewhere new, somewhere exciting where she's never been. I want to take her breath away and make her giddy with happiness, just like this.

The light over our heads goes out, and I'm jerked back to the reality that Ken's Bowl-o-rama is closing and the only thing that makes Violet this happy is beating me at something. The scoreboard over our lane flicks off. I try to tell myself it was just a dumb, meaningless bowling match. Even with the coffee bet, meaningless.

But that's never been true of anything between Violet and I. Nothing is ever *meaningless*.

We return our bowling shoes to the bored teenager without talking, but Violet is practically glowing. I can hardly look at her straight on.

"I'm gonna hang out here for a while," she says when I head for the door.

"They're closing."

"They'll be closing up for a while. I brought a book, they won't mind," she says, still seated on the bench by the rental shoes.

I turn, frown, and stick a hand in my pocket as I count up the number of beers she's had. The cups they gave us were tiny, but the answer is *enough to get her tipsy*.

"I'll give you a ride," I say.

"I'm—"

"I'm already your coffee slave for the summer, accept a ride, for Christ sake," I say. "You already know I won't get you killed."

"You're mad because I won."

"Yup," I say, crossing my arms in front of myself. "And I'll be even more pissed off if you make me talk you into accepting a ride, so come the hell on."

"My car's here."

"Ken's not gonna tow you."

"Then how am I—"

"Violet, I swear to God, I've been back in town for three months and I've already spent two of them convincing you to get in my car so I can get you home safely," I say. "Don't make me threaten to pick you up and carry you out of here."

She narrows her eyes, but I swear she blushes again. I ignore the thought pricking at me, that picking her up and carrying her somewhere wouldn't be so bad.

"I'll do it," I say.

"Okay, okay," she says, standing. "Fine. Thank you."

CHAPTER EIGHTEEN

ELI

We wind the windows down and let the warm night air drift in as I drive. Violet pushes the passenger seat all the way back and props her feet on the dashboard, still wearing brightly colored socks I can't make out, her hands over her head.

It's distracting. I'm tempted to spend more time looking at her than at the road in front of me, even though I know I'll be seeing plenty of her when I hand her coffee every morning for the next three months.

Ugh.

"Where'd you even find a car this old?" she asks, poking at a spot in the ceiling. It looks like a cigarette burn, a singed circle in the fabric that stretches over the roof.

"Maddy Thompson was using it to haul her dogs around her farm," I say. "And when I moved back she'd just gotten a slightly newer pickup that was better for dog-hauling, so she let me have this for two hundred bucks."

"You paid that much?"

"Hey now," I say, patting the console. "She passed

inspection on the second try and hardly ever breaks down in the middle of nowhere."

Violet shifts in her seat and sticks a hand out of the window, her fingers waving through the wind. She watches them, head turned away from me, like she's thinking.

"Why *did* you come back?" she finally asks.

I take a hand off the wheel and lean my elbow on the door frame, let wind lick my hair. Of course Violet would ask the question I don't know how to answer. Not really.

"The chef at *Le Faisan* went on maternity leave, and she asked if I could fill in for her for a few months," I say. "She's a friend from culinary school."

Violet looks over at me, her hand still dancing out of my car window, fingers slowly waving in the wind.

"That's all?"

"That's not good enough?" I ask.

"If you were just here to do a friend a favor, you wouldn't still be around," Violet says.

"I decided to stay."

"Why?"

I feel like my spine is slowly turning to iron and it's ready to come through my skin and become armor at any second.

It's my own fault. I know better than to leave myself unguarded around Violet, however briefly.

"Why not?"

Violet finally turns and looks at me. Her eyes are colorless in the faint glow of the Bronco's instrument panels, but I've got that familiar feeling: sharks in the water.

"Because you always hated it here," she says, like it's obvious. "Remember the day you got the admission letter to the University of Chicago?"

I grin in the dark, looking out the windshield.

"You still mad about that, Violet?"

Now it's her turn to laugh.

"Not anymore, but you sure were a dick," she says.

"You got into every other school you wanted," I said. "You got into Yale, Duke, Georgetown, all the state schools, and you couldn't even let me have Chicago."

"Probably because you acted like Jesus Christ himself had come down and personally handed you that admission letter," she says. "And it's not like getting into Yale did me much good."

"Well, neither did Chicago," I say.

She's quiet, but I can feel her watching me. Waiting, like she knows I'll say something if she gives me long enough.

I wonder if I should tell her. I wonder if she already knows.

"I left halfway through my second semester," I finally admit, because the darkness in the truck feels like armor. "It was that or get kicked out for failing everything."

A beat of silence: contemplative, oddly gentle.

"That was true?"

"As the gospel."

"I always thought the gossip mill was exaggerating," she says, shifting in the passenger seat. "Was everything they said true?"

I pass my hand over my hair, my elbow still on the frame.

"Depends on what they said."

Violet held up one hand, her thumb out, counting.

"You joined a hippie commune in California."

I laugh.

"Not really."

"But you were in California?"

"I was. I rented a room next to an organic farm and

used to exchange pastries for fresh eggs, does that count?" I ask.

"Did you wear flowing white robes and do lots of chanting?" she says, sounding hopeful.

"No on both counts. White's not my color, and I can't carry a tune."

She holds up her forefinger.

"You were in prison in North Dakota."

"What for?"

"Some kind of fraud, usually, but the rumors could never quite decide," she says.

"I was bartending," I tell her. "But I did have to break up a fight once and I got a scar from it."

"Is it a cool scar?"

I pull up my right sleeve with my left hand, find the slightly raised line on my shoulder. Violet leans in.

Instantly I'm aware of her closeness, of her eyes on me. I keep my own straight ahead, drinking in every detail of the road, spine rigid. Armor on.

"Touch it," I say without thinking, the words borne of nothing but the desire to feel her skin on mine.

"Why, so I know it's real?" she teases.

She touches it anyway, her finger cool against my skin. I hold my breath and watch the road like the answer to every question I've ever had is written on the asphalt, like keeping my eyes ahead means my heart isn't pounding, my pulse hasn't quickened.

"What else?" I ask.

Her finger leaves my arm and she sits back in her seat.

"You just like hearing about yourself."

"I want to set the record straight," I say, letting myself glance over at her and grin. She's turned halfway toward me in the passenger seat, lit only by the reflected glow of the headlights, the green lights of the LED clock.

"You joined the mafia while you were in Sicily," she says, ticking it off on her fingers.

I just snort.

"You were part of an opium smuggling ring in China."

"Also no."

"You hit it big in the drag racing circuit in Tokyo."

"That's the plot of a *Fast and Furious* movie."

"You were in a Mongolian princess's harem."

I look over at her, incredulous.

"People said that?"

"I heard it."

"From where?" I ask. "Who the hell thought that one up?"

"You haven't denied it yet," she points out.

"I think Mongolia's a democracy," I say.

I have no idea what kind of government Mongolia has, just like I'm not one hundred percent sure that moose are ungulates.

"Maybe they got it wrong and it was the prime minister's harem," Violet laughs. "You *were* in a harem, weren't you?"

"It doesn't sound like the worst life," I admit. "Lay around on cushions all day, eat bonbons, wait for the prime minister to send for you."

Violet just laughs.

"What?" I ask. "You don't think someone would keep me in a harem?"

"I can't imagine you chilling out and waiting for someone to send for you," she says. "I can't imagine you getting along with the rest of the harem. You'd get kicked out for bad behavior inside of a week, Eli."

I grin.

"I don't think harems kick you out for being naughty."

"You'd know, apparently."

We come up on Pine Ridge Estates and I slow, turning into the trailer park, tires crunching on gravel. Violet goes quiet as I navigate to her trailer, the same place she's lived for as long as I've known her, and pull up in front.

"You still haven't told me why you stayed," she says.

I cut the engine and the headlights. A warm breeze blows through the truck, carrying the smell of pine and grass, a whiff of cigarette smoke from somewhere, a hint of asphalt after rain.

"I got homesick," I finally admit.

It's the first time I've admitted it out loud. It's almost the first time I've admitted it to myself, but there it is: the tedious, mundane truth.

I can practically feel her thinking, her fingers still out of the window, waving in the air.

After a moment she says, "That's all?"

I prop my head against my hand and look over at her. Our eyes meet, lock, and this time I don't look away.

Violet's always gotten under my skin, like she knows exactly what to say or do that will get to me.

No one else has ever gotten to me like she does. Not my other friends, not my brothers, none of the girlfriends I've had over the years. No one's ever even come close.

She still gets to me, but something's changed. It feels like she's lifting up my top layer and peeking underneath, examining, critiquing.

It feels like she's seeing me raw and naked. Exposed.

The strange thing is that I don't hate it.

Stranger still, I'm starting to like being seen the way only she can see me.

"It felt more complicated at the time," I finally say. "I missed my mom. I missed my brothers. I missed knowing the names of practically everyone I saw walking down the street. I missed the way the air smells here after it rains."

It might be my imagination, but I think she sniffs the air.

"Dirt and pine trees and rocks," I offer.

"Do dirt and rocks smell different from each other?"

"They do here."

She puts her hand on the door handle, like she's about to get out, but then she looks over at me again.

"What's it like?" she asks.

"The smell of dirt?"

"Being homesick."

I swallow, thinking.

"I've never felt it," she says, staring straight ahead. "I've never been away for long enough."

"Maybe you're just not the homesick type."

"I doubt that."

I watch her. She watches her trailer, eyes glued to the light over her tiny porch like it holds all the answers. Like she's refusing to look back at me.

I want to reach out and touch her. I want to feel the curve of her cheekbone under my fingers, let her warmth infuse my skin. I want to see if she smells like home, like pine and dirt and rocks, or whether she smells new and wholly different.

I haven't gotten our kiss behind the brewery out of my mind yet. I might never.

"It's the feeling that everything around you is slightly wrong and you can't fix it," I say, still staring at her. "It's a bone-deep desire to bury yourself in the familiar."

She turns and looks at me, her face unreadable.

"It's wanting what you already know and can't have," I finish.

Violet just watches me. I have that feeling again, the feeling that she's peeling me back layer by layer. The feeling that she knows me like no one else does.

Then she opens her door and breaks the spell. The cool night air rushes in. Her seatbelt clanks as she unbuckles it.

"Thanks for the ride, Eli," she says, and hops out.

I hop out too, both doors slamming.

"Then it's Eli again?" I say.

Violet looks over her shoulder as she fishes her keys out of her purse, eyes crinkling at the corners.

"Do you have some other name?" she asks.

"Back at the bowling alley I was *Loveless* all of a sudden," I say as we mount the steps to her tiny front porch, barely big enough for two adults to stand side-by-side. She's got lights strung back and forth over her tiny lawn area, and we're both saturated in the ambient glow. "Glad to know I got my first-name privileges back."

She turns her key in her lock. I lean against the aluminum siding of her trailer, right next to her front door.

I shouldn't have followed her up here. I should have stayed in my car until she got inside safely, and then just left.

Being this close to Violet unchaperoned feels dangerous.

"You called me Tulane first," she counters. "Like you're my high school track coach."

"If you're comparing me to Mr. McLeod, I'm gravely insulted."

"Then don't call me Tulane, *Loveless*," she says. She's teasing me.

"Don't call me Loveless, *Tulane*. At least when I call you that I know who I'm getting. Shout 'Loveless' in a crowd and you could be getting any of us."

"What if you're not the one I'm calling?" she says.

I frown, my hands in my pockets.

"And why would you be summoning one of my brothers?"

"Why would I be summoning you?"

"For a car and a sober driver, apparently," I say. "Because you want to know all the sordid details of being in a Mongolian harem."

"I thought you said you weren't," she teases.

"I neither confirmed nor denied."

"Then what *are* the sordid details?" she asked, taking a step closer, her blue-gray eyes looking up at me with a challenge. The key in the lock is forgotten.

"Let's hear them, Eli."

I know I should leave. I should say goodnight and leave right now, and I don't. I'm going to do something I regret, and I can feel it coming like it's a train and I'm standing on the tracks.

I kissed her once already, and she ran away the second it was over. I know better than to do it again.

But I like the way my name sounds when she says it. I like the way she looks at me, the way she practically dares me to do something, the way my heart thunders with every inch she comes closer.

I lean in, like I'm about to whisper a secret, and she tilts her face upward like she expects something else. Every thought of walking away flies from my brain.

"Unless you weren't actually in a harem," she says, her voice suddenly softer. "Unless you're just lying to impress me."

"Would you be impressed if I'd been in some princess's harem?"

The breeze blows a strand of hair across her face, and without thinking, I catch it and push it back behind her ear, my fingers against the soft skin of her neck.

"I'd sure be surprised," she says.

I don't move my hand away. I just keep it there, feeling her pulse thump under her skin.

"I'll take it," I say, my voice softer now, matching hers. "What else would surprise you?"

"If I knew, it wouldn't be a surprise," she says.

We're too close. Now my hand is on the back of her neck and I'm barely breathing for anticipation, my blood's rushing through my ears with a steady stream of *don't do this, don't do this.*

I know exactly how to surprise her.

I lean down and plant my lips on hers, reveling in this bad idea, her mouth soft and warm and pliable, her body slowly crushing against mine as I step in, bringing her against me.

She kisses me back, and it's different this time – softer, sweeter – but it's every bit as good, her mouth fervent under mine, opening as she slides a hand onto my waist and tugs at me.

It's softer but no less intense, the heat of it pounding through me; sweeter but I don't want her less, still dizzy, still ravenous for her.

Her teeth brush against my lip, ever so slightly, and I'm reminded that this is dangerous. It's even more dangerous than I knew, because my other arm's around her too, because I'm already swiping my tongue along her lip, because I'm already thinking of how to open this door without pulling my lips away from hers, getting inside, finding out if she's this willing in the dark of her bedroom, too.

We move against each other. Our lips part, millimeters, a split second. Her hand closes around my shirt and then we meld again and this time there's a renewed urgency, an undercurrent that wasn't there before.

I pull a hand from her, find the doorknob, push it open when there's a loud BANG from somewhere beyond her trailer.

We both jerk back, Violet nearly stepping off her porch, though I grab her before she can go. She's flushed and open-mouthed, lips red and slightly swollen, her hair even more wild than after her bowling victory.

We look at each other. I've already forgotten the noise, my mind too filled with everything that just happened and what's going to happen next.

Violet swallows.

"I think it's the—"

Another crash, this one on her roof. I pull her toward me, my arm protectively going around her back as we look up, following the noise.

There's an unmistakable scraping sound of something sliding down the trailer's aluminum roof. I pull her in harder.

A moment later an empty, crushed beer can falls, landing with a hollow *clunk* on her stairs.

"—Rednecks next door," she finishes.

I look at the fallen beer can, Violet still in my arms. I'm rattled as hell, far more by Violet than by the redneck almost-assault.

"They seem to make a lot of things explode," Violet says, talking fast, shoving her hair behind her ears. She doesn't look at me, but she steps out of my arms. "The other day they—"

"Y'all okay?" a voice says from behind me, and I turn. A guy wearing torn camo pants and a white undershirt comes around the corner of her trailer, looking concerned.

"We're fine," Violet says. "I think we've got your can."

She points at it, still lying on her steps.

"Sorry 'bout that," he says, loping over to the can and picking it up. "I told Jim not to light that thing but you know he don't listen when he's drunk. I'll try to get them to tone it down a notch so y'all can have your privacy."

He grins, winks, then ducks back around the corner of the trailer.

Violet's hand is on her doorknob again, and suddenly the space between us feels like a chasm.

"Thanks for the ride," she says, already pushing the door open. "I gotta get — you know, work — and it's kind of cold out here? And I'm sure you also need to get home…"

"Violet."

"And I have to figure out how to get my car back?"

"*Violet.*"

Finally, she looks at me. Dead in the eye.

"It's a bad idea, Eli," she says, her voice still and quiet. "Thanks for the ride, though."

Then she's through the door and gone, and I don't even get to tell her that maybe it's *not* a bad idea before it closes on me.

Not that I've got evidence to back that up. Not that I've even got reasons beyond *hey, that was pretty fun*, but in this moment that sure seems like reason enough.

Her trailer's dead quiet. No lights go on. No floorboards squeak from inside.

I turn around and walk down her steps, her lights still glowing softly overheard, the rednecks next door hooting and hollering even though it's a damn Tuesday night.

I get in my truck and drive back home to my mom's house, and I spend the whole drive trying to convince myself that Violet's right, marking the first time I've ever done such a thing.

CHAPTER NINETEEN
VIOLET

I shut the door and don't move. I don't even lock it, I just get inside my trailer and freeze, hoping that in a few minutes I'll thaw out and figure out what the hell just happened.

After a moment, I hear Eli descending the steps outside. There's the deep rumble of his truck starting up, the crunch of the tires biting into gravel, the low coughing hum as he drives away.

Once it fades, I can move. I lock my door. I drop my purse on the floor right behind it, not bothering to hang it on its hook, and I walk into my tiny bathroom.

I don't even turn on the light, I just run the water and then splash it on my face because I need to do *something* to negate the shock.

Splash.

That wasn't supposed to happen.

Splash.

You liked it, though.

Splash.

Eli's a terrible idea. You don't even like each other, why would you make out with him?

Splash. My face is getting *really* clean.

And you're forgetting the maid of honor.

I pause my hands halfway to my face. For the first time in days, I'd forgotten about it, but now the scene comes rushing back full force: elevator, snuggling, smug look, doors closing, and now all my thoughts are crashing into each other, a confusing jumble.

He kissed you and then banged her and then kissed you — but maybe he didn't — but maybe he did — and if he did then what? You're just another girl on a list a mile long?

You could just ask.

You could just be an adult, for the love of God, and ask.

I don't want to ask. I don't want Eli to know that I even noticed that he was in the elevator with her, because then he'll know that I *care* that he was in an elevator with another girl, that I'm jealous and wish I wasn't, and I just don't want any of that.

I stand up, dry my face off, and wander back into my living room, putting my purse on the hook, then I head to the kitchen to drink a glass of water. I text Adeline and ask if she can give me a ride to the bowling alley in the morning. It's her day off, and also, God knows she needs an update.

Thank God for the rednecks because if they hadn't done whatever the hell they did, I'd probably have invited Eli in and then I'd really have done something I'd regret later.

Or not, I think.

No, I'd definitely regret it. Yes, Eli mysteriously got hot during his time away from Sprucevale, and yes, he's changed slightly, but he's still Eli. Earlier today we both acted like a bowling match was the final round of the world chess tournament, and it was just a dumb bowling match.

Eli and I are not compatible, even if kissing him is really nice. He will hurt me and I will hurt him, because how are you supposed to have a relationship with someone who you actively want to see crash and burn?

I'm pretty sure that's not how any of the great love stories start.

Pride and Prejudice kinda does, I think.

"Eli is not Mister Darcy," I say out loud to my empty kitchen, as if that settles anything.

Then I shut off the lights and go to bed, where I don't think any more about the things that I'd like Eli to do to me.

Not even a little.

· · · · · ★ ★ ★ · · · · ·

I SIT up with a jolt in bed. The clock says five a.m., and I've just had a horrible realization.

Eli's bringing me coffee this morning. To my office. First thing. Because that was the deal we made, and I won bowling, and oh my God this is going to be so awkward. *Why is this happening to me?*

Unsurprisingly, I don't go back to sleep, and at five forty-five I just get out of bed and try to clean my kitchen.

Adeline pulls up at seven forty-five, and the second I'm in her car, she frowns at me.

"What did you do?" she asks.

"I kissed Eli again," I say.

"Good, finally," she says, and puts her car into drive, pulling out of my driveway.

Then she stops in the middle of the gravel road that goes through the trailer park.

"*Again?*"

"I might have drunkenly made out with him that night at the brewery," I admit.

"*That's* why you were so weird," she says, the car moving forward again. "Also, you weren't drunk. You didn't even finish your beer."

"Let me believe my lie," I say.

Adeline just sighs, turning onto the main road.

"Fine," she says. "You got super duper trashed, got it on with Eli in the storeroom at the brewery —"

"We didn't *get it on*, we kissed," I correct. "And we were outside."

"And then you did it again last night."

I sigh dramatically, leaning my head back against my headrest.

"Yes," I say.

"I am *so* sorry you kissed a hot guy twice," she says. "How terrible to have to put aside your plans for spinsterdom."

"I have *not* put aside those plans," I say. "We're not dating. We can't stand each other."

"It sounds a little like you're dating," she says.

I pause, wondering if I should tell her about the maid of honor, because it's possible that even Adeline will think I'm insane.

"He might have slept with someone else in between," I say slowly.

That gets her attention.

"What?" she yelps. "Eli's a slut? Okay, I could see it. He did get hot."

"Stop saying that," I grumble.

"All the Loveless guys are hot," Adeline says, like that makes it better. "Even Levi. And, you know, there's always at least two girls fighting over Seth—"

"I'm not fighting anyone over Eli," I say, sitting up straight. "No. Hell no."

"I wasn't suggesting that," she says calmly. "Tell me about the floozy he might have slept with."

I tell her: the drunk maid of honor, the elevator, her hands all over him, maybe even grabbing his butt, the look he gave me. When I finish, we're sitting in the parking lot of the bowling alley right next to my car, and Adeline's shaking her head.

"Yeah, that's nothing," she says.

"Don't tell me that," I say. "I've been making myself crazy."

"That's kinda your thing," she admits. "Not all the time, but you do tend to get in your head with stuff like this. Remember the time you told Ellie Barker that her Shar-Pei puppy was adorable when she showed you a picture of her new grandson, and then you agonized about whether to send an apology card or flowers or something for a week?"

"No," I say. "I've wiped that from my memory, and also, that was a very bad picture and the baby was wrapped in a blanket and really did look like a puppy."

"Ask him if he banged the maid of honor if you're so upset," she says, unlocking my door. "It's not a weird question if his tongue's been in your mouth. Twice."

I sigh. She shoos me.

"Go be an adult!" she says, and I finally get out of her car.

· · · · · ★ ★ ★ ★ ★ · · · · ·

I HAVEN'T EVEN GOTTEN to my office yet when there he is, sauntering down the hallway, a cup of coffee in each hand.

Act normal, I tell myself, even though the heat is already starting to creep up my neck.

He reaches my office door before I do, then stands there, coffee in hand, waiting. He's got that same half-smile on his face as always, his hair still slightly mussed, his chef whites not on yet and his undershirt highlighting exactly what I'm missing out on.

"You wanted skim milk and ten packets of Splenda, right?" he says as I walk up to him.

I must make a face, because he just laughs.

"Kidding. Cream, no sugar," he says, and I take the coffee from his hand, sip it.

It's exactly right.

"Just the way you like it," he says, one eyebrow barely raised.

"Yep," I say, my face heating up more. "No sugar. None at all. Sugar's really bad for you, you know."

Eli gives me a long, searching look. He raises his own coffee cup to his mouth and drinks, even that simple motion somehow really hot.

"Well," he finally says. "If you ever change your mind about needing something sweet, just let me know."

Then he winks, turns, and leaves. My insides turn into goo. Thank *God* there's no one else in this hallway right now, because now I'm staring at Eli's back as he walks away, kind of looking at his butt and mostly wondering what on earth I've gotten myself into, regarding coffee deliveries and offers of sugar at eight o'clock in the morning.

I open my office door, toss my purse into a drawer, and flop into my chair.

My job is about to get *interesting.*

· · · · · ★ ★ ★ · · · · ·

THE MOMENT I see the boxes on Friday afternoon, I know I'm in trouble.

First, they were delivered in an old Subaru, and I was expecting at least a pickup truck.

Second, there are only five of them, each labeled '100 cranes' in careful, spidery handwriting.

"Where are the rest?" I ask the robed man.

He just tilts his head and looks at me curiously. Calm radiates from him, every movement absolutely infused with it.

"They're all here," he says.

I bend down to look into the Subaru, but aside from a few fleece blankets and one dog leash, it's empty.

"This is only five hundred," I say. "Unless they're mislabeled?"

Please be mislabeled. Please be mislabeled.

I know they're not. I've seen a thousand origami cranes before, and this is not a thousand cranes.

"Yes, the order was for five hundred," he says, completely unruffled. "We thought it was a strange number, so we double-checked it. One moment."

He ducks into the passenger seat of the Subaru and comes out with an invoice.

I read it twice, then three times, just to check.

It's for five hundred cranes.

I feel nauseous.

How the hell did I only order five hundred? Was it a typo? Did I not proofread this?

More importantly, what the hell do I do now?

Small, strange things have been going wrong all week. The CEO of a small midweek corporate retreat got booked into a room on the third floor after requesting a room on the fourth. A car service that we'd scheduled to pick someone up at the airport in Roanoke showed up fifteen minutes late.

In the kitchen, a hundred tortillas went missing.

Also, on Tuesday night Eli and I kissed after making a bet that means we have to see each other every morning for the rest of the summer, so even though I'm kind of trying to avoid him right now, it's not working great.

I still haven't worked up the courage to ask about the maid of honor. I know I should. I know I'm not being an adult, but every time I come close there's a tiny voice that whispers *yeah, but what if he did, do you really want to know?* and then I don't ask.

It's been a hell of a week, is what I'm saying.

"Right," I say, still staring at the sheet of paper. "Yup. Five hundred. Says it right there. In ink."

Oh God.

"We did think it was a smaller order than usual, but thought perhaps you were getting more cranes from elsewhere," he says, still serene as fuck.

I want to scream *why didn't you call and double-check?!*, but I don't.

One, I know perfectly well it's not his fault, and two, screaming at a Buddhist monk seems like it's especially bad, even though I imagine he'd take it better than most people.

"The mistake is ours," I say, my voice oddly formal as my mind starts racing, already a hundred miles away from this parking lot. "Thank you for the delivery."

I need five hundred more cranes.

It's six o'clock on Friday night.

I might be screwed. What if I'm screwed?

Where the hell can I get five hundred cranes?

With a sinking feeling, I realize the answer.

"Peace be with you," the monk says, his shaved head shining dully in the fading sunlight.

He gets back into the monastery's Subaru and drives off, leaving me standing outside a converted barn with five hundred less cranes than I need.

· · · · * * ★ * * · · · ·

THE ANSWER TO, "Where do I get five hundred cranes on a Friday night?" is pretty simple, at least on the surface. There's only the one answer.

I make them myself, of course.

Have I ever made an origami crane before? No. Am I particularly crafty or good with my hands? Also no.

But do I have another choice, besides *disappoint a bride and probably lose out on $20,000*?

Nope!

I call up Betsy, the owner of Betsy's Craft Emporium, and promise to buy her out of origami paper if she stays open an extra half-hour. Bless her heart, she does it, and by seven-thirty, I'm back at Bramblebush, set up in a conference room, armed with a giant stack of origami paper and an iPad loaded with origami tutorials.

By eight, I've made three janky cranes and two good ones. By nine, that number is six and fifteen, so I've only got four hundred and eighty-five left to go.

I take a break, put my head down on the table, and do some quick math. I need to get these done by nine a.m. Tomorrow, when I'm supposed to be here to set up for the final walkthrough with the couple and their wedding planner. That's twelve hours.

Four hundred and eighty-five cranes in twelve hours is…

…slightly over ninety seconds per crane. I don't need to do more math to know that I have *not* been achieving that goal, nor do I need math to tell me that taking a break with my forehead on the table isn't getting anything done, either.

You know what gets things done? Coffee.

Coffee gets things done.

Lots of coffee.

I hop up, newly determined, and head to the employee break room, flipping the lights on as I head in. It's deserted, obviously, because I'm the only one here at this time of night, the component pieces of the coffee maker drying in a dish rack by the sink.

It's then that I realize I've never made coffee at work before. I don't even know who does it, I just know that every time I've come in here, looking for a caffeine hit, I've gotten it.

I approach the machine, arms folded over my chest. It's one of those big silver cylinders with a spout at the bottom, not the Mr. Coffee-type that I've got at home, and I have to admit that it's a bit of a mystery.

I tackle it, obviously. It's just a coffee maker, and I have a college degree. I graduated summa cum laude. I got this.

I fill it with water. I balance the basket-thing on top of the metal-tube-thing, because I'm pretty sure that's how that goes. I locate the top and set it aside, then grab a new five-pound bag of coffee, and pull at the top.

And pull. And pull, because apparently these days they're closing bags of ground coffee with gorilla glue. I grunt. I grit my teeth and use all my might.

Suddenly, the bag flies open. It tears down one side and launches ground coffee into my face, all over me, and onto the floor.

"Dammit," I say through clenched teeth.

"There's scissors in the drawer," Eli's voice says behind me.

I whirl around, the coffee grounds beneath my feet

making the floor more slippery than usual. He's standing there, framed by the doorway, that irritating (and hot) half-smile on his face.

My heart thumps stupidly. Something flutters in my stomach-region, and before I know it I'm checking him out for about the thousandth time: dark hair just a little wild, green eyes just a little bit teasing, and a shirt that fits him *very* well.

Why do all his shirts have to fit him that well?

It's unprofessional. Can I report him for being too hot at work?

"Thanks," I say, as sarcastically as I can.

"Rough day?" he asks, shoving his hands into his pockets, eyeing the coffee-grounds-covered floor as he does, leaning against the door frame.

"I'm fine," I answer reflexively.

"You're trying to make a giant pot of coffee at nine p.m."

"That's just how I party," I say.

"What happened?"

I sigh. I blow a strand of hair out of my face, then toss the busted coffee package into the sink.

"I screwed up an order with the monks and now I have to fold four hundred and eighty-five origami cranes by tomorrow morning," I admit.

Eli whistles low, still looking at me.

"Yeah," I say, brushing coffee off myself.

"All right," he says, straightening. "Where are you folding?"

"Cumberland conference room."

He nods once.

"Perfect," he says, and then walks away.

"It's not!" I shout after him, confused.

Is he just being a dick? For a minute there I thought he was being nice…

His head pops back around the door frame.

"Don't make that coffee," he says, and disappears again.

I frown at the door, then at myself.

"I'll make coffee if I want to make coffee," I grumble to myself as I find the dustpan. "I'll make as much coffee as I want."

CHAPTER TWENTY

ELI

The coffee cups clink softly as I walk down the dark hallway, carrying the tray. It's got two full French presses, two coffee mugs with saucers, and a little pitcher of cream for Violet, since I know how she takes her coffee.

Call me Martha Stewart, I guess.

When I enter the conference room, she looks up from a half-finished crane, both hands anchoring opposite corners of it on the table.

"How's your craft project going?" I ask, setting it on the table.

She looks around. The table is half-covered with cranes, though it's clear that there aren't nearly enough.

"I'm in hell," Violet admits. "I'm not even good at this kind of thing. I'm all thumbs. Adeline tried to teach me to knit once, and I almost accidentally strangled myself on my own yarn."

I pick up one French press and plunge it, careful to keep the coffee from rushing through the spout.

"Adeline knits?"

"Of course Adeline knits," sighs Violet. "She also

bakes, sews, and can probably even make a Christmas tree look good with that weird fake snow stuff."

I pour coffee into one mug, then the other, wondering what the story is with Violet and fake snow.

"Though she's also the one who set me up on that terrible date, so she also has her faults," Violet goes on, frowning at the paper in front of her, then flipping it over.

"That was Adeline?"

"He was her cousin's cousin," Violet says, hands still busy.

"Poor thing," I say, pouring cream into her mug. I put it back on the saucer, then slide the saucer over to her.

"Me, or her?"

"Her."

I raise my own mug to my lips and take a long, slow sip. It's espresso, and it's slightly stronger than I meant for it to be, but at least it'll keep us both awake until we finish these birds.

"I'm the one who wound up doing dishes in heels and it's *poor Adeline?*" Violet says, and she's trying to sound stern, but I can tell she's laughing.

"You can handle being run out on and doing the dishes in heels," I tease back, sitting opposite her in one of the big leather office chairs. "But I bet Adeline feels really bad."

Adeline's always been nice to me. She's a nurse, for crying out loud. She even had pity on me in high school and invited me to a party.

Violet is, well, Violet. She finishes the crane and grabs her coffee mug.

"I thought our agreement was only for the mornings," she says.

"This is honoring our other agreement," I say, grabbing a piece of origami paper and holding it up. I wonder if I still remember how to make paper cranes.

Violet looks up at me, briefly, and I can't help but remember our kiss again: her lips on mine, needy, urgent. Her arm around my waist. My fingers in her hair.

"The one where we don't let Martin win," I say.

"Right," she says, and takes a sip of the coffee.

Then she nearly spits it out, her eyes going wide.

"It's espresso," I tell her, already folding my origami paper in half diagonally.

"You sure it's not paint thinner?" she gasps. "You should find out if someone's got a heart condition before you give them that."

"Got a heart condition?"

"I think I do now," she says, but after a moment, she takes another sip, and this one stays down just fine. "Look, Eli, you don't have to — holy shit, Martin."

I turn to look at the door, but there's no one there. I look back at Violet.

"No, this was him," she says, pointing at the cranes. "He did this. We were supposed to get a thousand cranes folded by monks, but someone changed the order form to five hundred, and it sure wasn't me."

"Does he have access to those?" I ask, taking another sip.

"Yeah, of course," she breathes. "He's the other coordinator, he can do everything I can do."

There's a brief pause.

"This sounds insane," Violet says, half to herself. "I'm sure I just had a temporary lapse of sanity and I did it myself."

"The man hid oysters," I say. "It's not insane. *Insane* is offering your employees one twenty-thousand dollar reward for being the best instead of, say, ten two-thousand-dollar rewards for good teamwork. I'm surprised no one's been hit by a car yet."

Violet snorts. It turns out that I still remember how to fold cranes, and we fold in silence for a while. Companionable silence, like maybe we're finally starting to get used to each other. We don't even race to see who can make the most cranes, we just work together.

"Let me guess," Violet says after a long time. "You learned crane folding in the harem."

I finish the head of a crane and launch it into the air, dropping it on a pile of its paper brethren.

"You're really stuck on this harem thing," I say. "Is it so unbelievable that some princess would want to put me up in the lap of luxury just so I was available to her every so often?"

Violet turns red, but she tosses her hair back over her shoulder and glances at me before folding more.

"It's the most salacious rumor," she teases. "And you haven't denied it yet."

Obviously it's not true. I don't think harems exist anymore, and if they do, no one's inviting a scruffy, difficult southern boy into one.

Besides, there's no way in hell I could share a woman I like. I'd lose my damn mind.

"I think the cult's pretty interesting," I say, still teasing her. "What did we supposedly worship? A spaceship or something?"

"People join cults all the time," Violet says, like cults are *so* passé. "There's a monastery up in the hills, for Pete's sake. They're the ones who didn't make me enough cranes."

"I don't think the monastery would appreciate being called a cult," I point out.

"They wear robes," she says.

"So do judges," I say. "So do I, after a shower."

"Is it fluffy?"

"I'll never tell."

There's another span of silence. I sneak a glance over at Violet, bent over the cranes, her dark honey hair spilling over one shoulder, unruly at the end of a long day.

She's barely spoken to me since we kissed. I've barely thought about anything else since then. I've laid awake many nights, imagining her lips underneath mine, the way she grabbed me, the way she pushed her body against mine. I've done a lot of very quiet jerking off in my attic room.

I'm starting to think I imagined all that. All the same, I want her again. Here. Now.

I want to pull her onto the table, her skin against mine, her nails raking down my back. I want her so bad it's a physical sensation like a weight on my chest.

"Why were the monks making cranes?" I ask, just to get my mind off of what I want to do to her.

"Because we gave them money in exchange for services," Violet deadpans.

"Doesn't the bride usually fold them herself?"

Violet shrugs.

"Some do," she says, finishing a crane and grabbing another piece of aquamarine paper. "Some outsource it."

"That does run counter to the point," I say. "Isn't the whole idea to demonstrate the patience and commitment you need for marriage?"

"You're asking the wrong person," Violet says. "I don't know the reasons, I just put in the orders."

"It's supposed to be a labor of love, not something you pay someone else to do."

I don't know why this is the thing that's getting to me, but it is. Sometimes things are about the experience, about putting in the work. Paying someone else to do it just doesn't get the job done.

"Why do you know so much about origami cranes?" Violet asks.

"I married into the Yakuza while I was in Japan," I tell her.

I've never been to Japan. Violet looks up for a moment, then starts laughing.

"How gullible do you think I am?"

"Wasn't that a rumor?" I ask. "That's at least as believable as *I was in the Sicilian Mafia*," I go on.

"I didn't hear that one," she says. "But I didn't particularly pay attention to rumors about you, so it could have been."

"You sure know a lot of them for someone who didn't pay attention," I say. "And it's unfair, given that I don't know any of the rumors about you."

"Well, there's the rumor that I go to bed at 9:30 sometimes," she says. "And Adeline says that she once heard from an unnamed source that they overheard me on the phone, talking about how much I like using my turn signals."

Of course Violet is a stickler for turn signals.

"Do you?"

"They make me feel prepared."

I believe that. What I don't believe is that there's nothing salacious about her, or that she's always the boring good girl she wants me to think she is.

Violet's a lot of things, and *boring* sure isn't one of them.

"So everyone in Sprucevale thinks they know that I was in prison in North Dakota, and you won't even tell me one wild rumor about yourself," I tease. "You may have everyone else fooled but not me, Violet."

There's a long, long pause, like she's focusing on the origami.

"I've never really left town," she finally says, her voice

quiet. "I mean, I've gone on trips, but I just stayed here and took care of my mom while you were off traveling the world, and then after she died I stayed in the same trailer, in the same place, with the same friends, doing all the same things…"

She trails off and meets my eyes. Her gaze pins me down, holds me still, robs me of my words.

She's arresting. She's intense, serious, teasing, playful. Violet's a diamond in a room full of coal: beautiful, interesting, always the most fascinating thing around.

Even though that's not always good. Even though I spent half my life wishing I never had to see her again and when I got my wish, the world was that much duller.

I didn't know it then. I didn't come back for her, but she makes me glad I came.

"We wound up in the same place," I point out.

"At least you know what you're missing," Violet says.

"Who says I'm missing anything?"

She gives me that look again, the look that says *I see straight through you*, the look that makes me feel stripped down to my skeleton. No one else has ever looked at me this way, and I hope they never do.

"Did you have sex with the maid of honor?" Violet blurts out.

I blink, because that's not what I was expecting. I've probably had sex with someone's maid of honor, but nothing is leaping to mind.

"What maid of honor?" I ask.

Violet swallows. She's paler than usual, and I search her face, looking for handholds into the conversation, because right now I'm just falling.

"The one the elevator," she says. "The wedding with the arancini. You took her upstairs."

"Susan?" I say, surprised. "The drunk one?"

I almost laugh, but Violet looks so serious that I force myself not to.

"Yeah, she had a few," she says.

"She could barely walk," I say, remembering how I'd practically had to carry the poor girl to her room. "I put her to bed so she didn't pass out in the hallway."

"But did you also —"

"No," I say. "I'm not in the habit of sleeping with women who're too drunk to know what's going on. I *did* leave her a trash can, though, because I didn't want her to puke on the nice carpet."

"Oh," Violet says. She's bright pink and looks back down at the crane she's folding.

"Is that why you've been avoiding me?" I ask her.

She doesn't answer right away.

"You thought we made out on Saturday, I had sex with someone Friday, and then kissed you Tuesday?"

"I didn't think that."

"*And* you think I'd fuck a girl who was falling down drunk."

"I don't know!" she says, finally looking at me, shoving away a half-finished crane. "I don't know you, Eli, I don't know how drunk she was, I just know that you took her upstairs and she was wrapped around you like a — a giant squid on a sperm whale."

"And you didn't like it," I say.

"It's unprofessional to —"

"That's not why you didn't like it," I cut her off. I'm smiling, despite myself, taunting her even when I know better. I can't help myself. I never could. "You didn't like seeing me with her because you were jealous."

Her jaw clenches. I've succeeded in pissing her off, twin spots of anger pink in her cheeks, beautiful and fiery and breathtaking.

"I was avoiding you because this —" she points to herself and then me, "is obviously a terrible idea."

I lean back in my chair, folding my arms, waiting.

"We don't even like each other," she says. "We can't even talk without fighting. We're coworkers, and fraternizing is definitely against company policy. We'll just make each other miserable until we inevitably crash and burn, so I say we avoid all that and just don't make each other anything."

She's right, but I still want her worse than anything. I watch her for a long moment, both of us silent and still though we should be furiously making birds if we want to be done by tomorrow.

"Right?" she finally says, like she wants me to agree.

So I do. I give her that. She's right about the details even if I think she's wrong about the big picture. I give her this, even though what I want more than anything at this moment and every moment is just to kiss her again.

"Right," I say, lean over, and grab her iPad. "Want to watch a movie?"

CHAPTER TWENTY-ONE

VIOLET

"Ninety-two," Eli says. "Ninety-four, ninety-six, ninety-eight…"

There's a long, long pause. I tear my gaze from the dots in the drop ceiling and raise my head off the floor to look at him.

"I can't make two more," I say. "I'll die of… paper."

Eli holds up two more cranes.

"One thousand," he says, and tosses them into the box.

I flop my head back onto the floor. It's seven a.m, and I know I should be doing *something* — someone still has to string all the cranes together, we have to get them out to the wedding barn, get them hung, not to mention that there are ten thousand other things to do for this crazy six hundred person wedding — but I'm lying on the floor, letting Eli count.

I'm pretty sure I look like a wreck. I know Eli does, though even with circles under his eyes and wild hair, he's hot as sin. The messy, disheveled look is good on him, but I'm not thinking about that right now.

It's been a hell of a night. We folded five hundred

cranes and, between the two of us, drank thirty-two ounces of espresso. I feel like I might simultaneously fall into a dead sleep and run a marathon.

Eli walks over and stands by my feet.

"You getting up or are these my job now?" he asks.

"Are you offering?"

"Only if you're making scallops for six hundred," he says.

I'm pretty sure I couldn't make scallops for one. Macaroni and cheese, sure, but I don't even know which end of a scallop is up.

"Okay, okay," I say, even though the floor feels really good. "I'll do my job."

Eli leans down and holds a hand out. There's a part of me that wants to refuse it and get off the floor by myself, but that part is dumb.

I take his hand, and when he pulls me up, I just about fly off the ground, landing on my feet and stumbling into him. Apparently those muscles aren't just for show, a fact that does not appeal to me one single bit.

Nope. Not one bit.

"Sorry," he says, but he's grinning.

"No, you're not," I say, not moving away.

His eyes roam my face. I realize that up close, they're more than just green: they're dark turquoise around the pupil, mossy further out, flecked with a gold-tinged seafoam. They look like an impressionist painting.

"Violet," Eli says. I realize I was staring.

"What?" I ask, already defensive.

I think my heart punches my ribcage. He's so close, and he's got that infuriating-but-sexy half-smile on his face, and I've now been blatantly staring at him for several seconds, our bodies touching, and I still haven't moved away.

I don't want to move away. I like touching him. I like it a *lot.*

There, I said it.

"You better not kiss me," he murmurs.

I swallow hard. My heart feels like it's in a boxing match, and I just hope Eli can't hear it.

"Don't worry, I won't," I say.

I don't move, one hand still on his, the other on his shoulder.

"Good. We agreed it was a bad idea."

"It's a terrible idea."

"Besides..." he says, and trails off. He raises one eyebrow.

"Besides what?"

"It wasn't even that good of a kiss," he says.

I know he's fucking with me. I know it, and yet it works. That's maybe the most infuriating thing about Eli: even when I can tell what he's up to, it *works.*

It was a great kiss, and that's God's own truth.

"And if you're thinking about trying it again to prove yourself, don't bother," he goes on. "That one was dead bottom of my list, right underneath the time a golden retriever licked me on the face and got her tongue in my mouth."

"Gross."

"It was. And yet," he says, eyes sparking, "it wasn't the worst."

"I'm sorry you had to suffer through that," I say in mock-sympathy.

"Me too," he says. "Thank God we had a rational talk and won't be doing it anymore."

I'm on my toes now, my fingers digging into his shoulder, pulling myself up to get closer to him.

"Violet," he says, his voice bottoming out. "Why do I get the feeling you're not listening to a word I've just said?"

"Do you ever shut up?"

The grin is back, lopsided. I realize his other hand is on the small of my back, my body pressed against his.

"Only when my mouth is otherwise occupied," he says. "And since there's no way you're going to kiss me right now, I guess I'll just keep—"

I kiss him. It's the wrong thing to do for about a thousand reasons, but it feels like walking out of the shade and into the sunlight, that warm full-body bliss.

He kisses me back, hard. Our bodies crush together, his hand on my back, his mouth opening, the kiss deepening.

"Liar," I whisper, pulling back.

He grabs my hips and spins me, walks me backward, eyes blazing, a teasing smile on his face.

"You can't say I don't know you," he says.

My butt hits the conference table and he kisses me again, boosting me up onto it. I've got his shirt in one fist and I draw him in, closer, his body between my knees.

His tongue's in my mouth. My other hand is in his hair, fingers woven through the unruly strands, his body firm against mine as his fingers knead my spine, like he's trying to draw me in even closer.

God, bad ideas feel so good. I let his shirt go and run my hand over his torso, the muscles flexing under his shirt as I do. Heat pools inside me, dangerous and overwhelming.

He nips at my bottom lip, and my eyelids flutter open.

"You're right," he murmurs. "This is a terrible idea."

We kiss again, mouths open. He slides one hand under my shirt, his hand warm on my back.

"Awful," I agree, gasping for breath.

I wrap my legs around him, pulling him in. I realize with a shock that he's already hard, his thick length pressing against me and without meaning to, I rock my hips against him.

Eli groans. It's quiet, but the noise vibrates through me like a symphony and I pull at him harder. I want more: more of that noise, more of this kiss, more of *him*.

His hand under my shirt slides up. I squeeze him with my thighs, my nails digging into his back, and he traces the bottom of one underwire with his thumb. My back arches and I gasp. Eli chuckles, taking my bottom lip between his teeth.

"Right," says a voice outside. "So we'll move the chairs first, and then when the other two get here we'll tackle—"

I practically leap off the table, shoving Eli away with both hands and sliding off, landing on one foot. I manage to pivot and land in one of the chairs, where I instantly cross my legs and lace my hands together over my head in the world's most casual pose.

Eli leans against the table.

"—The tables, and then we can deal with the center-pieces — oh hey, guys!"

Monica, one of our coworkers, walks past the open door of the conference room and waves at us.

"Hi," I call back. Eli waves.

"—So I think can get that all finished by nine…"

Eli starts laughing.

"What?" I hiss, adjusting my shirt. I'm pretty sure my face is bright red.

"You," he says, still grinning. "That's the most suspicious I've ever seen a person look."

I rake my eyes down his body, aftershocks still running through my own. He looks perfectly casual, like we've been standing here and talking about oyster sliders or something.

"I told you not to do it," he says, grinning, his words a slow drawl. "You should listen to me more often."

See? Infuriating.

I stand, running a hand through my probably-insane hair, and look him straight in the eye. Shivers prickle down my spine.

"Don't you dare —"

"Fool me once, Loveless," I say, and walk past him, to the boxes of paper cranes against the far wall. "Don't you have a job to get to?"

I'm very, very tempted to close the conference room door, lock it, and go back to what we were doing. *Insanely* tempted. Instead I stand in front of the boxes, staring at a blank wall, my arms folded over my chest.

"I guess," he says, his footsteps coming closer. "You need help carrying those somewhere?"

I shake my head, still facing the wall. I'm a little afraid that if I look at him I'll do something crazy, like tear all my clothes off.

"We've still gotta string them up," I say, and pause. Now he's standing right behind me, and I can feel him there, even though we're not touching. "Thanks, though. For everything."

"Any time, Violet," he says, his low, slow voice sending shivers down my spine. "Just holler."

Gently, he takes my hair in one hand, moves it to the side. Before I can ask what he's doing he presses his warm lips to the back of my neck.

I gasp. My eyes shut, but it's already over and he walks away. I turn my head and look at him, just as he gets to the door.

Eli looks at me. He winks.

Then he's gone.

I think I'm in for a very long day.

CHAPTER TWENTY-TWO

ELI

This wedding is the wedding from hell.

It's not just because I stayed up all night drinking espresso and folding cranes with Violet. It's not just because my mind wanders back to the conference room every ten seconds, to the way she grabbed my shirt and pulled me in, the way she rolled her hips against my dick.

None of those things make the day feel any shorter, but it's just a bad wedding.

At nine that morning, I learn that the groom wants to make an eleventh-hour menu change. At eleven, after scrambling for two hours to try and make this fool happy, I learn that the bride has forbidden the menu change and the original item is back on, only now we have two fewer hours to make it.

Other reports trickle into the kitchen, ones that have nothing to do with me: the mother of the bride is furious that the rose gold aisle runner is too rose and not enough gold. The mother of the groom insists on moving the entire ceremony last-minute, for fear that the glare of the sun will give her a migraine.

Time flies. I run the kitchen. Violet darts in and out, here and there, and every single time I catch her eye I wink at her and she looks away instantly, turning pink.

Then I watch her walk away in a pair of pinstriped pants that I guess she had in her office. Wherever they came from, her ass looks spectacular.

The ceremony starts. The kitchen kicks into high gear. There are reports that the bride's grandmother threw a fit about where she was seated and the rows at the ceremony had to be rearranged; the groom got his vows wrong; someone's cousin was sobbing so dramatically that she had to be escorted out.

We cook halloumi bites with mango chutney, crispy duck mini-tacos, and coconut shrimp skewers. We make a gallon of salad dressing. Zane sets out hundreds of salad plates and Naomi meticulously arranges organic micro-greens on them.

They can't find the groom for pictures. The bride is crying. When he turns up, he's in his brother's suite in the lodge with all his groomsmen, and they're smoking cigars in the strictly-no-smoking building.

Salads go out. This development seems miraculously drama-free, but then again, it's just salad. We start searing scallops and plating them, ready for the next course.

The word comes out: we have to wait, the groom's father is making a toast. It's not when he was supposed to make a toast, but we wait any way.

And we wait. The scallops get cold.

His toast lasts half an hour. We try to send the scallops out while he's toasting and the groom's mother is so angry that a server comes back pale and visibly shaken. When he's finally finished, we re-sear so they're not cold, but now they're overdone.

Plenty of people send their scallops back. I don't bother

hearing why. Violet comes into the kitchen again, nods at me, asks Janice something about the cake. I wink at her.

She winks back. I burn a filet mignon and have to throw it away.

I swear that wink gets me through the rest of the night. I'm still thinking about it an hour later when we're cleaning up, service finished, and she comes in again. She looks at me. I wink. She raises one eyebrow, heads back toward the walk-in freezer.

I follow her.

When I close the door behind us she turns around, surprised.

I cross the tiny, cold space toward her. I take her face in my hands, her eyes widen.

Before she can say a word, I kiss the hell out of her. Violet's arms go around me. I kiss her harder. I kiss her like I've been to war. I kiss her like I haven't seen her in years, her soft warmth flooding through me, bright against the cold room.

I kiss her like I won't be sleeping much tonight, either.

Finally, I break the kiss, step away. She looks bewildered for a moment, her lips parted and slightly puffy, and then she smiles.

I head for the door again, open it, wink at her, and leave.

CHAPTER TWENTY-THREE
VIOLET

I stare at *Re: Re: Re: Fwd: de la Rosa wedding requests.* It's ten o'clock on Saturday night. I've been at work since eight o'clock *yesterday morning*, and yet I'm blankly staring at an email about a wedding that's not happening for two more weeks like it's important.

It's got nothing to do with the fact that ten minutes ago, when I popped my head into the kitchen "just to check on everything," Eli winked at me and mouthed the words *five minutes*.

It's got nothing to do with the fact that I'm a bundle of nerves and anticipation for what's about to happen.

I could just leave. If I were making better decisions today I'd just leave, but I'm not about to start that *now*. Not after I've spent today either kissing the hell out of him or thinking about kissing the hell out of him.

It turns out that kissing Eli has two advantages: one, he's not talking if we're kissing, and two, it's really, really fun. Fun enough that, technically, I've read this email ten times now and I haven't absorbed the information even once, because I'm thinking about what else Eli and I could do that might be even more fun than kissing.

My door darkens. My heart spin-kicks. I raise my eyes.

"Still here?" Eli asks, sauntering in as if he didn't know I would be.

He looks like hot rough hell. There are circles under his eyes and stubble on his face, and his hair looks like someone's been running their hands through it. He's wearing a white undershirt with his jacket tossed over his shoulder, and it's still clinging to him slightly with the heat of the kitchen he just left.

And now I'm no longer thinking of kissing Eli. *Now* I'm thinking of that shirt balled up in the corner of my bedroom while he's on top of me, my legs wrapped around his waist, feeling the muscles in his back ripple beneath my touch…

"Just catching up on emails," I say, tilting my head to one side, still entranced by the way his shoulders swell against the sleeves of his shirt.

Eli just grins. It's full of swagger and slightly feral, exactly the grin that would normally irritate me to no end.

It does irritate me, just a little. But it thrills me more, especially because he comes around my desk and leans on it, right next to where I'm sitting, while he's grinning. I look up at him, still in my office chair, mouth dry.

"Must be mighty important emails," he says.

Our legs are touching, and that single point of heat sets off fireworks inside me.

"Most of my emails are life or death situations," I deadpan.

God, I want to lean forward and touch him, run one hand down his muscled chest, pull up his shirt and lick his abs. Instead I glance at my open office door, certain that the moment I make a move someone will walk by.

"Once we got the wrong kind of tablecloths and someone *died*," I say.

"Did they?" Eli says, still teasing. "Then don't let me distract you from your important, lifesaving work."

I glance at my office door again. I feel like one of those hand-cranked spinners you pick bingo numbers from, jumbled and spinning.

Anyone who caught me would totally understand, right?

"Unless you're looking for a distraction, of course," he goes on, voice lowering. "Then I'm happy to be of service."

I swallow, heartbeat rising, but I manage to raise one eyebrow at him.

"Well, this email is about what kind of fabric to use for napkins, so I'm not sure what you could *possibly* do that would tear my attention away—"

Eli kisses me again, right in front of my open office door.

God, it's nice.

It's needy and ferocious. It's barely restrained. It's incendiary, and already I've got one hand winding through his already-mussed hair, the other closing around the front of his shirt as I sit up straighter, leaning into him.

His strong hand is already on my cheek, sliding into my hair. I kiss him back as hard as I can, despite my open door. I kiss him back with abandon because for half the day I thought about our kiss this morning and for the other half I thought about our kiss in the kitchen, and I already decided I'm not making good decisions.

Everything about this is a bad idea, and I couldn't care less.

After a moment we separate and I pull back, one hand on Eli's chest.

He narrows his eyes.

"If you're about to tell me again all the reasons we

shouldn't be doing this I have to admit I'm not terribly interested," he drawls.

He takes my hand and pulls me to my feet.

He pulls me right into him, our bodies pressed together from shoulder to toe. He's already hard and I'm sure he knows I know. I'm filled with slow-burning fire, ready to shove him down on my desk and climb on top of him.

"Are you interested in my open door?" I tease, twisting his shirt in my fingers.

"Less than I should be," he says, his hand sliding along the top of my waistband, where my blouse is tucked into my pants.

He kisses me again. I lean into him. My fingers find their way under his shirt and onto his warm skin, muscles flexing and bunching underneath, sending shivers of anticipation down my spine.

He palms my ass, my ache intensifying. I bite his lower lip and his breath catches, his other hand wandering up my torso, his thumb stroking the spot right below my underwire.

I gasp softly. He squeezes harder and I press myself against him.

You're at work. Stop it.

I don't stop it. I tug lightly at the waistband of his pants, pulling his hips forward against mine, his hardness against my belly as fire pools inside me. He groans, running one thumb over my nipple. Even through my blouse and bra, I shiver.

"— See if Violet's still here, she might want to come."

I jump back so fast that I fall into my chair again. It spins slightly as Kevin appears in my door.

"Hi there!" I say, hoping that I sound perfectly normal.

If Kevin thinks it's weird that the hot chef is standing

very close to me right now, his face doesn't betray it, bless him.

"A bunch of us are going out to McMahon's to celebrate today being over," Kevin says, jerking one thumb over his shoulder. "You two are welcome if you want to come."

"Thanks, but I think I'm going to call it a night," I say, heart still pounding so hard I'm afraid my intern can hear it from across my office.

"I was just about to walk her out," Eli says over his shoulder.

"Cool," Kevin says, nodding. "See you Monday!"

Then he's gone. Eli's laughing silently, his arms crossed over his beautiful torso. I roll my eyes at him and flip him off. He grabs my wrist and pulls me upright again.

"Okay, I care about the open door a little," he teases. "Come on, I'll walk you out."

I shift my hips against him. A muscle in his jaw ticks, like he's trying to control himself.

"And then?" I ask, my hands lightly against his stomach.

"Well, since I live with my mother, my brother, and my niece, I think our options are the back of my Bronco or your place, Violet," he says.

His hands are on my ass again, pulling me in. Desire slices into me like a hot knife.

"Your choice," Eli says, grinning.

· · · · · ★ ★ ★ ★ ★ · · · · ·

I PAW through my underwear drawer, mercilessly shoving aside bras I haven't worn in months, panties I didn't know I still had, and a few stray pairs of tights that aren't with my winter things yet.

Please be in here, I think. *And please be unexpired.*

I shove some more. My fingers find lace, and I frown, pulling something out.

It's a black lace bra. Basically see-through, dainty and alluring and sexy.

I stare down at it, wondering when I bought it and how long I've had it, because God knows I haven't had a reason to wear black lace in quite a while.

Should I put it on? Is this a black lace bra kind of tryst, or —

Then there's the sound of heavy tires crunching on gravel. My heart stops, then speeds up. I cram the bra back in the drawer and shove my hand to the very back, elbow-deep in unmentionables.

A Bronco door slams. My stomach twists.

Last chance to make a good decision.

I almost laugh out loud at the hilarious joke I just told myself as my fingers finally brush against foil. I yank two condoms out in victory, just as footsteps come up my front steps.

I throw them on the bed, slam the drawer shut, wonder what the hell I'm doing one last time, and leave my bedroom.

Eli's standing on the other side of my screen door, fist raised to knock.

"That wasn't ten minutes," I say.

"Nope," he says, and opens the screen door, stepping inside.

It hasn't shut when he kisses me.

He kisses me so hard it nearly lifts me off the floor, the kiss vibrating through my whole body. I manage to swipe at the front door behind him and swing it shut.

Then I'm up against it, just like that. His mouth is still on mine and my hands are fisted in his shirt, then under it. He grabs my ass again and hoists me, still pressed against my front door, my legs going around his hips.

"Did you really think I was going to wait ten whole minutes?" he says, his mouth still half on mine.

He shifts his hips, pressing me harder against the door, the thick ridge of his cock slipping over my clit. Even though there's God knows how many layers of fabric between us, it sends a thrill of pleasure through my body.

"I didn't want anyone to know we were leaving together," I murmur.

His lips work their way along my jaw, to my ear. He's got one hand in my hair, the other on my side. My legs tighten around him of their own accord.

"You think anyone would naturally assume that because we left at the same time, we were driving to your place to fuck?" he says, his lips brushing against my ear.

"Well, weren't we?" I say.

"Hell yes," he says, biting my earlobe. "But no one else thinks that."

I gasp, gritting my teeth together. I've got one arm around his shoulders, and I start tugging at his shirt. It needs to come off, *now*.

Eli obliges. The shirt lands somewhere in my kitchen and his lips land back on mine, his hands quickly undo my blouse. The moment it's off he pulls my bra straps down over my shoulders, leaving my bra half-on and my nipples exposed and stiff.

He pinches one. I gasp again, and he rolls it between his fingers as my head goes back against the door, my eyes shut.

It feels really, really good. I bite my lip and clench his arms in my fists, trying not to make a noise because despite all this, I don't want to give him the satisfaction.

I don't know why, other than by now it's baked into my DNA.

Then my bra's off, on the floor. I stand on my own

again and I grab the waistband of Eli's pants, pull him in toward me, his mouth capturing mine again.

He's hard as a rock, his thick length insistent against me. I'm a puddle of desire, wet as hell.

I slide one hand down the length of his cock, through his pants. Eli *growls*, grabbing one hip and shoving me back against the door, an untamed flash lighting through his green eyes.

I do it again, but harder. Now he's wild, one hand in my hair, his lips on my neck. He bites my collarbone and I yelp, but he just laughs, the sound rough and low as he bites me again. This time the sensation sends a thrill through me, every hair on my body standing on end.

I grab his cock through his pants. He's big — *really* big, actually — but desire rushes through me again as he keeps me pinned.

Eli yanks on my pants, undoing the button, forcing the zipper down so roughly I'm afraid he'll break it.

"Don't break it," I hiss.

"It was stuck," he says, his mouth back on mine.

"Finesse it, don't force it," I say.

He slides his hand underneath my panties, his fingers slipping through my folds. I'm wet as hell and I know it, and from the way his kiss suddenly gets rough, even more fiery, he does too.

"Finesse it?" he murmurs, sliding a finger between my lower lips.

I gasp, my breath catching in my throat.

"How's this?" he asks, sliding another finger between my lips. He pushes them both inside me shallowly, and my hand on his waistband tightens, tugging him toward me.

"Does that count as finessing?" Eli teases me, drawing his fingers back out of me, sliding them forward until they're on either side of my clit. My whole body jerks as he squeezes it lightly. I think I moan, so he does it again, harder.

He kisses me, his tongue in my mouth. I squeeze his cock again, my fingers tight around him through the fabric. He groans and pinches my clit, white heat arcing through my body.

"That's two questions you haven't answered yet," he growls, his lips still against mine. "Unless moaning counts as an answer."

That cocky smile is there in his voice as he rubs me faster, fingers sliding back to my lips, teasing entry before moving away again.

I take a deep breath and force myself to focus for a moment.

"I'm just impressed you know where the clit is," I say.

He pinches it between his fingers. This time I definitely moan, and Eli grins.

"That?" he asks, and does it again, then again. I'm standing on my tiptoes, pressed against my front door, because we haven't managed to get any further into my house.

"I saw a diagram once," he teases, his voice still low.

We kiss. He keeps strumming me, over and over again. I'm trembling from the tension, rubbing his cock through his pants, listening to his breath catch in his throat every time I do.

"You know me, I like to study things real good," Eli goes on, his fingers still moving, now faster. "Be properly prepared just in case Violet Tulane wants to take me home."

I can barely listen to what he's saying. What he's *doing* feels way too good, and I know that if he keeps it up, I'm going to come hard and fast and without so much as taking my pants off. He kisses me, his tongue in my mouth, his fingers working me.

"Seems like it was worthwhile," he says. "Since you're wet as fuck and about thirty seconds from coming, and I've barely gotten past your front door."

"Forty-five," I gasp.

He raises his eyebrows.

"Is that a challenge?" he murmurs.

His fingers move faster. I kiss him and bite his lip. I moan and I can't stop, my body closing in on climax.

He slows, then he stops, his fingers teasing my lips one last time before he pulls his hand out of my pants completely, his lips still on mine.

"What the *fuck*?" I hiss, but he laughs.

"You're pretty when you're mad," he says. "And I always did like pissing you off."

I grab the waistband of his pants, jerk his hips toward mine until they meet, his erection straining against me.

"Don't tell me that's the point of all this," I say, looking up at him through my eyelashes.

He kisses me hard, one thumb on my nipple again. I unbutton and unzip his pants, find his boxer-clad cock, and squeeze.

Eli laughs in my ear.

"The point of this is to see how loud I can make you come," he says. "Pissing you off a little is just a fun bonus."

Now I'm grabbing his cock and blushing at the same time. I reach through his boxers and stroke him, skin to skin. He's even bigger than I realized, and as I do he groans again, pushing me harder against the door.

"I'm gonna make things *real* awkward with your neighbors," he whispers. I stroke him again longer, harder, feeling like I might burst out of my skin with heat and desire, the sheer uncontrollable *want* I feel right now.

"You think you can?" I ask, still stroking him. His hips move in rhythm with my hand, unfettered growls coming from somewhere deep in his chest.

"I told you I studied," Eli teases me. I squeeze his cock, precum gathering at the tip, and I bite the inside of my cheek to keep myself from making a noise. "Plenty of diagrams. Even a moving picture or two."

He slides his hands down my body. By now he's shoving his cock through my hands, our lips together, our tongues tangled. My pants come down and then his, and suddenly his cock is bare against my belly and we're pressed together, skin to skin. I shiver and it's wonderful, the combination of his warm body and the cool door at my back.

He tweaks a nipple. He moves his hand between my legs again, thumb flicking expertly past my clit, fingers just barely delving into my wetness. I moan and he withdraws.

Then he takes a moment. He presses his forehead to mine, our noses tip to tip. We're both breathing hard, our chests expanding and falling together, his hands still exploring me.

"Violet."

"Eli."

He laughs. My eyes are closed but I can feel it.

"Which door is your bedroom?"

"Right behind you," I say.

The second the words are out of my mouth I'm in the air, slung over Eli's shoulder like I'm a bag of flour as he strides into my bedroom, ducking slightly as he goes through the doorway. He tosses me gently on the bed, and I bounce once before he's on top of me, between my legs, his body covering mine.

I wrap my legs around him, arch my back. His cock slides against my mound and belly, and I squeeze tighter, feeling like I might explode.

I want him. *Now*. As much as I can't believe that I'm naked with Eli Loveless, not to mention having a great time, here we are and I. Want. Him. *Now*.

There's the sound of foil crinkling by my head, and Eli's lips pull back. He's leaning on one elbow, his other hand on my thigh, stroking it while it's wrapped around him.

"Twice, huh?" he asks, grinning.

I glance over at the two condoms in his hand. Frankly, right now, they don't seem like enough.

"If you need a second chance," I tease.

He tears one open with his teeth, looking me in the eye the whole time. It's the first time I've ever found opening a condom sexy, but right now, I'm mesmerized. He rolls it on, and I grab him in my fist, arching my back, guiding him to my slick entrance.

Eli groans, his face against my neck, the sound vibrating through my whole body. I'm aching and desperate, but he pauses for a moment with his tip right at my opening, teasing me.

Then he sinks in. My eyes slide closed and I grab his hair in my fist, a noise I've never heard before coming from my mouth. He's big — bigger than I realized, definitely bigger than any previous boyfriend — but he hilts himself in one long, slow stroke and it feels fucking *perfect*.

It feels like we were designed to fit together like this, hand in glove, heat coursing through my whole body.

"Oh, *fuck*," Eli whispers when he's buried, and pauses.

I kiss him and he kisses me back, oddly slow and sensual. I feel like he's touching somewhere deep inside me that's never been touched before, something that touches a live wire, a raw nerve, and I need a minute or else I might simply dissolve.

The kiss gets harder. Faster. His tongue is in my mouth

and I bite his lower lip, a little harder than I mean to. I slide my hand down his neck, to his shoulder and then he catches it with his, fingers encircling my wrist, pushing it down onto the bed, his weight on me.

I tighten my legs. I roll my hips, and he might be on top of me but that makes him move inside me, and he exhales hard, squeezing my wrist even harder.

I do it again, and this time in response he plows into me. I swear his cock hits every nerve I've got, including some I've never found before. My eyes slide shut and I whimper with pleasure.

I'm *definitely* going to feel weird talking to my neighbors tomorrow.

We do it again, then again, still wrapped in each other, each movement harder and faster than the last, desperate and needy. I'm using his body for pleasure and he's using mine and nothing in my entire life has ever felt better.

He's still holding my wrist, my legs still wrapped around his waist, and with every stroke he growls, groans. He drops onto one elbow and whispers *Jesus fucking Christ, Violet* into my ear over and over as he crashes into me and I invite him in.

I bite his shoulder. I claw his back with my other hand and we fuck harder and harder, the whole world obliterated except for the pure physical movement of our bodies, raw and hard and rough and like nothing I've ever even imagined.

I climb sky-high. I'm trying to tear Eli apart just to get *more* of him, more of him faster and harder and deeper until I can't stand it anymore.

"Don't stop," I hear myself say, half whispering, half moaning. "Don't stop don't stop don't—"

He kisses me savagely as he buries himself again and I moan into his mouth.

"As if I would," he growls. I bite his lip and his fingers dig into my wrist, my thigh. I'm cracking apart at the seams, close to coming unstoppably, uncontrollably. "I said loud, Violet."

Harder and harder, my comforter digging into my spine with every thrust.

"I fucking meant it," he whispers.

I grit my teeth together. I'm cracking, unraveling, my whole body tense as a fist, closed around Eli. He's relentless, taking, giving, holding me tight as I rise to meet him, keeping him.

Suddenly, the fist opens, and I fall. I think I shout. I know I tremble, shaking, the climax like a thunderclap in my body, the sound wave fast and vicious.

Seconds later, Eli falls into me. He buries his face in my neck and shouts, moans, and I wrap my legs around him harder, keeping him buried as we rock together. He jolts inside me and my body responds, aftershocks still rippling through me, the electrical impulses of nerves having their own way.

We slow. He releases my wrist, his hand slides up mine until our fingers interlock and then he closes it, intertwining our hands. I wrap my other arm around his back, holding him close, unfurling my legs from around him.

I kiss him, or maybe he kisses me. It's lazy and unhurried, thoughtful, slow. He pulls back, runs a thumb over my lip, kisses me again. I trace a finger down his spine, feeling every notch.

Finally, he rolls off, and we both crawl to the head of my bed, flop onto my pillows, exhausted. I close my eyes, his touch still singing through me. I feel like I'm melding with my bed, I'm so tired.

I sense Eli turn toward me, and after a moment, I open my eyes and look over. He's in the same position I am: on his back, panting for breath, looking as if he might never move again.

"What?" I murmur.

He smiles. It's teasing, taunting, a promise of something wicked glinting in his eye.

"Not bad," he says.

I start laughing, and the glint intensifies, the smile going full-on sexy and dangerous.

"Yeah, that was okay, I guess," I say between giggles. "If you want to try again there's one condom left."

Eli looks down at his dick, then up at me.

"Five minutes," he says, and winks.

CHAPTER TWENTY-FOUR

ELI

I wake up to sunlight in my eyes and the sensation that I'm being dragged up from the depths of the ocean against my will, like some sort of captured giant squid.

I've never exactly been a morning person.

I throw one arm over my eyes. When that's not good enough, I roll over, bury my head beneath a pillow, the sheets twisting around my hips. My elbow bumps something soft and warm.

"Ow," it says. "That's my face."

I crack an eye open to see a barely-awake Violet looking at me, lying on her stomach, my elbow right in front of her nose.

I remember where I am *instantly*.

"Morning, sunshine," I say, grinning.

Violet grabs my forearm with both hands and shoves it away, out of her face. I let her.

"You're on my side," she mutters.

"You're on *my* side," I counter, just for the hell of it.

"The whole bed is my side," she says, still shoving. "You're just a temporary guest."

"This is how you treat guests?" I tease, still not moving. "How about a little southern hospitality?"

Violet raises one eyebrow, and her eyes go instantly wicked.

"I was plenty hospitable last night," she says, the corners of her eyes crinkling. "You're the one who's over-stayed his welcome."

"Have I?"

"It's nearly ten."

"And I'm sure you're raring to get up and start your day."

Violet lifts herself on her elbows, her pillow under her chest. The sheet slips down her back, still covering her ass, the curves of her breasts pressing outward.

I stare. I already had morning wood, but now it's quickly becoming *Violet is naked underneath that sheet* wood.

"Don't let me stop you from your planned Sunday of productivity," I go on. "I'll just be here. Let me know if my services are required."

Now Violet laughs.

"What, if I need a jar opened?"

"Come on, Violet, you know what I'm good for."

She just raises one eyebrow.

"Cooking and fucking," I say.

Violet turns pink, the color flushing down her neck. It's gratifying as hell, even though she looks away for a moment.

"I'm not bad at jars, either," I admit after a moment. "But I imagine I could be of service somehow."

Violet looks at me. She's not laughing anymore, not blushing. Actually, she looks a touch worried.

"Is there some skill I haven't covered?" I ask after a long moment.

"We should talk," she says.

"Aren't we?"

"About *this*," she says, circling one finger over the two of us. "About what exactly *this* is."

"Pretty sure *this* is us naked in your bed, unless this is some kind of prank show and one of these walls is about to fall down and reveal a studio audience," I say, still in a punchy mood. I don't want to talk about our relationship at the moment. Maybe in an hour, after I've had some coffee and breakfast.

Right now, I'd like to roll Violet over on top of me and watch her ride my cock like a cowgirl. In fact, that's pretty much the only thing on my mind.

Violet ignores that studio audience thing and looks at me seriously, the sharks darting back and forth.

"I still don't think we should date," she says, her voice suddenly serious and quiet.

I push myself off my stomach and onto my side, my elbow under my head, the sheet still haphazardly draped over my waist. Violet's eyes dart down, then back up just as quickly.

I let the words settle for a minute, watching her, an odd twinge of disappointment working its way inward, somewhere behind my sternum.

I don't know why. She was right yesterday morning and she's right now. I don't like her. She doesn't like me. We don't get along. We can't have a conversation without arguing, and that's pretty much the bare minimum for dating.

If we tried, we'd both end up miserable, and that's for damn sure.

I just wish she'd said this when she was less naked.

"All right," I say, cock still throbbing. "You picked a hell of a time to say it, though."

She glances down again. I roll onto my back, arms

behind my head, erection pointing heavenward. Her eyes dart back to mine.

"I don't think we should *date*," she says, valiantly looking me right in the eyes. "It's clearly not going to work. We can't stand to be around each other, we can barely talk without—"

"Yeah, I've noticed we don't like each other," I say. "And I'm well aware of all the things you don't like about me, no need to repeat them since you outlined them all yesterday."

"I think we should be friends with benefits," she says.

I admit, it takes me by surprise.

"Are we friends?" I ask after a moment.

She's still looking deeply into my eyes, her gaze not wavering for a moment.

"It's just a phrase," she says. "I just mean that… there's no reason not to have a physical relationship, even though an emotional one clearly wouldn't work. But I'm not seeing anyone, you're not seeing anyone…"

She trails off, like she's looking for confirmation.

"Is that a question?" I say.

"You're not, are you?"

"You don't think you should've asked that at some point before last night?" I tease.

Violet rolls her eyes and adjusts the pillow underneath her. I almost see nipple. *Almost.*

"You know, Eli, there's a lot wrong with you—"

"I do love it when you sweet talk me."

"— But you ain't the cheatin' type," she finishes, an extra twang in her words and a smile in her eyes.

"For once, you're right," I finally tell her.

I look at her. She looks back, clearly determined not to look at my dick, tenting up the bed sheets like there's a circus in there as my capacity for talking gets shorter and shorter.

"All right, Violet, let me get this straight," I say, slowly, letting my eyes trail down her body. "You want to bang me like a screen door—"

"Oh, my God," she mutters.

"— and then kick me out, and I don't have to take you to dinner and a movie or anything?"

"Right."

The twinge digs a little deeper, and I continue to ignore it.

"You're not gonna be mad if I don't get you flowers on your birthday, or Valentine's day," I say.

Violet just snorts.

"You're not gonna pester me to meet my family?"

"Eli, I already know your family," she points out. "They're all much nicer than you."

I slide one arm underneath her, grab her by the waist, and pull her in toward myself as she yelps.

"There's gotta be some catch," I say, pulling her onto my chest.

She just laughs.

"We don't even have to talk," she says.

"Then what the hell are we doing?" I ask, and pull her lips down to mine.

The kiss is lazy and slow. I grab her leg and pull her until she's straddling my hips, pressing my aching cock against my belly. She rolls her hips against it and I groan out loud, my fingers digging into her flesh.

Right now I'll do anything she says, so long as she doesn't stop.

"We're good, right?" she asks, coming up for air, her hands on my chest. I slide my hands up her torso until her stiff pink nipples are between my fingers, and then I squeeze, watching her eyes slide shut, her hips rolling again, the pressure on my cock delicious.

She's already wet as she rubs herself on me, her lips slippery against the base of my shaft. I pinch her nipples again and she sighs, a tremor moving through her body, grinding against me harder.

It's beautiful. *She's* beautiful. The only time she's prettier than when she's angry is when she's like this, flushed and rapturous and wet as hell.

"We're good," I tell her, ignoring the twinge again.

Violet just moans. The sound makes my cock twitch as I watch her undulate on top of me.

"Thanks," she whispers.

I slide my arms under her legs and grab her ass.

"Don't thank me yet," I say, pulling her forward.

Violet yelps again, but seconds later I'm beneath her, her thighs on either side of my face, my arms holding her down.

I lick her once, just to taste, and she gasps.

She's delicious. I lick her again, my tongue between her lips, nudging against the tightness of her entrance, moving up to her clit.

She moans. I write my name on her like I'm marking my territory and her body jolts with every flick of my tongue. Violet leans against the wall, her eyes closed, one hand buried in my hair, her nipples stiff pink peaks poking out beyond the swell of her breasts.

It's a great view.

I write my name again. The whole damn thing, ELIJAH LOVELESS, and now she's gasping in between moans. I slide two fingers into her and her juices drip down as she clenches around me. She's closer than I thought and I lick her again, crook my fingers, stroke that spot inside her that makes her thighs tremble.

Her hand tightens in my hair. Her moans are high-pitched, breathy. It sounds like she's biting her lip, trying not to make any noise, but I'm winning that battle as I lick her harder, faster, because if this relationship is purely physical then it's at least going to be goddamn *good*.

Her legs tremble. She gasps, the sound echoing off the wall, her hips bucking as she presses herself into my face like she can't control herself. I'm lost in her sweetness, in her beautiful musky scent, in the tremors that move through her with every flick of my tongue as I write my name on her again.

Violet comes on the final S. I've got two fingers buried deep, her whole body shaking and trembling. She flutters around my fingers, her body tensing, her toes curling as she moans against her trailer's thin wall.

Oops.

I meant to tease her, get her close and then pull away, but then I couldn't stop. Violet's intoxicating, addictive. She moans, her pussy clenches again, and I flick my tongue softly past her clit, her whole body jerking as I do.

God, that's satisfying. She doesn't say anything but she's breathing hard. My eyes are open, watching her chest heave as I pull my fingers out and lick them off.

She's still leaning against the wall and gathering her wits as I reach up and grab the second condom from where I left it on the nightstand last night. I roll it on, because I've still got every intention of watching her ride my cock.

I scoot her down. She leans in and kisses me, her hand still in my hair, her taste still on my lips. If she notices, she doesn't seem to mind as she drifts her other hand down my body. Everywhere she touches lights me up, tiny fires trailing from my shoulder to my stomach, down my treasure trail until she finally wraps her hand around my cock.

I wrap my hand around hers, let her stroke me a few

times before she finally sits up, her hands on my chest, and she guides me to her entrance.

I brace myself just before she takes me in a single stroke, plunging me deep and Jesus tapdancing Christ, I swear it feels even better than it did last night.

And the view. She starts riding me, slowly, and I don't think there's any sight in the world like Violet naked and on my cock.

I put my arms behind my head so I can watch her. Her tits bounce with every stroke. Every time she hilts me, a little moan escapes from her lips, her pussy clenching slightly, her eyes fluttering closed. Violet is warm, tight perfection, and every stroke makes it harder to breathe.

She moves faster. She bites her lip, her eyes closed now, her movements harder, more demanding. I move my hands to her thighs, her hips. I meet her with every thrust, feeling her quiver, listening to her moan even as I clench my teeth.

I can't last much longer, not like this. Not when it feels this good, like we were designed to fit together so well.

Violet leans back, her hands on my thighs, and I gasp. She moans explosively with the new angle, slows, pauses. She clenches around me, muscles quivering, fluttering as I close my eyes, take a deep breath against the heat gathered in my belly.

She arches, takes me. It takes all my force of will not to come, and I slide one thumb up to her clit, and start circling her.

"Oh, God," she whispers. "That feels good."

"That's the idea," I manage to say.

"Don't stop," she murmurs.

My balls tighten, the liquid heat in my belly threatening to spill out so I pull her hips down onto mine harder, circle her clit faster with my thumb.

"You don't have to say that," I tell her, my voice coming

out rough and low. "I do know full well not to stop when you're seconds from coming on my cock."

"Shut up," she whispers, body flexing, tits bouncing. I hold my breath, reaching the very end of my rope, barely able to hold back any longer.

Then she proves me right. Violet comes hard, her head back, her pussy clamping around me, even tighter than before as she sighs and moans, not stopping for an instant.

I'm two seconds behind her, drawing her down onto me, shooting myself deep inside her as she coaxes it out of me, coming in jolt after jolt, totally at her mercy.

Violet leans down to kiss me when she's finished. Right now she's all softness and warmth, her prickles and hard edges gone. She's willing and molten, practically gooey in my arms.

Maybe we don't have to talk, I think, practically high as a kite on her. *Maybe we never have to talk again. We get along just fine like this.*

After a long, slow kiss she rolls off of me and onto her back, my arm under her neck. She's still breathing hard, her skin flushed, her hair spread over her pillow and my arm, wild.

Shit, she's beautiful. I'm sure it's got something to do with the fact that I came so hard I feel like I might never walk again, but she's beautiful. A man could just about go blind looking at her.

Finally, the sharks make their way over to me, and she studies my face. I wonder what she's thinking but don't want to ask, so instead, I let this moment play out for a long time.

At last she clears her throat, looks down, licks her lips.

"See?" she says.

"See what?"

"I was right," she says.

I put my other arm behind my head, narrow my eyes, study her.

"About what?"

"That this was a good idea."

"I don't remember disputing that," I say. "In fact, I think you could take my actions as enthusiastic agreement."

"I didn't say you were *wrong*," Violet says. "I just said I was right."

"That implies that someone was wrong and I'm the only one here," I tell her.

"Fine. We were mutually right, happy?"

The answer is *yes*, actually, because I can't think of anywhere I'd rather be right now than post-coitally arguing with Violet. If nothing else, she's always interesting.

"Sure," I confirm. "Is this the part where you kick me out, or did you want to exploit my other talent first?"

She rolls over, toward me, her hair tickling my shoulder as she puts her face down on my bicep, eyes laughing.

"That did make me hungry," she teases.

CHAPTER TWENTY-FIVE

ELI

Daniel turns his head as I enter the kitchen, tossing my keys on the table.

"Call Mom, she thinks you're dead," he says, still washing dishes.

I glance at the clock. It's coming up on one in the afternoon.

He puts a final mug in the drying rack, grabs a towel, and turns around, wiping the dishwater off his hands.

"Are you?" he asks.

"Hilarious."

"You forgot to call last night. She's convinced you're face-down in a ditch somewhere right now. I barely talked her out of calling the cops," he says. "She wound up taking Rusty to the park to get her mind off your death."

I lean against the table.

"She knows I'm twenty-nine, right?" I ask.

"And yet you're living at home."

"If that ain't the pot calling the kettle black," I say as Daniel dries his hands off.

"I've got a good reason," he says. "You, on the other hand, have been freeloading for three months now."

"I wasn't sure I was staying," I say.

"Are you?"

"I've got no plans to leave," I tell him.

Not that it hasn't crossed my mind. Sprucevale is the exact same small town I left ten years ago, with all the good and the bad that comes along with it.

"But you haven't signed a lease or even bought a couch," he points out.

"I bought a stand mixer because Mom didn't have one," I say. "It's right there."

"What a commitment."

"It's a really nice stand mixer."

Daniel sighs. He leans back against the counter, arms crossed loosely over his chest, dressed in lazy Sunday gear — sweatpants and an old t-shirt that says GO WITH THE FLOW! SPRUCEVALE RIVER FEST on it in faded letters.

"Are you deliberately changing the subject from you not coming home the last two nights?" he asks.

Yes. Yes, I am.

"I called Friday," I protest.

"True," he says, in a tone that still demands explanation.

"I had to work late last night," I say, narrowing my eyes at him. "And I actually came home around two, then went out again—"

"Nah," he says.

"I got drunk with some coworkers—"

"You know I'm not going to believe any explanation that doesn't involve Violet, right?"

I lean back in my chair, drumming my fingers on the table.

"Fine. I slept with Violet," I finally say.

Daniel just nods. I've never seen anyone look less surprised.

"I'm not sure it was a good idea," I say, slowly, studying the back of my hand on the table.

"Because it was bad, or because it's Violet?" he asks.

Daniel has always had my measure the most of all my brothers. It's probably because we're so close in age, but I've never been able to get much past him. Thankfully, he's also the chill one.

"Because it's Violet," I say. "It wasn't bad at all."

Understatement of the year.

"She thinks we should just be fuck buddies," I say.

"Are you buddies?" Daniel asks.

I just spread my hands and shrug dramatically.

"I don't know," I say. "Usually I at least like the people I have sex with. This is new territory."

Not that I've had sex with tons of people, or any at all in the past six months. But the women I date and sleep with usually at least get along with me.

"So you and Violet Tulane, the girl whose name I've heard come out of your mouth more than anyone else since time immemorial, are just casually having sex and that's it," he says.

I don't like the way he says it.

"Right," I say.

"You had a two-night sex bender and it was no big deal."

"Friday night I really was at work," I say. "Violet's order of origami cranes came in low so I helped her fold…"

Daniel's eyebrows shoot upward.

"…five hundred more and don't fucking give me that look," I finish.

"I'm giving you the look you deserve."

I drum my fingers on the table. I stare at Daniel. He stares back, the world's most skeptical look on his face.

"What does Mom want me to make for Sunday dinner?" I finally ask.

"She said something about spaghetti and meatballs, I think."

"Is Charlie coming?"

"Yeah, she's back in town."

"Is Silas?"

"Ask Levi."

I stand and walk to the fridge, opening it to survey my Sunday dinner options.

"Have you noticed that I haven't hassled you *even once* about Charlie?" I ask. "Not once, Daniel."

"I think you just did."

I pull two packages of ground beef from the fridge and toss them in the sink.

"That's not hassling. When I hassle you, you'll know you've been hassled," I say.

"We've been friends since we were like ten," Daniel says. "Charlie is basically my sister. Screw off."

I snort.

"*Screw off?*"

"Shut up," he sighs. "Force of habit. Rusty overhead me tell Seth that someone was being a real dickhead and I got calls from her kindergarten teacher for a week. Apparently that's what she wanted to name the class iguana."

I start laughing.

"*And* she convinced half the other kids it was a good idea," he mutters. "I was not popular at the next PTA meeting."

"Are you ever?" I ask, hunting through the cupboards for stale bread.

Now Daniel grins.

"What?" I ask.

"I'm one of the only men who ever goes to those things, and I'm *definitely* the only single one," he says. "Yeah, I'm popular."

I find a can of breadcrumbs, which will also work, and look over at Daniel.

"Well, shit, stud," I say. "Back to your old ways?"

"One of Rusty is plenty," he says dryly.

"You could be smarter this time around," I point out.

"I'm being smarter by not even going there," Daniel says. "Crystal makes sure I've got plenty of drama in my life."

"How *is* Crystal?" I ask.

"Same as ever," he says darkly. "Hasn't seen Rusty in weeks. I arrange for her to have a weekend, she cancels two days before and then chews me out for keeping her from her daughter."

Crystal, Rusty's mother, is not a good parent. She's also not a good person.

"Sorry," I say.

Daniel just shrugs.

"It's neither new nor surprising," he says. "Can I help with dinner or should I stay out of the way?"

I grab a head of garlic and toss it to him.

"Chop that," I say.

CHAPTER TWENTY-SIX
VIOLET

"What about roses?" I ask, trailing after Adeline. "I like roses."

She gives me an are-you-crazy look over her shoulder.

"No," she says definitively. "Roses are hard. They're very picky and bugs love them."

"Ranunculus?" I ask.

"I don't think so."

"Hydrangea?"

"Those come from huge bushes," she says, and stops.

We're at Manny's Farm Store and Nursery on Monday afternoon, thirty minutes outside Sprucevale, wandering through the wide outdoor aisles, looking at all the plants on display. I volunteered to help Adeline with a flower bed project she's doing, and she's helping me find something that will make the front of my ugly trailer look halfway decent.

"You've gotta think smaller," she says, stopping in front of a table. "Most of the stuff in wedding bouquets is hard to grow. Here, what do you think of geraniums?"

They're bright red with dark green leaves, short, and look kind of like a kid's drawing of a flower.

"Okay," I say.

"They're not fancy, but they're hard to kill," she says. "They'll do well in pots, so you can take them with you when you move."

"Whenever that is," I say.

I checked the listing on the lake cottage again this morning, which I do a couple of times a week. It's still active. It's been up for nearly a year, and no one's bought it.

I should probably stop checking until I'm ready to actually move on it, because at this point if someone else buys it, I think I might cry. I've gotten very attached to a house I've never even visited.

"I had to spend five thousand dollars fixing the roof last winter," I say sourly as I pick up some geraniums and examine them. "I told you that, right?"

"Yeah, that's the worst," she says. "I hate when you spend money on something like that. It's not even fun. If you have to spend five grand on something, you should at least enjoy it a little bit."

"I guess I enjoy not being rained on," I admit. "But it sucked, and that's five thousand dollars I can't put toward a new place."

Adeline is well-acquainted with my housing woes, and nods along with me.

"How about those?" she asks, pointing. "African violets. Also hard to kill."

"Am I that irresponsible?" I ask, and she laughs.

"Only sometimes," she says. "Did you ask Eli about the maid of honor yet?"

"Will my answer determine which flowers you let me buy?"

"It probably should," she says.

"He didn't," I say. "And also I slept with him."

"Unlike the maid of honor," she says, grinning.

I sigh.

"I told you so," Adeline says. "People get into elevators together all the time and don't have sex."

"But she was touching him!" I protest. "He made that face at me, and I think she was grabbing his butt—"

"Don't worry, I love you even though you're crazy," she says, cutting me off and handing me a geranium. "Was the sex a direct result of you asking? Was it like, 'Hey, did you bang this chick?' 'No.' 'Take me right now!'"

She's grinning. I'm blushing.

"I never said *take me right now*," I tell her. "And there were more steps to it than that."

"Well, I don't have to be at work until seven," she says. "Come on, your foray into mature adulthood has earned you a look at the begonias while you tell me what it's like to boink a Loveless."

I give Adeline the rundown while she decides which flowers I'm equipped to handle. I can't tell whether her flower choices are made based on the story I'm telling her, but they might be.

"…so we just decided to be friends with benefits," I conclude.

"Are you friends?" she asks, one eyebrow raised.

"I don't know. We're something," I say, leaning against the cart and looking down at the flowers inside: a few easy ones for me, and then the pretty, dramatic ones for Adeline's flower bed. Apparently she's earned the difficult flowers, presumably by being incredibly mature.

"We obviously can't date," I say, still looking down. "You need to at least like someone to date them, right?"

"Usually," she says.

"And I don't like him, and he definitely doesn't like me, but we have a lot of chemistry—"

"*Bow*chicka."

"— so why not just do the part that works and not the part that doesn't?"

She brushes her hands against each other, getting dirt off.

"If we dated we'd just get attached and hurt each other sooner or later," I say, still defending myself. "I don't think we've ever had a conversation that didn't end with one of us angry. You can't date someone like that, it's ridiculous."

"And it's well known that sex rarely leads to attachment," Adeline says.

"Not with *Eli*," I say. "We don't even—"

"—Like each other, yeah, I heard," she says, one eyebrow raised.

"Exactly," I say. "Do I need dirt or anything for these flowers?"

CHAPTER TWENTY-SEVEN

VIOLET

"The smoked chicken isn't bad, but obviously, what you want is the pulled pork," Eli says. "You like spicy?"

"I do."

"Get the jalapeño hush puppies," he says, nodding at the menu over the counter. "If you think you can take it, anyway."

"Of course I can take it," I say, even though I have no idea if that's true. "What else is good?"

"The mac and cheese is eh," he says, tilting one hand side to side. "The coleslaw's just average, the collards are all right…"

He trails off, reading the menu. There are no printed menus at Ace in the Hole Barbecue, only the big plastic one over the counter that looks like it's been there since the 1970s. Half the stick-on letters are black, half are red, and there's a variety of different colors represented. The interior is entirely unfinished plywood, and it seems to be a design choice, not an accident of laziness.

Eli swears that this is the best barbecue in a three-hour

radius. He also swears that we won't run into anyone we know, since we're forty-five minutes outside of Sprucevale in Grotonsville, which is several towns away.

It's Thursday night. He's slept over every night but Sunday.

We both order at the counter: I get the hush puppies, Eli gets baked beans, we both get the pulled pork.

"You folks together?" the cashier asks as he rings me up.

"No," I say, just as Eli says, "Yes."

The cashier just looks up at me expectantly.

"We're paying separately," I tell him, already handing over a twenty.

"Really?" asks Eli.

"Yes, really."

"I can't even take you for barbecue?"

The cashier quietly takes my twenty-dollar bill and makes change. I look at Eli like he's lost his damn mind.

"Why would you take me for barbecue?"

"Because you had a shitty day and I'm trying to be nice for once?" he says. "Because barbecue was my idea so I figured I'd be paying for it?"

"This isn't a date," I say.

Even though I'm about ninety-nine percent sure we're going to have sex later.

"No one said date," Eli says.

"The last time someone else offered to pay for my dinner I ended up washing dishes until midnight," I point out. "Fool me once, et cetera."

I don't like this. I don't want to feel beholden to Eli. I don't want to feel like I owe him anything, like he's got some advantage over me that he could hold over my head.

I don't want to give Eli an edge, ever, for any reason. With sex, everything is even: we both want and we both take until we're an exhausted heap in my bed. But out here, in the real world where there are manners and clothes, it feels different. It feels like I need to be on my toes.

"How would that even work at a place where you pay up front and *then* get your food?" he says. "I'm not going to jump out of a window *after* I pay, I'm going to eat my damn barbecue."

The cashier clears his throat, holding out my change. I attempt a smile in his direction and take it from his outstretched hand.

"I'm just saying, I haven't had the greatest experience with men paying for things lately," I say, taking my number and stepping aside so Eli can pay for his meal.

"Besides," Eli says, ignoring my last statement and taking out his wallet, "I can't imagine you being any more of a pain in the ass than you already have been, so I wouldn't even have a good reason to jump out the window."

"Wow, I can't wait to share a meal with you," I dead-pan, and Eli laughs, taking his change and grabbing his number.

"Besides, I'm pretty sure you'll sleep with me," he says as we walk away from the counter.

I pretend he didn't say anything. We sit. The topic changes. We talk food. Eli goads me into predicting how long the couple from last weekend is going to stay married (I say a year, he says nine months).

We talk about whether Montgomery is wearing a toupee. We talk about whether that's his real accent. Eli tells me his theory that Montgomery is actually a New Yorker who saw *Gone with the Wind* one too many times and decided to come try it out for himself.

The food comes. We dig in, and for once Eli's right: this place is great.

"Or maybe," Eli says, pausing with his barbecue sandwich held in front of his face, "he's got that accent so he can be shitty to his employees and it still sounds cultured and genteel."

I dunk a hush puppy into barbecue sauce.

"Does it sound genteel?" I ask. "Usually, when something gets screwed up and he's giving me hell for it, it just sounds shitty."

"I wonder if we could get him to crack," Eli muses. "Do something that makes him drop the act and go back to his carpetbagger accent. What?"

"Did you just say *carpetbagger*?" I ask, a hush puppy halfway to my mouth as I give Eli a *look*. "Are you ninety? Did you time travel here from the 1870s?"

"People say that," he protests.

"They don't," I tell him, biting in.

"My granddad did."

"I'm pretty sure that only proves my point," I say around a mouthful of hush puppy.

"Fine, we do something that makes him reveal his *yankee* accent. Better?" he teases.

"Maybe we start talking with ridiculously over-exaggerated Brooklyn accents," I muse. "See if that gets him to switch."

Eli grins, laughing, and I can't help but grin back. He's handsome as hell even here, in a hole-in-the-wall with a dot of barbecue sauce on his chin.

"He's going to think we've had strokes," he says.

"Well, we have to study," I say, like it's obvious. "We'll practice for a few months first, really nail it, and then one day—"

"I've got better things to do than practice a Brooklyn accent just to see if my boss is faking it," he says.

"Like what?" I tease.

Eli's sticks his thumb in his mouth, licking the last of the barbecue sauce from it.

"Take me home and I'll show you," he says, grinning, his dark hair flopping over his forehead, his eyes ablaze.

It's unfair. He's sitting here, at a tiny table in a hole-in-the-wall barbecue joint, eating off of paper plates, and he's so sexy that if he wanted to bend me over and do it right here, I'd probably say yes.

Seven billion people in the world, and Eli Fucking Loveless is the one I can't help myself around.

I lean forward, across the tiny table, and grab his wrist. I close my eyes and bring his fingers to my mouth, sucking the barbecue sauce off of them, running my tongue along the rough pads.

When I finish, he looks at me, that feral look that I've gotten so familiar with in the past few days. I flick my tongue over a fingerprint one more time, my core already heating up.

"That was weird," he murmurs, his voice low and rough. There's another couple on the far side of the room, but I don't think they're watching us. At any rate, I don't know them, so who cares?

"You liked it, though," I say, smiling.

He slips his hand into mine. Tingles rush over my skin because we're in public, because I like the way everything he does feels, because Eli feels like driving a pickup truck too fast over a narrow bumpy road, like every swerve and jostle might be the one that does me in.

"You gonna take me home or what?" he asks, the pad of his thumb rubbing over the back of my hand, even that small amount of friction causes heat.

"You're driving," I point out.

"Think we can make it?"

That smile. The half-hitched one that makes his eyes

light up, the one that makes him look rakish and dirty and everything I thought I didn't like in men.

"I think we better," I say, and stand up.

We toss our trash and tell the owner thanks. Eli opens the back door for me and we practically run across the gravel parking lot to his Bronco. When he opens the passenger door for me, his hand is already on my ass and he turns me around to face him.

"You should wear this skirt more often," he says, pressing against me, my back against the seat, both of us standing between the open door and the side of the car.

"Don't tell me what to wear," I say.

He bends down, kisses me. It's slow but rough, needy, his erection already throbbing against my hip. He pulls back and bites my lip as he does, leaving me breathless.

"It was just a suggestion," he says lightly, his eyes sparking. "I know better than to tell you what to do."

He kisses me again. Harder, his hand digging into my hip. Behind him are the lights of the Ace in the Hole, the road beyond that, this spot anything but private.

I kiss him back. I can't help it. I slide one hand around his waist, feeling the warm muscles under his skin, and pull him into me.

One hand on my thigh, Eli tugs at my skirt, finding the hem, his fingers slip beneath it.

I put one hand on his chest and push him away.

"We should go," I whisper.

He just grins, moving his hand higher.

"Eli."

"Your house is forty minutes away," he says. "That's an awful long time."

"So drive fast," I say, sliding one finger beneath the waistband of his pants.

"I can't drive *that* fast," he says. "Besides, nobody's out here."

"Eli," I say, my hand moving down.

Somehow, it finds its way to the bulge in his pants, his grip on me tightens.

"You can't say my name in that tone of voice while you're grabbing my cock," he says, sounding absolutely wicked. "You know that, don't you, Violet?"

"Think of it as a preview," I say, squeezing.

He shuts his eyes and groans quietly.

"For what'll happen once you drive me home," I tease.

"I've got tinted windows."

We kiss, slowly. His hand moves up my leg and I squeeze his cock again.

"The backseat's pretty big," he goes on. "I've got a tarp I can use to protect your honor if anyone catches us."

"The words every girl wants to hear," I tease him, our lips still touching.

He just laughs. He kisses me, his other hand now in my hair, my heart racing.

"I'll put it over us," he goes on. "Anyone who looks in will just think I've got some dogs under there."

I can't help but laugh, even as he presses himself against me, so hard I can feel the ridge around the head of his cock through his pants.

"I don't know how I can refuse an offer like *that*," I say.

Eli swipes one finger under my panties and along my swollen lips, his tongue curling into my mouth.

"Doesn't feel like you want to," he teases.

My fingers find the zipper on his pants. His thumb flicks past my clit and I gasp, my whole body going rigid.

Just do it right here, I think. *Bend over the passenger seat, hike up your skirt and maybe no one will notice.*

Apparently, I'm so horny I've lost my mind.

"Eli," I growl, taking my hand from his cock.

"Say it again."

I clear my throat, pull back.

"*Eli.*"

I grab his wrist, pull his hand out from under my skirt.

"I like the way my name sounds in your mouth," he teases.

Behind him, a door slams. I stand bolt upright, pushing at Eli's chest. He glances over his shoulder casually.

The other couple from the restaurant are walking through the parking lot, toward another car, parked at the far end. I take the chance to recollect my senses and tug my skirt down. Eli pulls away. I hop into the passenger seat, and he stands next to me, one hand on the doorframe, every muscle in his arm called into high definition.

"You sure you're passing up the tarp in the backseat?" he asks.

"Positive," I say.

I lean back against the seat.

"You taking me home or what?" I ask, as sweetly as I can.

He leans in to kiss me one more time, but that's all he does.

"Fast as I can," he says, and shuts the door.

CHAPTER TWENTY-EIGHT

ELI

We don't make it past her kitchen table. We don't even get our clothes all the way off, because for the whole twenty-five minute drive I'm glancing over at her and she's laughing, teasing me, the hem of her skirt a fraction of an inch higher every time I look.

The moment I pull into her driveway she leans over, kisses me, grabs my cock with one hand. I nearly explode right there in front of her house, in full view of the entire trailer park.

It's hard and fast, her skirt pushed up over her hips, her shirt unbuttoned. I don't even get my pants off before she's bent over the table and I'm rolling on a condom.

But it's good. It's so fucking good that the rest of the world may as well cease to exist, because it feels like there's nothing but me and Violet and this kitchen table, two bodies somehow made to fit together like clockwork.

Violet's a revelation. Every single time we kiss it feels brand new, like I've never been kissed before. Every time we touch, her skin is electric. I want her like I've never wanted anyone. I haven't been a virgin for a long time, but she makes me feel like one.

It feels almost like a cosmic joke, that we're so physically compatible.

If only we never had to talk, we'd be the perfect couple.

I come buried deep inside her. I pull her hair, her head drops back as she moans my name, back arched, my other hand pinching a nipple while her pussy is still fluttering and clenching around me. Violet rocks back against me like she still wants more.

"I like it when you come that hard," I murmur in her ear.

I soften my grip on her hair, suddenly aware that I could hurt her. She turns her head, takes me by the back of my neck.

"I like it when you fuck that hard," she says.

I lean over and kiss her. The angle's awkward, but I couldn't care less right now.

"Who are you?" I ask between kisses. "And where the fuck is Violet, who would never say that?"

She laughs, her nose grazing my cheek.

"What, that I like fucking?"

"That you like anything I do."

I pull out before I go soft inside her. Violet leans against the table for a moment, looks around, and then sits on her kitchen floor and leans back against a table leg.

"Just this one thing," she teases. Her shoes are off, her skirt hiked up, her shirt unbuttoned, her bra unhooked and loosely shoved over her tits so her pink nipples are on display, her hair disheveled.

It's the hottest, most beautiful thing I've seen in my life. I just look at her, my mouth going dry.

I join her on the floor, leaning back on my hands, the

scarred linoleum cool beneath my palms, my leg nuzzled against hers.

"I'll take it," I say. "And here I thought you were impossible to please."

"I'm perfectly reasonable, Eli," she says, her eyes laughing. "You've just got a difficult personality."

"You know what's not difficult?" I say.

There's a strand of hair strung across her face, and without thinking, I tuck it behind her ear, her skin soft and flushed under my fingers.

"What?"

I just point to my dick, which is still out. Violet laughs, running a hand through her hair.

"For once, you're right," she says, then sits up straight. "I'm gonna go put on pajamas. You staying over?"

She says it so casually, like it's a natural part of our four-day-old non-relationship. Sure, I slept here once, but it was an accident.

"I don't have clothes here," I say, watching her stand.

"You wear the same thing every day," she says, shrugging out of her blouse. "No one will notice."

"If I didn't know any better I'd swear you were trying to talk me into it," I say.

She pulls her bra off, unzips her skirt, lets it puddle on the kitchen floor and she's suddenly, gloriously naked in her kitchen.

"I like it when you make me breakfast," she says, winks at me, and disappears into her bedroom.

· · · · ★ ★ ★ ★ ★ · · · ·

That night stretches into two, then three. A few days becomes a week, ten days, a fortnight, and before I know it, Violet and I have been friends with benefits for a month.

Well, "friends." It'll have to do as a moniker, because I don't know another word for "person who irritates the living daylights out of me until she takes her clothes off, at which point she becomes my own personal sex goddess, custom-built to satiate my physical desires."

"Friends" is at least shorter.

I spend about five nights a week at her house. She gets me a toothbrush. I start leaving clothes over there. It's all purely for convenience, because it would be stupid to carry shirts and a toothbrush with me every day.

We fuck in nearly every room in her house, on nearly every surface. I learn her inside and out: that she likes watching me fuck her from behind in the mirror. That there's a spot deep inside her pussy that makes her legs shake. That we both like fucking in the shower, her detachable showerhead aimed at her clit.

It's an informative month, is what I'm saying.

I don't tell anyone besides Daniel, even though I'm clearly no longer spending much time at my mom's house, other than our weekly Sunday dinners. My mom has to know that something is up, but she hasn't said anything to me. Maybe Daniel's covering for me.

At any rate, she seems to stop worrying.

· · · · * * ★ * * · · · ·

"TELL me one more time what sliding rocks are," Violet says. She's sitting in the passenger seat of my Bronco, her feet on the dashboard, her legs stretched all the way out. I'm studiously ignoring them, as well as the fact that all she's wearing is cutoff shorts and a bikini top.

If, at any point in the last ten years, you'd told me that one, Violet Tulane would go *anywhere* in just shorts and a bikini top, and two, that I'd be impossibly distracted by it,

I'd have laughed. Except here we are: she's doing it, and it's driving me a little crazy.

"They're rocks," I explain, very slowly. "And you slide down them."

Violet doesn't even look at me as she flips me off, and I laugh.

"There's moss so you don't get too scraped up," I say. "It's fun. My father used to take us here sometimes when we started driving Mom a little too crazy."

Then I stop. There's a silence like I've dropped something over the top of us, and I keep my eyes on the road.

It's the first time I've mentioned my father to Violet. She knows the story, of course. Everyone here knows the story, but it's something that's always existed between us unspoken.

We're just fuck buddies, two people scratching each other's itches, and that's all. We don't get too personal, and discussing our respective dead parents seems pretty personal.

"He take all five of you?" she asks, like it's nothing at all.

"A couple of times?"

"And none of you ever died or drowned?"

"Levi did hit his head on a tree branch once," I admit.

"That explains a lot," she says.

"And Caleb broke his arm."

"Next you're gonna tell me that actually, there were six of you and the sliding rocks are the reason there's five now," she teases.

"I think five was plenty for my parents," I say. "I think they kept going because Mom wanted a girl, but after a while she decided a sixth wasn't worth risking another one of us."

"She's a wise woman."

"I'm sitting right here, Violet. I can hear you."

"I should hope so," she teases, and we lapse into silence for a moment, the dappled sunlight filtering through the trees, speckling the car as I drive. I turn off of the main road onto an unlined pavement, then off the pavement and onto a dirt road. After a while it ends in a big dirt patch, and I park.

"All right," I say. "You brave enough for this?"

Violet's not looking at me. She's looking through the windshield, at the bright green foliage in the hard sunlight, the forest so dense it looks like a wall. We had the windows open, so the dust from the road filters into the car, making the air around her shimmer.

Suddenly she turns and those eyes settle on me.

"I'm sorry I called you a moron the day after he died," she says.

I'm literally speechless. Even though I'd carried that with me for ten years, even though when I saw her washing dishes it was one of the first things that popped into my mind, I'd forgotten about it in the past month.

Or, at least, I'd forgiven it. Ten years is a long time and despite her numerous faults, Violet's not that girl anymore.

"Thanks," I say.

"I didn't know he'd died," she says, still wide-eyed in the passenger seat. "I like to think I would have been nicer if I'd known."

I don't point out that calling someone a moron isn't nice ever.

"I only went to the geography bee because I didn't want you to win by default," I admit.

"There were other people competing."

I half-smile at her, and she half-smiles back.

"What, like Dwayne Carson and Mabel Lean? Those morons didn't stand a chance," I say. "Someone had to stop you and it sure wasn't going to be them. Until I got Trinidad and Togo backward, at least."

"And then, none of it mattered," Violet says, looking through the windshield again, grabbing her left arm with her right hand like she's cold. "You flunked out of college. I got into Yale but had to go to the state school instead, and now we're both here."

"I'm sorry about your mom," I tell her. It feels like the right thing to say in this sun-dappled, quiet, raw moment.

"Thanks," she says. "You know how sometimes you hear about parents whose kids died, and they keep their rooms exactly the same for years and years, like they're gonna come back?"

I don't answer her, I just wait.

"I did that with her room," Violet says. She sounds far away, strange. "I took all the medical equipment out because I had to give it back, but everything else I just… kept. It's that door by the kitchen. I never go in there."

"I know the door," I tell her.

"It's not that I think she's coming back," Violet says. "I know she's not. I've got her ashes. It's that…"

"You don't have to explain it," I say. "I know."

She's frozen, staring forward. Without thinking I unbuckle, slide across the center console, and then she's in my arms. I press my lips to the top of her head and she leans into my chest, her seatbelt still on.

This is dangerous. It's dangerous the way drugs are dangerous, because it feels too good. It feels warm and right, soothing, like there's a deeply tangled piece of me coming untwisted in this moment. It feels like the world outside my Bronco has stopped so that we can be here, together, warm and safe.

But getting drunk feels good. Cocaine feels good.

Heroin feels good, and everyone knows those are dangerous.

I ignore the danger and don't move. We stay that way for a while, until finally Violet takes a deep breath, pulls away, gives me a quick kiss on the lips and the moment is over.

"Come on," she says. "Let's go slide down some rocks or whatever."

CHAPTER TWENTY-NINE

VIOLET

"Where are you?" the bride demands, stomping away from us, one finger held out in our direction.

Lydia puts her clipboard down, holding it in front of her with both hands folded over each other, her lips thin. I glare daggers at this woman's back as she walks away, having just answered her phone in the middle of Lydia's sentence.

"She didn't even say *excuse me, I need to take this*," Lydia mutters to me. "She just stuck her finger in my damn face."

It's been a long afternoon. A *really* long afternoon.

"It'll be over soon," I promise.

"Cool, then we can deal with some other bitchy princess who thinks all other humans are her servants," Lydia huffs.

"Oh, it's not always like that," I remind her. "Sometimes it's the groom who's the nightmare."

She snorts, but I think it does the trick.

In reality, most of our brides are lovely, delightful people who are perfectly easy to work with.

They're just not the ones that make an impression.

"Send me a video!" the bride shouts. She's now holding her phone away from her face, and even though we're outdoors in the rose garden, I'm pretty sure they can hear her in West Virginia.

"Someone's in trouble," Lydia mutters.

"Video, Edgerton!" she screams. "I want to know where you are and who you're with!"

"Uh oh," I mutter to Lydia.

"Edgerton, I swear to God — who is that?"

"She got a video?" Lydia whispers.

We exchange a glance, then both turn partially away from our screaming, shouting bride, like we're giving her privacy.

We're not. We could probably hear her clear across the garden, and besides, she's the one who started this phone call in front of us, not the other way around — not to mention that she's been a demanding asshole all afternoon.

I am not looking forward to this wedding.

I *am* looking forward to getting drunk after it's over.

"*Reginald's yacht*?" she screams. "Get off that boat right this instant! You know how I feel about Reggie, and if his whore of a — was she wearing a bikini?"

Lydia and I cringe in unison. Payton — the angry bride — already spent several minutes this afternoon detailing how she likes to punish her fiancé, Edgerton, by withholding sex for a week whenever he does something she doesn't like.

Apparently, when she discovered a Victoria's Secret catalog at his house, she wouldn't sleep with him for a month.

I have no idea why they're getting married. They don't even seem to like each other.

"—Betrayed and *humiliated* right now," she's saying.

"First we had to get married at this shithole while I wanted that private island in the Maldives, then you send me out here to the asshole of nowhere, surrounded by inbred hicks—"

"We're standing *right here*," Lydia hisses to me.

"—While you party in the Greek Isles with Reginald and a bunch of sluts?"

"At least we're not sluts," I murmur to Lydia.

"Speak for yourself," she whispers, and I have to bite my lip so I don't laugh.

"Baby—" the man on the phone says. She's got the volume cranked up loud enough that I can hear.

"Don't you *baby* me," Payton shouts. "I want you off that boat right this instant—"

"—But, baby—"

"—Or I swear you won't be getting any of this pussy until Christmas —"

Lydia and I make *what the fuck* goggle eyes at each other.

"—Come on, baby—"

"—And you can forget about my lips coming near your dick until this time next year—"

I'm holding my breath and Lydia's doing the same, both of us turned away from Payton like we're giving her privacy. We're not. There's no such thing as privacy when you're screaming about your pussy in public.

"Should we leave?" I whisper.

"What if that only makes her angrier?"

"—I swear, it's like you don't even want to get married, Edgerton."

There's a long, long, silence.

It gets longer. I desperately want to leave, only based on today's events, I think that might just make her start screaming at me instead of him. You know that scene in

Jurassic Park where the kids are in the Jeep, and the T-Rex is coming, and if they move they'll get eaten?

I feel kind of like that.

"Edgerton!"

"Maybe I don't," he finally says, sounding like a sulky thirteen-year-old.

"Don't you dare start that," she says. "You're coming out here tomorrow and we're getting married like you wanted to—"

"This was all your idea," he says, in the same tone of voice. "I just wanted to hang out for a while, but you wanted to get married."

Lydia and I exchange a glance. I start sidling away from Payton and her phone conversation, because I just can't take this anymore. There's schadenfreude and then there's enjoying someone else's misery, and I've got no interest in the second.

"Reginald's whore of a sister tried to seduce you again, didn't she?" Payton says.

Lydia joins me in sidling away, toward the Lodge, where at least we can close a door and hear a little less of the shouting.

"She puts out even if I use the wrong fork at dinner," Edgerton says.

Lydia and I look at each other, and suddenly we're power walking towards the Lodge, for the sweet, sweet door that will separate us from this horror show.

"*What?*" Payton screeches. I swear she's so loud that a flock of birds startles out of a tree.

Lydia reaches the door, pulls it open, and I dart through. She follows, shutting the door behind us, leaving Payton alone in the rose garden, shouting into a video call with her fiancé. The receptionist looks up, sees it's us, and looks back down at her computer.

"I don't think we're having a wedding this weekend," Lydia says.

· · · · · ★ ★ ★ ★ ★ · · · · ·

TWO HOURS LATER, I walk into my office to find Eli sitting at my chair, behind my desk.

"This place is cute," he says. He's sitting sideways, his legs out, lounging in my chair and looking at something on the screen.

"Don't look at my computer," I say. "And especially don't look at the folder labeled 'Plotting Eli's Downfall.'"

I don't actually care if he looks at my work computer. What's he gonna find, seating charts? I'm not dumb or crazy enough to keep anything remotely interesting on there.

"I don't see that one," he drawls. "I just see this one called 'Very hot porn,' and it's… all drawings of me, naked?"

"Dammit," I hiss, glancing at the door.

"It's nearly six, everyone's gone," he says, lowering his voice.

"Still," I say, and come around my desk to see what he's looking at.

It's the listing for the lake cabin. The dream house, with the high ceilings and lots of light and subway tiles over the farmhouse sink.

"You thinking of buying a place?" he asks, idly flipping through the pictures.

I reach over and use the keyboard to close the window.

"I live in a trailer, of course I'm *thinking* of buying a place," I say. "I'm always thinking of ways to get out of there."

"That one's got a nice kitchen," he says thoughtfully. "Wasted on you, obviously, but…"

Eli shrugs, trails off like there's something he thought better of saying.

"But what? Get out of my chair," I say, shooing him.

"But I'd know how to use it," he says, not moving.

He makes a *sit on my lap* gesture.

I give him my *fuck no, we're still at work* face.

He rolls his eyes playfully and stands up, ceding my chair back to me. I sit, flipping through my one thousand open windows, saving and closing and making a few last-minute notes for tomorrow.

I don't think Saturday's wedding is going to go well, which is probably the understatement of the century. Having worked here for a few years, I've witnessed more than a few weddings that nearly blew up in the days before, and every single one of them was *deeply* unpleasant as an employee.

"Nine?" he asks.

I write one last note — *ranunculus!* — stick it to my desk, then look up at him. It's been over a month since our arrangement, and somehow, every time he asks me about coming over my heart *still* beats faster.

"Nine sounds good."

"I promised my mom and Daniel I'd make them dinner tonight," he says, keeping his voice low.

"They still think that you're getting drunk every night and sleeping on some coworker's couch?" I tease.

"That was a good story once," he says defensively.

"And how many times have you used it, now?" I ask.

Eli nudges a giant box in the corner of my office with his foot.

"That's beside the point. Please tell me this mechanical bull is for a rodeo-themed wedding this weekend?"

"This weekend's wedding is hell-on-earth themed," I tell him. "And I think the mechanical bull is punishment for something terrible I did in a past life."

"Bonus drink floats?" he says, crouching to inspect the box. "This mechanical bull floats?"

"I don't know," I say, warding off any questions. "Whoever stole my wallet bought it, but it got shipped here anyway."

"So whoever stole your wallet was more fun than you," Eli says, standing.

I come around my desk and stand right in front of him. We're much closer than coworkers should be standing.

"I'm not fun?" I tease him.

Eli takes his time, letting his eyes wander down my face, pausing on my lips, that familiar light coming into his eyes.

"*Now* who's getting us in trouble at work?" he finally says.

"I'm doing no such thing, Eli Loveless," I murmur, looking at him through my eyelashes. "We're having a completely professional interaction right now."

I still hate how much I want him, for the record. I also hate that, at least once a day, I have to shake myself out of the dirtiest daydreams I've ever had.

One hundred percent Eli's fault. He's distracting.

"Well, do you need me to carry your mechanical bull to your car for you, Miss Tulane?" he offers.

"No, Mister Loveless, I'm leaving it here because I need to return it anyway," I say.

"There goes my excuse to walk you out."

"You could just be a gentleman."

He gives me that half-hitched smile. It does things to me, just like it does every damn time.

"Who'd believe that?"

I lean one millimeter closer. I swear Eli has his own

gravity field, like he's the earth and I'm a meteor, circling inward until I crash and burn.

"True," I say. "I guess you'll have to—"

"Oh good, you're still here," Montgomery's voice says from my doorway.

I jump away from Eli so fast I trip over my own feet and have to catch myself on my desk. I clear my throat, righting myself. I push one hand through my hair, doing the worst job of acting cool and collected that I've ever done in my life, adrenaline stabbing through my veins as Montgomery casually walks into my office.

It's not a big office. Three people is too many, particularly when two of those people are having a covert affair and trying to keep it under wraps at the workplace.

"I was just about to leave," I say, my voice slightly higher-pitched than usual.

Eli just nods in agreement.

"Well, you may as well both hear this," Montgomery says. "Saturday's wedding has been canceled."

There's a beat of silence in my office, while I just blink at Montgomery.

"It has?" I ask.

I'm genuinely surprised. Not because I think that Payton and Edgerton are a match made in heaven, but because people rarely cancel events that cost them half a million dollars. Months and months of work go into planning a wedding. Hundreds of people fly in. It's a huge undertaking.

Generally speaking, people elect to have the party and then get the union itself annulled a month later if things aren't working out. But they always have the party.

"Indeed it has," Montgomery says. "And given the extremely late notice we've been given regarding the dissolution of this union, we've elected to throw the party anyway and invite the good people of Sprucevale."

Eli and I look at each other, then back at Montgomery.

"It'll be a considerably more casual affair, of course," he says. "But there's no point in letting everything go to waste, right?"

"Right," Eli echoes.

"Besides," Montgomery smiles. "We'll call it a charity event and get the tax write-off. It's win-win. Go home, we'll work out the details tomorrow."

And just like that, he leaves.

"I don't think that's what win-win means," Eli says, keeping his voice low so Montgomery can't hear him. "Who's the other winner?"

I just shake my head.

CHAPTER THIRTY

ELI

"Which one's your new best friend?" Seth asks.

I flip a steak over on the grill and take another pull from the beer he just brought me.

"My new best friend?" I echo, like I'm not really paying attention.

I'm standing on the grilling patio outside my kitchen at work, finishing up my part of the All Sprucevale Block Party that Montgomery sprung on us with thirty-six hours' notice. Thankfully it's much more laid back than any wedding — which is why Seth is here, hassling me, instead of being served hors d'oeuvres next to an ice sculpture or whatever this weekend was supposed to be like.

"According to Daniel you're spending most of your nights getting tanked and then sleeping on your coworker's couch," Seth goes on. "It's just so nice to see you making friends that I was wondering whose couch it is."

I sigh and look over at my younger brother. Seth looks back at me with a perfectly straight face, but I'm not stupid.

"I just need to tell Mom something when I don't come home," I say, hoping it'll be enough explanation. "She worries, but staying there gets a little old sometimes, and I haven't found my own place yet, so…"

"So you're letting her and Daniel think you routinely get too drunk to come home?"

I pretend to check the steaks, cursing myself for using that excuse more than once. Problem is, I haven't come up with a better one — the second I tell them there's a girl, they'll all want to know who and I'll never have a moment of peace again. Mom might start planning a wedding. Rusty will want to be a flower girl, but it's not that kind of relationship.

What am I supposed to say to *my mother* about that? *Don't worry, we're just fucking*? I can't say that to my mom.

On the other hand, there's no way that she doesn't know something is up. I'm lying, they know I'm lying, and can't we all just live in this nice world we've created without Seth sticking his nose into the middle of it?

"I promise I'll get my own place soon and my getting-drunk-every-night phase will end," I tell Seth. "Did she send you over just to ask me about this?"

"I came to see if I could get the truth out of you," Seth says, grinning. "Guess not."

I take another long pull from the beer, then start taking the filet mignon off the grill and stacking them onto a platter. It feels weird to serve all this top-tier wedding food buffet-style for a few hundred of our closest friends, but we already had all the food, and it wasn't like we could return shrimp and steak.

"Don't you have somewhere to be besides harassing me?" I ask Seth, still removing steaks, piling them on the plate.

"No," he says.

"Pretty sure I just saw Mindy Drake heading toward

the bar," I say. "Isn't it about time for you two to make up again?"

"Hilarious," he deadpans.

"Or, who'd you leave her for? Amber Stremp? Though right now I can't remember if you were most recently with her or her cousin, what's her name..."

"Oh, fuck off," Seth says, but I can tell I'm getting to him. "I can't date around?"

"You call it dating now?" I say, getting the last steak off and shutting the grill. "That's not the word I heard."

"There were some misunderstandings."

"What was it that got spray-painted on your car, again?" I ask.

Seth glares. I grin, reach out, and click my beer against his.

I drink. He glares a little more.

"Was that before or after Mindy got your name tattooed on her—"

"That's not true," Seth says quickly. He quits glaring at me and drinks his beer. "At least, I'm pretty sure it's not true."

It's fair to say that Seth has a reputation. He's got enough of a reputation that even though I've only been around for a few months, I could name at least three girls who he's charmed and then dumped.

"I thought we agreed on *casual*," he says. "Apparently that word doesn't mean what I think it does."

"It must be rough being a serial heartbreaker," I tell him.

"Shut up, Eli," he says, but there's no heat behind it now. "Least I'm not telling my own mother I'm an alcoholic just to get out of admitting where I really am."

Admit nothing, I tell myself. *He's bluffing.*

"I'm doing no such thing," I tell Seth. "I'm drunk. Constantly. Irreparably."

He just raises one eyebrow.

"That *is* exactly the sort of thing an alcoholic would say," he deadpans. "Always telling people how drunk they are when they're clearly sober."

"I can call Mindy over here if you like," I tell him. "I think I see her over there, and she's putting her hand on Bradley Thompson's arm, squeezing his bicep? She's got two margaritas in her other hand?"

"Good, he can deal with her mess," Seth says, perfectly straight-faced. "Meanwhile, you can keep on—"

"Seth, we discussed this," Levi's voice suddenly says from behind me. "We were going to let Eli keep his secret."

He steps up to us. Now we're forming a triangle, Seth, Levi, and I, all drinking beers, standing around. Someone's taken the last of the steaks to the buffet tables, so I'm officially free to party.

Though this is feeling less like a party and more like an inquisition.

"I don't have a secret," I say. "And if I did, I wouldn't tell you two what it was, for fuck's sake."

"Well, I'm convinced," Levi says, looking at Seth. "Aren't you convinced?"

"Utterly," says Seth. They're both trying not to laugh. I cross my arms over my chest and keep drinking my beer, trying not to let them see how much they're getting to me. "This man has got no secrets at all."

Levi glances at me furtively. I ignore him, stone-faced.

"He must not be sleeping with Violet, then," Levi says.

I choke mid-sip. Beer goes up my nose, and I have to turn away, coughing. My asshole brothers just watch me, both smiling without smiling.

They don't know. Do they know?

I'm going to kill Daniel. And then Violet's going to kill me.

"What are you talking about?" I finally say, once I've recovered. "Violet? Tulane?"

"You know another Violet?" Levi asks Seth.

"Wasn't that the name of one of Ricky Camper's barn cats?" Seth says. "Or was that some other color name?"

"I do believe there was a cat named Violet," Levi answers, stroking his beard for effect. "But that was at least twenty years ago and I'm quite sure she's passed on by now."

"I'm not sleeping with Violet," I say, pulling myself together. "That's crazy. We don't even like each other. I just see her at work, that's all. We work together. We're coworkers. Coworkers who work together."

Shut up, I tell myself.

"As opposed to coworkers who sleep together?" Seth asks.

"Why would I sleep with Violet?" I ask, gesturing wildly. I try to make it sound like the thought of sex with her has literally never crossed my mind, not even once.

They're not buying it.

"She's pretty," Levi says.

"She's hot," Seth says. "Last summer I saw her at Wilson's Fourth of July barbecue, and she had on this bikini that really—"

"Okay, okay," I growl, cutting him off before I have to hear any more about how hot he thinks Violet is. "Fine, she's pretty, I'm not sleeping with her, could you just drop it?"

"That's not your Bronco outside her house most nights?" Levi asks calmly.

I feel like he's felled a tree on my head, only the tree is made of information.

I look my older brother dead in the eyes. I swear they're

sparkling with the sheer joy of being difficult. I try to think of an explanation about why my truck is always outside Violet's house, and I can't.

"No," I lie.

I know full well how many twenty-year-old Broncos there are in Sprucevale.

One. There's one.

"That's not you leaving her house most mornings?" Seth adds.

I look my younger brother dead in the eyes this time, and double down.

"No," I lie again.

I don't have a plan. I know it's not working, but total denial is all I've got right now.

Seth turns dramatically to Levi. They're both enjoying the hell out of this. Fuckers.

"We've got a problem," Seth says, his voice dead serious.

"It's the doppelgänger scenario," Levi agrees.

He puts one hand on my shoulder.

"Eli," he says. "Someone's been impersonating you. For weeks, now."

"Fuck off," I say, resigned.

"It does make the most sense," Seth concurs. "I can't imagine Violet sleeping with this grumpy asshole. She's such a nice girl."

"Violet is not *nice*," I say.

"Always been nice to me," Levi says.

"Me too," agrees Seth. "I also hear that she's *real* nice to that doppelgänger you got."

I open my mouth. No sound comes out. My face heats up.

I shut it.

"Did Daniel tell you?" I ask. "He swore—"

Seth grins and claps me on the shoulder.

"I love that you thought it was a secret," he says. "Fifty people drive past your car in her driveway every night, and you know that nobody in this town can keep their mouth shut."

"According to Clive, the two of you exchange morning greetings several times a week," Levi adds in. "That's her next-door neighbor."

They're right, obviously. I don't know how I thought I could keep this a secret in a town the size of Sprucevale, where everyone and their mothers know what kind of car everyone else drives.

"Fine," I say. "We've hooked up a couple of times, it's not a big deal."

Seth and Levi look at each other, but mercifully, they don't say anything.

CHAPTER THIRTY-ONE

VIOLET

I've had too much to drink.

Or, more accurately, I've had more to drink than I probably should at a work function. But then again, the number of drinks one *should* have at a work function is zero, and that's no fun.

It's no fun at all. I, on the other hand, am lots of fun.

"Pivot tables," Clarabelle Loveless is saying, gesturing with her whiskey glass. "I'm telling you, Violet, once you start using them you're never going to look back."

"That's not the question," I say, gesturing as well. "The question is, I've got all these brides who can only, you know, use SnapFace or GramChat or whatever on their phones to take selfies, how do I get *them* to use the pivot tables when they don't even know what Excel is?"

"Everyone knows what Excel is," Adeline objects, standing next to us out on the lawn. Dinner's over — it was the first time I'd ever eaten filet mignon off a paper plate — and now everyone under the age of fourteen is sprinting around, screaming their heads off. It's that kind of party.

"Don't they?" she says. "Tell me they do."

I take another sip. I don't usually drink whiskey, but I don't usually have this kind of week. I've earned it, and besides, my responsibilities here are over. I plan and execute, I don't clean up.

I just shake my head at Adeline, who looks dismayed.

"Mrs. Loveless, I cannot let them near my data," I say. "It would be chaos."

She looks horrified.

"I told you already, it's Clara," Eli's mom says. "And Lord no, child, you don't let *them* use your spreadsheets. Just get the information from them and input it yourself. Don't let other people touch your data."

I just nod sagely. Of course not. How could I be so silly?

"You know what I've gotten really into lately?" I ask her. "Using conditional formatting to color cells. I figured out how to set it up so that the closer a date is, the darker it is, so it's easy to see what's the most urgent at a glance."

"That would also make it very easy to see outliers in a data set at a glance," Clara muses. "You know, that might be very useful for calibrating the — hello, who's this?"

"ANKYLOSAURUS!" shouts Rusty, plowing into her grandmother's knees.

"Goodness!" Clara exclaims, laughing.

"Ankylosaurus says come get ice cream," Rusty says, grabbing Clara's hand.

"All right, baby," Clara says, then holds up her whiskey glass to Adeline and I. "We'll talk more later. Sweetheart, I'm *coming*. Violet, you should come to Sunday dinner. Are you free tomorrow?"

"Sure," I say, my mouth agreeing before my brain can give approval.

Wait, what?

With Eli? And his brothers? And his mom, and his niece?

That's not our agreement. That's not our agreement at all.

"Perfect," Clarabelle says, letting Rusty lead her off. "Four o'clock!"

Then she's gone. Rusty leads her off, excitedly discussing the sorts of ice cream they're about to eat.

When she's out of earshot, Adeline turns to me.

"I have bad news," she says.

I scrunch up my face, waiting for it.

"I feel like she knows," Adeline goes on. "It's just a theory but I'm pretty sure it's right."

"Yeah," I admit.

"I also have more bad news," she says, taking another sip of her drink.

"Go on," I say.

"I think everyone might know," she says.

There's a spiky ball somewhere in the vicinity of my stomach, sharp points dulled by whiskey but still vicious enough to be felt.

"You think," I repeat.

"Mindy Drake was pestering me about it maybe ten minutes ago," she says, making an apologetic face. "She'd had, like, two margaritas but she was saying something about having open arms when he inevitably left you for your cousin? Though she shouted that last part at someone else, it seemed like it wasn't meant for me."

She takes another sip. I think I'm not the only drunk person here right now.

My mind is racing, but it's useless, just *people know, Mindy knows people know, oh shit Mindy knows* over and over again.

I'm in no state for this.

"I don't think I have any cousins he could leave me for," I finally say. "Though I don't really know, my mom didn't talk to her sister anymore and my dad, I mean, who the fuck knows where he got to? You could be my cousin."

"If your dad got around you'd be my half-sister, not my cousin," she points out.

"Whatever."

"Right, so everyone in your trailer park knows that Eli's Bronco has been parked outside your house, like, every night for a month," she says.

The simplicity of it smacks me in the face.

Of *course* everyone knows. We would have had to practically build underground tunnels for this to actually be a secret. Sprucevale is a tiny, incestuous, gossipy town and I really should have known better.

"Fuck," I say.

"And Mindy was trying to get me to tell her details and I will have you know that I gave her *nothing*. Even though she was being super weird. So technically it's all still speculation because even though I know you two are fucking like bunnies, I haven't said a thing."

She looks very pleased with herself.

I hold out one fist. She bumps it with hers.

Everyone knows, I think again. The spiky ball gets pricklier. I swallow, trying to ignore it.

"I think she had a thing with Seth for a while," I tell Adeline. "Does that sound familiar? And she might still be mad about it?"

Adeline rolls her eyes dramatically.

"Who *hasn't* had a thing with Seth?" she says.

"Me," I say.

"Well, also me," she says. "But I think it's just us. Should we be offended?"

"No," I say. "I'd claim that we prefer a better class of men, but the other residents of my trailer park totally just busted my fuckbuddy and you set me up with Todd in the first place, so I think he's just not our type."

"I'll take it," she says, shrugging.

I close my eyes for a second. Things are… unsteady.

"I just agreed to go to his family dinner, didn't I?" I ask.

· · · · · ★ ★ ★ ★ ★ · · · · ·

A FEW MORE HOURS GO BY. I don't get drunker, but I do maintain my current level. I know where the couches are at Bramblebush, and I can crash on one for a while tonight, at least until I sober up.

Apparently *all* of Sprucevale knows about Eli and me. Apparently they've known for quite a while now and tonight's the first time anyone has bothered to tell me that my secret is, in fact, not even slightly secret.

If Mindy knows, I have to assume that everyone knows. His brothers. His mom. Lydia and Kevin. Zane and Brandon. The cashier at the grocery store. The driver who waved me through an intersection this morning.

Probably even Montgomery, though he doesn't live in Sprucevale itself like the rest of us so there's a slim possibility that he doesn't know yet.

My solution is to avoid Eli for the next hour, like that'll keep people from talking.

"I wish they'd widen thirty-nine," I say to Lydia. We're drinking by the fire pit at the far edge of the lawn, the party slowly switching over from 'family fun' to 'after dark drinking.'

"You know they never will," she says, leaning back in her Adirondack chair.

"Every time I drive down it I swear I get stuck behind an eighteen-wheeler doing fifty-five," I say. "It's such a pain."

"Write a letter," she says lazily.

"I'd rather just complain," I say, leaning back into the bench I'm sitting on.

There's a shadow across the fire, a dark space that slowly takes shape.

The second I see it I know it's Eli. I know how he moves, how he walks. I know how he stands, the way he runs his hands through his rumpled hair when he's got something he wants to say and is trying to figure out how to say it.

"I don't think letters work," Lydia admits.

Eli comes around the fire. My stomach twists, flips, excitement charging through me at his mere presence. A knot pops and sparks fly past his face, his eyes never moving from mine, the heated look in them pooling somewhere inside me.

"This seat taken?" he asks, sitting next to me on my bench without waiting for an answer.

"What if I said yes?" I say, lazily. I slouch on the bench, my head against the back of it, and I turn to look at him. My field of vision sloshes. "Would you actually get up and sit somewhere else?"

"Probably not," he admits.

"Then why ask?"

"Because we live in a society where manners are expected," he says, that note of amusement in his voice that drives me up the wall. "Even though it's obvious that no one's sitting here, I say *is this seat taken* and you say *no, please sit down*, but only one of us managed to do it right. Hi, Lydia."

She's trying not to laugh at us.

Does she know? She must know. She knows that this is basically foreplay.

Oh, God.

"Hi, Eli," she says. "Good party."

"Thank you," he says. "Same to you."

"Thanks," she says, and heaves herself out of the chair. "You guys want anything?"

We both decline. Lydia leaves the ring of light cast by the fire, and then, for the first time all night, Eli and I are alone together.

"You're such a dick sometimes," I say, relaxing against the back of the bench, no heat behind my words.

"You wouldn't like me if I weren't," he says.

Something pops in the fire, sparks shooting upward.

"*Do* I like you?" I ask, finally looking over at him.

His smile's slow, deliberate, cocky. He's drunk too. It's in his voice, his exaggerated movements, in the way he looks at me with the raw, naked lust he usually saves for in private.

"You like me plenty," he says. "And there's plenty of me you like."

For once, I don't argue, just look at him and let him know I'm looking: black t-shirt tight around the biceps, across the chest, bulge in the jeans, that easy, relaxed posture that screams *I know how to fuck.*

I want him to touch me and I don't. I want him to take my hand where no one can see. I want one stolen kiss.

I want so, so much more.

But I feel like every single person left at this party is looking at us. I'm fire-blind and can't see more than five feet, right to the edge of the circle of light, but I know I'm easily seen.

We're easily seen.

"Eli," I say, unnecessarily.

"Violet."

"Everyone knows," I say, my voice hushed.

"Knows what?" he asks, his voice low as gravel, secret and quiet and meant only for me, the voice he uses when we're alone together.

I pause. Maybe it's the whiskey but I suddenly realize that I don't know how to answer the question, not exactly.

Or, more accurately, I realize that there are multiple answers.

I could say *they know we're sleeping together.* Simple and true, but in this moment, firelit and drunk, it feels incomplete.

I could say *they know we're dating.* I could say *they know we're together.*

I could say *they know you're my boyfriend* or *they know we're in love* or any one of a hundred other things, and I think they'd come true, just like that.

Words have power. Labels have power, and right now, it all lies with me. I can name what I want and form reality.

But then I remember what and who I'm talking about. It's Eli. If I said *they know you're my boyfriend and we're in love* he'd laugh and say *then they're wrong.*

So I go ahead and strike *boyfriend* and *together* and *in love* out of my lexicon, because none of those things are true.

We're not in love.

We're not even in *like.*

"That we're sleeping together," I say.

Eli just sighs. If he senses the weight of everything I didn't say, he doesn't show it. If he thought, for a moment, that I might label us differently, I can't tell.

"I know," he admits.

"Then why'd you ask?"

"Levi and Seth discussed it with me," he says, ignoring my question.

"Mindy Drake asked Adeline about it," I say.

"You told Adeline?"

"Of course I told Adeline. You didn't tell your brothers?"

Eli sighs, running one hand through his hair.

"Just Daniel, for obvious reasons," he says.

"Not the others?"

He looks at me, green eyes serious. The fire makes the bones of his face stand out, makes his cheekbones and jawline sharper. He looks like a painting, breathtakingly beautiful.

Maybe it's just the whiskey, but suddenly I want to trace every angle with my fingers.

I don't touch. I can't touch. I don't dare.

"I thought you didn't want me to," he says.

"I didn't," I say.

"And now?" he asks me, the syllables low and quiet, secret.

"Now it's not up to me anymore," I say.

Whenever I'm in his orbit, I always feel too far away and right now is no exception. I want him, his touch, his skin on mine. I wake up wanting it. I go to bed wanting it.

"That's not an answer."

"It's a pointless question," I say.

"Violet."

"Does it matter what I want if it runs counter to reality?" I say.

The truth is, I don't know what I want besides *him*. I want him whispering dirty nothings in my ear while he fucks me. I want him teasing me with kisses in a parking lot behind a barbecue shack. I want his arm slung over me as I fall asleep at night and I want him there in the morning, his weight on his side of the bed soothing.

"Look at me."

I do it.

Eli slides his hand into mine, hidden in the valley between our legs where the light doesn't reach. My heart dips and rolls, my head swimming, my impulse control nearly gone with the whiskey.

"Kiss me," he says.

"We're in public," I murmur.

"And?"

"And everyone can see us," I whisper.

My eyes drop to his lips.

"Let them watch," he says. Shivers roll down my spine, the rough pads of his thumb move over the back of my hand. "I've been waiting all night to kiss you. I've been waiting since I left your house this morning."

Me too, I think.

A pause. I don't breathe. His thumb keeps moving, tracing small circles on the back of my hand.

I want it. I want him, his kisses and more, so much that the wanting is palpable, physical, like a cloak I've wrapped myself in.

"Not here," I whisper, my voice barely audible.

"Where?" he asks.

I swallow. My mouth is dry. I know the right answer to this question: *at my house, after we both sober up enough to drive home*.

It's not the answer I give.

"The wedding barn's right over there," is what I say.

"Can we make it?" he asks, his thumb still circling. I swallow hard, shutting my eyes for a moment so I don't have to look at him.

"I have a key," I whisper, still breathless, eyes shut. "I'll go first. Follow me after a few minutes."

I can feel him lean in, the heat that radiates from his skin.

"You won't kiss me in public but you'll fuck me in the barn?" he asks, teasing.

"You make this sound so dirty."

"That's because it is."

I open my eyes, drink him in again. Lord, he's beautiful.

"You promise?" I ask.

Eli just laughs softly.

"All this time together and you still want a promise?" he teases. "And here I thought maybe I'd proven myself."

He leans in by millimeters. If anyone's watching, there can't be any doubt about what we're up to, but I can't stop it. I don't want to.

"Yes, I promise," he says. "I promise that I'm drunk enough to throw caution to the wind and fuck you in the barn. I promise it'll be dirty and perfect and you'll think about it every ten minutes for the next week."

His eyes flick to my lips.

"And I promise that if you don't go right now we're going to do it on this bench," he whispers. "Get outta here."

In the last sensible moment I have that night, I go.

CHAPTER THIRTY-TWO
VIOLET

The wedding barn is dark. I hadn't thought that part through very well. It's dark and possibly full of spiders, because even though we hold events in here all the time, don't spiders naturally gravitate toward barns?

Seems like they would.

I step inside, wait for my eyes to adjust. The barn has high windows and skylights, and after a moment I can see in the moonlight filtering in. Tables and chairs stacked at one end, audio equipment, other various wedding accoutrement.

I walk in. It still smells of hay and dirt, even though there hasn't been an animal in here for twenty years, even though there's a chandelier over my head and a wooden floor under my feet.

And, at the far end, a couple of couches, artfully arranged in a lounge shape, because they needed something to fill the space when the barn was converted. My heart pounds as I walk toward them, wondering exactly how stupid I am, wondering whether I should find the throw pillows and arrange them nicely or just take the dust covers off the couches.

I settle for taking the dust covers off. Motes fly everywhere, caught in the moonlight, and my vision swirls again. I stare for too long.

The door opens, shuts. I hear the bar slide over it and turn toward the sound, not moving.

Soft footsteps on a wooden floor, a pattern I've come to recognize by heart. A dark shape saunters toward me and even though I can't see the smile, I can feel it vibrate through the air.

And then: Eli's lips are on mine. His thumb is on my cheekbone, his fingers in my hair, his body against mine.

There's a moment of sweetness, tenderness. His hand skims along my waist. His tongue darts at my lower lip. There's a moment where his fingers sift through my hair gently, where his touch is tentative, gentle.

Then he pulls away. He traces his thumb under my lower lip.

"I've had too much whiskey," he murmurs.

"For what?" I ask, suddenly alarmed.

Eli laughs.

"For kissing you like this," he says, his other hand sliding down my arm, taking me by the wrist. "For all this sweet foreplay bullshit where we kiss like we're lovers and not like we're trying to destroy each other."

He plants my hand on his cock. It feels like steel beneath denim, and reflexively, I grab it through his jeans.

"Don't worry, Violet, I'm not too drunk to fuck," he rasps, right into my ear.

I slide my hand along his thick length. I'm already wet as fuck and getting wetter by the second.

"Is this too much sweet foreplay bullshit?" I ask, the heel of my hand on his cock.

"You could do better," he growls.

I kiss his neck, then bite it. He's smoky from the grill, his skin salty beneath that, and I yank his pants unbuttoned, shove my hand inside without even unzipping him.

He groans when I find his cock, hard and hot and thick in my hand.

"Still too sweet?"

"You're getting there," he says, and pulls my shirt off. My bra follows and then I reel backwards, onto the couch, where I fall, his zipper now undone as he leans over me and pumps himself into my grip.

Eli kisses me hard. He pinches my nipples until I moan into his mouth, pushes my knees apart, kneels on the edge of the couch.

I squeeze him harder, faster. Precum runs down his shaft now as he unbuttons and unzips me and I arch my back, our mouths still together roughly, his hand under my panties.

There's no teasing. Eli slides two fingers into me and I moan, biting his lip. His other hand pinches a nipple, my hips rising off the couch until I'm gasping and moaning in the same breath.

He thrusts forward, his cock moving smoothly through my hand, its tip almost at my chest. His fingers move inside me and I grip him tighter.

"You don't even need foreplay," he growls. "All I had to do was say *let's fuck in the barn* and you're soaking wet."

"I've also had plenty of whiskey," I remind him.

His fingers move again, crooking, stroking my sensitive inner wall, the heel of his hand against my clit.

"That's not the whiskey," he says, that cocky smile on his face. "That's the promise of getting bent over this couch with my cock buried in you."

He kisses me again, hard and rough, his hand still moving inside me while I moan into his mouth.

"Told you I was drunk," he murmurs. "There I go, telling you all my plans."

I pump his cock again. Eli groans.

"Tell me your other plans," I say.

"You want me to talk dirty to you, Violet?"

"I want to know what I'm in for," I gasp.

He shifts. I stroke his cock, and he slides a third finger into me. I whimper with pleasure.

"I'm going to take you right to the edge and then I'm going to stop," he murmurs. "I'm going to get those pants off of you, flip you over, and lick your pussy while you scream into the couch cushions so no one outside can hear you."

Heat pools inside me, desire and pressure swirling. I tremble with every motion of his fingers, my whole body tense and taut, ready to explode.

"What else?" I whisper.

"Then I'm going to fuck you as hard and deep as I possibly can," he says.

Every inch of my skin tingles.

"And when you're finally begging me to make you come, maybe I'll let you," he goes on.

There's that half-hitched smile, the cocky one, the I'm-in-control-here smile that drives me crazy in every single way.

"Maybe," he says.

I draw his head down to mine, kiss him again, hard and slow as his fingers move inside me. I roll my hips, still stroking his length.

"You want me to beg?" I murmur into his mouth.

"I want you to at least say please," he murmurs back.

I bite his lip, sitting forward. Eli growls in response, his fingers sliding out of me.

Then I lean forward and wrap my lips around the thick head of his cock.

"Oh *fuck*," Eli hisses.

I grab his hips, dig my fingers in, slide my lips down until I can't take any more of him. He grunts as he bumps the back of my throat and I flatten my tongue against the smooth underside of his cock.

I move my head back. I go slow, teasing him, listening to his breathing quicken. His fingers work their way through my hair again, the ridge of his head under my lips as I swirl my tongue around him.

He groans. I suck him in again, my hand wrapped around his root. Before I know it I'm off the couch, on my knees in front of him, sucking his cock as hard as I can.

Eli's fist closes in my hair. He pushes my head down on his shaft, until he hits the back of my throat. I swallow, my tongue moving against him. We do it again and again. I lose myself in the rhythm, in the pleasure of listening to him.

Without meaning to, I reach down, between my legs. I find my own soft heat, so wet my thighs are sticky, my pants already unbuttoned but not off, and I circle my swollen clit the way I have a thousand times before.

As I pull back, I moan into Eli's cock.

"More," he murmurs, and I move my fingers faster, do it again.

This time I moan louder, harder. Eli's hand in my hair gets rougher, more insistent with each stroke. It's not sweet and it's not gentle, but my God, it's satisfying.

Suddenly he pulls me back until my lips are just barely touching him. I lick him slowly, ridge to tip, savoring the shudder that moves through his body.

"You don't like it?" I tease.

"I can't fuck you properly if I come in your mouth," he says. "As much as I like doing that, too."

His other hand is on my face, his thumb on my chin. It still smells like me, and without thinking, I suck his thumb into my mouth, lick the pad with my tongue.

Eli watches me, mesmerized. He pulls his thumb out and I take his finger, still sticky with my own juices, lick it clean.

"You're beautiful," he murmurs.

I pause for a moment, mid-lick. It's not what I was expecting to hear.

"And you're getting yourself off," he says, finally noticing what my other hand is doing. "Do you like sucking my cock that much?"

I don't answer, just lick his fingers while he watches me, his cock pulsing in my hand.

"Maybe," I finally say.

Eli takes my wrist, and then he's on his knees in front of me. He pulls his fingers from my mouth and licks them himself, eyes sparking, then pulls my other hand from where I'm pleasuring myself.

"Can't a girl have fun?" I tease.

I pull at his shirt and instantly it's off, his hard muscles shining in the dim moonlight.

"This isn't fun?" he says, his voice low, playful with an edge. He finally pulls my jeans off with one motion, his hand instantly sliding up my thigh, finding my wetness, his thumb already on my clit.

He kisses me. I have one hand on his back, one on his cock, his tongue in my mouth. I'm on the floor, leaning against the couch, and he's on his knees in front of me.

I want him. I want him like I've never wanted anything before: I want to be taken, ravished. I want him to open me up and write his name on the inside of my skin.

"Enough sweet bullshit," I whisper.

"Is this too much foreplay for you, Violet?" he says, his mouth still on mine.

He reaches behind himself, momentarily distracted. A soft thunk, the sound of something ripping. I put my hand on his just as he's rolling the condom down his huge length.

He grabs me, heaves me off the floor, my back still against the couch, pinning me there with his legs under mine, his jeans still on.

Oops. I think I meant to get those off of him.

Eli kisses me roughly. He grabs my hips, shoves me against the couch, and I grab onto his shoulders, dizzy with his raw power.

His cock's against my entrance. His lips are still on mine as he slides it along my pussy lips, circling my clit with the tip, drawing himself back down until he presses against my tightness.

"I thought you said no sweet bullshit foreplay," I whisper. I buck my hips against him, uselessly.

I want him inside me. I want him there, as intimate as can be, past all my defenses.

I want all the things no one else has ever made me feel.

"This isn't sweet bullshit," he says.

He captures my mouth with his, the head of his cock entering me, his fingers digging into my hips as he stops.

"This is fucking you slowly," he says. "Feel the difference?"

I don't answer, because he moves, sliding in further, just until he finds that sweet spot on my front wall. Then he pulls back as I rake my hands over his shoulders.

"Don't," I whisper. "Just — oh, *fuck*…"

He does it again, slow, just a little deeper. Then again,

and again, each time deeper and harder. Finally he hilts himself, pulling me against him, our bodies melding.

"I tried to talk myself out of this," he whispers into my ear.

I wrap my legs around him. He pulls back, pushes himself in, his arms tight around me.

"Out of fucking me in a barn?"

"Out of fucking you at all," he goes on. "I know danger when I see it, and you're nothing but."

Harder, deeper. I find his mouth with mine and he groans into me.

Faster, harder.

"I'm no such thing," I whisper.

"Then why are we fucking on the floor of a barn?"

"A bed was too far," I say.

I bite my lip. Our bodies meet again and again, every thrust more urgent. I wrap myself around Eli, feeling like I might burst at the seams. I get higher and higher, closer, at the edge as we move together frantically, tangled and wordless.

And he stops. He hilts himself and stops, pinning me against the couch. I pant for breath, and finally, I open my eyes and look at Eli.

He doesn't have to speak for me to know what he wants.

"Please," I say, the word coming out a hoarse whisper.

He gives me the half-cocked smile. He kisses me roughly.

Then he pulls out. We move as one, untangling, until I'm on my knees, on the floor, elbows on the couch and he's behind me.

He slides into me in one smooth thrust. My toes curl and I moan, clutching the couch fabric in my hands.

We fuck. We don't *sleep together*, we don't *bang*, and we

sure as hell don't *make love*. We're on the floor of a barn and this is fucking, pure and raw and simple.

Eli wraps an arm around my chest, pulls me upright. He covers my mouth with one hand and finds my clit with the other while I moan onto his fingers.

It doesn't take long before I'm shaking and shuddering. Eli knows exactly what I need, how to touch me. He's had weeks of near-constant practice, and he's always been a quick study.

But there's something else. There's the fact that Eli fits me like a glove. There's the fact that he feels custom-made for me, the fact that what I need always seems to be exactly what he wants.

I come so hard I see stars. Eli's hand is still over my mouth, his other fingers strumming my clit, and he doesn't stop for anything. I come in wave after wave, my climax rocking through me.

Seconds later, Eli follows. His grip is like iron on my body, and he holds me there, using me as his cock strains and throbs, my pussy clenching again in answer.

Finally, we relax. He doesn't let me go but we relax, on our knees on the floor. He takes his hand from my mouth and I put mine over top of it, winding my fingers between his.

"Violet, I have a confession," he says, his lips next to my ear.

"I don't already know all your sins?"

"At the moment, you *are* most of my sins."

"Then what have you got to confess?" I ask.

He pauses, his thumb stroking my ribcage absentmindedly. I'm still on my knees, sandwiched between him and the couch, in this state of post-coital reverie where everything seems unreal except for the warmth of his body against mine.

"Sometimes I wish we weren't us," he says.

I lean my head back against his shoulder. I'm drunk and he's drunk, my mind swirling, bits of words and feelings and things I should say crashing through my brain, presenting themselves and disappearing.

"That doesn't make any sense," he says after a while. He strokes my bare ribcage with one thumb.

"You wish I wasn't me and you weren't you," I say.

"I wish I wanted someone who got along with me," he murmurs into my hair. "Wouldn't that be nice?"

He finally pulls back. We unwind, tumbling to the floor. I'm still naked, my back against the couch. Eli puts an arm around me, his pants still on and undone. I lean my head against his shoulder.

"I get along with you just fine," I say. "You're the one who doesn't get along with me."

He just laughs.

"How on earth could that be?" he muses. "You're so damn agreeable, Violet."

"You'd hate it if I were."

"No, I wouldn't," he says. "I like nice girls."

"I'm nice," I say.

Eli kisses the top of my head, his arm still around me.

"You're something," he says.

CHAPTER THIRTY-THREE

ELI

I should have kept my mouth shut. I don't know why I think I have to say everything out loud that runs through my brain when I get drunk, but I do.

I press my lips into her hair and try not to think, because that's clearly no good right now. I'll think tomorrow.

Right now, I'm here and she's here against me, wrapped together on the floor like lovers.

"What time is it?" Violet asks.

"You got a date?" I tease.

She just laughs.

"Yeah, my next barn sex appointment's at eleven," she says lazily, not moving. "Just tell me what time it is."

I know it's a joke, but I don't like it. I don't like it the same way I didn't like it when Seth said she was hot. Neither statement has any real significance, and yet…

I pull out my phone.

"Almost eleven," I tell her. "You about to tell me that we should go?"

"I'm about to tell you we should stagger our departure," she says, even as she slides an arm around my waist.

"I should buy you one of those fake glasses with the nose and the moustache," I tell her. "That way we could sneak around all sorts of places and no one would ever know it was you."

"They'd just think you had a Groucho Marx fetish."

"There are worse things," I say.

"Such as?"

"Such as people thinking I've got a Harpo Marx fetish."

I find the camera on my phone and open it.

"Which one was he, and what are you doing?" she asks. She pulls me closer.

Times like this I don't know what to make of Violet, of the way she tells me one thing with her mouth and something else with her body. I don't know what to make of the fact that everyone knows what we're doing, that we're together in some kind of way, and she wouldn't kiss me in public.

I want that. I want her to kiss me in front of people, admit what we are, whatever that is.

I didn't even know I wanted that until she wouldn't do it.

"He was the boring one, and I'm taking a selfie," I say. I reverse the camera, but it's so dark that there's nothing more than vague shapes on the screen.

"I've never seen a Marx Brothers movie," she says.

I snap a picture, but it's nothing.

"You need the flash," Violet points out like I don't know.

"My dad loved the Marx Brothers," I say, flipping my phone around. "*A Night at the Opera* was his favorite movie."

Violet draws an arm across her breasts, but she doesn't move.

"Not *Duck Soup?*"

"You've seen it?"

I hit the button. The flash goes off, and Violet turns her head into my chest.

"Ow. No, I've just heard of it. Why are you taking selfies?"

I take another one. I'm sure they're terrible — dark, shaky, my thumb probably in the frame somewhere — but I don't really care. I just want to document this moment, because I have a feeling that someday I'll want proof that it happened.

"I need a new profile picture on Facebook," I tell her.

"Not funny," she says.

"Everyone already knows," I point out, taking another one.

"I don't have anything worth blackmailing me for," she says.

Snap. Snap. Snap.

"Kiss me," I say.

Her face turns upward. I can barely see the outline of it, flash-blind.

"Don't argue about it, just kiss me," I say.

She does. I take a picture. I take five, and then I put my phone down and just kiss her back.

It's good. It's nice. It's better than nice; it's a thousand things that I don't want to admit to myself. It's enough to make me wish that I was someone else, or that she was. It's enough to make me wish this could actually work.

I kiss her long and slow. I kiss her like we're in love. She kisses back the same way, her hand soft against my face, her lips gentle.

The kiss ends. I press our faces together, say nothing.

I'm trying to formulate a thought into words, something like *what if this was really what it feels like it could be*, but it's not working.

"I don't want to leave," she murmurs.

"Any reason we can't sleep here?" I ask.

"About a thousand," she says. She traces one finger along my collarbone, my whole attention suddenly focused on that singular point of contact.

"You're coming over, right?" she says.

"That wasn't enough?" I tease, and Violet laughs.

"Just come over," she says. "I need someone to make me breakfast in the morning."

I kiss her hair one more time, my arms back around her.

"Sure," I say. "I've got two skills, may as well—"

I stop. I listen. There's a wail in the distance, rising and falling. Getting louder. Violet tenses.

They're sirens, getting closer.

"Shit," I whisper.

· · · · · ★ ★ ★ ★ ★ · · · · ·

THE GOOD THING about the pandemonium is that no one sees us leave the barn together.

The bad thing is everything else. When we come out there's already a fire truck in the parking lot by the Lodge, a herd of people milling and running around, everyone looking slightly worried and unsure.

"Is there a fire?" Violet breathes.

"How am I supposed to know?" I ask her. "There's a fire truck."

We start walking toward the Lodge. Despite the truck, it doesn't look like anything's on fire.

"Sometimes they just send whatever first responder

they've got," she says, walking faster. "A lot of times that's the fire department."

"If you know everything about this, why'd you ask me if there's a fire?"

There's another siren in the distance. We walk faster toward the Lodge, where it doesn't look like there's a fire and no one is acting like anything's on fire.

An ambulance winds its way up the driveway. The sirens are turned off, but the lights keep flashing as it pulls up near the fire truck. People are standing around in swimsuits and towels, dripping wet in the warm night.

"Oh no," Violet whispers, and breaks into a jog.

There's a heavy, sickly feeling in the pit of my stomach as I follow her. We skirt the parking lot. Paramedics jump out of the ambulance, head toward the pool area.

"It wasn't even supposed to be open," Violet says, slowing to a walk. "It was locked, we didn't have a lifeguard on duty or anything, and with all these kids around there's so much liability…"

She trails off when a stretcher appears, coming from the pool area. We both stop in our tracks. Violet covers her mouth, steps out of the way.

I pray that I'm not about to see a dead kid. I think of Rusty and my heart twists, because I can't help but imagine my feisty, wonderful niece on that stretcher.

I swallow hard. *It's not her*, I tell myself. *Someone was with her all night.*

The paramedics come closer with the stretcher. They're hurrying, not walking, not running. The person on it isn't covered up.

A foot moves on the stretcher, and relief prickles through my body. It's an adult, not a kid, someone who's still moving, someone with sandy blond hair and bandages wrapped around his head.

Someone I know.

"Kevin?" Violet says, taking her hand off her mouth.

The stretcher goes past, Violet's intern laid out on his back, wearing nothing but boxers and a head bandage.

As he looks at us, he weakly lifts one hand as if to wave. Violet watches him go, then turns and walks toward the pool.

It's full of guilty-looking Bramblebush employees. Zane, Brandon, and Naomi are sitting on lounge chairs, looking shell-shocked. Lydia and Martin are there, fully-clothed. Lydia's wide-eyed and pale, and to his credit, even Martin looks concerned.

On one side of the pool is a big bloody spot. Everyone's giving it a wide berth, the blood slowly seeping through the cracks in the tiles.

Bobbing gently nearby on the surface of the pool is a huge, dark inflatable… thing.

"Oh no," Violet says again, and now she's moving toward the pool, arms held out, careful not to slip. "No, no, no."

I follow her coming around the side of the pool, until finally I can see the behemoth straight-on.

It's unmistakably a floating mechanical bull. Bobbing next to it in the water are four more floats, each about six inches across, with a can of beer firmly wedged in the middle.

"How did this get out here?" Violet says, mostly to herself, crouching at the edge of the pool. "What happened? Is Kevin okay?"

Zane clears his throat, or maybe it's Brandon. They're both wrapped in towels, wide-eyed and pale.

"He fell off," Zane says.

"No shit," Violet snaps. "What the hell are you doing at the pool?"

No one answers.

"This was closed off for a *reason*," she goes on. "There's no lifeguard. There's no one watching, and you're not supposed to be here and you're absolutely not supposed to be drunk out here!"

"Violet," Lydia says, stepping around the blood to put her hand on Violet's arm.

"Did you do this?" Violet snaps.

"I got here five minutes ago," Lydia says.

"Kevin?"

"Probably just a concussion, but they're taking him in just in case," Lydia says, her voice still low and soothing. "Head wounds always bleed like crazy. He'll be fine, Violet."

She takes a deep breath, presses her fingers to her eyes, and without thinking I step forward and put my hand on her back.

If anyone sees me or thinks something of it, they keep their mouths shut. Violet takes a deep, shaky breath, and I realize that she's trying not to cry.

"Okay," she says. "Okay, we need to get a mop and lots of bleach out here, and I think we're going to have to drain the pool because this is definitely—"

The door from the lodge opens, and Montgomery walks out.

We all freeze, like teens caught smoking in the basement.

"What the hell is going on?" he demands, his accent thick as syrup even now.

Lydia shoots Zane, Brandon, and Naomi a dagger-filled look.

"This was to be closed off," he thunders.

Zane stands. He wobbles slightly on his feet, but he keeps the towel on and he doesn't fall over.

"A couple of us sneaked in to take a swim," he says, uncertainly. "And… Kevin fell."

Montgomery gives Zane a withering look, then glares at the mechanical bull.

"Off of that thing?"

Zane just nods.

"That yours?"

"It was just here," Zane says.

Under my hand, Violet's back muscles tense.

"Where did it come from?" Montgomery barks.

"Um," Zane says, rubbing his head. He sways again, one hand clutching his towel, but valiantly stays upright. "I dunno?"

"There's a box in the corner over there," says Martin. "That might have a clue."

"It's mine," Violet suddenly says.

Over her head, I catch Martin's eye. He betrays nothing, his gaze flat and dark.

You fucking shitweasel, I think.

"Yours?" Montgomery says. "Care to explain why you thought this was a good idea?"

"Last time I saw it, it was in my office," Violet says.

Montgomery just waits.

"It showed up here because there was a… misunderstanding when my credit card got stolen," she says, rubbing her forehead with one hand. "I was supposed to send it back. I don't know how it got out here."

"No?" Montgomery asks quietly.

"Someone must have brought it," I say, looking right at Martin.

Nothing shows in his face.

"Thank you for that, Elijah," Montgomery snaps. "Yes, someone must have brought it. All of you, get the hell out of here. Close the pool off *now*. No one comes out here until biohazard cleanup is finished, and I want all of you in my office first thing Tuesday morning."

With that, he turns on his heel and strides back into the lodge. Violet slumps onto a chair, her face in her hands. I sit next to her, Lydia on the other side, Zane still standing awkwardly.

Martin melts into the darkness, presumably because he can turn into slime at will.

"Shit," Violet whispers.

CHAPTER THIRTY-FOUR
VIOLET

The next morning I wake up with a hangover and Eli's arm draped over me. It's not the worst hangover I've ever had, but it's unpleasant. My mouth is sticky. My limbs feel like lead. My head feels like it's filled with cotton.

Eli rolls over, looks at me. There are circles under his eyes, and his hair's an unholy mess.

"You look rough," I say, half my face still smashed against the pillow.

"Well, you look like Miss America," he says, rolling onto his back, his arms under his head.

I flip him off, and he laughs.

"You want breakfast?" he asks.

· · · · · ★ ★ ★ · · · · ·

I DRINK APPROXIMATELY a gallon of water and a gallon of coffee. I eat the bacon and eggs that Eli makes. I didn't know I had bacon and eggs in the house, but apparently he's started stocking my fridge when I'm not looking.

That probably means something. It probably also

means something that I've given him a key and that he has his own toothbrush on my sink, but I'm too tired and hungover to think about any of that right now.

I'm also too tired to think about the fact that everyone in Sprucevale knows about us, too tired to think about the mechanical bull incident last night, and very definitely too tired to contemplate what my chances at the twenty grand are looking like right now.

I drink another gallon of coffee. Eli kisses me and leaves. As I watch him go, I wonder how I could ever think that we were keeping us a secret.

After another hour, I finally force myself to put on jeans and leave the house. I go get flowers, then take them to the hospital.

"Mom, it was my fault," Kevin's saying when I reach his room. "You don't need to sue Bramblebush. I got on the bull myself, I swear—"

"That gate should never have been unlocked," she's saying, steel in her voice, when I step in. "Someone's going to pay for this."

They both look up: his mom's mouth a thin line, Kevin looking absolutely mortified.

"Hi," I say. "I just wanted to see how you were doing."

"I'll be fine," he says. "They're releasing me in a few hours, they just kept me overnight as a precaution."

His mom glares at me. I vaguely recollect that she's some kind of lawyer, and I wonder if I've already said too much as she goes back to rearranging his pillow.

It's familiar, in a way. I'm acquainted with hospital rooms and I'm acquainted with endlessly rearranging someone's pillows, though in my case, the roles were reversed.

A quick, sharp pang of jealousy spikes in my chest, but I

banish it. I step into the room, give Kevin his flowers. He apologizes to me over and over again for sneaking into the pool. I think he's still apologizing even when I finally say goodbye.

There. I accomplished something, one single, simple task. I head back to my trailer, turn on Netflix, and zone out, because I have too many things to think about and I don't want to do any of it.

It's three when I suddenly remember Clarabelle's invitation.

I'm on my couch. I'm comfy. I'm half-asleep and watching old episodes of *House Hunters International*, avoiding my problems by getting annoyed at people with million-dollar budgets.

"No," I say out loud, to no one. "That's not today."

I sit up, press the heels of my hands into my eyes, try to remember what Clara said yesterday.

She said Sunday dinner. She said four p.m.

And, yeah, she said it was today.

"Why?" I ask my empty living room.

Then I roll myself off the couch and finally take a shower.

· · · · · ★ ★ ★ · · · · ·

At 4:05, I climb the wooden stairs to the Loveless homestead with an apple pie in my hand, bought last-second from Kroger because nothing else is open on a Sunday. In my defense, I at least put it on a nice plate, and I'm pretty good at putting things on nice plates.

The house is an old farmhouse, probably at least a hundred years old if not older, and it's huge. I've been inside a few times before, since Eli and I have always been in the same class and there's an age when you have to invite everyone to your birthday, but it's been at least twenty years.

As I raise my hand to knock, it suddenly occurs to me: I didn't tell Eli I was coming. Last night I was, you know, *distracted*, and then this morning I completely forgot.

Clara told him, right? Or is Eli about to be surprised that I'm showing up at his house with pie?

I shrug and knock, because the last twenty-four hours have thrown everything pretty askew, and whatever happens, I'm just going to roll with it.

I wait. Footsteps. Someone hollers.

Then the door opens and Eli is standing there, the screen separating us.

I hold up the pie.

"Hi," I say. "By the way, your mom invited me for dinner."

He pushes open the screen door and holds it for me as I step through.

"So she told me about an hour ago," he says. "Here, I'll take that."

Eli takes the pie from me. He glances around, craning his neck to see down the hall and into the kitchen.

Then he kisses me hello. It's quick, familiar, a nothing kiss, except that his brothers and mom can't be more than a hundred feet away.

"Sorry about this," he says.

"Sorry about what?" I ask.

He sighs, pushing a hand through his hair. There's a streak of something down his forearm, and it suddenly occurs to me that it smells *amazing* in here.

"This whole Sunday dinner rigamarole," he says. "I know it's not your thing. Come on, I'll show you in."

He turns away before I can ask him why he thinks I

don't want *this whole rigamarole*, padding down the hallway with bare feet.

"Everyone is on the back porch," he says when we reach the kitchen. He puts the pie on a sideboard, tucking it neatly away next to a bundt cake. "You want a drink before you head out?"

My stomach recoils at the thought.

"I'm good," I say, and finally, Eli cracks a smile.

"Yeah, thought you might say that," he says. "You ready?"

"I don't know why you're acting like I'm about to face the inquisition," I tell him, leaning one hip against the sideboard. "You know I know your family already, for Pete's sake."

He folds his arms, looks away for a moment.

"I've never brought a girl home before," he admits. "I moved away when I was eighteen and I never exactly introduced my family to any of my girlfriends."

"You didn't bring me home either," I point out. "Your mother invited me. You found out about this an hour ago."

I leave unspoken *and I'm not your girlfriend*, but I know we both hear it.

"They all know," he says, keeping his voice low. "Well, I think they do. My brothers know. I'm sure Charlie knows. I don't know what my mom knows."

"Charlie's here?"

Charlie — Charlotte — is Daniel's best friend and has been since they were kids. I don't know her all that well, but she's always been nice.

"Yeah, she comes a lot," Eli says.

"Eli," I tell him, putting a hand on his arm. "Chill out. It's fine. I'm a big girl. What do you think is going to happen?"

"If I knew I wouldn't be so worried," he says, half smiling.

Before I can do anything, he leans forward and kisses me. It's brief, sweet, over in a second, a *calm down your girlfriend before she meets your family* kiss, though neither part of that applies here. I'm not his girlfriend, and I've met his family before.

"They can be a lot," he says. "Come on, let's get this over with."

CHAPTER THIRTY-FIVE

ELI

I open the sliding door onto the back porch and step out, Violet trailing me.

Six sets of eyes turn our way, and silence falls over the group.

I already wish I'd told her not to come.

"Violet's here," I say, as casually as I can. "Everyone, this is Violet. Violet, you remember my brothers Levi, Seth, and Daniel, his daughter Rusty, Charlie McManus, and my mom?"

Seth, Daniel, Charlie, and my mom are sitting in a semi-circle, a low table in front of them, beers on Loveless Brewing coasters atop it. A few feet away, Levi and Rusty are playing some sort of card game, sitting on the wooden planking of the back porch.

"Violet!" my mom says, standing and coming over. "I'm so glad you could make it. Eli, you didn't get her a drink?"

"He offered," Violet says as my mom envelops her in a hug. "I declined."

"Are you sure?" my mom says. "We've got the boys'

pale ale that they just finished bottling, we've got lemonade and iced tea…"

I glance over at the chairs. All three of my brothers are staring at me, varying expressions of amusement, interest, and just general nosiness on their faces.

Charlie's also looking, but she's very nice and not related to me.

For a moment, I'm just glad that Caleb's off in California, doing his thing, instead of also sticking his nose in my personal business. If I had to deal with all four of them right now, I might actually lose my shit.

"You're sure? You know what, just come look," my mom says to Violet. "I don't even remember what all we've got right now…"

"I'm fine, really," Violet says, but moments later my mom's leading her back into the house so she can read the contents of the fridge aloud to her.

As soon as they disappear, the eyes feel like lasers. I wander over and take a seat, pretending to ignore them.

"You owe me five bucks," Daniel says to Seth. "I told you she'd show."

Seth sighs dramatically, reaches into his pocket, pulls out his wallet, and hands Daniel five dollars.

"I thought that when Mom told you she was coming, you'd tell her not to," he explains.

"You think Violet listens to anything I say?" I ask.

"That's what I said," Daniel offers. "I knew she'd show if Mom invited her."

"Thanks for telling me," I say.

"You weren't here this morning when we were discussing it," he says smoothly. "Otherwise I would have."

"Violet didn't tell you?" Seth asks.

"She forgot," I say, doing my best to keep my composure.

"Or you were too busy to talk," Seth says, lifting his beer to his lips and grinning.

Sitting next to Daniel, Charlie frowns and leans forward.

"Seth, you swore," she says.

"I didn't say a thing."

"Then why's poor Eli blushing right now?"

Shit, my face *is* getting hot.

"I'm not blushing," I say.

"Don't make Eli blush, he hates that," Levi adds, out of nowhere. "Go fish."

"He really thought no one knew," Daniel says, his voice calm and gentle as always. "And now his… woman… is looking through the fridge with his mom."

He reaches out and pats my shoulder. I glare at him and the stupid smile on his face. He's definitely enjoying this too much.

"Be gentle with Eli," he admonishes.

"She's not my woman," I mutter.

Where the hell is Violet?

They'll lay off when she gets back.

"That's patently untrue," Levi says from the floor. "Give me all your lanternfish."

I lean forward, rubbing my face with my hands, trying to find the simplest way to explain to all of them — including a six-year-old — that we're nothing more than frequent sex partners.

"Violet and I have an arrangement," I say, as delicately as possible.

"An *arrangement*," Daniel says, mostly to himself.

"Yes," I say, glancing down at Rusty. "We, uh, spend some time together, but we're not dating."

Silence from the brother squad. Silence and interested stares.

"We don't even get along otherwise," I point out.

"You're saying you're friends with benefits?" Seth asks.

"Are you even friends?" Levi asks.

"I know, right?" I say.

Seth leans forward, looking thoughtful. His eyes narrow.

"You've been spending most nights at her place," he says.

"Yes," I confirm, wary.

"Are you seeing anyone else?"

"No."

"Do you eat meals together?" Levi pipes in.

"I bet he cooks for her," Daniel says, leaning back in his chair. "You cook for her, don't you?"

I do. More often than not I make us dinner in her kitchen while she has a glass of wine and helps out. Her onion-chopping skills have come a long way in the past month.

"I cook for everyone," I say. "I cook for you assholes—"

"Eli." That's Daniel.

"I cook for you *jerks* and you're not giving me the third-degree about it."

"Eli," says Charlie, leaning forward. She's sitting cross-legged in her chair, a beer in her hand, her curly hair spilling over her shoulders. "These boys are all missing the point. Do you enjoy one another's company?"

Yes.

I think I like arguing with Violet more than I like talking to anyone else.

"Where exactly are you going with this?" I ask.

"She's your girlfriend," Charlie says, putting the beer to her lips.

"Enjoying someone's company doesn't make her my girlfriend," I point out. "You're not Daniel's girlfriend."

I swear to God Charlie turns the faintest pink, but maybe I'm imagining things.

"Daniel and I aren't fu—"

"*Charlie.*"

"—uh, we're just platonic friends," she finishes, rolling her eyes at Daniel.

"She is *always* listening," Daniel mutters.

"Uncle Levi, what's platonic mean?" Rusty asks, still sitting on the floor.

"It means they're not in love," Levi says. "Give me all your giant tube worms."

Rusty sighs dramatically and tosses three cards onto the floor in front of Levi, who chuckles. I lean over and look at Levi's Go Fish cards.

They look like something out of a horror movie: all jaws and teeth, some weird eels, some shapes that look nothing at all like animals.

"What are you playing?" I ask.

"Abyssal Zone Go Fish," Levi says, tossing another card of giant tube worms on top of the three he just got from Rusty.

"They're weird fish who live at the bottom of the ocean where it's always dark," she explains. "Charlie gave it to me."

I look over at Charlie, who's drinking her beer again, any imagined blush gone.

"Cool, right?" she says. "Anyway, your girlfriend."

"Violet is not my girlfriend," I say, as calmly as I can. "We are not—"

"You should probably let Violet know she's your girlfriend," Daniel interrupts.

"She's not."

"She is," pipes up Seth.

"She's not! She's the one who doesn't want to be my girlfriend!"

I'm met with total silence, including my own.

I've never said that out loud before.

I've never exactly *thought* that out loud before.

They're all staring at me. Even Rusty, a six-year-old, is giving me a look.

"Uh oh," Seth says, just as the sliding door opens again.

Violet and my mom step through, chatting about something, holding bottles of Cheerwine. They don't seem to notice that we're all totally and completely silent.

"We have Cheerwine?" Seth finally asks.

"It's in the basement fridge," my mom says breezily. "You'd know that if you listened to me."

"What's going on out here?" Violet asks, walking toward us.

She takes a seat next to me, then leans over and looks at Levi and Rusty's game.

"Are those giant tube worms?" she says. "Cool."

CHAPTER THIRTY-SIX
VIOLET

To my great relief, I'm having a lovely time. Not that I thought I'd have a bad time at Clara's house, but I did have some concerns. It's hard not to when you spend time with the mother of the man you're banging like a screen door.

I'm coming to appreciate that phrase, by the way. It has a certain ugly, redneck charm.

Dinner is delicious. Eli made lamb, mint, braised brussels sprouts, and some sort of refreshing, crunchy salad that apparently his brother, Levi, foraged all the ingredients for. I sit next to Rusty, who tells me all about bioluminescence and geothermal energy at the bottom of the ocean. I think I impress her by knowing that the gulper eel's jaw accounts for a quarter of its body.

But most of all, I sit back and listen. There's a rhythm to this family, a back-and-forth between the brothers that's as easy and natural as the tides. One second they'll give each other hell and the next they're passing the gravy, all with the kind of ease that comes with living with someone for a lifetime.

I don't have any siblings. My dad left while I was still a baby, so it was always just me and my mom, and now it's just me.

When the meal's over, I stand up and try to help clear the dishes, but Clara shoos me away.

"Hell no, Violet, you're a guest here," she says.

"*Mom,*" Daniel calls from the kitchen.

Clara rolls her eyes at me.

"I don't know how I raised such a tight ass," she whispers. "You know, studies have shown that people who curse more are happier, smarter, and more creative than people who don't?"

"The studies weren't on six-year-olds," Daniel calls.

"Go sit for a spell in the living room," she says. "Where's Eli? Eli, go give Violet a tour while we clean up before dessert."

"Well, which is it?" he asks. "Sit, or a give tour?"

Clara just sighs exasperatedly and walks away.

"Give me the tour," I say, and loop my arm through his.

· · · · ★ ★ ★ · · · ·

"THIS FLOWERBED RIGHT HERE IS where I broke my arm because Levi convinced me I could fly if I ate thirteen dandelions," Eli says, pointing at a row of flowers around the side of the house. "I jumped off the roof. In his defense, I think he wanted to see if it would work as much as I did."

"How'd you get up there?"

"There used to be a trellis on the side of the porch with some morning glories," he says. "I was six and he was eight, so we were light enough to use it like a ladder."

"With zero supervision, of course," I laugh.

Eli just shrugs, grinning.

"There were five of us, one of my mom, and my dad

was still working all hours back then," he says. "Levi was practically considered an adult while he was in grade school."

The tour of the house has been light on architectural details ("I think this was built sometime around 1860 or something like that," Eli told me,) and heavy on memories of childhood incidents where one or more of the Loveless boys got hurt.

I have no idea how Clara's maintained her sanity this long, let alone started an academic career late in life. The more I hear of the time that Caleb fell from a tree, Seth ate a slug, or Daniel somehow impaled his shoulder on a sharp stick, the more impressed I am with her.

Apparently Daniel's never told anyone *how* he impaled his shoulder on that stick when he was twelve. To this day, he refuses, though Eli thinks Charlie knows.

"And way back there in the woods is the bootlegging shed," Eli says, pointing off. "It's kind of falling down now, though Levi keeps threatening to restore it."

"Who bootlegged?" I ask. According to Eli's very sketchy history of the homestead, it's been in his family since it was built.

"Who didn't?" he says with a grin. "Mostly my great-granddad Lowell, I think. At least he was the one who got into the most trouble, but then he married the sheriff's daughter so it all worked out in the end."

"Worked out how, exactly?" I ask.

"He stopped getting in trouble," Eli says.

"He stopped running hooch?"

"I don't believe he did," Eli says, laughing. "He died before any of us were born, but I've been led to believe that I'd have gotten along with great granddad Lowell pretty well."

We mount the steps to the front porch. It's actually all

one porch, wrapping around the outside of the house, and we walk across it and go inside.

"I don't even know what I'm supposed to be giving you a tour of," he says, glancing around the entryway. "Though I'm fairly certain that when we're done there'll be a quiz and I'll fail it. Come on."

He leads me up the stairs.

"These are stairs," he says, helpfully. "Up here are most of the bedrooms, that's a bathroom. It's got a shower that works okay."

"So informative," I murmur.

He points at a door.

"I shared that room with Levi for a while, then Daniel for a while," he says. "Now it's Daniel's, and Rusty's across the hall. I'm staying upstairs in the attic bedroom."

"Do I get to see that?"

"And why would you want to?" he asks, casting a glance back at me, and I laugh.

"Curiosity," I say. "You've been to my house a thousand times by now and I've never been here."

He stops at the bottom of the next staircase, gives me the grin that I always feel in *places*.

"That the only reason?"

"Yes," I say. "If you think I'm going to get up to any hanky-panky with all your brothers, your mom, and your niece downstairs, you've got another think coming."

"Hanky-panky," he says, his voice going low as he reaches out, takes me around the waist. "The hell is that, Violet?"

"Oh, shut up," I say, climbing the stairs in front of him. "It just slipped out."

"I do like the sound of it," he teases, and lightly smacks my ass. "Hanky-panky. You know, I doubt they can hear us all the way up here."

The attic's small, a short hallway with just two doors on it. Eli opens the left one and leads me into a space with windows at either end, a sloping roof, a bed, and a desk.

And… that's pretty much it.

"Ta da," he says, closing the door behind him. "Impressed?"

"You do remember that I live in a trailer, right?" I ask. "And this is way nicer than anything in my house?"

"Yeah, but does yours come with a six-year-old alarm clock who has no regard whatsoever for late nights?" he laughs.

"True," I admit as Eli slides his hands around my waist, his thumbs rough against my skin, under my shirt.

"I gotta find my own place," he murmurs, bending to kiss me.

It's a nice kiss. A restrained kiss, one full of barely-held-back heat, a kiss that's not leading anywhere.

After a moment, he pulls back.

"Thanks," he says, thumb playing over my back. It's a habit he has, like he can't ever quite sit still. "You didn't have to come."

"I wasn't about to turn down an invitation from Clarabelle Loveless," I tell him. "I'm not that brave."

"Seriously," he says. "I know it's not what we discussed."

I almost ask him if that still matters. I almost say that *what we discussed* a month ago doesn't have any bearing on where we are, right now, but I shy away from it. I'm afraid that it still matters to one of us, and ironically, it's not me.

Besides, right now — these stolen moments in his attic bedroom while his entire family mills around two floors below — isn't really a good time or place.

"It's fine," I tell him instead. "They're nice. I like them. I never had brothers."

He laughs. Kisses me. Hands on my back, desire moving through me slow and steady, but I ignore it.

"Occasionally I wish I hadn't either," he says. "But overall they're pretty all right."

We kiss again. His hands move higher. His thumbs are on my ribcage, that soft skin right below the underwire of my bra, and without meaning to I press against him, our bodies flush.

I force myself back.

"No hanky-panky," I tease.

"How about just panky?" he asks, that half-smile on his face. "I'm probably good for another five minutes, I bet we could get up to some over-the-clothes stuff like teenagers—"

"ELIJAH!!" a voice bellows from below.

Eli shuts his eyes for a moment, then walks to his door.

"WHAT?" he shouts.

Footsteps pound up a flight of stairs.

"Where's the cake knife?" Seth's voice asks from the second-floor landing.

"I don't know," Eli says. "Who used it last? Ask them."

"Daniel says it was you," Seth says.

I wander further into Eli's room. There's not much in here: a dresser, a bed, a desk, a small bookshelf. I mosey to the bookshelf, run my fingers along the spines. It's half novels and half travel guides, their spines striped with use: Iceland, Spain, Thailand, France, Egypt, Italy, Mongolia, China, Turkey. They're well-worn, the pages grimy.

It's a list of places I've never even considered going. A trip to Mongolia may as well be a trip to the moon, as far as I'm concerned. I've never been to Canada. I've never even been west of the Mississippi.

"I wasn't even here Thursday night," Eli says. "I was at — I wasn't here, I don't know what he's talking about…"

I pick up the book on Thailand, curious. It opens to a page about how to haggle in marketplaces, and idly, I flip through it a little.

Some of the pages are flagged. Some have notes in them in Eli's handwriting, and the page on the best time of year to go has both.

So does the page on living in Thailand as an expat. According to a quick scan, it's affordable, the quality of life is decent, and the rest of Asia is a short flight away.

I put the book back. I'm not doing myself any favors, snooping through his stuff and reminding myself that while he traveled the world and went to Thailand and China and Egypt, I was here. This bookshelf is a list of places that are all probably a hundred times more interesting than Sprucevale.

I wonder when he'll realize that.

"Then use another knife," Eli is saying, still shouting down the stairs. "That's not — you did what?"

"She said it's not whipping," Rusty's voice says.

"We don't even — you know what, hold on, I'm coming down," Eli says, then turns to me. I tear my gaze away from the bookshelf, away from the thought that sooner or later, he's going to realize the mistake he's made coming back here.

"Sorry," he says. "I gotta head back down, I think my mom is trying to make whipped cream with half and half."

"That's not how you do it?" I ask.

"Not you, too," he says, opening the door. He puts his hand on the small of my back as I leave, descending the stairs in front of him.

"I don't know how to make whipped cream," I say. I force the books and the doubt to the back of my mind. "As far as I'm concerned, it comes in a tub from the grocery store."

Eli laughs.

"That's Cool Whip, and you've just committed heresy," he says. "Come on."

CHAPTER THIRTY-SEVEN

ELI

"Careful," I say, offering Violet my hand. She takes it, holding onto the window frame with the other, ducking under the panes and stepping carefully onto the roof.

"This'll hold?" she asks, looking down at our feet in the dark.

"It's a roof."

"I wouldn't go on my roof," she says.

I keep her hand in mine and lead her up to the ridge of the roof, to the spot with the best view. The trees out here are too thick to see most of the sky, but we can see a little.

We lay down, the shingles still warm from the day, my arm under her head.

"This where you came to drink and smoke pot in high school?" she asks.

"You know I wasn't that cool," I say.

"Yeah, I do," she agrees, her voice lazy. "Not that I can talk."

"I came up here to read," I say. "It felt like the only time that I could get some time and space to myself, though

I finally got busted when I left *The Hitchhiker's Guide to the Galaxy* up here, it got rained on, and Levi found it."

"Was *he* coming up here to smoke pot?" she asks.

"More likely than me," I admit. "But I think he just liked the quiet, too."

We're both silent for a long moment, savoring it. The noise of people in the house below is vague buzz, voices occasionally breaking through.

This feels like a small miracle: that Violet came at all, that my brothers didn't frighten her off before we even ate, that she's managed to hold her own against them and even impress Rusty with her esoteric knowledge of deep-sea fish. I love my family, but they can be a lot sometimes.

Plus, I'm fairly certain that not one of them has cornered Violet and asked her probing questions about the nature of our relationship. I have no idea why they care so much whether I call her my girlfriend or not, especially since I don't even care that much.

We have a lot of sex. We spend time together. Sometimes we go to restaurants in other towns, where no one knows who we are. Right now we're cuddling on a rooftop, away from the eyes of my nosy brothers.

Who cares what we call it?

I don't. Really, I don't.

Violet points up, toward the stars glimmering beyond the leaf canopy, her head turning against my shoulder.

"Is that one Orion?"

"Orion's not up there," I tell her.

"That's the belt."

"That's just three stars, they're not even in the same constellation," I tell her. "Those two are in Draco," I say, pointing, "and that one's in Hercules."

Violet sighs.

"Fine," she says.

"Orion's a winter constellation," I tell her.

"What's that one?" she asks, pointing.

I have no idea what she's pointing at, so I just start naming constellations.

"That right there," I say, waving my finger at the sky, "is Cygnus, the swan—"

"It looks like a cross."

"Well, it's a bird. See, it's got a neck and wings?"

Violet considers this for a moment, a slight breeze moving her hair against my arm.

"I'm not seeing it," she says. "Show me a better constellation."

"Cygnus is a perfectly good constellation," I argue back, but I'm laughing.

"It's a B minus constellation at best," she teases. "Come on, you can do better."

I sigh dramatically and point at something else.

"There, that one's a dragon," I say, pointing at Draco. "It's got a tail, and a head, and it's kinda wrapped around Ursa Minor there."

Violet shifts against me, tilting her head. Then she tilts her head the other way, the side her body against mine, her warmth radiating through me.

I like this. She's soft. She smells good. She's here, on my roof, keeping me on my toes like she always does. Violet's not always the easiest person to get along with, but who wants easy? I'll take interesting any day.

"That's your tattoo," she finally says. "Right?"

"Right," I confirm.

She looks up at me.

"You gonna tell me about it?"

"Are you gonna ask?"

"Is it weird that I never have?"

"Not really," I say. "Half the time I forget I have it."

"I figured people must ask you about it all the time, so you're probably sick of explaining it," she says. "Or that you got it so people would ask, and I didn't want to give you the satisfaction."

"It's on my back, no one ever sees it," I point out, amused. "How often do you think I take my shirt off?"

"Seems like pretty often to me."

She has a point.

"And yet you've never asked about it."

"Okay, okay," she says, but she's laughing. "Eli, please tell me about your tattoo."

"Well, now it's built up to be this whole big thing," I say. "It's just a tattoo. I got it with my brothers once when I was visiting home."

"You all got tattoos?"

"Different constellations, but yeah," I say.

"*Daniel* has a tattoo?"

I just laugh.

"Earlier tonight he fussed at me for saying *hell*," she goes on.

"Do you not remember him when he was twenty-two? It's a miracle that he only ended up with one tattoo and one surprise baby."

"True," Violet laughs. "Which ones did they get?"

"Daniel got Serpens, the snake, because, and I quote, 'snakes are badass,'" I tell her. "Levi's got the crow, Corvus; Caleb's got the sextant because he's a nerd, and I think Seth has… shit, he changed his at the last minute, and I can never remember what he ended up with."

"Why'd you get this one?"

I stare up into the night sky, right at the constellations that are also tattooed on my skin. The truth is, I don't really know. I just always liked them: the dragon wrapped around the bear, the bear escaping anyway, led by the North Star in its tail. There's something in there about keeping my bearings and finding my way home, but I can't quite grasp it right now.

"Well, I was twenty-three and thought dragons were badass," I say.

Violet just laughs.

"I liked the idea of tattooing the North Star on myself," I say, my voice getting quieter. "It made me feel like I could always find my way when I was lost as fuck."

"Could you?"

"Hell no."

She's quiet. Quiet for a long time, a little too long.

"What was your favorite place?" she asks. "Of everywhere you went."

I go through the possibilities: mountains and oceans and rivers, busy cities and small quiet towns, safe places and dangerous places and everything in between.

"I liked the food in Chiang Mai and Saigon," I say. "I spent a Christmas in a village in the Swiss Alps and I swear it made me think Santa Claus was real. I spent a month living in Istanbul as a politician's temporary personal chef and every morning I'd go to the market and find something new to try. I went to Peru and once I got over the altitude sickness, it was the most beautiful place I'd ever seen."

"So you liked everywhere," she says.

She's even closer to me now, one leg draped over mine, my hand on her ribcage. I stroke her with my thumb, thoughtlessly, the feel of her warm skin beneath her skin anchoring me even when I feel like I could fall into the sky.

"Not everywhere," I say.

"But you miss it."

"I miss it and I don't," I say after a moment. "I worked a lot of shitty jobs and lived in a lot of sketchy apartments. I kept moving because nothing was ever like I thought it would be. Nothing interesting stays interesting. Everywhere has the same problems after a while."

"You can't convince me that Bangkok and Sprucevale are anything alike."

"You'd be surprised," I say. "They won't fix the damn potholes there, either."

That gets a laugh. She slides her hand over mine, winding our fingers together. I turn my head and kiss her hair softly, so softly that maybe she doesn't notice.

"I like them," she says suddenly.

"The potholes?"

"Your family," she says, like that was obvious. "They're fun."

"They're fun because you're their guest," I say, sounding grumpier than I really am. "You don't get shouted at about cake knives and you're not the one facing the inquisition later."

"What inquisition?"

"Are you serious right now, Violet?"

She twists against me, her eyes looks up into mine.

"Well, the first question is going to be *how come Mom had to be the one to invite her?*" I say. "Next it'll be *when's she coming again* and after that *so are you moving out yet* and *why don't you take her somewhere nice and —*"

I stop, because I almost say that the next questions are *when are you getting married* and *what are you going to name your kids* because if there's something my brothers don't know, it's how to shut up sometimes.

"And none of that applies here," she says, her voice flat, like she's far away.

It could, I almost say. *What if it did?*

But then I remember last night. I remember practically begging to kiss her by the fire, holding her hand.

Not here, she said.

Because I'm only good for two things and being a boyfriend isn't one of them, no matter how many times I ask.

"Nope," I say. I say it like it's a joke, my voice light against the weight in my chest.

We're quiet for a while, the air slowly cooling around us. The trees move in the breeze, the stars wink in and out and she stays there, nestled against me, her hand in mine.

I force my mind to quiet. None of this bears thinking about it. It simply is, and that needs to be good enough.

"Tell me more constellations," she finally says.

I shift on the roof, my arm still around her, fingers still through mine. Her hair is soft against my chin, but I don't think about any of that.

"Why?" I ask. "So you can give them B minuses?"

"Only if they deserve it," she says.

I sigh dramatically, for effect. Then I point at the sky and start telling Violet stories.

CHAPTER THIRTY-EIGHT
VIOLET

"You mean turtle doves," I say, scrolling through a seating chart. This one's more complicated than most: color-coded by nobility rank, something I had to crash-learn in the past four days.

I swear, I don't understand why brides want me to do their seating charts. I must have sent the princess's people fifty emails, trying to figure out whether an English marquise was higher in rank than a Swiss baron or not.

And did you know that a marquess is actually a male title? Thank God for America, where we at least pretend that we don't have different classes.

"No, I mean turtles," Lydia says on the other end of the phone.

She sounds stressed.

"They're very slow," she goes on. "They have shells. In fact, they're mostly hiding in their shells right now, and I have a feeling that they're not going to suddenly take flight at the correct moment in the wedding ceremony."

I'm still staring at the seating chart, but I'm not seeing it.

"You're kidding," I say.

"No!" Lydia yelps.

"We got reptiles and not birds?" I ask. I'm baffled. I have literally no idea how that sort of thing happens.

"That's what I'm telling you," she says.

I stand from my desk, because the seating chart is just going to have to be good enough as it is.

"I'll be right there," I say.

· · · · · ★ ★ ★ ★ ★ · · · · ·

Five minutes later I'm standing next to Lydia, staring at several crates filled with turtles.

I'm well and truly speechless.

"What?" I ask. "How?"

She just shakes her head.

"Did you…?" I ask.

"Martin was in charge of the turtle doves," she says. "I haven't seen him since these showed up."

It's a small, cold comfort, but it's comfort: at least he screwed up his own responsibility for once, and not mine.

In one of the crates, a turtle sticks its head out and glares at us. It's kind of cute — about six inches in diameter, some okay colors on the shell — but then it pulls its head back in.

"All right," I finally say. "If you figure out where to put them and how to care for turtles until someone comes and gets them, I'll tell Montgomery and see if we can find any birds in the next—"

I check my watch.

"—Three hours," I finish.

"Montgomery knows," Lydia says. "He's the one who took Martin off."

"Oh," I say.

I keep my voice as neutral as I can, though on the inside I do a cartwheel.

"I hate that slimy turd," Lydia mutters.

"Same," I admit.

· · · · · ★ ★ ★ ★ ★ · · · · ·

"FIFTEEN POUNDS OF LETTUCE?" Zane asks. "How much lettuce is that, even?"

"I think it's fifteen pounds," Brandon says.

I can't tell if he's being sarcastic or not. He's perfectly straight-faced.

"Do you have it? I'll take any greens you have," I say, because beggars can't be choosers.

They look at each other, then Zane shrugs.

"Sure," he says. "Why do you need this?"

I explain about the turtles as they lead me to the walk-in fridge. I grab a bunch of greens and try to answer their questions about *why* there are turtles, but God knows I don't entirely understand the situation either.

On the way out, I walk past Eli. He's wearing an apron that's covered in splatters, holding a thermometer, and focusing on a pot on something.

We nod at each other, and then I'm out of there with my lettuce.

· · · · · ★ ★ ★ ★ ★ · · · · ·

AND THEN, the most surprising thing of all happens: the princess's wedding goes perfectly. The only problem is the lack of dove release — unsurprisingly, we couldn't find replacement birds in time — but I don't think anyone notices, and Her Highness sure doesn't seem to care.

The ceremony is beautiful. The day is gorgeous. The

food is great. I got the seating chart right, and if I didn't, there's so much imported vodka that no one notices. There are toasts and dancing and more drinks and more dancing, and as far as I can tell, everyone's having a great time.

The couple is glowing. She's radiant with happiness. Her new husband can't take his eyes off her, and every time I look over at them, they're leaning together like they're sharing some secret, laughing with each other.

Weddings like these more than make up for the terrible ones.

I'm standing in the corner, about to go find Eli and leave, when I suddenly see the princess making a beeline for me.

I straighten up. It seems like I should stand up straight for royalty.

"Violet?" she asks.

"What's wrong?" I ask, my default state.

She laughs, her hand on my arm.

"Vhat? Nahssing eez wrong," she says, her accent made heavier with vodka. "Zees is beautiful. Eet's perfect. Zee best day of my life, and I vanted to sank you for making eet happen."

Then she takes my shoulders, leans in, and gives me a kiss on each cheek.

"Vonderful," she says, flushing pink.

Then she winks.

"And I vill be sure to tell your boss," she says, and gets back to her party.

I decide that's my cue to leave, because nothing better is going to happen.

· · · · · ★ ★ ★ ★ ★ · · · · ·

"Then she kissed me," I say.

"Should I be jealous?" Eli asks.

I'm facedown on my bed, the sheet wound around my feet. He's on his back. We're both naked, sweaty, satiated.

Would you be? I think.

"It was very platonic," I say. "Hardly any tongue at all."

"What are you gonna do with the money?" he asks. Just the question makes my nerves prickle.

"Don't jinx it," I tell him. "There's two more days. Anyone could win."

"Come on."

"Are you somehow going to use this conversation against me?" I tease. "Are you wearing a wire, and now you're going to bait me into saying I've embezzled thousands of dollars from Bramblebush or something?"

Eli just laughs.

"Am I that bad?" he asks.

"You told people I liked to smell my own farts," I say.

He laughs harder.

"That was pretty good," he admits.

"Kids called me the fart sniffer for *months*."

"Then it was effective."

I grab my pillow and smack him with it.

"Ow," he says, his voice muffled.

I push my pillow further under my chest, punching it in to make it puffier.

"I'd use it as the down payment for the cabin by the lake," I say. "You know that. I'd move out of this place. I'm sick of being trailer trash."

I sigh, stretching.

"The roof would never leak," I say. "I'd have a bathtub. The AC would work properly in the summer and the heat would work properly in the winter. My next-door neighbors would be a quiet retired couple whose interests include five hundred piece puzzles and gardening."

He's quiet for a moment. Then he looks over at me, his face suddenly earnest, unguarded.

"Let's go somewhere," he says. "To celebrate. A weekend away."

"Didn't I just tell you not to jinx it?"

"Come on," he says. "We'll rent some charming cabin with a good view and a hot tub in some mountain town where no one knows us."

I hear the subtext, loud and clear. I play it back, make sure I got it right. I examine it for pitfalls.

"Just the two of us for a weekend," he says. "Come on."

My heart sputters, kicks, restarts, hammers away.

"Where?"

"Anywhere," he says. "Please?"

I hold my breath for a moment, nervous despite everything, nervous even though I know I shouldn't be.

"I'm sorry I didn't kiss you last weekend," I say, getting the words out before I can stop myself.

His eyebrows hitch upward.

"You kissed me plenty," he says.

"In front of everyone, I mean," I say.

My chest feels like balloon about to burst, just waiting for him to say *oh, I was only kidding about that* or *I was just drunk* or another of a hundred phrases that would pop me like a needle.

"I wish I had," I whisper.

Eli takes my hand in his, winding our fingers together.

"How about instead of that, I take you to dinner Tuesday after you win?" he says.

"Don't—"

"Jinx it, I know, can I take you to dinner or what? Here. In town."

My heart feels like a bellows.

"What if I don't win because you jinxed it?" I ask.

"Then I'll take you out to get your mind off it," he says.

"What if Martin wins?"

Eli makes a face.

"If Martin wins I say we get sloppy drunk and make out at the bar until they have to call someone to come pick us up," he says, and I laugh.

"Okay," I finally say. "Dinner if someone good wins, shots if Martin wins."

"Exactly."

My hand is still in his, and he absentmindedly taps my knuckles with his fingers in that restless way he always has, and I watch him. I already can't remember what I was so nervous about, but that's the way it always goes.

"Eli," I say.

He stops tapping for a second, his eyes flicking to mine.

"Violet.

"I like you," I say.

There's more to it than that. There's desire and lust, obviously, and there's everything that's between us. But there's also these quiet moments. There's also him showing me the constellations on his roof or holding me in the car while I told him about my mom. There's making pancakes for breakfast and bringing pies to his family dinner.

"I like you, too," he whispers back, his eyes crinkling with a smile as he brings my hand to his lips and kisses it. "A lot."

CHAPTER THIRTY-NINE

VIOLET

Tuesday morning, I wake up at five a.m., like I'm a kid on Christmas. After thirty minutes of trying to go back to sleep I give up, get out of my bed quietly, toss on my robe, head into my kitchen, and make some coffee.

Two hours later, Eli wanders in, pillow lines on his face, hair mussed and wild, in nothing but his boxers.

It's a very good morning sight.

He gives me a suspicious look, then shakes his head and pours himself some coffee.

"You're that excited for this meeting?" he says, sleep still weighing down his voice.

"I just couldn't sleep," I say, pushing aside the book I was reading.

"You do know there are other employees at Bramblebush who do good work," he teases. "Like me, for example. I did okay this summer."

"I didn't say I couldn't sleep because I think I'm going to win," I say, truthfully. "I just said I couldn't sleep."

If I really thought I were going to win I'd have slept like

a baby. I hate to admit it, but it's the thought of not winning that's kept me up.

I don't like losing. I really, really don't like it.

"Mhm," he says, lifting the coffee to his lips. "I'm sure that hasn't crossed your mind at all."

I just roll my eyes.

"Just remember us little guys when you win," he says. "Name some of us in your acceptance speech."

He leans against my counter, sipping. I take a minute to ogle, because I can.

"Are you suggesting I name you?" I ask. "And to Eli Loveless, thanks for keeping my bed warm?"

"I did better than that," he teases, grinning. "A heating pad could keep your bed *warm*. Besides, I do have professional accomplishments. Several, in fact."

"You gonna thank me in your speech?"

"Does the winner really have to give a speech?"

"I didn't last year or the year before," I admit. "It would be weird."

"Good," he says. "I hate giving speeches."

"You'd love doing it if you won," I say. "Don't lie, Eli, I know you too well for that."

He laughs.

"Maybe," he admits. "Mostly, I'd want to revel for as long as I could in the fact that I beat you at something."

I lean my head against my hand.

"Still, Eli?" I say lightly. "Even now?"

He drinks the last of his coffee, puts the mug in my sink, and crosses the kitchen toward me.

"Especially now," he says, and kisses me on top of the head. "I'm gonna take a shower. Leave without me if you want, I've got my key."

· · · · ★ ★ ★ ★ ★ · · · ·

I DON'T SEE Eli again until the all-staff meeting starts, and then it's from across the room. I stand around, having my fourth cup of coffee, trying to make idle chatter with Lydia and Kevin when he walks in.

He saunters straight over to us. My heart flutters and I brace myself, all at once, remembering our conversation from last night. We're real now. I'm fully prepared to admit to the world that Eli Loveless is my boyfriend.

But I don't think I can kiss him in front of my coworkers. That's just weird, right? Weird and wildly unprofessional? And against several workplace guidelines?

Eli just nods at me, like he can read my mind. Maybe he can by now, who knows.

"How's your head?" he asks Kevin.

"It's been better," my poor intern says. "Montgomery did chew us out pretty good."

Lydia makes a face.

"I heard," Eli says dryly. "Zane and Brandon have had their tails between their legs all week."

"He said the only reason he didn't fire us is because this is our last week, so there was no point," Kevin admits. "So that's... something."

A hush falls over the assembled staff, and Lydia's eyes snap to the front.

I turn, heart already thumping.

Montgomery is standing in front of everyone, looking as self-important and well-dressed as ever in a white linen suit and an ascot.

An *ascot.* How is this man real and not a cartoon character?

"Good morning, everyone, and thank you so much for coming to this meeting," he says, as if it's not mandatory. "First off, I'd like to thank you all for a wonderful, outstanding wedding season."

Polite applause.

"Before I get down to things, I'd just like to share a few statistics about the past three months," he says, unfolding a piece of paper. "Did you all know that this is the busiest wedding seasons Bramblebush has ever had?"

Murmurs from the assembled employees.

"That's right, folks," he goes on. "Between Memorial Day and today, we have hosted seventeen weddings, including four on Fridays, plus one community block party!"

Polite laughter. I feel like something's clawing at the inside of my chest, so I take another sip of coffee, trying to play it off.

"That's nearly seventy-seven hundred guests at Bramblebush," Montgomery says. "With the largest wedding being…"

He keeps talking numbers, the noise becoming a dull roar in my ears. I can't stand this. I feel like Montgomery is doing this to hurt me, personally, because every moment that I don't find out whether I beat Eli is another moment that I feel like I'm suffocating on my own anxiety.

Eli's standing next to me. He shifts his weight from one foot to the other, and I swear, I feel like he's just rubbed porcupines on me.

I can't help it.

I really want to beat him.

I know I shouldn't feel like this about it. I know that he's also worked his ass off this summer. I know that I should be preparing myself to be a gracious loser, that competition isn't everything, that the true prize is real friendship or some Sesame Street bullshit like that.

Yeah, no. I've spent my entire life wanting to beat Eli Loveless at everything and despite everything, today's no different.

"Isn't that fascinating?" Montgomery asks the clearly un-fascinated crowd. "I thought that was really something. Thanks to Rosa Garcia for those facts."

A smattering of applause.

"All right, I've kept you waiting for long enough," Montgomery says, folding his hands together. "I know you're all really here to learn who's won the Most Valuable Employee prize this summer."

A buzz zips through the crowd. I clench my coffee mug a little tighter.

It doesn't matter, I lie to myself. *Be happy for whoever wins, and if you're not, fake it.*

"Well, this year's winner is someone who really earned it," Montgomery says. "An employee who embodied the spirit of a team player, but who went above and beyond when called upon to do so."

I'm going to die waiting for this announcement.

"And that employee is…"

My hands are shaking.

"Elijah Loveless!"

Oh.

Everything stops for a split second. I hold my breath, hands still clenched around my coffee cup, and I wait.

I wait for the announcement to feel like a punch in the stomach. I wait for it to feel like all my efforts are futile, like I'm not good enough and I'll never be good enough.

But there's no punch. There's no overwhelming feeling of failure.

I look at up at Eli. He looks down at me, grinning, and I'm surprised to realize that I'm smiling, too.

"Good job," I say softly. "You deserve it."

Holy shit, I meant that.

"Thanks," he says, and then everyone is applauding, people turning around to congratulate him, people patting him on the back and cracking jokes about what he should do with the money.

I swallow, tuck my coffee mug under my arm, and applaud along with them.

I'm disappointed. I'm bummed. I'm sad I didn't win, and yeah, there's a part of me that's annoyed that Eli did. But there's a bigger part that knows he deserves it, and that part's actually happy for him.

What is *happening*?

"Congratulations, Elijah!" Montgomery says. "Here's to your first wedding season of many."

Eli holds up his coffee mug, like he's toasting Montgomery.

"Thank you," he calls, looking a little lost for words.

I keep my hands on my own coffee mug, even though he looks over at me again. I have the urge to put my hand on his arm, lean in, kiss him, but we're at work in an all-staff meeting, so I keep my hands to myself.

Eli just smiles at me again, and then Montgomery keeps talking.

"Now that that's over, we have just a few more things to discuss…" he says, still standing in the front.

"Dinner's on me tonight," Eli says into my ear, leaning down.

· · · · · ★ ★ ★ ★ ★ · · · · ·

I HEAD BACK to my office in a slight daze. I lost something — to Eli, no less — and I don't actually mind that much. Don't get me wrong. I still wish I'd won. I'd still love to be twenty grand richer right now.

But I am, at best, *fairly* disappointed, and that's all. Eli deserves it. He folded cranes. He saved a cake. He made good food for impossible people, and he did it all without making a big deal of it.

When I wake my computer up, the lake cottage's listing is still up on my browser.

That gets a twist in the stomach. A twinge of regret, a brief lump in my throat, a brief bout of intense desire. I hate my trailer. I hate it. I hate that it's too hot in the summer and too cold in the winter, I hate that it's where my mom died, I hate that it keeps costing me money even though it's barely worth anything.

More than anything I hate that it's a trailer in a trailer park and that, despite everything, I haven't managed to get out of there.

I close the window and take a deep breath. I'll get there. I've been steadily saving for ages now. I'm close to a down payment, even without the prize money. If this house goes off the market there will be other houses, and life goes on.

Just as I fire up Excel, my phone rings.

"Violet," Montgomery's voice says. "Could I see you in my office?"

"Of course," I say, my heart skipping a beat. Maybe there's some sort of secondary prize. Maybe I'm getting a pay bump or a promotion.

"Sit," he says when I knock on the door, his face grave.

I do. My stomach suddenly clenches. My lips feel cold.

This is not a good office visit.

Montgomery sits. He clicks something with his mouse, not making eye contact.

Then without a word, he turns the monitor to face me.

I'm on it.

I'm sitting on the floor, against a couch, my skin totally washed out by the flash. I'm laughing, leaning back.

I'm naked. Visible from the waist up, my nipples hard and brownish pink.

I'm clearly in the wedding barn.

I think I'm going to throw up.

Montgomery calmly turns the monitor back around. I have both my hands over my mouth. I'm shaking, shivering, suddenly cold and hot at the same time.

"I got that from an anonymous email account Saturday night," he says, folding his hands on the desk. "And I don't mind admitting that until I did, I considered you and Elijah neck-and-neck for the award. I even gave serious thought to giving you each ten thousand dollars."

I just shake my head, hands still clamped over my mouth. He saw me naked. Montgomery, my boss, saw me topless.

I close my eyes. I can't look at him.

"Violet, I want you to understand that the only reason I'm not firing you for blatant impropriety on Bramblebush grounds is that you've got a long history of excellent work here," he drones on.

I force myself to nod. There's bile rising in my throat. I feel like someone put whiskey in my veins, every pump of my heart burning worse than the one before it.

"I won't tolerate something like this again," he says. "And frankly, Violet, I'm shocked at you. I half-expect idiots like Zane or Kevin to do this, but you?"

I don't answer him. I just breathe because that's all I can manage.

"Violet?" Montgomery asks.

I swallow hard, grit my teeth, try to pull myself together. I sit up straight, though I keep my eyes closed because I absolutely cannot look into the face of my boss who just saw me naked.

"I'm sorry," I whisper. "I—"

My stomach heaves, tightens.

I run. I run out of his office and to the bathroom, where I throw open a stall door and barely make it in time. I throw up until I'm dry heaving. I flush the toilet again and again, tears streaming down my face, and when I'm sure I'm done I sit on the toilet, still clothed, and lean my head against the side of the stall.

My whole body is shaking. I sit there for a long time. People come and go into the other stalls, and I don't leave.

It feels like I've been stabbed in the heart.

I should never have let him take that picture.

I should have known that people don't change. I should have seen, somehow, that instead of mellowing out Eli's only gotten colder, more ruthless, more willing to fuck people over to get what he wants. I should have learned my lesson when we were kids, but I didn't.

Instead I slept with him and for fuck's sake, I let myself *like* him and here I am, now, crying in a bathroom stall while there's a picture of my tits on my boss's hard drive.

I throw up again.

CHAPTER FORTY

ELI

Twenty thousand dollars.

It might be the most money I've ever seen at one time. It's definitely the most money I've ever had at my disposal, right here in my hands in the form of a check from Bramblebush.

And I have no idea what to do with it. I didn't think I'd win. I thought Violet would, and despite everything, I was strangely okay with it.

I still wanted to win. Wanting to beat Violet at something is baked into my DNA at this point, but in truth, I was ready to be happy for her.

But now I get to be happy for me.

"Congratulations," Montgomery says, patting me on the shoulder one more time. "Don't spend it all in one place."

Then he turns and leaves the kitchen. I realize that everyone's looking at me, and I quickly slide the check into my pocket.

"You're at least gonna take us for drinks, right?" Naomi

says. "Try to remember the little people after you've hit the big time."

"Fancy drinks," Brandon adds in. "At that new cocktail bar downtown."

"Are you even old enough to drink?" I ask.

"Bet twenty grand could buy a decent fake ID," Naomi adds in.

"Drinks are a maybe," I tell them, faux-sternly. "I'm not buying anyone a fake ID. Get back to work."

"Whatever you say, Uncle Moneybags," Naomi teases, pulling out some huge mixing bowls.

I stare around the kitchen, trying to remember what's happening. I think we're preparing for some corporate event that's tomorrow night — a textbook manufacturer who wants an old-world Italian feast — though, for the first time since I started here, there's no Saturday wedding.

Take Violet somewhere she's never been. Forget a bed and breakfast in the mountains. Go to Paris.

Put a down payment on a house of your own so you can move out of your mom's house.

Buy a new car, for the love of God.

What does Italian food need? Probably tomato sauce. Maybe I should just make several gallons of tomato sauce and then figure out what else later.

Open a brewpub with Daniel and Seth. Expand the brewery, have your own kitchen. Quit working for Montgomery, because twenty grand aside, he's a terrible boss.

That's actually not a bad idea.

I'm lugging three gallon-sized cans of whole tomatoes back from storage when the kitchen door opens, and Violet steps in quietly.

She looks like hell. Her hair's a mess. Her eyes are red, puffy, glassy, her face splotchy.

And she glares at me like she's trying to set me on fire with her mind.

I drop the tomatoes on the counter with a bang. Everyone else in the kitchen looks over at the noise, looks at her, looks at me, and quickly goes back to whatever they were doing.

The bottom's already dropped out of my stomach. She walks over to me.

"Eli," she says, her voice a rough whisper, her eyes flat with anger.

Before I can answer, she walks away. I don't know what else to do, so I follow her though the kitchen, around the corner, into the cold storage room.

In a flash, I remember the time I kissed her here. In the middle of that awful wedding. We'd been up all night and just made five hundred cranes together, and when I saw her come in here, I had to follow her. I had to kiss her just that once or I thought I might die.

Violet turns. The sharks in her eyes snap their teeth. We're not here for a kiss.

"Why?" she asks, her voice breaking.

I don't know what's happening, but I go to take her by the shoulders. I want to comfort her, tell her that whatever's happened, it'll be okay.

She steps back before I can touch her.

"Don't," she says. "Don't you *dare* right now."

Panic stabs at me. Anger blossoms in the wound, a gut reaction, a pure and simple reflex at Violet's fury. I haven't even done anything. I keep myself in check.

"What are you talking about?" I ask.

"I should have known," she says, her arms crossed in front of her chest. She's shaking. She looks away and a tear runs down her cheek, her jaw flexing. "Of course you didn't change. Of course you'd fuck me over for that much money, you fucking asshole."

Her words feel like bricks, hitting me one by one.

"You think I fucked you over to win?" I say, cracking the knuckles on my right hand, anger booming inside me, hot and dark. "I win one *goddamn* thing and you can't handle that?"

She snorts, derisively. She looks at me like I'm something she found on the bottom of her shoe, tears streaming out of both eyes now.

"He showed me the picture," she says, like I'm stupid.

I feel like something gets yanked out from under me.

"What picture?" I ask.

"I can't believe I was this stupid," she says, ignoring my question. Her voice wobbles, but she keeps control. "I can't believe that after everything I knew about you, all the shit you used to do to me, how much I knew you *hated* me growing up, that I would fall for this just because you got hot. Well, good job, joke's on me, you win."

"What picture?" I say, louder this time.

"No," she says looking me dead in the eye. "Fuck no, I'm not falling for that."

"Goddammit, Violet, *what picture?*" I say, stepping forward, clenching my teeth so I don't shout. Violet stands her ground, crying and glaring.

"What picture, Violet?" I ask, my voice deadly calm.

"The picture of me in the wedding barn, Eli," she says, like I'm an idiot, her voice so quiet I can barely hear her. "The one you sent to Montgomery."

Black tendrils curl around my windpipe, choking me.

Montgomery has a naked picture of Violet.

I feel like the wind's been knocked out of me.

"The one I let you take when we were drunk last weekend?" she says. Now her voice has a mocking edge to it, lashing out. "The one I told you wouldn't work as blackmail? Tell me, did I give you the idea myself?"

"I swear to God I didn't send Montgomery anything," I tell her. The panic knife turns, opens a hole in my chest. "I promise you I would never—"

"Did you think I wouldn't find out?" she hisses, her eyes wide. "Did you think you'd just win and he'd never tell me and we would just keep fucking until you got bored of me and moved on? Or did you not mind that I'd find out?"

"I didn't fucking do anything."

"You made up this whole Martin story," she whispers. "You fucked with the cranes, you made shit go missing, you put the bull in the pool and I *fucking* believed you about all of it because you're hot now and Martin's always been a douche."

I turn away from her. I have to. I want to punch something: the door, the wall, a side of beef, throw fifty pounds of potatoes at the wall. I want to absolutely wreck some shit right now.

"You really think I did this?" I ask, my own voice shaking.

"I think you fucked me over for twenty grand? Yeah, it tracks," she says like she's spitting daggers.

"Two months," I say, turning back toward her. I feel like I'm crumbling. Turning to rubble.

She swallows, sniffles, her face furious, her arms still locked in front of her.

"We were together for *two months* and you don't believe me?" I ask. My voice rises.

"We weren't together."

It stings. It shouldn't, but it does.

"I don't get the benefit of the doubt for one second."

"Not you, no."

I just stare at her, because I feel like I've been thrown

into a pit with no rope, no ladder, no way out.

"You think that's who I am?" I ask. "I did all that in some plot to win money?"

"I don't think you minded the sex."

"I can't fucking believe you," I say. I turn away again. I can't look at her right now.

"A naked picture of me magically gets transported from your phone to my boss, you win twenty grand, and after all the shit you did to me for years and years I'm supposed to think that it *wasn't* you?" she says.

Fuck this. Fuck her. Fuck me for thinking there was something between us.

"Yeah, I thought maybe I'd earned two seconds of trust," I say, walking for the door. "I forgot you only like people when you think you're better than them. Fuck you, Violet."

I open the door, warm air hitting me in the face.

"Fuck *you*, Eli!" I hear as it closes.

I storm back through the kitchen, rage radiating through my bones from a black supernova somewhere in the vicinity of my heart. I want to smash every piece of glass in this place, knock over every appliance, throw every pot. I want to shout at Violet until she hears reason.

And I want to kill whoever sent that picture. It never once occurred to me that someone might find my phone and go through it, even though I don't have it on me most of the day. Jesus Christ, it's not even locked.

Fuck me, this is all my fault.

I shove through the kitchen doors. I know everyone's watching me. I know they probably just heard the fight Violet and I got into, but see if I give a damn.

I'm at Montgomery's office door in thirty seconds flat. I ignore his secretary and push it open.

"Who sent it?" I ask, not bothering with preamble.

He goes red. There's a woman sitting across his desk from him, her mouth a small O of surprise.

"Excuse me—"

"Who sent the picture of Violet?" I ask.

"Elijah, you can't just barge in here—"

"I took it," I tell him, stepping to the desk, both my palms flat on it. "In the barn. Last Saturday. We were drunk. You want to see the rest?"

"No," he says, his face bright and his voice cold. "I'm not interested in your lovers' quarrel, Elijah."

"This is not a lovers' quarrel," I say, fighting to keep control of myself. "This is someone stealing a private photo from me—"

"A photo which clearly shows her acting inappropriately on company property."

"—and sending it to you without her permission or knowledge. Tell me who sent it."

"Get out."

"Tell me—"

"Get out before I fire you both and cancel that check," he says, standing slowly, adjusting his tie. He's still bright red with anger. "I don't want to lose either of you, Elijah, but so help me God if you don't leave my office this instant you will both be out of a job."

I don't give a shit about my own job. I'm seething with rage, tempted to just grab his computer and leave with it, see if I can't find out myself.

But I can't do that to Violet. As furious as I am, I can't get her fired, too.

I turn and leave without another word. His secretary goggles, and I ignore her, stalking back into the hall, winding through the maze of offices.

I have a pretty good idea who did this. I don't know how he knew there were pictures like that on my phone. I usually leave it in my locker. Maybe he's been going through my things this whole time.

When I get to Martin's office, my rage has simmered to a slow, even boil. I walk inside and he looks up, then looks worried as I shut the door behind myself.

"Congratulations on the—"

I grab him by the front of the shirt and pull him bodily from his chair, his arms windmilling.

"What the—"

"I know it was you," I say, and shove him against the wall. "You're a vile fucking piece of trash."

His eyes go wide in fake shock. I know a liar when I see one.

"Know what was me?"

His hands grab at my wrists, but I'm locked on, rage-fueled.

"Don't fucking play," I say, keeping my voice down. "I know it was you, I know what you did, and you're going to fucking pay for it."

Martin's breathing hard. He's average-sized, but I'm bigger, and more importantly, I'm angrier. His eyes search mine.

And then, I swear to God, he smirks at me.

"Prove it," he says.

It takes all my self-control not to strangle him. I want to. I want to give him two black eyes and a broken nose for what he did to Violet, for going through *my* pictures of her, for sending them to her boss. Nothing seems like enough for violating her like that.

"I will fuck you up," I say, getting right in his face. "If you ever so much as look at Violet again I'll rip your heart out and serve it as an appetizer."

Then I let him go, turn around, and leave his office before I can do something that could land me in jail.

CHAPTER FORTY-ONE

VIOLET

"Everyone heard it," I say through my hands, leaning both elbows on Adeline's kitchen table. "Everyone. The kitchen staff. The planning people. They probably heard it out in the Lodge. Jesus, they probably heard us fighting in Roanoke—"

"There's too much road work on Interstate 81," she says. "Don't worry."

"I can't go back there," I say, taking a deep shuddering breath. "My boss has seen my tits because my ex-fuckbuddy screwed me over for twenty grand."

Adeline just strokes my hair, but I see her fist clench on the table.

"I can't believe that's all it took," I say, and by the time I get to *took* my voice is nothing more than a high-pitched squeak. "Who does that? Fucking Eli couldn't just dump me, he had to—"

I break off and take a deep breath.

"He's a fucking snake," she says, and her voice is soft but there's steel in it.

"I told him I liked him," I say, miserably. "Like five days

ago. God, I'm so dumb. He said we were gonna go on vacation together to a cabin with a hot tub and I bet the whole fucking time he'd already sent Montgomery a picture of my tits in the barn."

"You're not dumb," Adeline says, pushing my hair out of my face. "You're human."

"For money," I say, for at least the thousandth time.

I start crying again. I don't know how the hell I haven't cried all the liquid in my body out today, but apparently there's more. *Fuck.*

"I knew how he was. I fucking knew, Adeline. And I went and let him take a picture of my tits anyway."

She doesn't say anything, but a muscle in her jaw clenches.

"And he fucked me over for twenty grand," I say.

My chest feels hollow, like someone's scooped it out, except I'm still breathing and my heart is still beating so I guess I'm fine, technically.

"Do you want me to help you hide the body?" she asks, her voice perfectly gentle.

I grab a tissue and blow my nose.

"Where?" I ask.

She leans her chin on her own hand, still stroking my hair. I let her, because it feels nice, and because my hair's a wreck right now anyway.

"A body of water is probably the best place," she says, her voice still so soothing and gentle. "It'll help get rid of any evidence, and the police almost never have the resources to properly search the deep ones."

I sigh a deep, shuddering sigh.

"Last week they pulled a car out of Evans Lake that had been there since 1977," she says.

"A car?" I say.

For half a second, I forget about Eli.

"Yup," she says. "I think it was a Buick."

"No one noticed it there?"

Adeline just shrugs.

"Apparently not," she says. "I think the trick is to make sure it doesn't float back to the surface. Because if someone finds a hand on the shore—"

"Okay, okay, you *have* to watch fewer true crime shows," I say.

"I'd be really good at murder, though."

"Adeline, you're a nurse," I say.

"Well, besides the murder part," she says. "I think I'd be really bad at that. Except with Eli."

I sniffle. I lean my forehead against my hand, a tissue wadded up in it.

"Murder is probably worse than sending someone's boss a naked picture," I say.

Despite myself, I replay it. The picture. Montgomery's face. The punch to the gut of knowing that Eli picked money over me.

"I thought he'd changed," I say, another wave of misery washing over me. "I mean, he was still kind of an asshole but I thought he was an okay asshole. But no, he just got worse and meaner and *bad* and fuck everything, Adeline, I quit. I fucking quit life."

I say that last part with my forehead against her kitchen table.

"It's okay to quit," she says.

"I am getting twenty cats and moving to the mountain," I say. "Cats don't even know what money is."

"Aren't you allergic to cats?"

"Don't ruin my plans," I tell her.

"Sorry."

I take another deep breath and look over at the clock on her stove. It's 6:30.

"You should go to work before you're late," I tell her.

"I've got a few minutes."

"I'm fine," I say.

She keeps stroking my hair, pulling it off my face where it's sticking to my tears.

"Stay here tonight, okay?" she says.

I just nod.

"Take a bath, watch a movie, you know where all my stuff is, right? Use a toothbrush from the hall closet, I just got a value pack of new ones."

"Thanks," I say.

Fuck, his toothbrush is still on my sink. His pillow probably still smells like him. I think there's bacon still in my fridge that he bought last week.

I let Eli into my life and he fucked me over. He fucked me over and he wasn't even sorry.

Pressure pounds at the back of my eyes, and I push at them with my fingers, like I can ward it off.

"Go to work," I say. "I'm fine."

"Violet," she murmurs.

"Fine-ish?" I try.

I look up into her blue eyes, her eyebrows knit together. She's been sitting here for almost three hours, listening to me sob the same stupid story over and over again. Adeline might be an actual angel.

"Seriously," I say.

She stands, glancing at the clock again.

"I think there's a relaxation aromatherapy candle under the bathroom sink," she says.

"Does that work?"

"No," she says. "Aromatherapy's bullshit. But it smells nice, and that's something."

"Thanks," I say.

She grabs her stuff, pulls her hair back, grabs some yogurt and an apple from the fridge.

"Try to sleep, okay?" she says, kissing me on the top of the head. "You know the Netflix password. No romcoms, promise?"

"No," I mutter.

"Violet."

"Fine, no romcoms."

"Movies with explosions only," she says, grabbing her purse. "I want to come back in the morning and find that you've watched The Rock's entire body of work."

"Yes, ma'am," I say.

"Eli's a shithead and an asshole and he'll get what's coming his way," she says. "I'll see you in the morning. Explosions!"

She shuts the front door behind herself. I rub my eyes. I blow my nose again, then put my mug in the sink and my tissues in the trash.

I don't feel better. I still feel like a hamburger wrapper that someone left on the side of the road, discarded and tossed aside. But I also don't feel worse.

I head into her living room, flop on the couch, fire up Netflix, and find a movie that stars The Rock, because I'll do anything to keep my mind off Eli.

CHAPTER FORTY-TWO

ELI

The guy who opens the door is heavyset, fiftyish, white, and has the bearing of someone who's accustomed to giving orders. I've never met him before. He must not live in town.

"Help you?" he asks, hands on hips.

"Hope so," I say. "We've been having a problem with some of our pantry items growing legs and walking off, and Montgomery thinks you might be able to give us some idea of who's to blame."

I smile at him, the easy, charming, good-old-boy smile I learned from growing up around my dad's cop buddies. I pretend my palms aren't sweating.

I look like hell because I didn't really sleep last night. I couldn't. I just laid there, watching the ceiling, trying to think about something besides Violet, furious at me and crying in cold storage.

When I was a kid, my dad used to take us fishing at this catch-and-release pond nearby. Usually, the fish would bite the hook, we'd take it out, and they'd go on their merry way. But every so often, the fish would swallow the hook, and if that happened it was all over for the fish. Either we had to pull it out or cut it out, and either way, the fish was a goner.

I feel like I've swallowed the hook, like something sharp and merciless is wedged behind my ribcage and I'm just waiting for it to destroy me. Every time I think about her, it tugs. Every time I remember her saying *I like you* or think of her on the roof, looking at the stars, it tugs.

Even though apparently the last two months don't matter, it hurts. Even though she thinks I could do this to her, it hurts.

It hurts and I have to do something to try and fix it, no matter what.

"Monty didn't say anything about that," the guy says.

Monty?

"It was just a suggestion he had," I say. "But we've had nearly a thousand dollars of saffron go missing in the past week, and I'm starting to think that someone might be selling it on the black market."

His brow furrows.

"Saffron?"

"It's a spice," I explain. "Sells for five thousand dollars a pound, so I'd hate to lose too much."

He emits a low whistle, then steps back from the door, letting me into the security office suite.

"Don't know how much we can help you, but you're welcome to look through the footage. Talk to Marcus over there. I'm Jim, by the way."

We shake hands. I introduce myself. I confirm that there is, indeed, a black market for spices, a fact which gets another whistle out of him.

Finally, he walks me through the small office suite to the reason I'm there: the monitor room. Inside is a young man, leaning back in his chair, hands behind his head, looking up at a bank of screens. There must be at least thirty.

"Marcus," Jim says. "This is Eli. Can you point him to the cameras on the kitchen? They're having a spice problem."

"Of course," he says, and I step into the room, sit in an empty chair. Jim leaves.

"What kind of spice problem?" he asks.

"I think someone's stealing the expensive ones," I say, and explain the problem I invented.

It's not real, obviously. I'm not going to find that anyone's stealing the saffron, or the vanilla beans, or anything else.

I'm going to catch Martin in the act.

Then I'm going to take this footage to Montgomery and get his ass fired.

It doesn't feel like enough. I want to get him fired and then scorch the earth behind him. I want to get him fired and make him unemployable. I want to get him fired, get him kicked out of his house, get his driver's license revoked. I want him to have to change his name and move to a new state, and once he's there, I want someone to take a picture of his flaccid dick and put it up on every street corner and signpost.

I want Martin to suffer. That's what I want.

For now I'll have to settle for getting him fired.

Violet might never talk to me again, but by God, I'm going to do something about this shitweasel.

"All right," Marcus says, and pushes a laptop toward me. "We store footage for the last week on this, but after two weeks it's deleted from there and stored on the cloud. See those folders that say 'Kitchen 1' and 'Kitchen 2'?"

"That's the kitchen?" I ask.

"You got it."

It's pretty self-explanatory, and I start going through the video files. They're each labeled with the camera and date, so I find what I need instantly.

Then I hit a dead end. There are only two cameras in the kitchen, and neither one is in the room where our lockers are. Neither is even pointed at the entrance to that room.

The hook digs deeper. It buries itself in my stomach and I swear I can feel the cold steel point digging into my spine.

I don't give up. I didn't lie my way into the security office to give up, so I diligently go through a week's worth of kitchen footage, skimming through it as fast as I can.

Martin comes and goes three times: Tuesday, Wednesday, Friday. Each time he's in the kitchen easily for long enough to head to the lockers, find my phone, go through my photos.

The thought makes me sick to my stomach. How many of them did he go through? Did he look at all of them? Did he deliberate over which picture to send to Montgomery? Did he go back and forth from one topless picture of Violet to another, deciding?

I take a deep breath. I unclench my jaw. I unclench my fists.

On the screen, Martin leaves the kitchen and I still have nothing and I lean back in the chair, rub my eyes. I look at the bank of monitors in front of us, and I try to think.

There has to be something, I tell myself. *He fucked things up for everyone all summer long.*

Somewhere, there's evidence.

Something catches my eye: a bright flash, a quick glint of sunlight on water. On one of the pool cameras, a kid wearing arm floats just did a cannonball into the water.

I sit up straighter. I lean forward again, like I've got a renewed interest in catching my saffron thief.

Marcus doesn't pay me much attention. I open the folder labeled POOL.

It's the same as the kitchen cameras: sorted by date. I scan for the 25th, two Saturdays ago.

The files skip from 8-24 to 8-26.

I blink. I double-check.

I'm not wrong.

I open a dialogue box and search the computer for 8-25. Marcus still isn't paying attention, but I find nothing. No pool footage from that day. Not even in the trash.

Tension prickles through my veins, even as my stomach twists.

Suddenly, Jim appears in the doorway. Marcus and I both look up.

"You find what you need?" he asks.

I found the opposite, I think.

"Camera's pointed at the wrong place," I say, regretfully. "Thanks for the help, though."

"No problem," he says, and I shake his beefy hand.

· · · · ★ ★ ★ ★ ★ · · · ·

I SQUEEZE a few more drops onto the whetstone, draw the knife through it, and then crouch down in front of the counter.

Shiiiick.

I adjust the angle and do it again. The sound raises the hairs on the back of my neck, but I ignore that in favor of the solid feel of steel on stone underneath my hands, the concentration it takes to do this freehand.

Shiiick. Shiiiick.

I have to do something or I'll lose my mind.

"Should you be doing that while you're drinking whiskey?" my mom asks from behind me.

I draw the knife across the whetstone one more time, check the blade, then look over my shoulder.

"I could do this in my sleep," I tell her.

She walks up to the counter, leans one hip against it, standing next to me.

"Yes, but should you be doing it while drinking?"

My mom eyes the mostly-empty glass of whiskey on the counter near the knives.

"I'm fine," I tell her.

"Are all those knives really ours?" she asks.

"They were in your kitchen," I say, holding the knife I'm working on against the stone again. "Maybe you stole them from a church potluck, I don't know."

"Are you planning on sharpening them all?"

I glance at the counter. It's mostly covered in knives: steak knives, carving knives, butcher knives, even a filet knife or two.

"If they're dull."

"Why's there an axe?"

"Because it needs sharpening," I say, drawing the knife over the stone again. "Or I assume it does. You ever sharpened that thing?"

"Do you want to talk about it?" she asks, still leaning against the counter.

"About sharpening the axe?"

"About whatever's wrong," she says.

Shiick. Shiiick. Shiiiick.

"Everything is fine," I say, not looking at her.

I'm lying. She knows I'm lying, and I know she knows I'm lying. Clara Loveless is a very smart woman — she got her Ph.D. in astronomy when she was fifty-three, after raising five boys — and there's not much fooling her.

"Bullshit," my mom says. "You're sharpening every blade in a ten-mile radius while drinking whiskey, and moreover, you're home at six o'clock on a weeknight. The sun's still shining, for Pete's sake, Elijah."

I put the knife down, sigh, pick up the whiskey, and down the rest. I don't particularly want to tell my mom all about the problems I'm having with the girl I was fucking, but the alcohol's making me want to talk.

"I got into a fight with Violet," I say.

"A fight? With Violet? Surely not," my mom deadpans.

"If that's how you're going to be then—"

"I'm sorry, sweetheart, you're right," my mom says, putting a hand on my arm. "That was unkind of me."

"She thinks I sent our boss a picture of her so I'd win the twenty grand," I say, walking back to the bar where the whiskey is. I pour myself another glass.

My mom grabs a glass, comes over, and holds it out. I pour her some whiskey too.

"What kind of picture?" she asks.

I drink and don't answer.

"I see," she says, and I have to look away as my face heats up. "Did you?"

"No!"

She takes my elbow and leads me to the back porch, sitting us both down. I let her, even though I feel a little like a child. A whiskey-drinking child.

"Then this is just a misunderstanding," she says.

"She thinks I'm a sociopath."

"Does she have a reason to think that?" my mom asks.

I drink. I want to say *no*. I want to have only ever been nice to Violet in my life. I want there to be no reason for her to think ill of me, but I know that's not true.

"Not a good one," I finally say.

My mom looks at me. I drink again. The alcohol feels good, like it's dulling my brain.

"Violet hasn't had a lot of kindness in her life," my mom says. It's not what I expected her to say.

"Well, she's not very kind," I mutter into the whiskey.

"I once went over to her mother's house when the two of you were in first grade," my mom says, ignoring my input. "I forget why I was there. The place smelled like a chimney, but anyway, I noticed something. There was nothing on the fridge. Not a single piece of artwork."

I frown. I take another drink. My mom is looking at me expectantly, like she's waiting for something.

I stand and walk to the back door, look in at the fridge.

It's covered with Rusty's drawings. You can barely see the fridge between pieces of construction paper decorated with crayon.

I sit back down.

"So Daniel's a better parent than her mom was," I say.

"Not to speak ill of the dead, but yes," my mom admits. "But besides that, there's a reason why people are the way they are."

"Then how come I'm like that?"

"That's your father's genetics," she says, smiling slyly. "Not to speak ill of the dead."

I roll my eyes.

"My point is, I like Violet and since sometimes you're too stubborn to know what's good for you, I don't mind telling you that you'd do yourself a disservice to lose her."

"She's the one who lost me."

"What I'm suggesting," my mom says, ignoring me again, "is that maybe you don't worry about what you think she deserves or what she's earned. Just be kind because you like her and everyone deserves kindness sometimes."

I run a hand through my hair and look out at our back yard: a quarter-acre of grass before the forest starts.

"What if she's a jerk and I'm happy to be rid of her?"

"Is that why you're drinking whiskey and sharpening knives?"

Fine.

"Your good advice is just *be nice*?" I say. "Can't you tell me, like… what kind of flowers to get her?"

"No, because I don't know shit about flowers," my mom says, laughing. "And, for the record, my advice is to be *very* nice."

Be very nice.

Yeah. Sure. Great.

"Thanks," I say, and finish that glass too.

My mom stands.

"I'm going to go put the knives away," she says lightly. "You can keep sulking out here if you'd like."

"I'm not sulking."

"I didn't say it was a bad thing," she tells me, standing. "We all need it now and again. Have a good sulk, Eli."

I do.

· · · · · ★ ★ ★ · · · · ·

I SPEND another night not sleeping.

My own bed feels strange. My pillow feels wrong. My blanket is too hot, then too cold, then too hot, and worst of all, Violet's not here.

I miss her. I hate this.

I'm still mad. The hook is still deep in my chest, still jerking every time I think of her face. I feel it every time I remind myself that she doesn't trust me. That she never trusted me. That she kept me at arm's length, ready to think the worst of me at the drop of a hat.

And I miss her. That's all. As complicated as things sometimes feel between us, this is simple. I miss talking to her while I make dinner, I miss bringing her coffee in the morning, and I miss waking up in her bed.

I'm angry with her and I miss her and I wish she were here and I want to fight with her about why she doesn't trust me and how she could ever *possibly* think that I would send that picture to Montgomery, and I want to bury my face in her hair and hold her close and never let her go.

I want to hand her Martin's head on a platter, but I can't even do that. I can't even metaphorically do that.

My mom's advice bangs around in my head. *Be very nice.* It's probably good life advice in general, but I don't know if it'll work with Violet.

To be honest, I'm not sure I've ever tried being nice to her. We've been a lot of things to each other, but nice? Not really.

I give up on sleeping and on my sheets that are always the wrong temperature, and I start pacing, running through the same things over and over. I feel like I'm spinning my wheels in mud, but I can't stop revving the engine.

The hook. Her hair on her pillow. The look in her eyes when we argued.

Be very nice.

Mid-pace, my door creaks open. Daniel sticks his head in.

"If you're not going to sleep, at least sit the fuck down," he hisses.

"Language, Daniel," I hiss back.

He frowns, leans in, taking a closer look at me.

"Jesus," he says.

I just glare.

"That bad, huh?" he asks.

"I'm fine," I say, crossing my arms in front of myself.

He just sighs.

"Come downstairs," he says, turns, and walks away.

· · · · ★ ★ ★ ★ ★ · · · ·

"—SO SHE HATES ME NOW," I say, my half-empty tea mug between my palms. "She hates me. She must have hated me all along, because apparently none of it mattered."

I take another swig of the peppermint tea Daniel made me. I wish it were bourbon.

"She didn't even want to date me," I say, mostly to myself. "I should have known. What the hell is wrong with me, Daniel?"

Daniel just watches me. He's spent this whole time listening, nodding along without saying much, but that's fine.

"I'm sorry," he says.

"Finally, there's a girl I like — really *like*, for fuck's sake — and she's an asshole," I go on. "She thinks I sent that picture to her boss. She thinks I would fucking show *anyone* else that picture of her. That's insane. Every time I imagine him opening that email I just — ugh."

"That's rough," Daniel agrees.

He's as calm as ever. When he was twenty-three Daniel found out he had a one-year-old daughter, and two months later he had full custody of a child he barely knew, so he's pretty much impossible to freak out.

"Can you prove you didn't do it, or is that not the point?" he asks, drinking his own tea.

"That's not the point," I say. "The point is—"

I stop. I don't even know what the point is, anymore. The point is that I'm hurt she could even think that and I'm hurt she wouldn't listen to me for one second and the point is also I'd probably take her back in a second if she walked in here right now.

"—well, I also can't prove it," I say.

I tell him about the kitchen cameras being pointed at the wrong thing. I tell him about Martin and what a shitweasel he is. I tell him about the cranes, the oysters, everything he tried to ruin this summer. I tell him about the mechanical bull and the deleted files.

"Okay," Daniel says, pointing at me. "That. Right there. I don't know shit about relationships but this, I got."

"What?" I ask, mystified.

"Deleted files. You can get those back."

There's a glimmer of hope. It's small. It's fragile. But it looks like Martin's head on a platter and even if Violet never speaks to me again, I want that.

"Rusty once managed to wipe everything from the computer at the brewery," he says. "It's a long story, and the moral is that we should have been doing regular back-ups, but we managed to recover all our files."

I sip my tea, mind already racing.

"You can probably do it yourself, honestly, but we called one of Silas's military buddies who does IT stuff now—"

"Do you still have his number?"

"Probably."

I pat my pajama pockets, looking for my phone.

"Eli, it's three in the morning."

"I need that number," I say.

"I'm not giving it to you if you're gonna call now," he says, sounding irritated. "Wait until morning."

"I will if you give it to me," I say.

"You also will if I don't give it to you," he points out, standing and taking our mugs. "My phone's in my room, can you make it that long?"

"I guess I'm waiting until morning," I say.

Daniel puts the mugs into the sink, then sighs, turning to me.

"C'mere," he says, and holds his arms out for a hug.

I step in. I don't hug my brothers that often but he's firm, solid. He pats me on the back, his short beard just barely tickling my ear.

"This sucks but it's gonna be okay," he says. "Try to get some sleep, you look like shit."

"Thanks," I say, and for once, I'm not even being sarcastic.

"You know what I mean," he says.

"I do."

We hold each other for one more second, and as we separate I tousle his hair. He makes a face at me.

"Go the fuck to bed, Eli," he says, but he's smiling.

CHAPTER FORTY-THREE

ELI

There's some contraption on Silas's head. I stand next to my Bronco, arms crossed, and watch as he and Grady get out of their vehicle, and try to figure out what in the blazes Silas is up to.

They're both wearing all black. Grady has on cargo pants, and Silas, in addition to the head contraption, has on something that looks like the cargo pants of fanny packs.

I finally walk over to them.

"Hi," I say to Grady, holding out my hand. "I'm Eli. Thanks for coming."

"Happy to help with your problem," he says, shaking my hand. "Hope you don't mind that I brought Silas along, he can be very useful in a tight spot."

I glance around the Bramblebush employee parking lot, wondering what tight spots exactly they think we're going to get into. There's one nighttime security guard, and so far tonight, he's spent most of his time watching *The Office* on his phone and occasionally walking around the grounds.

It's a former farm in the middle of nowhere, and it's not like we're storing gold bullion here. The cameras are mostly to watch the employees and guests, not the building when no one's around.

That doesn't make what I'm trying any less stupid. If I get caught — and since I'm a chef and not a cat burglar, there's a decent chance that I will — I'm definitely getting fired.

I'm fine with it. Montgomery can fire me all he wants. I already cashed the check.

"Not a problem," I say, regarding Silas, who looks like a kid in a candy shop. "What's that on your head?"

Silas grins and points to the big black bulky thing strapped to his head.

"Night vision goggles," he says. "I haven't gotten to use these things in years."

"No," I say.

Silas crosses his arms in front of himself. Grady glances over at him, an *I told you so* look on his face.

"These can give us a serious tactical advantage—"

"Anyone who sees you is going to wonder why the hell you look like you're waiting for the aliens to land," I say.

"That's the point," he says, raising one eyebrow. "No one is going to see me."

I realize that maybe I haven't been clear about our plan tonight. I rub my hands together, looking from Grady to Silas and back, and I feel a little guilty because they're very, very excited for a secret operation.

"This is where I work," I explain. "I'm here at weird hours sometimes, like a few weeks ago when I had to marinate a pork shoulder for exactly—"

They're both standing in a perfect line, feet planted shoulder-width apart, arms crossed in front of their chests. I feel like they're about to salute me or something.

"—the why's not really important, but the important thing is, it's completely unsuspicious that I'm here, and it's not even suspicious that I've got some people with me. So act like you're some buddies of mine and I had to make a quick stop here to check on something, and we're golden. Got it?"

"Got it," Grady says.

Silas is quiet. The goggles are still on his head.

"Silas?"

"I'm telling you—"

I shove one hand through my hair. I thought he'd make things easier, not harder, because I just want to get in, find these deleted files, ruin Martin's life, and get back out.

That's what I need right now. I need vengeance. I want justice for Violet. I've seen her twice since our fight, for about one second each time, and the way she looked at me felt like it was tearing my heart out.

Even if she's mad at me forever, I need to do this. I'm not sure it's the nice thing my mom wants, but it's something.

"Can you put them in a briefcase or something?" I finally ask.

"Roger that," he says, and opens the car door again.

Five minutes later, we walk through the side door of the Bramblebush office barn. I spent some time today doing a little recon, to the best of my not-very-good ability, but I think I at least know where the cameras are.

"Okay," I say as we walk, going over the plan one more time. "We need to get into the security office, where the camera feeds are. There are keys in the janitor's closet, which is usually unlocked."

Grady just sighs. Silas shakes his head.

"Do people around here not know how to lock a door?" he asks, rhetorically. "I know we think it's safe and everything, but…"

"We're in this whole mess because I didn't password protect my phone," I say.

"Eli," Silas says, horrified.

Grady just shakes his head.

"It has a password *now*," I grumble. "Anyway, we get into the security office, you get the files back, we put them on this thumb drive, we leave."

"Do we delete the footage of us breaking into the security office?" Grady asks.

"…yes," I say, trying to act like I'd thought of that.

"What do we do if the security guard hears something suspicious and decides to check it out?" he asks.

"You get the deleted files and I'll distract him by talking about how perfect Pam and Jim are together," I say. "We just need the files. That's all I care about."

"I care about not getting arrested," Grady says.

"You won't get arrested," I say, and I'm at least eighty percent sure I'm right.

There's no one else around right now. It's a Thursday night in the off-season, and though there's a small event tomorrow, it's not the sort of thing that anyone's staying late for. We walk through the halls without meeting another soul and get to the janitor's closet undetected.

It's unlocked. I open it, lean inside, reach for the keyring on the hook where I saw Hank leave them earlier today.

There's no keyring. I frown. I lean further in, my hand scrabbling at the wall, but there's nothing.

I turn on the lights. I go in. The closet is nine feet square, maximum, so it doesn't take me long to look around, my heart pounding.

There are no keys. My heart rises in my chest, the hook in my ribcage twisting.

"No keys?" Grady asks. Silas is behind him, his back to us, keeping a lookout.

"They're not here," I say.

"It's fine," Grady says. "Come on."

Now he's smiling. I'm starting to wonder if asking Silas and his military buddy for help was the greatest idea I've ever had, but I turn out the light, close the door, and lead them to the security office.

There's only one camera on the hall, and I point it out before we walk past it. For a moment I'm afraid that one of them is going to whip out a can of spray paint and black out the lens, but thankfully, they both just nod and turn their backs to it.

When we reach the door to the security suite, Grady stops. He holds his hand up. Silas and I both stop short. My palms are sweating, and there's a single bead of perspiration making its way down the back of my neck.

I'm not cut out for this. I'm not the sneaky type. I'm not good at doing things undetected and unseen, and all the quiet and subversion here is making me ten times more nervous.

Without warning, Grady goes down on one knee. He pulls something from one of his many cargo pockets, a tube about a foot long, sticks it under the door, and puts an earbud in his ear.

I look at Silas. Silas is standing practically at attention, fully alert, both hands on his belt.

I close my eyes briefly and pray he didn't bring a firearm. This is *not* a firearm situation.

"Clear," Grady murmurs, putting the tube and the earpiece back into his pocket, pulling out a small black pouch from another one.

He unrolls it. It's full of small silver tools. He selects a few and gets to work.

The door's open in twenty seconds. He nods at Silas, and Silas slips through, into the dark. I follow, and practically trip over Silas the moment I get inside.

"Sorry," I whisper.

The door closes. A red light shines on the ground, and I jump.

We set something off, I think. *Not now, we're so close…*

"You don't lose your night vision with a red flashlight," Silas explains, and waves the light around the room as I try to still my heart. "Where to now?"

I point at the back room where the monitors are glowing. We go in. We sit. The monitors are all quiet and still, except for the ones on the Lodge, and even those are boring: the receptionist typing at her computer, someone in the lounge reading a paperback.

Grady opens the laptop, and the desktop comes up.

"You've gotta be kidding me," he mutters. "Do you people even know what a password is?"

"You can get it, right?" I ask.

"If you give me a second," he says.

Silas is outside the door to the tiny monitor room, standing at attention again. He has a laptop bag slung over one shoulder, and he has one hand on the zipper like he can't *wait* to get those night vision goggles out.

"Sorry," I apologize.

Grady says nothing. Silas says nothing. I point out the folder with the pool's security footage. I point out the missing date. Grady just nods, then pulls a thumb drive from yet another pocket.

"Two minutes," he says, and gets to work.

I stand up. I can't keep sitting. There's not enough room to pace in here, so I just stand there, arms crossed, watching the monitors, my stomach in knots.

It'll work, I keep telling myself. *This will work.*

What if the camera doesn't show anything?

What if Martin knows how to really delete something?

And what if it works? What then?

I don't know *what then*. I know I send Montgomery the security footage anonymously — Grady gave me detailed instructions on that when we spoke on the phone.

He'll get fired. I'm almost positive. There have been rumors swirling about Kevin's mom, a personal injury attorney, suing Bramblebush for negligence. If the footage shows that Martin unlocked the pool and brought the bull, that means he opened Bramblebush up to a nasty lawsuit.

A lawsuit.

That gives me another idea. It's sneakier. It's more devious. It might even be mean.

I shove it aside for now.

"Is it working?" I ask.

"Yes," Grady says, tersely.

I swallow hard and take a deep breath. All I need is that file in my pocket, and I'm done. I don't care what happens after that, though, like Grady and Silas, I'd prefer not to get arrested.

Then Grady leans in, frowning, his face lit by the laptop screen.

"Huh," he says, and my stomach lurches.

"Boys," Silas says, before I can ask Grady what's wrong. "We got company."

He points to the bank of monitors. I look up. Grady doesn't.

The lone security guard is walking through the halls. I watch him come down one, then another.

I think he's coming here. It's a little hard to tell with the layout of the monitors, but I'm pretty sure—

He passes the bathrooms, then the breakroom.

He's coming here.

"Shit," I say, and turn to Silas. "Okay, if I—"

He's already strapping the goggles to his head, a huge grin on his face.

"I got this, kid," he says.

Then he's gone.

"Oh, fuck," I say, my hands over my face. "Fuck."

"He's fine," Grady says, still leaning in, totally unconcerned. "He's happier than a pig in shit right now."

Silas is on the monitor. Silently, I watch him stalk a hallway, then sidle around a corner.

A second later, the guard rounds the corner at the opposite end of the hallway. He freezes for a second. It looks like he shouts something.

Then Silas runs, and the guard runs after him. I turn my attention to Grady, who's still frowning at the laptop. There's a popup window with a progress bar on the screen, but the bar seems to be frozen halfway.

I just sit. I don't even bother asking Grady if it's working, because I don't think he wants to hear my dipshit questions right now. I just watch Silas and the security guard on the monitors, darting through hallways.

"That is not how I would do it," Grady mutters, mostly to himself.

Then, to me: "You're sure this was deleted?"

I try to swallow against the brick in my stomach.

"No," I say, truthfully.

"Huh," he says, and lapses back into silence.

I watch Silas and the security guard on the monitors. My heart pounds. I'm sweating, my stomach in knots.

What do I do if this doesn't work? I think.

I have to do something. That's not the question. There's always the option of beating the shit out of Martin, but bruises heal and I'd prefer not to face assault charges.

There has to be a way to trace that email he sent Montgomery, I think. *Maybe if I can find someone to hack into—*

"Is this it?" Grady suddenly asks, and turns the laptop screen toward me.

It's a video of the pool. It's daytime. There are a few kids splashing around, a yellow float bobbing in the water.

"It's labeled the 25th," he explains, and I reach for the computer.

I scan through the video. It gets dark. The float disappears. Everyone leaves.

I scan farther, and suddenly, there's Kevin on a stretcher, two paramedics attending to him. I sit bolt upright.

"Yeah, this is it," I say, and go back.

On the monitors, something catches my eye, and I glance up. It's a golf cart, wheeling around the side of the building. A moment later, there's another golf cart.

"What the fuck?" I say.

"We should probably hurry this up," Grady says, calm as can be.

I grit my teeth. I focus on the laptop, scan backward, skip through.

Pool closed. Nighttime. Nothing. Nothing.

Someone at the locked gate, carrying a box. We let it play.

He unlocks the gate. He comes inside. I can't see his face, but it's him. It has to be him. He comes round the side of the pool.

Show your face, I think. *Show your goddamn face.*

He sits on a lounge chair, pulls the mechanical bull out, and starts blowing it up. We skip forward. It takes him forever to blow the thing up, and his back is to the camera the whole time.

He knew it was there, I think.

I've gone through all this and I've still got nothing. Silas is leading a golf cart chase right now, and I've got nothing.

Finally, on the screen, he tosses the bull into the pool.

And then, for one second, he looks right into the camera.

It's definitely, without-a-doubt Martin.

"There it is," Grady says, and sticks another thumb drive into the laptop.

I look at the monitors again. The golf carts are still going, and my chest tightens. The guard *must* have called the police by now.

"How long does it take to — oh," I say, as he pulls it out and sticks another in.

"I'll make a few backups," he says, clicking a few keys. "You take some, I'll take some. Leave at least one in a secure location."

He hands me four thumb drives. On the monitors, the golf carts are stopped. The security guard gets out of one, but Silas is nowhere to be seen.

On another monitor, blue lights flicker. Grady glances up. He does something else on the laptop. A box of code pops up. He types something, and then the screen goes black.

On the monitor, the cops pull into Bramblebush's long driveway.

"Is there a back exit?" Grady asks. "Any way we can leave without being seen?"

"Come on," I say, and we leave the security offices.

· · · · · ★ ★ ★ · · · · ·

I COME out of the locker room and practically throw an apron at Grady. He puts it on without asking, standing in front of the stainless steel counter.

I put an onion and a cutting board in front of him, practically shove a knife into his hand.

"Do I cut this?" he asks, knife in one hand, onion in the other.

I open a refrigerator and heave a stockpot out, put it on a burner, and turn it on.

"Just look like you could," I tell him.

The kitchen doors open, and the security guard steps through, followed by two cops.

"Didn't realize you were here," he says. "Late-night cooking?"

Grady grips the knife and frowns at the onion, concentrating ten times harder than he did at the computer. I have no idea where Silas is right now. I haven't seen him since he abandoned his golf cart at the edge of the forest, so hopefully he's alive and not being eaten by a mountain lion or something.

"Forgot to put something in the consommé for tomorrow's event," I tell them, smiling. "Just need to add a touch of seasoning to this, let it simmer for a bit longer and while it's doing that, I may as well start proofing the rolls, right?"

Grady cuts into the onion, right through the middle. The skin is still on, and he's holding the knife like he's going to stab someone with it.

"Right," the guard agrees. "Sorry to bother you."

"Smells great," one of the cops says.

They turn and leave. Grady looks over at me. I touch my pocket where the thumb drives are, just making sure for the thirtieth time that I've still got them.

"Have you ever *seen* an onion before?" I ask.

· · · · · ★ ★ ★ · · · · ·

Silas is sitting in my Bronco. I don't bother asking how he got in, because it can't possibly be that hard to break into a twenty-year-old piece of junk.

He grins when he sees us, looking for all the world like a kid who's just been on a roller coaster for the first time. I touch the thumb drives in my pocket yet again, reassuring myself.

"Told you they'd come in handy," he says, holding up the goggles.

"Thanks," I say. "You all right?"

"That was the most fun I've had in months," he says. "Eli, anytime you need me to come do a covert op at your workplace—"

"I'm hoping that never happens, actually," I say.

"—just let me know because I am *all in*," he says. "You get what you need?"

"Yup," says Grady, and hands him a thumb drive. "Keep that just in case."

Silas just nods and puts it in a pocket. Grady and I shake hands.

Silas pulls me in for a hard, solid hug.

"Good luck, kid," he says. "Now go get her back."

CHAPTER FORTY-FOUR

VIOLET

I rub my eyes, stretching my arms over my head, seated in my office chair. For at least the tenth time that morning, I dig my right hand into the left side of my neck, trying to work out the kink that's in there.

For at least the tenth time, it doesn't work.

I should probably stop sleeping on Adeline's couch, but I hate being in my trailer. I threw away his toothbrush and washed my sheets, but everything still reminds me of Eli and how unimportant I was in the end.

It reminds me that I liked him. I really, really did. I told him I liked him. I opened myself to him — of all people, *him* — in ways that I never have with anyone else. I trusted him.

And he used it against me. For twenty thousand dollars.

I can't look Montgomery in the eye. I've been skipping meetings, making excuses, because I can't look *anyone* in the eye.

I feel naked. I feel like everyone's seen me topless and drunk in the wedding barn, and it's an awful, crawling feeling like I'm trapped in a swamp and can't get out.

Obviously, I've already started looking for a new job but Sprucevale is small and there aren't a ton of opportunities.

Just as I turn back to my computer, figuring that I should probably concentrate on something productive, Lydia runs in to my office.

She's out of breath. Half a second later, Kevin nearly collides with her back.

"What happ—"

"Martin's getting fired," she says.

I shoot out of my chair.

"For the turtles?" I say.

They come in and close the door.

"We don't know," Kevin says. "But Montgomery called him in this morning and when Martin left his office he was super pissed and then he went to his own office and started putting stuff in a box and there was a security guard by the door."

I start smiling, maybe for the first time in days. I cover my mouth with my fist, because I still have enough decency to feel slightly bad that I'm delighted at someone's misfortune.

Only slightly bad, though.

"Brandon tried asking what happened but he wouldn't say anything," Kevin says, walking through my office to join Lydia, who's already posted by my window, looking out at the parking lot.

"Of course he didn't say anything," Lydia says. "He's a slimy scumbag who got what he deserved."

I join them, arms crossed, waiting for Martin's walk of shame to his car. If he looks over here he'll see us watching, but I couldn't care less.

The cranes. The oysters. The bull in the pool. The thousand other shitty things he's done, making things go missing, fucking with orders.

"There he is," Lydia hisses, and the three of us crowd closer around the window.

It's classic. He's walking out with a single file box. There's a lamp sticking out of it. He's being followed by a security guard, all the way to his car.

None of us say anything. He opens the trunk and puts the box in. The guard watches. Martin opens the car door, and then, as he gets in, he looks straight at us.

He looks straight at *me.*

I flip him off. It feels *great.*

Then he gets in his car, closes his door, and the security guard watches him drive away.

"Good riddance," Lydia mutters.

"I hated him," Kevin admits.

"I hope he has to work a road crew now," I add.

"Ooh, in the summer," Lydia says.

"Pouring asphalt," says Kevin.

There's a knock on my door, and the three of us jump, like we're doing something we shouldn't be.

"Come in," I call.

Eli steps in. My heart slams against my ribcage, then falls through the floor. Lydia and Kevin are suddenly stock-still, rigid, like they're afraid to breathe.

"Can I talk to you?" he asks, his voice polite, quiet.

Part of me wants to say no and never talk to him again. Part of me wants to be angry forever and hurt forever and nurse my wound until I'm a crazy old woman living in a cave on a mountain, incessantly telling the birds about the man who broke my heart one time.

But I've been at Adeline's for three nights, and in between telling me all the places that we could hide a body — and I appreciate the support, I really do — she's also made the case that having a reasonable conversation one last time with Eli might not kill me.

"Sure," I finally say, feeling like all the blood has drained from my body.

"I've gotta go take care of that thing," Lydia says. "I'll be — you know, if you need me—"

"Same. Got a thing," Kevin agrees.

They practically trip over each other to get out of my office. Eli closes the door behind them.

I lean against my desk, arms folded in front of me like that'll deflect whatever's about to happen.

"You heard Martin got fired," he says.

"We just watched him leave," I say.

I pause. Eli watches me, rubbing his hands together in front of himself, like he's not sure what to say.

It's unlike him. Eli *always* has something to say.

"Do you know what happened?" I ask. I keep my voice low, for fear that if I don't, I'll start shouting.

"Apparently someone found security footage of him unlocking the pool and putting the mechanical bull in it," he says.

I hear what he's saying, loud and clear.

"So you did something else sneaky and underhanded?" I ask before I can stop myself.

His jaw flexes. I close my eyes, bite my lip.

"He did this," Eli says, his voice low, controlled. "*Someone else* just found the evidence."

"And did *someone else* make sure that this evidence came to Montgomery's attention anonymously?" I say.

"Yes," he says simply. "I wanted his head on a platter for sending that picture, and I got it."

My head snaps up, and I look at him.

He looks shitty. There are hollows under his eyes, and he looks like he hasn't shaved in a couple of days. His hair's messier than usual, but he's looking at me with the same intensity as usual.

Not that I look great. I've been crying and sleeping on a couch. I've been holding onto anger like it's my last remaining possession.

Eli rubs his hands together. He takes a deep breath. He looks to one side, like he's trying to formulate what he's about to say.

"I couldn't prove he sent the picture," he says at last, his voice soft, constrained, like he's fighting something. "I couldn't prove it to Montgomery and I can't prove it to you, but I could get his ass fired anyway, so I did."

I want to stay angry. I want to stay hurt, because somehow that feels easier than believing him and being sorry.

He reaches into his pocket and pulls out a thumb drive, hands it to me. His fingertips barely brush my palm, but that whisper touch sends a bolt of longing through me anyway.

"There's a rumor that Kevin's mom is suing Bramblebush over his injury," Eli says. "I bet she'd be interested in seeing this."

I close my hand around it.

"You know this is proof that you're a devious, ruthless asshole sometimes, right?" I ask.

"Only for the right reasons," he says. "I'd go to the ends of the earth to be a devious, ruthless asshole to anyone who hurt you. Even if you won't believe me."

I'm afraid. I'm afraid that I was right when I thought the worst of him. I'm afraid that it would be stupid of me to believe him. I'm afraid that the thumb drive in my hand is just proof that he's capable of doing what I thought he did.

I take a deep breath, and it shudders on the way out as I fight tears.

"Jesus, don't cry, you're at work," he murmurs. For the

first time in days there's that familiar teasing note in his voice.

"Then don't make me cry at work," I whisper.

Eli steps closer. A tear slides down one cheek and before I can do anything about it, he brushes it away with his thumb.

"Don't," I say, but there's no fire behind it.

"Get dinner with me tonight," he says. "After work."

I clench the thumb drive in my hand, trying to compose myself.

"Please?" Eli asks.

I just nod.

"Seven. I'll pick you up," he says.

I take a deep breath. I reassert some control over myself. I walk around my desk and sit down again, the thumb drive in my hand.

"Seven," I confirm.

The ghost of a smile passes over his face.

"See you then," he says, and leaves me alone in my office.

I look down at my desk. I feel like a maelstrom. I feel like an asshole. I feel like a gullible idiot. I feel like the past few days have dragged me through the desert.

And I feel like I might not deserve gifts like this.

Eli's head pops back around the corner.

"Don't watch that here," he says, keeping his voice low. "You'd be amazed at how bad security is at this place."

Then he's gone again.

I put the thumb drive into my pocket.

· · · · ★ ★ ★ ★ ★ · · · ·

He brought flowers. Nice ones. Bright pink peonies and pale pink ranunculus, interspersed with small white roses, eucalyptus stems scattered throughout.

It's gorgeous, classy, and I did not think that Eli knew what a ranunculus was.

He holds it out. I take it.

"I can't take much credit for that," he admits. "I just went to Blooms in the Vale and told Kate to make something you'd like, since I figured she'd know better than me."

"Thank you," I say. "She got it right."

"Good," he says, and I finally look up at him.

He still looks rough, but he's shaved since this afternoon. His hair looks better. I think he's showered.

I did. I showered and shaved my legs and scrubbed myself clean. I blew my hair dry and put on the nice underwear and a cute dress.

I called Adeline and told her everything. I talked her ear off, going around and around in circles like I do, until she finally cut me off on the third or fourth iteration and just said *Violet, it's okay to feel however you feel. Everyone's wrong sometimes. It's not that bad.*

I'm still nervous, though. I take a deep breath.

"Can I come in?" he asks, that hint of a smile in his voice.

"Right," I say, and step back. "And I should put these in water—"

"Wait," he says, catching my wrist. His hand is warm. The pads are rough, but he's soft underneath. He slides his hand into mine and it feels like getting into bed at the end of a long day.

He takes a deep breath.

"Violet—"

"I'm sorry," I blurt out. "I should have believed you. I

shouldn't have jumped to conclusions and I should've given you the benefit of the doubt for *one second* and…"

I trail off, a giant lump in my throat. Eli squeezes my hand.

"Dammit, I rehearsed this," I say.

I look away. I take a deep breath.

"I should have trusted you," I say, willing my voice not to shake. "That's all. You earned it. I should have believed you and I didn't. And I'm sorry."

"I get it," he says, simply.

I watch him, waiting. Despite everything I'm still nervous, the butterflies in my stomach pitching and rolling.

"We've always been… us," he says. "You've been at my throat since we were kids and vice versa, and it's hard to change that. It's hard to change, period, and it's even harder to believe that other people have changed."

He exhales, hard, squeezes my hand.

"But I want to be someone you can always trust. I want to always have your back. I want to always be there, behind you, and I want to be so constant you never have to think about whether I'm yours or not. I just *am*. I'm there. I'm there and I always am and you never have to wonder whether I'd hurt you, and can you believe I rehearsed this?" he asks.

I swallow hard against the lump in my throat.

"Maybe you should have rehearsed more?" I whisper.

"See, I'm not sure you *have* changed," he says, teasing.

"Of course I have," I say, even though I don't trust my voice. "I'm totally and completely different than I used to be."

"You were never boring," he says. "Never for a second have I found your company lacking. Not then and not now."

"Yours either," I admit. "I'd rather argue with you than do almost anything else."

"Are you done interrupting my speech?" he asks.

"You interrupted yourself to claim you rehearsed," I protest.

"I did rehearse," he says, and looks down at me.

We lock eyes, and there's that feeling again: that I'm not standing on the floor, that I'm somewhere above it. That I'm floating, drowning.

"I've been to a lot of places and there's no one else like you," he says, his voice suddenly low, serious. "You're it, Violet. You're all there is for me. It's you or a life of austere hermitude. Let me be yours."

I'm still looking into his eyes. I'm crying again, tears of relief and penance and sorrow. Tears of gratitude.

I try to say *yes*, but I can't get my voice out, I can only make my lips form the words.

In the end, I nod. Eli crushes me against him and I bury my head in his chest, my whole body shuddering as I hold him close.

It feels good. It feels right. It feels like I've just healed something that was much, much older than this fight, like a splinter I didn't realize I had until it was gone.

"I do have one question," I finally say.

I pull back. I look up at him. He brushes a tear from my cheek.

"Kiss me first," Eli says, and I do.

It's sweet, gentle. An *I missed you* kiss. An *I'm sorry* kiss. A *let's never do that again* kiss.

An *I'm yours* kiss.

It ends. He brushes his lips across my forehead.

"Okay, shoot," he says.

"Did you really get Martin fired?"

He looks down at me. A smile spreads across his face

until he's grinning. I raise both my eyebrows, not entirely sure what to make of it.

"Hell yes I did," he says. He takes my hand, links our fingers, kisses my knuckles. "And it's a great story that I'll tell you over dinner. You like sushi?"

CHAPTER FORTY-FIVE

ELI

I take Violet on our first date.

We've had sex in pretty much every position on pretty much every piece of furniture in her house, but this is the first time we've gone on an honest-to-God *date*. We hold hands. We drink sake. She eats too much wasabi and turns bright pink.

I tell her about getting back the deleted security footage, and about Silas's golf cart chase. She has a lot of questions about the night-vision goggles, and sadly, I can answer very few of them.

After dinner, we get ice cream and walk around downtown Sprucevale, holding hands. We sit on a bench overlooking the river and debate whether sprinkles are good or not; Violet is wrong, and they're not.

Halfway through the argument, she kisses me and it tastes a little like chocolate.

We go back to her place without even discussing it. She apologizes for throwing away my toothbrush and gives me a new one.

That night, I just hold her. It feels important, somehow, just being there. Just being with her.

Just being hers.

· · · · · ★ ★ ★ ★ ★ · · · · ·

When I wake up the next morning, Violet's already gone and the shower is running. I roll over and look at the bedside clock.

It's 10:30. Good *Lord.* I slept like the dead.

I roll back over and stay in bed, waiting for Violet to come back. Why get up when I'm fairly certain I'll just be back in five minutes?

I'm just being energy-efficient.

Five minutes pass. She's still showering. Then ten.

I should probably go make sure she hasn't been sucked down the drain or something.

I knock on the door before I go in, then crack the door.

"You still alive in here?" I ask, the steam hitting me in the face.

"Eli?" she asks.

"Who else would it be?"

"No one, I hope," she answers.

I step inside and close the door, watching her shadow behind the shower curtain. It's a small shower in a small bathroom, not big enough for a tub, but it's not tiny.

"You still in there?" I ask, locking my arms across my chest.

The shower curtain jerks back partway, and Violet peeks out.

"Do you have to leave?" she asks.

All I can see is her face, her side, one hip. The rest is in shadow behind the shower curtain but I swear to God she's teasing me, water running down her body in rivulets I want to lick.

"No," I say.

She steps back into the shower. The curtain stays partly open.

"I'll be out in a sec," she says.

I'm pulled forward. I know that by now I should be used to seeing her naked, that something I see nearly every day shouldn't hold this magnetic draw for me, but it does.

I lean against the shower stall, push the curtain back further. Violet sees me, smiles, head back as she rinses her hair under the spray.

"I hate waiting," I say, and reach out to slide my thumb across one stiff, pink nipple.

Violet's eyelids flutter closed. I do it again, take it between my thumb and finger, roll it. She bites her lip.

"C'mere," I whisper.

She comes to the edge of the shower stall, warm and wet and dripping, naked body slick. I can't stop touching her as she kisses me, my hands gliding over her body, slippery and supple. She bunches my shirt in her hands, mouth open under mine, water dripping onto my belly.

There's no resisting.

I shed my shirt, jeans, shoes in record time. I'm already rock hard as I step into her shower, my mouth on hers, pushing her against the cheap porcelain wall. It vibrates as her body hits it. A bottle of shampoo drops and clatters off a shelf, but we both ignore it.

I take her by the hips, slide a hand between her legs. It's even hotter and wetter than the rest of her, and Violet moans into my mouth as I skim my fingers between her soft, velvety lips.

It feels right, electric, secret and safe and holy. I shouldn't still get a charge from the way her hips buck against me when I brush my thumb across her clit, but I do.

When I'm with her, like this, the world falls away and nothing else exists. Reality is the heat of the water on my back, her mouth under mine, the way her body begs me for more. Reality is her nails on my back, my lips against her ear, her hand finding my cock and stroking it.

"I'm yours," I murmur into her ear as I slide two fingers into her tight, hot entrance.

She gasps, moans, her mouth open, her head back. Her hand tightens on me. I slide a third finger in, kissing her neck. Her pulse races and I nip at her neck. I move my mouth to her collarbone, lapping up the water that's collected there.

Her nipples are stiff but go soft in my mouth, between my teeth, her hand knotted in my hair. I stroke her inner wall with my fingers and her hips move with me, begging, pleading.

I love her like this, her defenses gone, still soft but demanding, all angles and curves. I fall to my knees, lips on her belly. Her breathing gets faster. I move my fingers harder, feel the shudder that moves through her.

I shift her weight, throw one knee over my shoulder and she grabs the curtain rod, steadies herself.

I tongue her clit, slowly, my tongue broad and flat and rough.

"Oh, fuck," she gasps, like it's a surprise.

I love her like this, too: foul-mouthed and rough, her hand too tight in my hair, her pussy clenches at my fingers, squeezing so hard it almost hurts. I love Violet when she wants everything I have to give her. I love her when she begs for it, no matter what. For her, I'd stay on my knees forever.

I lap her, slowly. Carefully. I lick her hard, her body

jolting with each pass, my fingers inside her stroke along with the rhythm. I don't write my name with my tongue anymore because I know what she likes. I know every shiver and nuance of her body.

Besides, she knows my name by now. It'll be on her lips soon enough.

My cock throbs. A tremor moves through Violet's body and in me it becomes an earthquake. I lick her faster, harder, want pounding through me. I push her harder against the wall, feeling the flimsy thing shake behind her. Something else clatters to the floor of the shower but I push myself deeper into her, drinking her in unceasingly.

"Eli," she gasps and there it is: three breathless letters shot straight to my core.

"Make me come," she whispers, and I'm helpless. Whatever I am in life right now, I'm her slave because I *need* this. I need her shaking and whispering my name, I need her trembling and coming and being utterly, completely mine.

I lick her rougher, harder, and she moans. She whispers my name like it's a prayer and she whispers it like it's a curse, and I never did know which I prefer. She trembles and she quivers and grips my hair until my eyes water and then, she comes.

And I love her like this. I love her undone and vulnerable, shaking against the wall of her shower. I love her in her pure animal state, thoughtless and wild. I love her when she's mine like this, when she gives herself over to me and I give her this back.

It fades. I pull my fingers out of her, take her knee off my shoulder, lean back into the slowly cooling water of the shower. I make sure she's watching me as I lick her off my fingers, one by one, because I like the way she tastes and I like the look in her eyes as she watches me.

I stand up. I tower over her. The water on my back is lukewarm at best and turning quickly, but I rest an arm over her head, teasing her lips with mine. She tastes herself in light, quick kisses, each one longer. Her hands wander over my body, leaving trails of fire all the way to my cock.

She gives me long, hard strokes, her tongue in my mouth. I groan and lean into her, seeking out the warmth of her body for what feels like the first time and the millionth. The water is cool against my back but she strokes me again and bites my lip, drawing me toward her.

Her other hand is on my back. It pauses.

"We used all the hot water, didn't we?" she murmurs.

"We? You're the one who was in here for twenty minutes," I tell her.

She gives me a slow stroke, tip to root, root to tip. There's a noise in my chest that I don't mean to make.

"I was trying to wake up," she says, and her hand leaves my back. She leans forward, turns the faucet and the water stops.

I kiss her one more time. I'm tempted to fuck her right here, against the wall, but it's not what I want. I don't want to worry about balancing or about slipping.

I want her hard and fast and deep. I want to make my body a part of hers and I want to never let go.

So I take her in my arms, carefully step out of the shower, and carry her to the bedroom. Violet laughs. I toss her onto her bed, still wet, and she bounces once, sits on the edge, pulling me in.

"I have legs," she teases.

"I know. They're great for spreading," I say, pushing her knees apart. She grabs my cock again and we kiss.

We move onto the bed. It's harder, rougher. She's on her back under me and I'm over her, cock in her hands, the tip bumping against her slick wetness with every stroke.

It takes all my self-control not to sink into that perfect tight channel, but I don't.

"Hold on," I murmur, and reach for her nightstand.

"Don't," she says.

I look down at her.

"I went on the pill a few weeks ago," she says. "I was gonna surprise you, so… surprise?"

"I'm surprised," I say.

I wander a hand down her body: shoulder, nipple, belly. I thumb her clit and watch her eyes go half-mast.

"Fuck me bare," she whispers. "Please?"

The words take my breath away. My cock aches, throbs. I thumb her clit once more.

"Say it again," I growl.

"Why?"

"I like hearing you say it," I tell her.

"Fuck me bare, Eli," Violet murmurs. "I want you inside me with nothing between us — oh, *fuck.*"

I'm inside her with one thrust, her tight channel enveloping me to the hilt, her legs locking around me. It's beautiful, perfect, overwhelming. I have to stop for a moment, afraid I'll embarrass myself.

"Like that?" I whisper.

"Yes," she whispers back, her breath catching in her throat. "God, Eli, you feel so good."

She could say it a million times and I'd never get tired of hearing it. I fuck her again, slowly, gently. I feel her melt as I hit every sensitive spot inside her, her legs tightening, her hips moving and rolling.

"Tell me I'm yours," I tell her, sinking in.

"You're mine," she says, stifling a moan.

Her breath catches. I find her knee, maneuver it over my shoulder. She pulls me deeper.

"Tell me I'm yours," she says, eyes at half-mast.

"You're mine," I answer.

We move harder, faster. She pulls me and I push together, bodies hammering together like pistons in an engine, smooth perfect machinery.

I want more. I need more. I know it will never be enough but I need more like I need air. I kiss her and she bites me, gasping, whispering *fuck me, Eli* into my mouth, and I know that's the signal.

I pull out and she rolls over as I hand her a pillow. She shoves it under her hips and I slide back inside her again, the rhythm barely interrupted. Violet arches her back, on her forearms, her ankles wrapped around my legs.

I bury myself so deep I see stars, my head on her shoulder, her channel gripping me like a fist.

"Eli," she whispers.

I slide my hand over hers, fingers tangling. I squeeze her until my knuckles are white and she squeezes right back, our bodies locked into a union.

This is love. I've known it for a while but the understanding flashes through me again as I move inside her, as I feel her body underneath me and worship it with my own.

It's love. It's dirty and rough, physical and tangible, but it's love. The way I need her like this is love. The way I feel her in my soul is love. The way she says my name, the way she moves, the way she shudders and moans and says *come inside me* is love.

It's hard. It's deep. It's ruthless, raw, primal and needy, but it's ours and it's love. Violet shouts my name into her mattress and I have my face in her neck and I whisper *I love the way you fuck me* over and over again.

She comes. It's cosmic, her body shuddering and bending and drawing me in, her hand in my hair, pulling my face to her shoulder. Her body arches into me as she tightens, squeezes, pumps me until I explode inside her and can't stop, draining myself in spasm after spasm.

I kiss the back of her neck, rising. I let her hand go and I kiss that, too, roll off and land next to her. She takes the pillow out and puts her hand in mine.

"I like this," she says softly.

"I like this too," I say.

"I like us," she goes on. "I always did, even when I didn't want to admit there was an *us*."

"You came around," I say.

"I slept at Adeline's the last three nights because my bed felt awful without you in it," she says, the words tumbling out in a rush. "I missed you so much, and I hated how much I missed you, but—"

I wait, our fingers laced together.

"I did miss you," she says.

I kiss her fingers. I open her hand and kiss her palm.

There's still something else. Something stupid and reckless, something that I never should have done but that I did anyway.

"Stay there," I tell her.

"Where are you going?" she asks, going up on her elbows as I pull on pants and a shirt.

"So many questions," I tease, and walk out of her bedroom, through the living room, out of her house to the Bronco.

On the backseat there's a manila folder with a bunch of paperwork inside it. I glance through it one last time, standing barefoot on her driveway.

Are you sure? I ask myself. *You might scare her off again. Maybe you should wait.*

I glance back at the trailer, think of Violet inside, her admission that she missed me.

I'm done pretending I feel casual about her. Fuck it.

I'm sure.

She's sitting up in bed when I get back, and I hand it to her.

"You got me paperwork," she says. "I love paperwork."

"Open it, smartass," I tell her, getting on the bed and curling around her, my chin on her shoulder.

She opens it. I hold my breath.

Violet freezes. She doesn't speak, her fingers drifting over the first page, her shoulders suddenly rigid.

I knew it.

"No," she says.

I don't answer her. I knew that would be the first thing, so I wait. She flips over the first page, the folder now lying in her lap.

"Did you…?"

"Yup."

"This is insane," she says. "What? No. Eli."

She flips through the pages, then turns around and looks at me.

I look back.

"You bought the house by the lake?" she asks, her voice quiet and still.

My heart thumps in my chest. I knew it was a lot. I knew that there was a big difference between *be my girlfriend* and *I bought us a house*, but it was reckless and impulsive, a late-night decision to write an offer letter and send it off.

"Technically, I just have an accepted offer on the house," I say, draping an arm over her shoulder. "I think there are like… ten more steps before it's mine."

"Why?" she asks.

"I need to move out of my mom's house," I say. It's technically true, but I can tell Violet's not buying it. "And I couldn't think of a better way to spend twenty thousand dollars than on getting us a place."

Her eyes go even wider, her lips parted.

"And because I love you and I want to live with you," I say. "That's pretty much it, actually."

She doesn't answer me right away, just flips through the paperwork again, slowly this time, and stops on the last page, her fingers floating across my signature.

"What's the H stand for?" she asks suddenly, pointing at *Elijah H. Loveless*.

"Hiram," I say.

"I never knew your middle name was Hiram."

"Well, I don't really advertise it," I say.

"It's a good name," she says, her fingers still on the page.

"Is it?"

"I like it," she says.

Then she turns her head suddenly, looks right into my eyes.

"I'm gonna say yes," she says, her voice serious. "But if there's something else you want to do with the money besides buying this house just because I like it—"

"Nope," I say. "This is what I want. I want it to be ours, and I want to live here with you, and I want you to wake up every morning knowing someone loves you."

She bites her lips together.

"And not because you're the best at anything. I love you for who you are. You're determined, you're smart, you're funny. You're never boring. I went around the world looking for someone like you and you were here all along."

"Michelle."

I just blink.

"My middle name's Michelle. It seemed like something you should know if we're moving in together," she says.

"Violet Michelle," I muse, mostly to myself.

It feels strange, like turning the lights on in a room I'd

never looked into before. It feels strange that all this time I thought I knew her, but I didn't even know this one basic thing.

"I love you, too," she says softly.

I hold her closer, nuzzling my nose into her neck, and kiss her softly below her ear.

"I already like being yours," I say.

CHAPTER FORTY-SIX

VIOLET

One Month Later

"And finally, if you'll initial there and there, and sign there, we're finished," Karen says.

Eli initials, signs, slides the paperwork over to me. I do the same.

"Fantastic!" she says, flashing her too-bright smile one more time. "Congratulations on becoming homeowners, y'all two! And don't forget, if you know anyone in the market, just point 'em my way. Lovely to work with you!"

She grabs her enormous purse, then holds out one perfectly manicured hand. We both shake it, saying our own thanks and goodbyes, and then Karen is out the front door, in her Mercedes, and driving away.

We're alone in the house.

Correction: we're alone in *our* house. We're both on the mortgage paperwork and we'll both be on the title, because once his grand gesture making was over, Eli did manage to see reason. There was no way I was letting him be entirely on the hook for this place if something went wrong.

Also, it's insane to give someone a house. I stand firmly by that. It might also be insane to buy a house with the guy who's only been your boyfriend for a few months, but I'm choosing to ignore that.

Eli slides his hand into mine, and we look around the house.

Our house.

It's small. The bed is in a loft, which is sort-of-but-not-technically a second story. There's one bathroom. The washer and dryer are in the kitchen. The kitchen and dining room / living room are all open plan.

But the main floor has big windows that look out over the lake. The loft is tall enough to stand in and cozy at the same time. The kitchen is way nicer than the one in my trailer, and the bathroom has a real tub and not just a shower. The previous owner replaced the HVAC system just last year.

And it's *ours*. His and mine.

"Where should we put the couch?" he asks, looking around the space, taking my hand in his.

"Do we have a couch?" I ask, leaning my head on his shoulder.

"You've got one."

"I hate that couch," I say. "I've been meaning to replace it for years, but then I figured, what's the point of getting a new couch when the whole house is so crappy, you know?"

"All right, so we'll put the couch nowhere," he says. "What furniture *do* we have?"

"A bed," I say. "That horrible kitchen table at my place. Some dressers."

"At least moving won't be too hard," he says. "All I've got at my mom's place is that bookshelf. Everything else is hers."

"I think that bookshelf is probably hers now, too," I say. "When's the last time you slept there?"

"Ownership isn't determined by how often you sleep in the same room as a thing," Eli says. "You've never once slept in the same room as your car but it's still yours."

"Possession is nine-tenths of the law," I say. "Your mom clearly possesses that bookshelf. What time are we supposed to be over there, anyway?"

Eli pulls out his phone and checks the time.

"Forty-five minutes," he says.

"We should go soon," I say.

"Few more minutes," Eli says.

I walk backward and heave myself onto the kitchen island. Eli comes and stands between my legs, his elbows resting on my knees, facing away from me. I drape my arms over his shoulders, put my chin on top of his head.

It's still nice. I don't know if I'll ever get over the simple pleasure of touching Eli casually like this, of small affectionate touches that are the constant reminder that we like each other.

"There's a storm across the lake," he says, leaning back. He puts his hands over mine, and we both watch the angry, steel-blue clouds bubble and churn, miles away.

"You know something?" I say.

"I know lots of things," Eli says, and I ignore him.

"I think I'm glad I lost the MVP prize. Not about the picture, but I'm glad I lost it in general."

There's a long pause.

Then Eli just whistles.

"I know, I know," I say.

"Someone get the New York Times on the phone," he says.

"Yeah, funny."

"Call CNN."

"Hilarious."

"Or maybe the Washington Post will want this exclusive," he goes on.

I just sigh.

"I'm about to be nice to you, you know," I say.

He just laughs.

"Then, by all means," he says.

"Such a dick," I murmur, mostly to myself.

"That wasn't the nice thing, was it?" he teases. I can feel his voice rumble beneath my palms, low and soothing.

"If I'd won, I'd just have a house," I say. "It would be mine, not ours."

"I'd probably be over a lot, though," he points out. "I've got more stuff in the trailer than at my mom's, which is theoretically my home."

"We'd still just be fuckbuddies," I say.

"Would we?" he asks, lacing his fingers through mine.

"I wasn't gonna end it," I say.

"I was already in love with you," he says, his voice suddenly soft. "Everyone already knew about us. It was a matter of time before I confessed and put myself at your mercy."

I just hold him closer.

"Did I ever tell you why I took that picture?"

"Which?"

"*That* picture."

He means the one Montgomery got, of course. I flex my fingers, then squeeze his hands.

"Because you were drunk and wanted spank bank material?" I say, lightly.

Eli pauses for a moment.

"Well, that too," he admits, and I smile into his hair, planting a kiss on top of his head. "But mostly, I wanted to remember the moment I realized I was in love with you."

"When we got drunk and had sex in the barn?"

"When you wouldn't kiss me in front of people, even though they already knew," he says. "I didn't know that mattered to me until then, but it did. I wanted you to be mine and I wanted people to know."

He pauses. The storm roils, flashes. My heartbeat picks up. I wonder if I'll ever stop learning new things about Eli.

I hope I don't.

"And that was when I realized that sooner or later, I was going to have to come to terms with that. So when we were in the barn, and I was drunk, I just… I wanted that moment. That memory. When we were in love and didn't even know it yet."

Another pause.

"That backfired like *fuck*," he says, and I laugh.

"There were a bad few days, but I figured it out eventually," I say. "And we got a house."

"And we got a house," Eli echoes. "I think this will be good, Violet."

I kiss the top of his head again, my lips linger a little this time, like I'm pausing this moment. He squeezes my hands, and I squeeze back.

"It's already good," I say.

EPILOGUE

ELI

Five Months Later

I crouch down in front of the oven, frowning at the food inside. I think the internal thermometer of my mom's oven is off, because this lamb roast has been in there for a good forty-five minutes already and it's nowhere near done, not to mention the potatoes are—

"Are you coming or what?' Violet asks from the doorway.

"Just a minute," I say, still frowning. "I think the temperature on this oven is wrong."

She walks over to me and bends down, peering over my shoulder.

"Looks fine," she says.

"Thanks for your expert opinion."

"My expert opinion is quit staring at the oven and come hang out," she says, landing a quick peck on my cheek.

"What are you even an expert *in*?" I tease, standing.

Violet doesn't answer me, but she grabs the kitchen

towel off my shoulder and tosses it onto the counter, then grabs me by the arm.

"You've been in here all afternoon, and I'm out of things I can ask Caleb about theoretical mathematics or long-distance trail hiking," she says. "C'mon. I need you."

I just raise one eyebrow at her.

"If you put it that way," I say, and wink.

Violet casts a quick glance over her shoulder, at the door to the living room, then steps in toward me.

I slide my hands down her back and grab her ass.

"Is this why you've been staying in here?" she asks. "So I'd come find you?"

"Sure doesn't hurt," I say.

We kiss. Her arm slides around my neck. I give her ass a good squeeze, move my hands under the thick sweater she's wearing and she gasps into my mouth.

"Don't tell me I've got cold hands," I say.

"Well, they're not warm," she laughs.

I kiss her more. There's a burst of laughter from the direction of the living room. After a long moment, Violet pulls back, keeping her arms around my neck.

"Stop cooking and come socialize," she says. "Please?"

I land a light kiss on her nose.

"Okay," I say.

· · · · · ★ ★ ★ · · · · ·

"THAT'S NOT EVEN what eminent domain is for," Seth is saying, gesturing with his beer, his other arm behind his head. "It's for highways, or parks, or... you know, things that actually benefit society. It's not for Walter Eighton to use to get richer."

"He's threatening it as leverage," Silas says. "He doesn't have much of a case for it, but he's trying to make the

Osbornes think that they can avoid a big legal battle by selling to him."

Sometimes, I forget Silas is a lawyer. It's not that hard to forget.

"Do you think it'll work?" Daniel asks.

Silas just shrugs.

"Hope not," he says. "They asked my advice and that's what I said, but who knows. When the easy way out comes with a side of a few hundred thousand dollars…"

"No," my mom says. "That's all he's offering? For three hundred acres right along the river?"

"It's what I heard," Silas says.

We're all sitting around the living room, ten people on two long couches, some rocking chairs, and the floor. I'm on the end of one couch, my arm around Violet. Seth is on the other end, Daniel, Charlie, and Silas on the other couch. Levi and my mom are in rocking chairs, and Caleb and Rusty are sitting on the floor, putting together a puzzle on a low table.

"What's he want the land for?" Caleb asks, squinting at a piece.

"An outlet mall," Seth says, sourly.

"I thought it was a ski resort," Daniel says. "Isn't that close to where Stony Mountain used to be?"

"I heard water park," Levi offers.

"So none of you know," Caleb says, still looking at the puzzle piece. He puts it down, picks up another one.

"One of us is bound to be right," Levi says.

"Are you?" Charlie asks. She's sitting cross-legged on the couch, her curls piled on top of her head, one knee touching Daniel's leg. They're both acting like they don't notice.

"You know the saying about monkeys writing Hamlet," Daniel says.

No one responds. They all just look at Daniel.

"He means that if you put infinite monkeys into a room with infinite typewriters for infinitely long, one of them will write Hamlet," I finally say, since I know what he means.

"Right," Daniel confirms. "And if you keep guessing, eventually you'll guess right. It's science."

"Nope," says Levi.

"Not science," Mom says at the same time.

"The infinite monkey theorem," Caleb says. "It's math. You're good."

"See?" Daniel says.

"He's not telling anyone what he wants the land for?" Violet asks. She sounds suspicious.

"Or he's telling everyone different things," Charlie says. "Which seems worse, somehow. Not telling anyone is just being difficult. Telling different people different things is…"

She trails off, frowning.

"Deceptive?" Daniel says, finishing her thought. "Backhanded? Sneaky?"

"Right," she agrees."

"He can say whatever he wants, and once the land is bought the use is between him and the zoning board," Silas says. "It's slimy of him to say that he wants to build a playground and then put a coal mine there, but if he can get it zoned and approved, he can do it."

Seth sighs.

"I hate him," he says. "He keeps calling the state alcoholic beverage control board on us and it's a huge pain in the a— uh, the butt."

"Thank you," Daniel says. Rusty giggles.

"Is dinner ready yet?" Seth asks. "It smells good."

"I'll go check," I say, and pull my arm from around Violet, looking down at her. "If I'm allowed."

She rolls her eyes at me, but she's smiling.

· · · · · ★ ★ ★ ★ ★ · · · · ·

When dinner is over, Levi and Silas direct everyone in kitchen cleanup, Mom and Rusty go to back to working on the puzzle, and Daniel slips out the back door.

I watch him through the sliding glass as he paces back and forth on the wooden deck. It's hard to see him in the dark, but it looks like he's on the phone.

I give him five minutes, and then I grab my jacket and follow him out.

He's standing there, poorly lit by the porch light, wearing nothing but his flannel shirt as a light dusting of snow falls in the backyard, his breath leaving his lungs in bright puffs as he looks down at his phone.

"Everything okay?" I ask.

He looks at me, running one hand through his hair, which may as well be the universal Loveless distress signal.

"Fine," he says.

"So you want me to drag it out of you," I say, leaning one hip against the wooden railing.

"It's nothing," he says, sliding his phone back into his pocket. "We should go back in."

"You checked your phone four times during dinner," I say. "You're the originator and fiercest defender of the *no phones at dinner* rule."

He crosses his arms in front of his chest. He plants his feet, sighs, the air leaving his lungs in a long white stream.

"Crystal called," he says. "Four times in forty-five minutes. She left me one voicemail that just says 'call me back,' and now, she's not answering."

Crystal is Rusty's mom, and she does *not* have a good relationship with Daniel.

"She's probably just drunk," I say.

"She didn't sound drunk."

"I'm sure she's good at hiding it by now."

"Do you know how many times she's called me in the past two years?" he asks. "Twice. She has called me twice. I've called her I don't even know how many times, because if Rusty's ever going to see her, it's going to be my job to set it up. It's my job to double-check that she's still available. It's my job to call her the day before a visit to remind her that it's happening."

"Is she in trouble?" I ask. "Would she call you if she were in trouble?"

"I hope not," Daniel says.

"It's probably nothing," I tell him. "I bet she just wanted to know Rusty's shoe size or something like that. Maybe she's buying her shoes."

Daniel snorts.

"She hasn't bought Rusty shoes in…"

He thinks for a moment.

"Ever. She's never bought Rusty shoes."

"Quit thinking about it and come inside," I say, taking him by the shoulder. "It's freezing out here and she was probably just drunk."

Daniel sighs and lets me lead him back in.

"I hope you're right," he says.

· · · · · ★ ★ ★ · · · · ·

VIOLET HOLDS a paper plate up in front of my face. On it is a slice of blackberry pie, covered with plastic wrap.

"Do you see this pie?" she asks me, her face and voice completely serious.

I just sigh and cross my arms.

"Eli."

"Yes, I see the pie."

"This is my pie," she says. "I nearly had to stab your

brother Levi with a fork to get it. And I love you, but if you try to eat it, I'll stab you with a fork."

"I understand," I say. "You want me to eat it while you're asleep."

Violet does not look amused. We're standing in our kitchen, putting away the leftovers that my mom made us take home.

My mom's pie is one of the eternal mysteries of the universe, because it's amazing. The woman is one of the worst cooks I've ever met, but an incredible baker. It defies logic.

"You already had a piece," she says. "I watched you eat it. This one is mine, and I'm saving it."

"For when?"

"For whenever I want."

I take a step closer. Violet narrows her eyes, but she doesn't move.

"A fork, you say?"

"Eli."

I consider this, looking down into Violet's shark-colored eyes. I'm trying not to laugh. I think she is, too, because she puts one hand over the pie

"Don't look at it," she says.

"Which fork?"

"All of them," she says.

"Okay," I finally say.

I grab the pie and hold it over my head.

"Worth it," I say, grinning at her.

"Dammit!" she yelps, grabbing one bicep and pulling.

I switch the pie to the other hand. I've got about seven inches on her, so she doesn't stand much of a chance.

"Don't make me drop it," I say. "Then no one gets the pie."

Violet turns and opens the silverware drawer. When she

turns back, she's got a fork in each hand. She brandishes them.

"I'll do it," she says. "Don't make me."

"Go ahead," I dare her.

She makes a half-hearted stabbing motion. I block her with my free hand, dodge the other fork. She gets the first one free, moves past my hand, and pokes me in the ribs.

It kinda tickles.

"Was that it?" I tease.

"Come *on*," she says. "You already had pie. Don't take my pie."

I grin at her again, then toss the pie onto the counter. Violet breathes a sigh of relief.

"Thank you," she says.

I lean back against the counter, grab her, pull her in. Violet falls into place perfectly.

"Did you really stab Levi with a fork?" I ask.

"*Almost,*" she says. "I only almost stabbed him."

I start laughing.

"Sorry," she says, looking off to the side. "It was the heat of the moment, I probably shouldn't have."

"I'm sure he deserved it," I tell her. "Besides, I'm glad you can hold your own against them, since none of you are going anywhere."

She stands on her tiptoes, tilts her face up and kisses me, and even though she's warm and familiar it sends a shiver of sparks down my body.

"I love you," she says. "And I'm sorry I stabbed you with a fork."

"I think I'll live," I murmur, kissing her again. "I love you too."

We stay there for a long time, kissing in our kitchen, in the house we bought, in the life we built together. The life we're still building.

She hasn't stopped surprising me. I don't think she ever will.

Violet pulls back, one thumb finding its way under the layers I'm wearing, sweet friction along my skin.

"Bed?" she asks, smiling, one eyebrow cocked.

"Ladies first," I say, following the love of my life into our bedroom.

THE END

ABOUT ROXIE

Roxie is a romance author by day, and also a romance author by night. She lives in Los Angeles with one husband, two cats, far too many books, and a truly alarming pile of used notebooks that she refuses to throw away.

Join her mailing list for release updates, free bonus scenes, and tons more!

www.roxienoir.com
roxie@roxienoir.com

Printed in the USA
CPSIA information can be obtained
at www.ICGtesting.com
LVHW091612200824
788780LV00007B/134